LOST IN THE FIRE

Geraint Jones is a New York Times and Sunday Times best-selling writer, a combat veteran of Iraq and Afghanistan, and host of the *Veteran State Of Mind* podcast. Since his debut in 2016 alongside writing's superstar James Patterson, Geraint has written 12 books ranging from historical fiction to war memoir. His work has been published by Penguin, Random House, Pan Macmillan, and Headline. *Lost In The Fire* is Geraint's second self-published book. He also writes for the screen, and is a lyricist for electronic dance music. Apparently Geraint likes to write, and he does so from his home in Wales.

ALSO BY GERAINT JONES

Ambush (Blood Forest)

Siege

Legion

Brothers In Arms

AS CO-AUTHOR

No Way Out by Major Adam Jowett

Relentless by Dean Stott

Uncaged by Paul de Gelder

Sugarman with Vincent Vargas

AS CO-WRITER UNDER THE NAME
REES JONES

Private Royals by James Patterson

Heist by James Patterson

Private Princess by James Patterson

LOST
IN THE
FIRE

by

GERAINT JONES

Acknowledgments

Usually this section would be at the back of a book, but given that this novel would never have happened without a Kickstarter campaign, I think that this is the right place for it. I'm so grateful to everybody who made this possible, including, but certainly not limited to:

Owain Brown

Jim Anthony

Lucien Manuel Tristan D'Artagnan

Jamie Waldron

Ken Emery

Anthony Reid

Chris Lewis

David McWhirter

Brian Painter

William Currie

Trish Tebbutt

Paul Grant

Bjorn Niclas

Karen DeGroot

Andrea Robinson

Chris Duffield

Lily Konstanznig

Viki May

Amy Gregory

Nick Wyrill

Ryan Connick

Grant Stevenson

Gareth Emery

Sam Mathews

Gareth Priestly

Carin Bouwmeester

Sebastian Calvo

Simon Cooke

Zakk Wedemeyer

Thank you all so much. I hope that you enjoy the story that you breathed life into.

Love you all,

Geraint

To the city and people of Las Vegas.

1

No one believes that they'll be eaten alive.

No one.

It's hard to accept that a car-driving, iPhone-toting human being can find themselves at the bottom of the food chain – a meal for something bigger, faster, stronger, and altogether more deadly.

With lattes in hand, and a spin class at six, it's a little difficult for members of the species to think of themselves as what they truly are:

Meat.

Delicious, edible, meat.

The surfer was no different.

He knew that the ocean was a dangerous place: riptides that would pull you under; crashing waves that could crush; hidden rocks that lurked beneath the surface. The surfer had heard of people going out that way, knocked unconscious and drowned when they'd come off of their board – he'd even heard of an older guy having a heart attack on a wave – but he'd never known anyone involved in a shark attack. Not at his usual spots in Malibu. Nor here, at Surf Beach in Santa Barbara County. Everyone knew that the sharks were out there – this was *their* ocean after all — but in twenty years of catching waves he had never even seen so much as a fin. That had changed quickly.

Today — *his last day* — the surfer found himself staring into the cavernous black eye of a Great White.

The vision was a surreal one. He couldn't believe how detached he felt from the whole thing, as if he was watching one of those shitty B-movies that his brother was so fond of. One minute he'd been paddling out, lying flat on his board and using his hands and feet for propulsion. The next he'd felt a bump, and a shock of pain had raced along his left side. When the surfer had looked back, he'd seen that his left leg and board were in the mouth of a silver-white creature.

Sheer disbelief and shock hit him like a train. *That's a fucking shark.*

'Shark!' He heard someone shouting, someone that sounded like himself. 'Shark! Shark!'

There was blood in the water. Lots of it.

Fight! his instincts suddenly screamed at him from the sidelines. *Fight! Hit that motherfucker!*

He tried. The surfer tried to twist and turn, but he was in a prehistoric vise of teeth and jaw.

'Help! Shark! Help me! Help!' No mistaking who was shouting now.

The shark's eye looked on, a black marble of emptiness. Perhaps it was wondering if it liked the unusual taste of polystyrene, fiberglass, flesh, and bone.

It bit harder to find out.

For the surfer, there was no more sense of detachment.

He screamed.

He screamed as every nerve in his body was set alight, pulled, twisted, and pinched. He could feel the creature's teeth against his bone. He could feel hot blood shooting from his sliced arteries.

The surfer screamed, and prayed, and cried. He let go of his mind, his bowels, and his hope.

And then the shark let go, too.

It didn't part with grace.

What followed was beyond agony. Beyond the surfer's comprehension of what it meant to suffer. The man brought his hands to his head as he howled against the pain, but instead of feeling the fingers of his left hand, there was the sensation of hot liquid spurting against his face – blood.

His hand was gone.

Eyes wild with adrenaline and misery, he saw that his hamstring had left with it.

The surfer had been eaten.

Eaten while he was alive.

There were no more screams.

2

Josh Kelly didn't scream as he woke from the nightmare. It was too familiar for that, an unwelcome and irritating neighbor rather than an armed intruder running riot in his mind. And yet, Kelly could feel that his heart rate was higher. He knew from experience that the sheets around him would be wet and growing cold with sweat, and that he was awake long before his alarm was set to rouse him.

'You never get any prettier,' he grumbled to the shark that had changed his life.

Kelly's words were part of a well-worn routine that went back years. A little light-hearted defiance to prime himself for the day ahead, because life had to go on.

The surfer looked around his room, and listened. The window was open, the air warm. A thin net curtain stirred with a breeze that carried the smell of the ocean. Kelly wondered why he was alone. He knew that he'd had company when he fell asleep. Her name was Caroline, and she was a volleyball coach at UCLA, Kelly's alma mater. Caroline's hair and skin were dark, and her tastes in the bedroom darker still. Kelly had met her the previous morning, after delivering a talk to the student-athletes of Caroline's squad.

Kelly's path to that meeting had begun fifteen years ago, when he made it on to UCLA's football team as a 'walk-on', the term given to players who earned a spot on the roster despite not having come to the school on an athletic scholarship. He'd remained a fixture on the team for the remainder of his time in college, and though he didn't have what it took to make it to the pros, his work ethic and personality had made him a favorite of the staff. A couple of months ago, the athletics department had approached him, asking if he could come in regularly to talk to the student-athletes about overcoming adversity. As Kelly liked to joke, he'd gone from fish food to sought-after inspirational speaker, occasional documentary presenter, and, of all things, a hard-working advocate for the conservation of sharks and the oceans.

Yesterday had been the turn of the UCLA volleyball teams to hear the talk that described that journey: the years of physio; the depression; a life that had seemed robbed of purpose.

It was a powerful story. Powerful enough that Caroline had not let him leave without the promise of dinner that night. Powerful enough that the shark had come to visit Kelly in his dreams. Without fail, the attack would play out in the nights that followed his talks. Now it seemed likely that his sweating and shouting had scared Caroline from his bed.

'You took my hand and leg, man,' Kelly muttered to the shark in his mind. 'Do you really have to cock-block me, too?'

5

He sat upright. The sheets had been thrown clear as Kelly refought his battle with the Great White, leaving him with an unobstructed view of his body. Kelly's left arm was gone from the middle of his forearm, the stump formed neatly where the surgeons had rounded it off to make the best possible fitting for a prosthetic limb - an animatronic replacement that worked off of sensors detecting twitching muscles in his forearm. Kelly'd always had the torso of a surfer, and dependency on his core strength since the attack had left him with a mid-section that resembled a Greek statue. His friends openly hated him for his abs, but there was nothing to be envied about Kelly's left leg – there was almost nothing of it. The White had taken his entire hamstring and his sciatic nerve with it, leaving Kelly with the choice of dragging around a useless lump of flesh for the rest of his life, or amputating the entire thing. For a man who lived and breathed an active lifestyle, the decision had been simple – chop it.

Not much had been simple after that. Even the act of getting out of bed was one that had to be learned with hour after hour of cursing, sweating, and shouting. Kelly was six foot three inches tall and, before the shark had taken part of him for lunch, he had weighed an athletic 220 pounds. That muscle had been a blessing and a curse. With most of it stacked on one side of his body, it had taken Kelly almost two years to recalibrate his center of gravity to the point where he could 'comfortably' exercise on his new limbs.

He began pulling on his prosthetics. Caroline hadn't batted an eyelid when he'd told her that he was taking them off to sleep. There *had* been a time when Kelly had felt . . . different. Ashamed. Half a man. But those days were long gone. 'Know your worth,' people seemed fond of saying these days. Kelly knew his, and though he was humble enough to know that he had flaws, he was comfortable enough in his own skin that he wouldn't lose sleep over a woman who took issue with his appearance.

Kelly stood, and tested the fit of the artificial limbs. They were the best money could buy, finished in a matt black. He liked to joke that the black gauntlet was the same model worn by Darth Vader, and that he could choke people from the other side of a room. More than once, a smiling woman had asked him to 'prove it.'

After savoring those memories for a moment, and wishing that Caroline was still in the bedroom, Kelly began stripping his bed. The sheets were damp with sweat, but Kelly could live with damp, rather than soaked - nightmares were acceptable, but sloppy housekeeping was not. Like so many things in his life, he knew from experience that things could always be worse. To be where he was now, from where he had been . . .

Kelly threw the sheets into his washing machine, and began his morning routine. He'd built order in a life that the shark had chewed into chaos, and now he walked through the kitchen and living area of his three-bedroom apartment, and stepped out on to the reason that had brought him here from the bedlam of Hollywood: his balcony.

A few hundred yards away, the deep blue of the Pacific stretched away to the horizon. A sense of calm and happiness washed over Kelly and his body as he felt the cool morning air tease at his skin, and the smell of sea air fill his nostrils. There was still a half-hour before the sun would come up behind him, but Kelly could make out the shape of the San Clemente Pier stretching out into the waters. He could hear the waves crashing. He could see them white and silver in the dawn. He could feel the energy in them. The power. A connection and a reminder that, no matter how bad things got, Kelly was not alone. He was a part of something bigger. A part of something that he did not understand, but that he had learned to trust.

Kelly sat, closed his eyes, drew in deep breaths, and meditated. It was a ritual that he had followed for years. It was one of the practices that he credited with saving his life, just as much as the lifeguards who had pulled him to shore and stemmed his bleeding, or the surgeons who had repaired his mangled body. When Kelly stood up ten minutes later, the memory of the shark had faded back into the ocean. Before Kelly's eyes were palm trees and peace.

He could never have imagined what was to come.

3

'Morning.' Caroline smiled. She was wearing yoga pants and a cropped T-shirt, and breathing deeply. 'I went for a run. You were sleeping like a baby so I didn't want to wake you.'

Heart thumping in his chest at the sight of her, Kelly felt on the verge of a coronary. After a moment, he recovered: 'I was just about to make coffee. Can I get you anything?'

Caroline stood her ground as he came towards her from across the kitchen. She smelt of sea air and sex. Kelly put the flesh of his right hand against her lower back. It was damp with sweat.

'Why are you smiling?' she whispered, teasing, in his ear.

'I was just thinking it was a shame that I already stripped the sheets.'

She laughed, and pushed him away. 'Pervert,' she joked, before tossing him a box from a countertop. 'I want to try this.'

It was a blend of mushroom coffee – the legal kind – that professed to be a source of mental focus and well-being. One of the many things in Kelly's life that his gung-ho brother condemned as 'woo woo.'

'I mix it with coconut oil,' he said. 'That work for you? Take a seat, and I'll make you a treat.'

'Promises, promises.' She smiled again as she straddled a chair.

Tearing his eyes away from her, Kelly went into the fridge, pulling out spinach, kale, berries, and ice. He blended these with a plant-based protein powder and a handful of nuts, making the nutrient-rich shake that helped him cope with the rigors of his injuries and lifestyle.

As he blended, Caroline got to her feet, and picked up a framed photograph. She brought it with her as Kelly walked back to the balcony, and placed it between the two smoothies on the table.

'You look so young and handsome,' she teased, pinching his stubbled cheek.

Kelly felt obliged to follow her eyes to the photograph. He saw a young man full of pride and promise and purpose. Josh Kelly, the LAPD recruit. His hair was cropped back then. Now, it fell thick and wavy to the back of his neck. His eyes had changed, too. They'd always been dark, but now they held a degree of intensity that hadn't been there before the attack.

'It was taken at the beginning of the police academy,' he explained. He didn't need to tell her that there wasn't a photograph of him at graduation. Caroline had heard his talk at UCLA. She'd heard how the shark had taken more than just Kelly's hand and leg.

Her smile slipped. 'You were a month from graduating?'

Kelly set his glass down. He wasn't as hungry as he had been. 'Two weeks shy,' he acknowledged.

Caroline recognized a trapped nerve. 'I'm sorry, Josh.'

Kelly shrugged, and straightened himself. Playing the victim was not his style, no matter how tempting it was when a gorgeous woman's eyes were promising to heal the hurt any way she could.

'Hey, don't be,' he told her. 'The universe has a way of working things out for a reason, right? If that day hadn't happened, I wouldn't be sitting here right now, enjoying this beautiful morning with you . . .'

'I guess.' She blushed, and Kelly turned to look at her in the eyes.

'. . . your name's Katie, right?'

He laughed as he ducked the lazy slap that came his way, Caroline letting her hand fall onto his shoulder. She worked her fingers into the tight muscle of his neck as he looked out to sea.

'Things work out for a reason,' Kelly continued.

She followed his gaze to the waters, tinted rose pink as the sky above them began to bleed with the sunrise.

'Do you say that because you really believe it,' she asked after a moment, 'or because you have to?'

He turned his head to meet her hazel eyes. There was more behind them than he'd given her credit for. Maybe if he'd known that, he would have said no to dinner.

'Would it matter?'

They sat in silence after that. The picture before them was a moment that could never be repeated. A second in life that was a secret known only to them. No matter if they never saw or spoke to each other again, they had shared a sunrise.

'We should surf today,' Caroline finally tried, having decided that she wanted more moments with this man, if only a few. Despite Kelly's profession as a speaker, Caroline felt as though he was sharing an edited story of his struggles. There was something else. Something he was leaving out. She hadn't realized something was missing until she'd spent a night and a dawn with him.

But then Caroline's instincts spoke to her, whispering that moments were as much as anyone could hope for from Kelly, and not because of any ill intent on his behalf. She'd seen his kind before. Elite performers who could never sit still. Good people who beat themselves up for not being better. Who could never accept the standard that they achieved, no matter how high.

'I can't,' he told her. 'I wish I could.' Kelly's lips were smiling, but his eyes were not.

She moved her fingers from his neck to his hair, playing with it gently. Something told her that he was about to be on the move again. Little though she knew of him, there was no doubting that he was an adventurer. Every smiling photo in his home was of Kelly at some exotic location: snowboarding in the Alps; a peak in Yosemite; cage diving in South Africa. It was why the somber young Kelly in his LAPD uniform had stood out so starkly. A regimented youth whose life then seemed at odds with the one he lived now, an existence that seemed so carefree, so different to the trials and regulation of life as a police officer. Her fascination with Kelly was growing. From the moment he'd walked into the athletic department yesterday, she'd known he was a rare breed. Caroline was one herself, and felt a pull towards him that came from someplace far deeper than simple physical attraction.

When he spoke again, she could see a spark in his eyes. A flicker of adventure. A desire for the chaotic, the unplanned, and the unexplainable. She wondered if Kelly was even aware of it, or that he was simply caught up in the riptide of his own life.

'I'm going out of town.' He smiled at the beautiful woman beside him. 'Just a few days, then I'll be back.'

'OK.' She kept playing with his hair. 'Maybe I'll see you when you get back.'

'I'd like that.'

Their moment was at its end.

She would never see the man again.

4

Forty-five years in the desert and Detective Tonya Sanders still hadn't gotten used to the summer heat. In fact, as she got older and air conditioning got better, she felt it more than ever. It was oppressive, a dry expansion of the air that seemed almost malevolent in the way it wanted to fill your throat and cook your eyeballs. At least in the city there was an escape from it through the nearest doorway. Out here, in the rocky canyons that shimmered and sizzled as though God had left open a gas valve? There was no respite. Just a constant beating down that reminded Sanders that she was mortal. Despite the phone in her pocket, and the new truck at the end of the hiking trail, she was just an animal on borrowed time when it came to the big bad backyard of Las Vegas.

'Who the hell would wanna come out in this?' she asked the patrolman who was waiting for her, his uniform soaked in dark patches around his armpits. The officer's body armor was held in his left hand, but Sanders was not about to reprimand him for that – in her book, department policy took a back seat to common sense.

The younger officer wore sunglasses, yet still the desert forced him to shield his eyes. 'No idea, detective,' he replied, and he was about to say more, but the words caught in his throat.

Sanders knew why. He had *the look*. The moment when a person clearly saw her face, and didn't know whether to look away, stare, or ask how she had come to look *that* way. It was a moment that Sanders dealt with daily, and had done for years. Her reply varied with her mood. Today, baking in a canyon, she had no desire for subtlety. Knowing from experience that the man's mind would keep wandering until she gave him the answers, she said calmly: 'I got shot. Nine millimeter.'

'Oh,' he replied. Sanders wondered if he was about to follow with, *I didn't notice.* That had happened before.

Instead, the patrolman told her that it was just about another hundred yards to go up the trail. The hikers who had called the police were waiting there, with . . . *it*.

They walked on in silence. Just the open-mouthed breathing of scorched air, and the crunch of ancient trail beneath their boots.

Sanders looked around at the Martian landscape. She had been here before. A lifetime before. She hadn't known much about gunshot wounds back then. She'd never held a bullet in her hand, let alone have one smash into her jaw, leaving half her face looking as if it'd been pieced together from broken glass. No, when Sanders had last visited Sloan Canyon, she'd been a teacher, here to show her class the Native American petroglyphs – etched drawings on the stone of men and deer, spear and combat. *Some things never change,* Sanders thought. The petroglyphs were telling stories of death in the Las Vegas valley long before the news.

Sanders smirked at that. She'd been born and raised here, but it was only when she came to sit at the head of a class that she *really* learned about her city: when the kids came in with bruises and black eyes. When they cried because their daddy was going back into prison. When they were taken by the state and put into foster care because Mommy loved meth more than her own kids. Sanders had soon come to realize that she was a history teacher who knew nothing of the present. She was teaching the Founding Fathers to kids who didn't even know their own dad. What use telling them what year the White House was built when the kids' own homes were crumbling around them?

And then it had come. She'd known that it would only be a matter of time. Empty chairs weren't rare, but this one was filled by a ghost. Jermichael. He'd been one of her favorites. He'd been one of everybody's favorites. His death was gang-related. His life had not been.

That day, Sanders had put her books back on a shelf. She'd gone to the Las Vegas Police Department, and told them that she wanted a badge and a gun instead.

The detective turned and looked over her shoulder. In the middle of the desert, a dusty metropolis rose from the sand and rock. Tourists called it Sin City. She just called it home. Sanders wondered if she'd made a difference to the place in the fifteen years since Jermichael had died.

Ahead of her, two hikers stood waiting. Despite the heat, they were white and shaking. Sanders could understand why.

There was a severed arm at their feet.

5

The morning had been good to Kelly. He'd driven two hundred miles behind the wheel of his Model S Tesla, beating the 'orange crush' that was Orange County's early rush hour, and escaping the Inland Empire before traffic could truly screw him. He was now cruising comfortably on I-15, the highway that dissects the Mojave Desert, and which would lead him to his home for the next few days – Las Vegas.

Cresting a rise, Kelly smiled as he saw a familiar sight. This was a drive that he'd once made often, and the view ahead of him was a sure sign that the journey's back had been broken.

To his right stretched the silver-gilded pan of the Mojave National Preserve. Ahead, sitting astride the highway, was a mile-long cluster of buildings. It was the town of Baker, a handful of gas stations dotting the road like vertebrae on a dusty skeleton. When Kelly passed the familiar turn off for Zzyzx Road, he knew it was time to make a final stop before Vegas.

He came off the highway, and pulled into a Greek fast-food joint. He watched the other customers eat as quickly as they could so that they could get back on the road, and on their way to fulfill dreams of adventure and riches. At the tail-end of weekends, this place would be full of groups of friends with bags under their eyes swapping war stories and insults as they remembered who had done what, and who had done who. It was a good place to be a fly on the wall. Right now, the restaurant was mostly empty except for a few knots of people in their twenties, heading to Vegas for the same reason that Kelly was . . .

Pandora, the biggest electronic dance music festival in the world.

Kelly looked at the bracelet on the flesh of his wrist. It was made from a brightly colored fabric, and fastened with a clasp that meant that it could not be taken off and swapped with other people. It was Kelly's entry credentials for the festival, a VIP band mailed to him weeks before on behalf of a friend. One of many that Kelly had made on his journey into dance music. It was a path that he'd taken accidentally, when he was lost, and wandering. Now he hoped that it was a part of his life that would never end. He found it hard to explain to those outside of the movement, but Kelly knew, in his own heart and mind, that electronic music had helped save him from his darkest days. Sometimes, when he shared that belief, he would be met with an empathic 'Me too!' At other times, there would be a subtle note of skepticism. Some, like Kelly's closest friend in law enforcement, would scoff and tell him that 'People only listen to that shit because they're on drugs.'

Clearing his tray and heading back outside into the furnace of the desert, Kelly's eye was caught by a forty-one-meter-high structure that stood like a needle against the cloudless blue sky. It was the world's largest thermometer, built to commemorate the record temperatures in nearby

Death Valley. Kelly had seen the thermometer on dozens of occasions, and it always made him smile. There was just something so *American* about it.

Kelly crossed the street, and took out his phone. Feeling the sweat begin to build around his lower back, he opened his Instagram app. Kelly's profile was a popular one, with 150,000 followers. They came to see Kelly's stories of shark conservation, or of his adventures across the globe in the name of sport and documentary making. 'They're just there to see you with your shirt off,' Kelly's mom would say, and that was probably true too.

Kelly hit record on the app's story feature, and smiled into the camera.

'Hi, guys, just wanted to share with you this fantastic piece of American architecture, the biggest thermometer in the world! I just had a quick stop in Baker on my way to Pandora Festival. If any of you guys are there, let me know! It would be great to meet you!'

Kelly set the video to upload and headed back across the simmering tarmac to his car. It was already day two of the three-day festival, and he didn't want to miss any more of it than he'd already had to. It had been a tough decision for him to skip day one in order to deliver the talk at UCLA, but he figured the universe had repaid him for that by introducing him to Caroline.

Kelly looked at his phone: there was an incoming call.

'Hello?'

His smile slipped. His shoulders slumped.

The universe wasn't doing him any favors today.

'*Fuck.*'

6

Tonya Sanders stood beneath the shade of a tent-top thrown up by the uniformed officers. A couple of hours after the hikers had discovered the arm on the hiking trail, the dusty parking lot of Sloan Canyon had come to resemble a very somber tailgate party. Sanders helped herself to a Gatorade from an ice chest, and tried to focus on the image in her mind: a severed arm belonging to a young woman. A jagged stump, as though it had been *ripped off*. A couple of nice rings on the fingers, fashionable, not matrimonial. A pair of fabric bands on the wrist.

The arm was now under the care of the Crime Scene Investigations team and the Investigative Services Division, to whom Sanders was attached. Meanwhile, search parties were beginning to comb the area for its owner. Sanders didn't expect that the body would be found quickly, or that the owner would be found alive – arm ripped off at the socket, there was no way that the victim hadn't bled out. The mountainous area was a labyrinth of nooks and crannies. One moment of slack attention and an officer could walk right by it. Sanders expected that the dogs would be the ones to save the day. They so often were.

The detective realized with a sigh that her plans for the next few days had died along with the owner of the arm. That sucked. She'd been looking forward to seeing her friend for a long time now. If she could count on anyone outside of family, it was he. He was there for her when the world had told her that she was no longer beauty, but beast. Those had been dark days. She'd shut out everyone, including Dez, who used to be called her fiancé. Sanders had pushed him so far that he didn't even have to walk away – he just had to stop moving. Now he was called husband by someone else. In the first two years following her shooting, Sanders had wanted nothing but to be left alone in her own misery. Her medical leave from the force looked like as if would stretch on indefinitely, but indefinitely didn't feature in Sanders's mind. So much of her identity – her *worth* – had been tied up in the way that she looked. If Sanders was going to be a monster, did she want to be anything at all?

She'd decided that she didn't. Sooner or later, she'd finish what the shooter had started. *She'd end her life.*

But one man had changed all that.

A stranger.

Sanders had found him on just another day when the blinds were drawn and the TV was on. Distraction from life, not the living of it. She was channel surfing when she came across a nature show. It hooked her immediately. Sanders couldn't have given two shits about the animals that the man was talking about, but she wanted to know about *him*.

One arm. One leg. A 'monster' like her. How had *he* made it out alive? How was *he* not only surviving, but thriving? The smile on his face almost made her want to hate him, she was so envious.

But she didn't.

Instead she searched out the show, and the man. She found that he was not only a presenter, but a speaker, and those talks were on YouTube for anyone to see. Within a day, Sanders had consumed every bit of content she could find from him. How he had gone from police recruit to amputee. How he had lost his identity. His dreams. How he had struggled with depression, and suicide. How he had come through it all with purpose, and pride. How he had built himself a new life that he loved every bit as much as the old one.

Sanders had to meet him. She knew that God had directed her to see that channel, at that moment, for a reason. This was her lifeline. Her way in from the dark waters that were getting deeper and deeper, and would eventually consume her. No one in her life understood what she was going through, but she knew that this man would.

And he had an event in Los Angeles.

She'd booked her ticket. It had been the first step in winning back her life.

'Shit.' Sanders dumped her recollections into a trash bag along with her Gatorade bottle. '*Shit.*'

Over the past two years that man had gone from mentor to friend. He was a little brother and teacher rolled into one. One of the few people that the introverted Sanders could never see enough of. And today, at last, he was coming back to Vegas.

But there was a body to be found.

'*Shiiit.*'

She took out her phone, and called Josh Kelly.

7

After being directed by the officer at the entrance to the parking lot, Kelly pulled to a stop on the hot tarmac.

He was only halfway out the car's door when she appeared, her arms folded and her jaw jutting out.

Kelly chuckled. 'God forbid Captain Badass cracks a smile when she sees her homie.' He grinned, pulling his friend into a bear hug.

Sanders let out a snort. 'I'm a detective, not a captain. No wonder you washed out of the academy.'

The tall man gave a belly laugh; then he took in his surroundings. 'Maybe for the better. It's hot as balls out here.'

'Says the guy who comes to Vegas in June for a music festival.'

'You got me there. I guess it's just more bearable with music. And the best bits happen after dark, anyway.'

Sanders rolled her eyes. 'You mean when they turn the power off?'

'Don't knock it until you try it! I thought today was gonna be the day?'

'Josh, I love you, and that's why I have to be honest with you . . . That bang-bang shit is for kids and junkies. I staged this murder just to get out of it.'

'Ooooooh, that's dark, T. A murder?'

Sanders shrugged. 'Murder, maybe. Too early to know. Pretty serious, though. Couple of hikers found something nasty.'

Kelly pulled a face. 'Who goes hiking in this heat?'

'*Right?* But anyway. They came across an arm. Now we're looking for a body.'

Sanders noticed how Kelly's eyes went a little wider at the detail. Not from fear, but with the kind of curiosity that seemed inherent in a select few. Those who could find a challenge in every aspect of life, including death.

Sanders shook her head. 'You're such a jock.'

'What?'

'You're thinking you could find the body before anyone else does. Classic jock.'

Kelly smiled in an admission of guilt. He'd been competing since he was a kid. Surf tourneys. High-school football, then college. At the police academy, he'd put himself down for every team, and driven his classmates on to accept nothing but victory.

But since the shark attack, most of his competition had been against himself.

'I'm bummed we won't get to hang out today,' he admitted, seeing his hubris for what it was, and letting it slip away.

'Me too.' Sanders smiled sadly. 'Here's the keys to my place. The guest room's good to go. Come and go as you like. *Mi casa es su casa*, but that doesn't mean you can go bringing back your skanky hos.'

'Skanky hos?' Kelly asked in mock horror. 'Not even if they speak Spanish?'

Before Sanders could open her mouth to reply, the pair were silenced by a shout:

'We got a body!'

8

Sanders knew that Kelly's dream had been to become a cop. She knew that the shark attack had robbed him of that future. She also knew that she wouldn't be alive to investigate the demise of the person in the canyon if it wasn't for Kelly. Her friend liked to talk about the universe and 'the law of attraction,' whatever that was, but Sanders believed in providence, and God's plan. Without doubt, she knew that Kelly had been brought into her life by God. It seemed only right to assume that Kelly, the man who had wanted to be a cop, had been with her the moment the body was discovered for a reason.

'You want to come with me?' Sanders asked him.

Kelly's answer was out of his mouth before he could even think about it.

Then, as they followed the heralding officer along a hiking trail, Kelly told himself that it wasn't morbid curiosity that made him do it, but simply a desire to spend time with his friend and see her at work. It would be a life lesson, Kelly told himself. An education.

It certainly was *something*.

'Are you OK?' Sanders asked as he took in the sight of the body.

Kelly nodded, but it was a lie. Having seen his own anatomy stripped bare, he'd assumed that the bodies of others would have no effect on him.

He was wrong.

Maybe it was her age: no older than twenty-five, she lay on her back, what would have been bright eyes now crawled over by ants.

Maybe it was her appearance: tattoos of flowers and poems wrapped around her, made visible where her T-shirt had been savagely ripped open. Piercings in her ears, nose, lips, and nipples made her seem so at odds with the rocky place that had become her burial ground. A designer bag lay by her side.

Or maybe it was her wounds; flesh that would have been sun-kissed was now stiff, bloodied, and dusty. The socket of her arm was a grotesque vision of torn flesh and sinew. One of her breasts had been torn away. She looked . . .

'. . . eaten.'

'What?' Kelly asked, snapping his eyes upwards.

'I said,' Sanders repeated, 'it looks like she's been eaten. Mountain lion, I guess.'

Kelly made no reply. He was a rookie. Less than a rookie. His mind was a million miles behind the professionals working over the scene. One of them joined him now, and put out a hand. He was short, and built like a football player, powerful shoulders and a short neck. 'Bobby Brovetski.'

'Josh. You guys work together?'

Brovetski nodded: 'Same department,' the lack of any embellishment making Kelly wonder at how close their working relationship actually was. He knew that Sanders didn't have a partner. She could be her own worst enemy, and had sentenced herself to exile following her disfigurement.

Brovetski took another look at the body. 'Mountain lion,' he said to no one in particular. 'Third attack in this stretch of mountain in six months.'

Kelly was stunned. His work with sharks had him crossing paths with many others in the conservation arena. He'd heard that attacks by America's big cats on humans were extremely rare.

'Three people *killed*?'

Brovetski shook his head. 'This is the first kill. The other two times, hikers got some injuries but the cat got scared away.'

Kelly made himself look back at the body, and soon wished that he hadn't. He could picture all too clearly, with the same bloody detail as his nightmares, how the girl would have been torn apart.

It was Sanders's voice that broke him from the violent vision. 'We'll see what the autopsy has to say,' was her take.

And with that, she gestured to Kelly that their time at the body was at an end. Sanders was needed in the parking lot.

Captain Wolford had arrived.

9

Kelly waited in the air conditioning of his car while his friend went to meet and brief Captain Wolford. As he sat alone, Kelly couldn't help but think of the body of the girl in the canyon. When he closed his eyes, he saw the ants that had crawled over hers. When he opened them, the image was still there.

'You should have stayed in the fucking car,' he scolded himself, before reaching for his phone. There were dozens of notifications from his social media, but Kelly ignored them. He thought about texting Caroline, but what would he say?

Vegas trip's going great. No luck on the slots but I did see a girl with her arm ripped off and her guts peeking out!

No. Kelly knew what he had to do. It had worked when his visions had been of his own bloody wounds. Maybe it would work when the butchered meat was of an unknown girl.

And so he meditated.

With his eyes closed, and his concentration fixed on his breath, it was the sound of the passenger door opening that broke Kelly from his mental escape.

It was Sanders.

She wasn't happy.

'I knew it was bad news when he showed up,' she said, taking a seat and closing the door. 'Captains don't show up at bodies, Kelly. He must have seen something he didn't like. Her age, maybe.'

Kelly didn't get it. 'Her age? Why would that bring him out here?'

'The same reason as you,' Sanders replied, helping herself to a water from the passenger footwell. 'The festival.'

Kelly didn't need to tell her that he still didn't get it. His face did that just fine.

'Something you may not know about your little disco is that it nets the city one point three billion in extra revenue,' she educated him. 'When it comes to young people dying this week, my bosses are going to want to triple-check the shit out of it, and hope that there's no fallout on the cash cow.'

Kelly gave himself a moment for the figure, and its implications, to sink in. Everything Sanders was saying made sense.

'So he's happy to say this is . . . an animal attack?'

Sanders shrugged. 'Hey, maybe it is. If you hear hoofbeats, think horses, not zebras. But anyway, animal attack is what the Captain Wolford's told Brovetski to brief them.'

Again, Kelly wasn't following. 'Them?'

Sanders pointed to the far end of the lot. As Kelly had been meditating, a handful of news trucks had entered.

'Tonya.' Kelly spoke up, suddenly anxious. 'They can't just go reporting this is a death from an animal attack. Not without evidence.' There was an edge to his words. An urgency.

'I'm kind of a fan of evidence, Kelly, but have you watched the news in the last five or six years? Facts are optional.'

The man beside her shook his head, and for the first time since she'd known him, Sanders saw violence in his eyes.

'Not to me they're not.'

Josh Kelly threw open the car door, and stepped into the sunlight.

10

Sanders walked beside Kelly as he made his way across the parking lot. He was heading towards the news trucks, the rolling gait of his prosthetic leg pronounced as he hurried to intercept Brovetski – the detective looked as though he was gearing up to give a statement to a half-dozen reporters and cameras.

'Can I get a quick word, please?' Kelly asked the officer.

Brovetski was taken aback. He looked at Sanders, who gave a small shrug and a nod.

'Sure . . .' the shorter man replied, moving out of earshot of the crews. 'What's up, man? It was Kelly, right?'

'Yeah,' Kelly said quickly. 'Look, I hear you're gonna tell people that this was a mountain-lion attack. I think that's a mistake.'

Again, Brovetski looked from the tall man to Sanders. If he was offended, he showed no sign. 'OK. Why's that?'

'I know how crazy this sounds coming from a guy who lost an arm and a leg to a shark, but that kind of stuff in the press, it's not a good thing. People start getting ideas. They start playing vigilante. I'm not saying they're doing it from a bad place, but before you know it, every cat from a cougar to your grandma's tabby is gonna have a bullseye on it.'

The detective took a second to digest the words, but Kelly could see that the man didn't like the taste. 'I hear what you're saying, buddy, but the proof is staring at us right there. You don't think those wounds are from a big cat?'

At first, Kelly said nothing. Then: 'Maybe,' he conceded. 'Could be post-mortem.'

'Could be,' Brovetski allowed. 'But could be that it's not. Captain doesn't want to risk it, so I'm gonna put out this warning to hikers, telling them there's a risk of deadly attack, and that they should avoid hiking alone, or at all. But thanks for your input, OK? I really do appreciate it.'

Kelly's jaw was tight. 'Sure,' he said through gritted teeth.

Brovetski was either oblivious to the tension, or didn't care. 'You really lose your arm and leg to a shark? I'd love to hear that story, man.'

'Yeah, OK. Let's grab a beer sometime.'

Kelly turned and walked back to his car. Sanders fell in beside him. 'You know he probably thinks you will? I don't think he understands sarcasm.'

Kelly turned, and looked back to the news crews and Brovetski. 'I don't blame him for thinking the way he does.' He shook his head. 'But look, Tonya, the things that people say matter, and . . .' He trailed off.

'And what?'

Kelly rubbed a hand over his stubbled jaw. Something had been bothering him, and it was about more than just a body.

It was about how the girl had come to be there.

'Hiking on her own? Out here? Did you even find ID on her?'

Sanders shook her head. Something in her manner told Kelly that he'd struck a chord.

'You said this to the captain, didn't you?'

Sanders nodded.

'And?'

She said nothing.

For a long moment, neither did Kelly. 'But I guess it's not my problem, is it? Shit. I'm sorry for getting myself caught up there, T. I suppose seeing the girl like that shocked me more than a little.'

'It would shock anyone.'

'You don't get used to it?'

'A bit, I guess. But I don't think that's necessarily a good thing.'

'Hey, well, at least I got to see you at work. Meet you back at your place?'

Kelly put out his arms and embraced his friend. It was only as they broke apart that Sanders's eyes went wide, and she grabbed at his arm.

'What are these?' she asked urgently, looking at the two bands of brightly patterned fabric on his wrist.

34

'They're my entry credentials for the festival,' Kelly explained, confused. 'Why?'

Sanders spoke slowly. 'Because I've seen them before,' she told him. 'They were on her arm.'

11

Who goes hiking after dark?

Kelly asked himself that question over and over as he drove into Henderson and parked outside of Sanders's three-bedroom home. He asked it as he let himself inside, took a juice from the fridge, and put his bag into the guest room. He asked it as he took a shower, changed his clothes, and ignored dozens of notifications on his phone. The festival finished every night at midnight, and yesterday was the first day of the festival. If the girl had been there, then . . .

Who goes hiking after dark?

Extreme athletes, Kelly had decided. The kind who run ultra-marathons at all times of day and night, and in all kinds of conditions. But while the girl had looked to be slender, nothing about her clothing said that she was out in the canyon as a matter of sport. Kelly hadn't seen a headlamp, water bottles, or rucksack.

Who goes hiking after dark?

Someone making bad decisions. Maybe the girl was drunk, or high, *but* . . . Sloan Canyon was twenty miles from the Strip. Ten from the south of the city. So why Sloan Canyon?

Kelly knew that people went out into the desert alone for 'vision quests' – he'd done one himself – and it stood to reason that if a person wanted to experience such drug-induced soul-searching in Vegas, then maybe they would do it in an area where the petroglyphs marked out a spiritual connection with the country's ancient inhabitants. Kelly's own experience with a vision quest had involved a shaman who kept close tabs on him, but it could be that, like many others in search of an adventure of the soul, the girl had taken an ancient rite of passage and enacted it recklessly. Through all of Kelly's reasoning, this explanation seemed the most believable to him.

But what about the festival bands?

The bits of brightly patterned fabric bothered him. Pandora was located at the Las Vegas Motor Speedway to the north of the city, *thirty-five miles* from Sloan Canyon. Kelly allowed that it was perfectly possible – though his gut told him highly unlikely – that the girl could have attended the festival, taken drugs, and then felt the need for a solo trip into the mountains. But if she was going to do that, why travel through all of Vegas to get there, when there were canyons and trails only miles from the Speedway? For that matter, where was her car? Sanders hadn't mentioned one. Was it sitting abandoned at the head of the hiking trail?

'Why are you even thinking about this shit?' Kelly scolded himself as he went back to the fridge. It was packed full of all kinds of food, Sanders having prepared for the big man's visit with a shock and awe campaign of grocery shopping. 'Just drop it,' he told himself as he spread peanut butter and jelly on to a bagel.

But he couldn't. Questions swirled in his mind. Kelly wished that he was by the ocean so that he could paddle out and clear his head. Nowhere else could he find such focus and serenity.

Who the fuck goes hiking after dark? he asked again.

How does someone wind up dead in a canyon, thirty-five miles from a festival that they had access to?

Did they even attend the festival?

Where's their car?

Were they alone?

Could a mountain lion really have killed her?

Why do I even care?

'You're an idiot.' Kelly finally chided himself gently. 'A fucking idiot.'

And not because he was playing Twenty Questions.

Kelly was an idiot because he had missed out the most important question of all.

Leaving his food half-finished on the kitchen countertop, Kelly took out his phone, and went in search of the answer to the one question that truly mattered.

Who is she?

12

It took Kelly just over an hour to discover the dead girl's identity.

It came in the form of a photograph. The girl was flanked by two friends, a young guy and a girl; all three were smiling. The girl that Kelly had seen in the canyon was wearing a pink bikini top and black hot pants. There was glitter on her arms and face. Her tattoos coiled around her torso like the inviting serpent of Eden. Behind the trio of friends was a huge stage and thousands of other ravers. The girl in the canyon *had* been to the festival and, from the look on her face, she had known happiness on her last day on earth. Something about that gave Kelly a little solace.

'How the hell did you find her?' Sanders asked when he called with the news.

'I searched hashtags,' he told her simply.

'Hashtags? What are you talking about, Kelly?'

'I figured there was a good chance the girl was at the festival,' Kelly explained. 'Judging by her age, chances are that she has an Instagram account, and you don't go to an event like Pandora without posting about it.'

'I still don't get what that has to do with hashtags,' Sanders said, and Kelly could hear her frustration through the speaker.

'Instagram has a function where you enter a keyword with a hashtag,' he told her, 'and it brings up all of the posts where people have included that hashtag. I started searching for #pandora, #pandorafestival, and then it was just a case of scrolling through the pictures that were posted yesterday.'

'There're over a hundred thousand people at that festival. Like you said, I bet most of them are of an age and inclination where they're going to be using these kind of pages. How the hell did you narrow that down?'

'I couldn't,' Kelly admitted, 'but the girls at these events don't wear a lot of clothes, T. I could skim through the pictures looking for girls who were as heavily tattooed as ours.'

'*Ours?*'

'You know what I mean.'

'I do, Kelly. And I appreciate your help. I mean, really appreciate it, but I know what you're like.'

Kelly frowned. 'And what's that?'

There was a pause before he got his answer. 'Sensitive.'

Kelly said nothing. It was true.

'I just don't want you ruining your trip and getting upset because of this, OK?' his friend told him.

'Yeah. Yeah, I get it, T, I just want to help out on this.'

'I shouldn't have taken you up there,' Sanders apologized.

'You know, I'm glad that you did. In a strange way. But look, OK? This is really gonna help, Tonya. Once I found the picture of Iris, I could click on it and it gave me the tagged usernames.'

'Iris?'

'Iris Manning. That's our – your – girl's name. I'm going to take screenshots of her profile and send them over to you. She's a popular girl. Sixty thousand followers.'

Kelly opened up the Instagram page and began to screenshot the details. He'd been so caught up in the chase that it was only now the realization hit him that the girl in these pictures was the same one that he'd seen as ant-food in the canyon. The thought made him gag. Looking at her pictures, most of which were in bikinis or lingerie, Kelly saw that Iris had been beautiful. So beautiful. It was hard to reconcile those images with the torn-up carcass that he was seeing when he closed his eyes.

'These are really helpful, Kelly,' Sanders told him as the screenshots began arriving on her phone. 'Is she a model or something? You understand this stuff better than I do.'

'An Insta-model, I think,' Kelly explained. 'Some girls use the app because it's a free platform, and they use it to try and get work or sponsorships from it.'

'Or attention,' Sanders replied coldly. 'She looks like a walking daddy-issue.'

'We all have our baggage,' Kelly offered gently.

Sanders said nothing, and Kelly didn't press the subject. Sanders was fighting her own war in a world where beauty supposedly equaled worth.

'I just don't get this,' Sanders finally said. 'Social media.'

'Of course you do. You're a detective, T, you understand human nature as well as anybody. Social media is just an extension of human desires.'

Sanders snorted. 'I can see what desires her pictures are extending.'

Kelly didn't laugh. 'I'm serious, T. It's the desire to be accepted. The instinct to be envious of others.'

'Bullshit, Kelly,' Sanders scoffed. 'You're not envious of others.'

'I'm envious of you,' he told her truthfully.

'Like my house that much, do you?' she replied, uncomfortable with the knowledge that she was carrying the badge Kelly had always wanted.

'OK, fine.' He thought of another example. 'Laird Hamilton. I'm envious of him.'

'Who?'

'The greatest big-wave surfer of all time, Tonya! Shit, I really do need to get you down to the ocean, but just listen, OK? Social media's just a window on to society, not a society itself. It's a magnifying glass on to human nature, not a change in it.'

Kelly could hear Sanders exhaling loudly down the line. 'It just doesn't look . . . healthy to me.'

'It's a tool,' Kelly concluded. 'It can be used for good or bad, but right now it's found Iris's name. It's told us she was at the festival yesterday, at least during daylight, and best of all, it's given us the names of two people who were with her.'

'How?' Sanders asked.

'There're two people tagged in the photo with her. I'll send you their profiles now. Wait.'

Within a few seconds, Kelly had sent the profiles of two young Asian-Americans to Sanders. They belonged to Adam Nguyen, and Amy Morgan. They were the two ravers who stood smiling alongside Iris in yesterday's photo.

'These kids need to be interviewed . . .' Sanders said.

Kelly said nothing back. He'd expected as much. What he hadn't foreseen were the next two words out of the detective's mouth.

'. . . by you.'

13

Traffic sucked on the Las Vegas Strip, but behind the wheel of his Tesla, Kelly was glad of the moment to catch his breath. Since he'd pulled up into the parking lot at Sloan Canyon, the day had spiraled. Kelly'd come to Vegas expecting to experience a music festival. Instead he'd seen a gruesome body in the rocks, and helped track down the dead girl's identity. Now he was a part of a plan hatched by Sanders.

'We've got enough here to get a rush on an autopsy,' she'd told him over the phone. 'I'll push and see if we can get it done by the end of the day.'

'So you don't think it was a mountain lion?' Kelly'd asked.

Sanders wouldn't say yes or no. 'But we know for a fact that she was at a festival thirty-five miles away. We haven't found a car, either. That's all I need to call this suspicious. I want to see that coroner's report, Kelly. What does your gut say?'

'That I should have gotten a hotel for the night instead of coming to pick up your house keys.'

'Bullshit,' Sanders had scoffed. 'If that's really how you feel though, tell me now. I'd like your help, but not with a gun to your conscience.'

If it really was how Kelly felt, it didn't matter. A young woman was dead. If Kelly could help to find the reason behind that tragic end, then he would.

'What do you need me to do?' he'd asked his friend.

Two minutes later, Kelly had sent a message from his phone. Five minutes after that, he was changed into a pair of black board shorts and white T-shirt that looked like it had been spray-painted on to his muscles. Within a half-hour, he was on the world-famous Strip surrounded by icons – the ominous dark pyramid of the Luxor; the emerald colossus of the MGM; the sleek and modern lines of the Cosmopolitan. On the sidewalks, obese men with frozen margaritas walked alongside shirtless, steroid-pumped bros. Aunt Peggy from Bumblefuck, Montana, waited at a crosswalk alongside a lady straight out of the Versace store, augmented from her hair extensions to her toenails. The Strip was a melting pot where the main ingredients were money and booze. So much booze. It was barely into the afternoon and already there were revelers staggering from casino to casino like casualties escaping a battlefield.

They never take the heat into account, Kelly thought to himself, but he was far from judging. He'd been there.

Kelly pulled out of traffic, and into the valet lane of a casino hotel. 'Welcome to the Cosmopolitan, sir,' the smiling valet greeted him. 'Are you a guest here?'

'No,' he replied, seeing the young man steal a glance at his prosthetic limbs. 'I'm just here for the party.'

14

Kelly walked inside the casino resort, and followed his way from memory to the section of the hotel that was known as Marquee – an umbrella for the nightclub and day-parties that operated in a special area of the casino's premises. Long before Kelly got to the line for entry, he was seeing groups of guys and girls in beachwear heading in the same direction as he was. Kelly smiled to himself as he saw some of those girls go straight to the head of the line. They were the Vegas locals, and they knew the system. Turn up early and looking hot, and they'd get right in free of charge. The more beauties the guys saw going in, the more that they'd pay to follow them, and the easiest way to skip the huge line was to pay for a VIP section. These packages ranged from four-person tables to twenty-person cabanas. On Pandora weekend, Kelly would be surprised if they started at any less than three thousand bucks. Vegas had a new cash cow, and the only gambling involved came from guys betting that their overpriced alcohol would get them laid.

'Excuse me,' Kelly heard from outside of the line. He turned, and found himself looking at a man who was every bit his equal in height, decked out in the black pants and polo shirt of the day-club's security.

'You serve?' the bouncer asked, taking in Kelly's prosthetic limbs. 'I was a Marine myself.'

'I wish I had,' Kelly admitted. 'But it was a shark that took these. Were you ever based down at Camp Pendleton?' he asked, referring to the sprawling Marine Corps base in Southern California. 'I live in San Clemente.'

'No shit? I was Fifth Marines for a couple of years.'

'That's infantry, right?'

'Hell yeah, it is. I was a machine gunner.'

'Sick. And thank you for your service, man.' Kelly smiled, offering his hand. 'Hey, did you ever go to a bar called Big Helyns? My friends work there.

'Oh yeah.' The bouncer laughed and opened the rope, gesturing for Kelly to skip the enormous line. 'Lot of crazy nights in there. Come on, man, come to the front.'

Kelly could feel the envious looks of dozens of men desperate to get in. 'I don't mind waiting in line,' he told the bouncer honestly.

'Tell me about the shark and we're all good. I saw some shit in Iraq but I never met nobody that got eaten by a shark.'

They laughed, and Kelly told his story. A couple of minutes later he was in an elevator on his way up to the pool level. It was crammed full of eager partygoers, and from the way one girl was pressing against him, Kelly guessed that one was impatient for a little more than music.

'I like your hair,' she told him. 'Do you have a table?'

'I don't,' Kelly replied, smiling inside as the girl's attraction to him vanished to nothing.

'Oh, well, maybe I'll see you later then.'

Kelly grinned. He wasn't used to being a last resort, but this was Vegas, and money talked.

Then, as the elevator doors opened, Kelly saw that it talked very loudly indeed.

'Like Caligula learned to DJ,' one of his friends had once said to sum up the Vegas pool-party scene, and Kelly found it hard to argue. Ahead of him, a swarming mass of people filled a pool, dancing maniacally to a mash-up of hip hop and savage dance music. Bikini-clad servers tried to dodge the splashing water as they shuttled bottles of vodka and champagne out to the VIP tables. Along the right-hand side of the pool were fabric-lined cabanas that offered some shelter from the beating sun. On the left were the more permanent 'bungalows,' solid constructions with their own private pools. Here were the most beautiful women and the deepest pockets. Everywhere there was shouting, dancing, and blaring music beneath a hot sun.

Kelly loved it.

So much so that, for a moment, he almost forgot why he was there. Snapping himself from the dream, he took his phone from his pocket and sent a message. Almost immediately, he got one back.

By the bar at the back. Blue bikini. White cap.

Kelly spotted her almost immediately. Her back was to him, but she must have realized he would be coming from the entrance behind her, and turned.

She saw Kelly and waved.

He waved back.

Her name was Amy Morgan and, so far as Kelly knew, she was the last person to have seen Iris Manning alive.

15

When Sanders had floated the idea that Kelly be the bait in a honey trap, he wasn't sure how he felt about the idea. After all, Amy was no suspect, if there even *were* any suspects at all.

'I don't want to mess with people's lives,' Kelly had told Sanders.

'But you do want to find out what happened to Iris?' the detective had asked him.

'Of course.'

'Well, that's police work and investigation, Kelly. I'd love to tell you it's precision surgery, but a lot of the time we're more like a Civil War surgeon with a saw and some pliers. I understand if you don't want to do it, though.'

'I didn't say that,' Kelly had quickly replied.

And so he'd listened again to Sanders's plan. She wanted him to contact Iris's friends from the Instagram picture. She wanted him to arrange a meet outside the scope of a police investigation. 'They'll talk to you,' Sanders assured him.

And they had.

Kelly was no stranger to meeting possible romantic interests through social media. He was a good-looking guy with a large following. Such things bought him a lot of social proof and credit, particularly with the younger generation, and he guessed that Amy was no older than twenty-three. He'd sent her a private message and, within minutes, the pair were talking.

Kelly: 13:10 Hey! This is crazy but I saw you at the Garuda stage yesterday, but before I got chance to introduce myself my friends went in the opposite direction!

Amy: 13:13 Hi. I think you have messaged the wrong person sorry. My friend is @IrisManning. I hope you enjoy the festival.

Seeing the girl's self-deprecating reply had made Kelly feel even worse about the honey trap, but the thought of Iris lying dead in a canyon made him feel sicker still.

Kelly: 13:14 Haha, no! It was you I'm talking about. What are you doing today? Maybe we could meet at the festival?

But Amy had a better idea, and had suggested the pool party.

'Hey.' Kelly smiled as they met in the flesh. 'It's really good to meet you.'

'You too.' Amy blushed a little. Kelly was over a foot taller than the young woman. 'This is my friend,' she added, indicating a short guy with two drinks in his hands.

'Hi,' he greeted Kelly awkwardly.

Kelly smiled, and once Amy had claimed a drink, he shook the young man's hand. It was a weak shake, and Adam Nguyen did not meet Kelly's eye. For a second, Kelly wondered if that was from a guilty conscience. Far more likely, he told himself, that it just came from growing up soft.

'How awesome is this place?' Kelly said, by way of starting conversation.

'So amazing!' Amy piped up. 'I love Joyryde.'

'Is that who's playing? He's sick.'

Amy finished her drink quickly. From the looks that she kept shooting Kelly's physique, he thought it a safe bet that she was building up her Dutch courage. 'So you were at the festival yesterday?' she asked after a hiccup that made her blush.

'I was.'

'Who were your favorite acts?' Amy said excitedly.

Kelly faked a smile. 'Honestly, I got so fucked up that I don't really remember.'

The younger pair grinned at that. Nothing to bind new friends like drugs and alcohol.

'We were rolling balls,' Adam admitted.

'You had a great day then?'

'Yeah, mostly.' Amy shrugged. 'It'll be better today.'

'Why mostly?'

The girl rolled her eyes. 'Ergh, just drama. So stupid.'

'Oh yeah? What kind of drama?' Kelly tried to ask without appearing too interested. 'And hey, can I get you guys a drink? I'm pretty thirsty.'

'Oh, are you sure? That's really nice of you.'

'Yeah, thank you,' Adam added. 'A vodka soda please, if you're sure it's OK?'

'It's fine,' Kelly assured his new friends, putting in the order to the bar staff. 'So what was this drama?'

'Oh, just a friend of ours.' Amy spoke with distaste in her voice. 'I'm not even sure if she is our friend any more, to be honest.'

'Did you guys fight?'

'Not really. She just ditched us.'

Kelly pulled a face. 'Why would she do something like that?'

'Because she got given a backstage wristband,' Adam said, as though it explained everything. 'They offered one to Amy, too, but she didn't take it.'

Kelly didn't need to be told that the only males getting the all-access bands would be friends of the DJ or festival staff.

'She's become such a bitch since she moved here,' Amy pressed on. 'We were all friends in Irvine, and this weekend was supposed to be our weekend together, but first chance she gets to upgrade and she's gone. She didn't even pay her share of the camping.'

'Camping?'

'We're staying on-site at the festival, but she bailed on that, too. We just came down to the Strip today for this.'

'She's not who she used to be, for sure.' Adam spoke up, his words more for Amy than Kelly. Now that the gates were open, the friends were discussing the betrayal that they had suffered as if Kelly wasn't there. Clearly it was a sore subject.

'We should have known she'd changed when she finished things with Blake,' Amy finished.

'Blake?' Kelly asked, but before he could get an answer, he saw Amy's eyes go wide. A second later, Kelly was shoved hard in the back.

When an arm wrapped around his throat, Kelly knew that it was time to fight back.

16

Kelly tried to turn, but whoever had jumped him was clamped tightly on to his back like a rucksack. Kelly looked back to Amy and Adam, expecting to see fear, but instead he saw the pair grinning like lunatics as they fumbled for their phones. That meant Kelly now knew the identity of his assailant, and so he reached around with his right hand . . .

And pinched the attacker's ass.

'All right, cheeky!' he heard in his ear, the accent unmistakably Australian. 'Do that again, but this time slip a finger in! Don't be shy, mate!'

Kelly laughed and felt the weight drop off his back. He turned and embraced the man before him: Chris Herbert, a heavily tattooed DJ who looked as if he would have been at home in Mötley Crüe and performed under the name CR1Z.

'Good to see you, Chris,' Kelly told him, meaning every word.

'Good to see you too, you good-looking bastard. Arm hasn't grown back then?'

'Can't say it has, man.'

'No worries.' Herbert grinned, turning to speak into the camera-phones that awestruck Adam and Amy were pointing their way. 'He told me that if he uses his fake hand on me it's not gay, but I don't believe him!'

He punched Kelly in the chest then, and for the first time the taller American noticed that Herbert had come with security, those big men being the reason that the popular DJ was not being swamped by the fans who looked on eagerly from behind them.

'Come over to my cabana,' the Aussie told his friend, seeing Kelly's expression. 'Can't get a moment's peace here.'

'Can we get a photo, please?' Amy shouted before one of her idols slipped away.

'Course you can.' Herbert grinned again, taking the phone and shoving it into Kelly's hand. 'Go on, mate,' he ordered, his arms over the two ravers, who looked as though they were about to die with happiness. 'Snappy snappy.'

Within a split second of Kelly taking the photo, Herbert was moving away. Kelly handed the phone back to Amy and told her that he'd be in touch, the girl just nodding in awe. If she'd wanted Kelly before, now she was enraptured by him.

With a bouncer leading the way and another bringing up the rear, Herbert and Kelly were escorted to one of the cabanas closest to the DJ's booth. It looked like the stage of a physique competition, all of Herbert's guests tanned and friends of the gym.

'Muscle beach,' he commented, catching Kelly's eye. 'Never hurts to have good-looking fuckers around. Good for the brand.'

The brand. Herbert had told Kelly about it before, when the pair had first met in Bali. Kelly had been there to surf and escape. So had Herbert. He had a wild side, that was for sure, but the DJ's persona and image were a carefully planned and executed marketing act that had lifted him from obscurity to headliner. He lived and breathed the music, but his true talent came in finding a way to infiltrate a saturated arena. Herbert had made a name for himself as being the 'mental' DJ, and now had legions of loyal fans across the globe. Not many of them knew what Kelly knew – that Herbert liked nothing more than to watch TV with his mum and dad, and to take the family dog for a walk.

'Bit different to Bali,' Kelly said, watching as a half-dozen beautiful women sprayed champagne out over the crowd.

'Sick though, isn't it?' The Aussie laughed. 'Fuck me, mate, we live some stupid lives.'

Kelly couldn't help but agree, and for a moment the two men simply stood together and watched the madness unfold. One of the reasons they had become friends was because they existed in a world that never shut up, but they could be perfectly comfortable in each other's silence.

'I was hoping we could catch up this week,' Kelly said honestly.

'Then why haven't you called me, you muppet?'

'I tried yesterday!'

'Did you? I was probably off my face,' the DJ conceded. 'It's day two of the festival, right?'

'Three!' Kelly teased, enjoying the moment of panic that passed over Herbert's face.

'You knob.' He laughed again, trying to tap Kelly in the nuts. 'I don't even know why I do things like this for you . . . Hey, Lisa! Jill! Come here and meet my chum Josh Kelly. He's famous.'

Kelly shot his friend a sideways look that Herbert returned. The Aussie always referred to Kelly as his 'chum' when introducing the man who'd provided a shark with its lunch.

'Josh,' Kelly said to the girls who shook his hand.

'Josh beat the shit out of the shark that tried to eat him,' Herbert explained to open-mouthed horror. 'Fetch us a couple of champagnes will you please, girls? Thanks.

'Are they fucking beauties or what, mate?' He beamed at Kelly, slapping his shoulder. 'Which one d'you want? We'll say after one, two, three. Or we can share if you want? Fuck it. It's Vegas.'

'How much coke have you done?' Kelly asked his jabbering friend.

'Enough to keep me awake. Who are you, my mum? The threesome's off the table then, you sick fuck. You're some dark pervert, you.'

Kelly laughed and looked around him. The party was everything that had brought him to Vegas. The music was infectious, the company was beautiful, and Herbert was the kind of wonderful maniac that Kelly loved being around, whether it was in a club, or on a deserted beach.

And yet . . .

'I can't stay, bro,' Kelly told his friend. 'Sorry.'

'*What?* Why the fuck not?'

Because he had to call Sanders, and tell her what he had learned from the friends of a girl who he had seen lying torn apart and abandoned in a canyon . . .

'Catching up with Tonya,' he said instead.

'The copper?' Herbert asked; he was familiar with Kelly's friendships. A lot of stories had been passed over rum on that Bali beach.

Kelly nodded.

'All right, mate, I'll let you go, but promise me you'll come to my set at the festival tonight?'

'I promise,' he said, meaning it.

'You better, mate. We're gonna fly in on a helicopter. I got a spare seat for you. Well, I maybe have to kick someone out, but fuck this lot, most of them are just here for free coke and backstage passes. Not like you, mate. So you'll come, yeah?'

'I will,' Kelly promised.

'Good. Fuck sitting in traffic with the peasants, mate, choppers are the way to go. I'll text you the details.'

Kelly smiled. 'If you can still see your phone.'

'Yeah, good point. I'll get my tour manager to do it. See you later, bro. Fuckin' love you.'

'Love you too, man. I'll see you at the heliport.'

'What the fuck's that?'

'Where you catch a helicopter flight, you idiot.'

'Oh.' Herbert grinned sheepishly. 'I think I could do with some more coke. Want some?'

Before Kelly could open his mouth, his phone began to buzz angrily. It was Sanders. 'I gotta take this,' he told the DJ, embracing him. 'I'll see you later.'

Then Kelly moved as quickly as he could through the press of bodies. He knew that he would never hear what Sanders had to say while he was still in the venue, and so he forced himself to be patient as he took an empty elevator out of the venue. After shaking hands with the former Marine who had let him skip the line, Kelly called in, and prepared to pass on what he'd learned.

'We can do that here,' the detective cut him off.

'Here?' Kelly asked, puzzled.

'I'm going to send you an address. Meet me there.'

'OK, sure. Why?'

'It's the home of a guy that's been talking a lot of shit about Iris online.'

'You found that?' Kelly smiled proudly.

'I don't like using social media, Kelly, but that doesn't mean I use two sticks to light a fire. I turned up some stuff, and I think it's worth checking out.'

'Got it. What's the guy's name?'

Sanders told him.

'Did you say Blake?'

She had done. 'Why?'

'Iris's friends mentioned that she'd dumped a guy called Blake,' he told her. 'I guess he's her ex.'

'Her ex,' Sanders confirmed. '*My suspect.*'

17

Kelly picked up his car from the valet, and made his way along the Strip so that he could join the I-15 heading north. His windows were rolled up tight and his AC was humming, but still he heard at least two cries of 'Vegas, baby!' as tourists rolled by the casinos in rented Mustangs.

Kelly smiled. It was good to see people so happy. Those tourists might have been waiting their whole lives to come to Vegas. The truth was that while Kelly had heard the sob stories of people coming to this place and losing everything, he had also heard a different side of the tale. There'd been a time in Kelly's life when he was a regular visitor to this city, and he'd met everyone from busboys to hedge-fund managers. It wasn't always the pit of despondency that some painted it to be. Kelly was a well-traveled man, and he reckoned that a person only needed to visit a handful of countries before stumbling upon a universal truth: every place on the planet has its own yin and a yang. No one place was truly pure. No one place was purely evil.

Kelly would have liked to put his foot down as he reached the highway, but the wide lanes were already beginning to flood with traffic heading to the Motor

Speedway and Pandora. Many of the ravers' cars had messages scrawled on their rear windshields in garish colors. Most common amongst them was the acronym *P.L.U.R.* Kelly was familiar with the message. It was something he had believed in since his childhood: Peace. Love. Unity. Respect.

Kelly tried to live his life by such ideals, but he also thought of himself as a realist. He was convinced that almost every person on the planet desired peace, but a minority was all it took to wage wars, whether that was on a global scale, in a gang-infested neighborhood, or in a broken home. That was why the world needed soldiers, and cops. They were there to teach the bad guys to respect the law and their fellow people. And if they wouldn't do that? Kelly had asked himself many times if he could have killed in the line of duty. He supposed that no one *really* knew until that moment, but, morally, he was at peace with the idea. He wouldn't have joined the LAPD if he hadn't been. With around eighty police-involved shootings per year, LA was not a city where you carried a gun as a fashion accessory.

Such thoughts of killing brought Kelly back to his destination, and his purpose for heading there. Sanders had told Kelly that the man at the address – Blake Mathews – was an ex-boyfriend of Iris's who had posted about her on his Facebook page. Sanders had described it as hateful poetry. Something that an angry teenager would write. Kelly wondered if he should be scared. Iris was dead, and nothing in Kelly's gut told him that her death was either an accident, or a mountain-lion attack.

Should he be scared?

61

Was he?

No.

He was excited.

And as he pulled off the highway, and watched the cars full of ravers continue to the festival without him, Kelly didn't feel a pang of jealousy about their destination.

He was heading right where he wanted to be.

18

Kelly pulled to a stop alongside Sanders's SUV a half-block shy of Blake Mathews's apartment. The area of northern Las Vegas was a flat expanse of concrete broken up with unchanging rows of housing that looked like a parade of short, unwanted soldiers in dusty uniforms. Kelly stayed behind the wheel as Sanders got in to sit beside him.

'Your AC's better,' she explained. 'You get stuck on the highway?'

Kelly nodded, and told her about the festival-goers.

'The Fifteen is like a parking lot after midnight, when Pandora turns out,' she said. 'At least every other one of those cars is a DUI.'

'But the police don't stop them.' Kelly knew that.

'Only a handful, for appearances' sake.'

'You're telling me this for a reason.'

Sanders nodded. 'You don't fuck with the festival.' Though it was clear from her tone that she didn't believe that the *you* applied to her. 'If they start busting every kid driving drunk or high back to their hotels, well, that's not good for business.'

'And neither's a murder.'

Sanders shook her head. 'Don't jump ahead of yourself, Miss Marple.' She grinned. 'Something doesn't sit right about this but let's not get crazy. People find all kinds of ways to get themselves killed. You should know something about that. I can't believe you still surf. And that free-diving shit?'

'Sharks aren't your enemy, T.'

'Pretty sure they're not my friend either, but what's it matter? The only ones around here are at Mandalay Bay.'

'And on the card tables, right?' Kelly joked, leaning in and winking like a bad lounge act.

She rolled her eyes. 'Stick to being pretty bait for the young ones, Kelly. Come on, even this AC isn't good enough for me to hang around for another of your zingers. You got something to change into?'

He had, pulling on jeans and a black shirt from the trunk of his car.

The heat enveloped him. As a ghost of a breeze came brushing along the asphalt, Kelly felt as though he was being followed by a malicious pack of blow-dryers.

'I miss the ocean,' he told his friend as they walked towards the nearest two-story apartments.

'You haven't even been gone a day.'

He smiled as he rolled up the cuffs of his shirt. 'Exactly.'

Sanders stopped, and looked around at their surroundings. There was no one in sight, but that was to be expected. The heat kept people shut down tighter in their homes better than a zombie apocalypse could have done. On the simmering asphalt of a large parking lot were a dozen cars and trucks. An Audi A4 was conspicuous amongst them. Its shining dark metal was almost obnoxious in the way that it stood out from its dusty companions.

Kelly saw Sanders take stock of it. 'You look excited,' she then said to him.

'I guess I am,' Kelly admitted.

'Put a neutral face on, OK? I shouldn't be bringing you along, but you met her friends, so maybe you can think of something that I miss. Don't ask him anything directly though, OK? Whisper it to me first.'

'Won't that seem kinda weird?'

'More weird than Scarface and a giant with one arm and one leg showing up at his door? Sure, Kelly. It'll be the whispering that freaks him out.' Sanders shook her head at him. 'Come on, rookie. Let's see what he knows.'

19

The door opened, and a thin, dark-eyed man in his twenties found himself looking at Sanders's police shield.

'Can we come in?'

Blake Mathews ran his eyes over her disfigurement, then Kelly's arm. He didn't say anything. He didn't need to. Kelly thought he heard the guy mumble, 'Sure,' before he led them inside.

The apartment wasn't small, but the man had done a good job of making it feel that way. Boxes cluttered the open-plan kitchen and living area. Blake Mathews sweated to move bags full of clothing from a sofa so that Sanders and Kelly could sit. Kelly wasn't surprised to see the man leaking. His AC sucked, and the ceiling fan was spinning with about as much conviction as the lazy wind turbines in the desert.

'I'm sorry about the mess,' Blake explained again. 'I just moved.'

Sanders: 'When?'

'Last month.' His back was to her, and so only Kelly saw the roll of her eyes.

He looked the guy over as he labored. Blake Mathews was about six feet tall, his arms the same thickness as his straw-like legs. He was no athlete, and had – in Kelly's school days at least – what would have been described as an emo look about him: dark, neck-length hair, pale skin, black clothing. Kelly put him at about thirty years old.

'Please, sit down,' Mathews insisted. 'I'm sorry about the mess. I just moved,' he said again.

Sanders remained standing. 'Why don't you sit?' she said to Blake, calm but authoritative.

He sat.

Kelly frowned as he saw that the man was shaking. Unsure of what to do with himself, Kelly decided to lean back against the front door. He could see no other way out, and Blake had that look of a rabbit caught in headlights on a dirt road.

'Do you know why we're here?' Sanders spoke, opening a notebook with careful deliberation.

'I do,' he stammered, before looking at his trembling hands. 'It's about Iris, isn't it?' he added, clamping them together.

Kelly's heart beat faster. He looked at Sanders; the professional remained unmoved by the near confession. 'It is,' she confirmed. 'Why don't you tell me about it? Why don't you start at the beginning?'

Blake nodded, more to himself than to the people standing in his home. He took a deep breath. Sanders' authoritative presence seemed to fill the room, and dragged the man's words out of him.

'I first met her at Rusa.'

'The club on the Strip?'

'Yeah. In the Grand. I was the resident DJ there, and when Iris came to Vegas, she started to work there too.'

'Iris moved here from Irvine, right?' the detective asked, primed with the information that Kelly had gleaned at the pool party. Blake confirmed that she did. 'What kind of work was she doing when you met her?'

'Bottle service,' Blake explained, and Kelly felt, more than saw, Sanders turn in his direction – this wasn't her area of expertise, but it was one that Kelly knew well.

'She brought out the drinks to the big spenders.' Kelly spoke up, leaving out the fact that Iris would have done so in lingerie. Sex sells in any industry, and when it came to selling alcohol, well . . . Kelly knew that a lot of club owners had gotten rich when they'd cracked that formula.

Sanders asked: 'So you guys were together?'

'We were talking for a while.'

'Explain "talking," Mr Mathews. I know the definition of dating changes every full moon these days, so help me out here. What does "talking" mean?'

The guy blushed and wrung his hands. 'We would go out on dates. Hang out. That kind of thing.'

'Did you fuck?' Sanders asked, shocking Blake and Kelly with her bluntness.

After a stunned moment, Blake nodded.

'So you were going on dates, hanging out, and fucking. That sounds like a relationship to me, Mr Mathews. It sounds like you were boyfriend and girlfriend.'

'We weren't,' the man replied meekly.

'Because she didn't want to be, right?'

Blake said nothing. His face talked enough.

'Sounds to me like Iris led you down the garden path.' Sanders sighed. 'We've all been there, Blake. It's nothing to be ashamed about.

'The thing is, we've heard a little different from what you're telling us. We've heard that you guys *were* together. Not "talking." But together. Why would we hear that?'

The man ran a hand through his dark hair. Sweat separated the strands.

'Because I told people that . . .'

'Why?'

Nothing.

'Because you thought that's what it was?'

Nothing.

'Because that's what you wanted?'

Nothing.

'Because you were embarrassed?'

He looked up. 'Wouldn't you be?'

'Tell me about that.' Sanders was asking gently, but behind the words was a tone of steel. An order.

Blake told her.

The young man had been as confused about the definition of their relationship as Sanders. Blake wanted to be exclusive, in mind and body. Iris didn't. She told him that she'd come to Vegas to make something of herself, not to be locked down.

'But you continued with this . . . arrangement?'

'For a while.' Blake nodded, and Kelly could see in the man's dark eyes how much that had hurt. How it still did.

'You put a stop to it?' the detective guessed.

He shook his head. 'She did.'

'Why?'

For a long moment, Blake said nothing. There was just the sound of his hands rubbing over themselves with anxiety, and the throb of the struggling AC unit outside of the flimsy window.

He exhaled. 'I got fired. From the club. As soon as Iris found out, she told me we should just be friends. She told me I'd embarrassed her. That I was a fucking junkie, and a joke.'

'Why would she say that?'

'Because I was?' Blake offered sadly, running his hands through his sticky hair. 'Vegas is fucked, man. I was playing at that place every night. I had drinks poured down my throat and coke stuck up my nose. I got used to it. I even thought it was one of the things that she liked about me!'

'But what she liked about you was the status.' Sanders shook her head, knowing enough about human nature to put the pieces together. 'A new girl in Vegas, dating the resident DJ of Rusa? That would have been one of the best clubs, right?'

'It still is.' Blake spat with more than a little acid. 'She saw me as something she could show off when she wanted to. Look, I know who I am, right, but a DJ in Vegas gets a lot of attention. She might not have wanted me, but she didn't want anyone else to have me either. At least not while I was at Rusa.'

'And now?'

Blake looked at his hands, then at Sanders. His eyes were red with misery, but there was something else in them, too.

Hope.

'I know deep down she still loves me. Sooner or later, she'll realize she's made a mistake.'

Sanders turned, looked at Kelly, and then back at the heartbroken man in front of her.

'Why do you think that we're here, Mr Mathews?'

The man's shoulders slumped. Kelly thought that he saw tears in his eyes. 'Because she told me she'd file a restraining order if I kept calling. But I couldn't . . . I couldn't just stand back and watch her ruin her life. I love her,' he said, his words choking on a sob.

Tonya Sanders put her notebook away. Kelly stopped leaning on the door, and stood upright.

Sanders took a breath. 'That's not why we're here . . .'

A moment later, and a stranger wept childlike into her shoulder.

20

Blake had cried for a long time. He'd only stopped when Sanders told him that they needed him to do something for Iris. Then it was as if a switch had been thrown, and the young man quickly pulled himself together – or at least, as well as could be expected to, given the circumstances.

He really did love her, Kelly'd thought to himself. *Even in grief, he's putting her needs before his own.*

'What can I do to help?' Blake had asked.

Tonya Sanders had told him. She wanted to know about Iris's friends. Iris's enemies.

Everyone and no one, according to Blake. Kelly wasn't sure if he believed that. No one went through life untouched by darkness, and he assumed that the guy was simply looking at Iris through rose-tinted glasses.

'Well,' Sanders had tried delicately, 'was she seeing anybody else?'

Kelly saw the words hit Blake like a punch in his stomach. For a moment, he looked physically sick.

Then he nodded.

'Who?'

Blake told them. 'He's a drug dealer,' he added, rubbing at his eyes. 'I told her to stay away from him.'

Kelly wondered at the choice of words. Blake had *told* her. Such statements didn't sit well with strong-willed women, and it was becoming evident that Iris fitted that description. Kelly wondered if 'telling her' could have meant actions stronger than words.

Sanders wondered the same, and she voiced her thoughts out loud.

'I've never touched her!' Blake protested, the use of present tense capturing Kelly's attention. 'I would never hurt her!'

'Do you think that *he* would?' Sanders asked, meaning her new man.

Blake nodded his head violently. 'He's a drug dealer,' he said again, as if that confirmed that the man was a violent one.

Sanders had a few more questions after that: where did Iris live? At the Sky Apartments on the Strip. Where do her parents live? In Irvine, but Blake had no contact details for them, and he didn't believe that they used social media.

'Blake. Was there . . . anyone else?' It took a long time for him to say no. 'Are you sure?'

He was. Kelly wasn't.

'Is that all?' Blake had finally murmured. 'I think I need to throw up.'

Sanders turned to Kelly. She'd read something in his stance, and knew that he had a question. She met his eyes, trusted what she saw there, and nodded.

73

'The Audi on the lot,' Kelly asked casually. 'Is it yours?'

Blake nodded. Kelly said nothing more, but Sanders had one question.

'The drug dealer,' she asked the trembling wreck alongside her. 'Can you tell us where he lives?'

21

They walked outside in silence. It was only when Kelly unlocked his car that he broke it.

'Hey . . .' he began, without getting into his open door. 'You handled that really well, Tonya. Really. I'm proud of you.'

Sanders raised an eyebrow. 'Practice makes perfect, Kelly,' she told him stoically. 'And fifteen years as a cop is a lot of practice.'

'But it doesn't get any easier.'

It was a guess, but a right one. 'It doesn't get any easier.'

'Well' – Kelly smiled sadly – 'that's why I'm proud of you.'

Sanders cracked her own smile then, and shook her head in some wonder. 'I love you, man.' She chuckled. 'Most times I've had to break news like that, the guy wants to wait it out outside, or makes a joke as soon as we leave. *You* say that you're proud of me.' She laughed. 'I'm surprised you didn't jump in there for a group hug and a meditation.'

'I thought about it,' he said honestly.

'You're a dick.' Sanders cackled, but there was nothing but love in the insult.

Kelly made no reply. He knew that his brand of masculine was outside the norm in America, maybe even in California, but it was *him*.

'Why did you ask about his car?' Sanders asked.

'It looks like it got washed today, and it's not like his place was in great shape. Seemed kinda at odds.'

She nodded. She'd picked up on the same.

'Why did you think he'd have the dealer's address?' Kelly asked her back.

'You tell me.'

Kelly shrugged his wide shoulders. 'Because he's clearly obsessed with the girl. If he's the kind to lash out and bleed emotionally online, he's probably the kinda person who's gonna follow his romance's new life to the nth degree.'

'Tragic, isn't it?'

'Have you never been in love?'

'That's what I mean, Kelly. Look where it gets you.' Sanders shook her head, pointing back to Blake's apartment. 'That guy got chewed up and spat out, all because he was unlucky enough to fall in love with the wrong person.'

Kelly ran a hand through his hair. He wasn't so sure, but love was a dangerous topic to tread with Tonya. It was the one part of her life that she had kept off-limits. 'There're two sides to every story,' he offered eventually.

She grunted. 'Maybe . . .

'Hey,' she added, 'I wanted to ask you something. What's the difference between a DJ and a resident DJ?'

Kelly thought on it for a moment. 'Kind of like the difference between a touring band, and a guy that opens at the same joint every week. The residents are on a fixed contract with the club. They're a paid employee, whereas the DJs are self-employed. The bigger ones may have contracts with the top clubs for regular appearances, but ultimately, they're responsible for themselves.'

'So Blake losing that job is a big deal?'

Kelly nodded. 'Huge. Getting a foot on the DJing ladder is so hard. The competition is massive, so he was doing well just to be getting paid for it. Think of it like basketball. There are tens of thousands of people who love playing, but how many get to turn pro?'

'And how much would he get paid for a gig like that? Say, as an annual salary?'

'Less than the headline act gets for a two-hour show. You either make bank in the industry, or you make shit. There's not much of a middle ground.'

'Explains why he's moving in here,' Sanders thought out loud. 'Shame Iris isn't in the same neighborhood.'

'What makes you say that?'

'He said that she lived in the Sky Apartments,' Sanders explained. 'Those are nice places. Rent probably starts at a couple of grand a month.'

Kelly still didn't get it.

The detective spelled it out. 'That means security, and tight regulation. It means there's no way we get a look at her apartment without permission of her next of kin. Not while this is still being called an animal attack.'

'And is it?'

Sanders nodded. 'I got told to keep my nose out. So far as the captain knows we're just looking for Iris's next-of-kin details, and confirming the girl's ID. When we get something he can't ignore, then I'll hit him with it.'

'Is that a good idea? Keeping him out of the loop?'

'He's my captain, Kelly. I know him. Trust me, OK?'

'All right. Cool. So what next?'

Sanders began walking to her truck. 'Meet me back at mine,' she told her friend, looking at his electric Tesla with a twisted grin. 'We'll drop your . . . car, and then we'll go talk to the drug dealer.'

'I get to ride shotgun?'

'Yes, Joshua, you get to ride shotgun.'

Kelly smirked. 'Does that mean we're partners?'

Sanders paused as she opened her truck's door, and tried hard to keep a twitch of a smile from off her face.

'We'll see.'

22

Traffic on the I-15 South was easy going, but even so, Sanders changed her mind about meeting Kelly at hers to drop his car there. Instead, she instructed him to leave it at McCarran Airport on the southern side of the Strip. 'This guy's on the opposite side of the city to me.' Sanders explained of the 'drug dealer's' home as Kelly climbed into the passenger side of her truck. 'Most of the gated communities are on the western side.'

'Works for me,' Kelly said. Despite everything, he intended to honor his promise to Chris Herbert, and watch the DJ's set at the festival. Kelly wasn't quite sure how he felt about that, wondering if he was abandoning Iris's ghost, but at the same time he had a duty to the living – Chris was his friend, and playing on the main stage at Pandora was a big deal to him. Kelly knew that the Aussie would be disappointed if he let him down.

Sanders could see that something was on her friend's mind, and asked him about it.

'You should go,' she insisted when he told her. 'When dealing with the dead is your job, you have to keep that line between what was their life, and what's yours. When it's *not* your job . . .'

'Yeah,' Kelly agreed. 'Thanks, T. I get it.'

Sanders shot him a look – did he?

'I do.'

But getting it was one thing. Thinking that way was another.

'I just can't understand how someone can hurt somebody,' Kelly told his friend as they crossed over the highway and into the western side of the city.

'Sometimes you don't understand,' the fifteen-year cop told him. 'And most of the time, you don't need to.'

Kelly shrugged. 'But don't you want to?'

'Not really.'

'Why?'

'Because there's a difference between seeing a case through, or a case seeing *you* through. Only a robot could just cut and snip these people off like they were ribbon, Kelly. You carry them with you. But the more you try and understand past what you need to solve the case, the more you carry. The more you carry, the sooner the weight's going to get too much. Then who do you help?'

For a moment, Kelly was silent. Then he asked gently, 'Can I be totally honest with you, Tonya?'

Sanders smiled to herself as she took a corner, pulling them into an immaculate road where houses peeked up from behind an eight-foot fence. 'Is there a version of Josh Kelly that isn't? Because I'd like to meet him.'

'I don't think you actually believe that. And even if you did, I'm not sure I agree with it.'

The truck came to a stop in front of a set of decorated steel gates, between which sat a small security office. If Sanders took offense at what Kelly said, she didn't show it.

'I'm just saying that the world's not yoga retreats and group meditations, Kelly.'

Kelly scratched at his jaw, and was forming his reply when a security guard appeared at the window of the office, and flashed Sanders a smile. Kelly noticed, to the man's credit, that he looked Sanders straight in the eye, paying no mind to her disfigurement. *Guy's a veteran,* Kelly thought, thanking the man mentally for his subtle behavior and his service. How many warriors of Iraq and Afghanistan were now manning barriers at gated communities? he wondered.

'Good afternoon, ma'am. Sir. Can I help you?'

'Hi. We're here for Number Fifteen, Rose Lane.'

'Be happy to help you with that, ma'am. Are they expecting you?'

Sanders took her police shield from her pocket, and handed it through the truck's window. 'I really hope not.'

23

The gated community numbered a few hundred houses, its immaculately tarmacked streets running like black rivers studded with palms and rock features. The driveways of the five-bedroom homes were a parade of SUVs and coupés, the occasional open garage showing motorbikes or jet-skis on trailers, playthings for the desert and Lake Mead.

'Do you ever go out there?' Kelly asked his friend, thinking of how long it had been since he'd powered across open water.

'We used to take field trips to Hoover Dam.'

Kelly's face broke out into a big grin. 'I would have loved to have seen you as a teacher,' he said; then he swallowed his pride. 'I'm sorry if I offended you back there. It's not my job to second-guess how you hold it together.'

Sanders laughed hard. 'Don't be such a pussy, Kelly. Shit. Do you ever get laid?'

He grinned. 'Last night.'

'She liked the "woo woo" stuff?'

Kelly nodded, and ran his hand through his hair as he pictured Caroline sitting astride him. 'Loved it.'

Sanders pulled the SUV to the curbside and snorted derisively: 'California girls.' She opened her door. Kelly followed from his.

The heat reminded him, with a slap in the face, that they were guests in the desert. It was past mid-afternoon, and Kelly reckoned that the temperature was into triple digits. 'You hear that?'

She did. The dull thud of bass was creeping out onto the deserted street.

Kelly led the way to the door, but Sanders stepped in front of him. 'I'm the cop,' she told the big man, eyeing a Maserati and Range Rover that were parked in front of the house's double garage.

Kelly admired them. 'Nice.'

'Lot of money,' Sanders replied. She didn't need to be a detective to work that out. They were high-end models, kitted out way above factory spec.

'Those alloy wheels are ten K a set,' Kelly confirmed. 'These don't have a scratch on them.'

'Doesn't look like they've been off-roading anytime recently,' Sanders agreed. 'But the roads out to Sloan Canyon aren't so bad. Not the Strip, but not bad.'

Kelly made no reply, and Sanders knocked on the door. It was time to meet the drug dealer.

24

It took a lot of knocking and ringing the doorbell before the door opened. When it was, Kelly found himself looking at a man in his twenties wearing a neon-green tank and ripped black trousers. Kelly guessed he was of Pakistani descent, with a neatly trimmed beard and hair tied into a topknot, patterns edged into the closely cropped sides of his head. His name was Zakhir Khan, and through red eyes, he took an appraising look at the people on his doorstep.

'What's up?' he asked them simply. 'Is the music too loud?'

'Zakhir Khan?' Sanders asked.

'Yeah. I'm guessing you're cops?'

'I am,' Sanders answered evasively.

Khan raised an arm and placed it on the doorframe. He looked at the floor, as if deep in relaxed contemplation. Kelly and Sanders shared a look. This wasn't the behavior either had expected.

'Look,' Khan told them after a moment, 'I feel bad about you standing in the heat, but I can't invite you inside. I just can't. I'm really sorry.'

Kelly didn't need to be told why. Behind Khan, a pair of similarly dressed ravers made their way downstairs, and helped themselves to drinks from a table. Kelly guessed that there was more than alcohol on offer.

'Hey, Amaan,' Khan called to one of them. 'Bring me a couple of waters, man. No, not those. Out the fridge.'

'Here.' He offered Sanders and Kelly the ice-cold bottles a younger man passed him. 'I know it's hot as shit out, but I can't invite you in. Sorry.'

Kelly cracked the seal on his bottle, and drank. 'Thank you,' he told the man in the doorway.

'You're welcome, man. Gotta look out for each other in the desert. I gave out so much water at the festival yesterday, man. I'm not trying to hype myself up, I'm just saying. People need to stay hydrated. They come into town for Pandora and they drop Molly and shit and they don't know how to deal with the desert. It's no good. You gotta take the horse to water and make it drink, man.' Khan smiled. 'So what's up?'

Kelly looked at Sanders. She hadn't been expecting to be allowed into the home of a man accused of being a drug dealer, but the rest of the conversation had thrown her. It took her a second to recover. 'We're here about Iris Manning.'

'Oh.' Khan shrugged. 'She's not here. There're just six of us, and we're getting a limo to the festival. I don't know how she's getting there.'

Kelly looked closer at the man's eyes. His answers made Kelly think that he had started the party early – or maybe hadn't stopped it from the first night – but he could detect no hint of deception. He wondered what Sanders, with her experience, was picking up.

'We've been told that you were Iris's boyfriend,' Sanders went on, without explaining why that was important, 'and that she stays here.'

'Boyfriend?' Khan scoffed, turning to look up at Kelly. 'I live in Vegas, bro. Why would I do that to myself?' He laughed in a high-pitched chuckle.

'So you're denying you were involved with her?' Sanders asked, in no mood for laughter.

'Course not,' Khan told the officer. 'We were "involved,"' he said, using air quotes. 'Like, we'd hang out, sometimes we'd . . . you know. She'd stay here sometimes. Like, in one of the rooms.'

'Not yours?'

'No. I like to sleep alone. You ever think about that, like, why do we share a bed as a couple? It sucks. You get all sweaty. You can't get comfortable. What's the point? It's just societal norms that say we should feel bad if we don't do it.'

Sanders shook her head. 'I'm not here to discuss societal norms with you, Mr Khan. Did Iris Manning stay here, and if she did, why?'

'OK,' Khan replied, putting drama into every letter. 'This is a five-bedroom house. It's my house, but I hate being alone. I let people come and go. Some stay for months and pay rent, some just crash for a few days.'

'And which was Iris?'

'She'd come and go.'

'She didn't pay rent?'

'No.'

'Did she pay you in other ways?'

Khan laughed. 'She fucked me because I'm a good time, man. Sometimes she'd stay and nothing would happen. She's a grown woman, she can do what she likes.'

Kelly bit his lip as he wondered if Sanders would correct Khan on that statement. She didn't, and Kelly found that he was relieved. Khan was clearly rolling on Molly, and if he was innocent of any wrongdoing, then he didn't deserve a bad crash on that drug. If someone could go as high as a plane they could crash like one too. Kelly knew that firsthand.

'Look,' Khan explained, his words directed equally to both of the unexpected guests on his doorstep, 'Iris is fun, but she's a bottle-service girl. I don't get involved with girls like that. Not at the level I think you're talking about. It just ends in trouble.'

'From what we've heard,' Sanders replied bluntly, 'you're not a stranger to trouble.'

At that, Khan scrunched up his face. 'What are you talking about? I've got no record.'

Sanders looked straight into his eyes. Kelly thought he saw her twist her face so that her scars stood out – more prominent and imposing. 'We've been informed that you're involved in supplying narcotics,' she stated as calmly as if she were telling the time.

Kelly didn't know what he expected Khan to do then. Run, maybe. Shut the door, certainly.

He definitely didn't expect the man to laugh.

'This *again*.' Khan shook his head. 'Fuck my life, dude, I hate this shit. Fucking haters, man,' he cursed, rubbing his hands against his temples.

'Look,' he said after a moment, pointing inside his home. 'You see that? The five computer screens? That's where I make my money. Fucking drugs, bullshit. I run affiliate marketing. Banner ads. That kind of thing.'

Khan could see from Sanders's look that she didn't understand. 'You know those adverts that pop up when you use Facebook?' he tried to explain. 'Those are coming from people like me. We buy your data, and then target you with specific advertisements based on what you've been searching for, or what pages you've been looking at.'

Kelly said nothing, but he knew there was good money to be made in such advertising and marketing. He had a friend in Hollywood who worked from home – a luxury penthouse – and put in a couple of hours work a day, before sitting back to watch the dollars roll in.

Sanders looked to Kelly. He gave the smallest of nods.

'We're gonna follow this up,' she promised Khan.

'Please do. Give me your email and I'll tell my accountant to get in touch. It's just fucking hate, man.' He shook his head again. 'As soon as people see a young guy with money they think drugs. Has it not occurred to them that maybe he just works hard and makes money in an industry they don't understand? Just because I'm not rolling out to do nine to five at a firm with three names over the door doesn't mean I'm not legit, bro. Fuck. Seriously.'

'You done?' the detective asked him.

'Yeah,' he replied, hands on his head. 'You?'

Kelly almost laughed at the man's easy manner, but Sanders held her untouched water out across the threshold, then crossed her arms when Khan took it.

'No,' she told him. 'When was the last time you saw Iris?'

'The night before the festival started. She came by. Wanted to borrow some stuff to go hiking. Me and my brother go in the winter. She was in and out.'

For a moment, no one said anything.

'We'll be in touch,' Sanders promised, turning away.

'Thanks for the water,' Kelly said, handing the man the empty.

'Hey,' Khan called after them as they walked away. 'You not going to tell me what this is about?'

It was Sanders who answered.

'No.'

25

'*Thanks for the water?*' Sanders asked Kelly as they shut the truck's doors.

'What? It was good of him to offer.'

'It would have been better of him to ask us inside.'

'You know why he didn't. That doesn't make him a bad person.'

Sanders shook her head. 'Dealer or not, there were drugs inside that house.' She pulled the car away from the curb and into a U-turn. 'So we know he's OK with breaking the law.'

Kelly turned to look at his friend. 'You're not equating doing recreational drugs with involvement in a girl's death, are you?' he asked defensively.

Sanders grunted. 'It's a slippery slope.'

'If those party drugs were alcohol you wouldn't be saying that.'

'But they're not.'

'OK then,' Kelly went on. 'There are a hundred thousand people a day at Pandora, T. Let's make a conservative effort and say that half of them are going to use a drug today. That's fifty thousand. How much of a spike in violent crime is there in Vegas during Pandora?'

Sanders said nothing.

'Look,' Kelly told her, 'I get it. What Khan and a lot of other people do is illegal, but you and I both know there's a big difference between illegal and wrong. Tell me that there isn't,' he challenged her.

Instead, Sanders told him something else. 'I know you've got your own past with that scene, Kelly, And I respect that. But you've got to respect that I have mine too. Whether you think they should be or not, those drugs *are* illegal, and there's no such thing as a victimless crime. The ravers at that festival may be all hugging each other, but people have been hurt – people have been killed – in the trade that got them those drugs.'

'It wouldn't happen if it was legal,' Kelly insisted. 'If that industry could be run legitimately.'

'But it's not,' Sanders said gently. 'And my job is to enforce the law, Kelly. Not interpret it. Not wonder how it could be better. Just enforce it.

'And,' she added finally, 'that would have been *your* job, too.'

Kelly sat back into his seat. It was true. 'Maybe it is better I didn't get it . . .' he mused out loud. 'I just can't accept something like that. It doesn't make sense. It doesn't stand to reason.'

Sanders spoke patiently. 'It stands to somebody's reason, Josh.'

Kelly said nothing as they crossed over the I-15, his eyes on a jet that was landing at the nearing airport.

'I hadn't really thought about it like that,' he admitted after a long moment. 'So where do we go from here?'

Sanders didn't look at him as she delivered her verdict. 'I think it's best for us both if you go to the festival.'

26

Sanders's decision to split up cut Kelly. 'So you don't want my help?' he asked in disappointment.

Sanders looked straight ahead at the traffic. She took a moment before replying. 'You see the best in people, Kelly. It's my job – a detective's job – to look for the worst.'

'So you *don't* want my help.' He said it again, this time with a little heat.

Sanders laughed. It was a sharp laugh, and she stole a glance across to the man beside her. 'So I *need* your help, you sensitive pussy.' She grinned. 'Look, when we went to Khan's place then, and much as I try to keep an open mind, I gotta be honest and admit to myself that I didn't like the guy. I hear drugs, I think of dead kids in the gutter because of some gang bullshit, you understand me? Now I'm not saying I condone anything to do with drugs – because I don't – but my mission is to do right by my victims. If I do that better with you sitting like a one-armed angel on my shoulder, then that's a good thing.'

Kelly snorted, but then smiled. 'It feels so good to be wanted.'

'Listen, though,' Sanders went on, 'there's something else, too. This festival, Kelly. There're over a hundred thousand potential witnesses to Iris's last day, and if it comes to it, *suspects* too. In two days' time, they're back to being spread out all over the globe.

'Maybe Iris's death really was an accident or an animal attack, but time's not on our side to find out. You know the festival world, Kelly, and people will open up in a way that they wouldn't to me. So yes, I want your help, totally off the books, and totally underappreciated by anybody but me and a dead girl. Does that work for you?'

Kelly reached out and put his hand on his friend's shoulder. 'It does,' he told her, deeply moved by her trust.

Sanders shook her head and laughed. 'Can we ever have a moment that you don't make weird?'

'No.' Kelly smirked back. 'Now take me to the heliport please, *partner*.'

'Ugh. I hate you.' Sanders spoke beneath her breath.

Kelly looked out ahead of them and grinned. For the first time in a long period of his life, he felt like the man he was born to be.

27

Sanders pulled her truck into an open spot in the heliport's parking lot. On the other side of a security fence, helicopters buzzed back and forth as though there was a military invasion in progress.

'Shuttles to the festival,' Kelly explained.

'I hate to think how much that cost.'

'About five K for the whole chopper, or eight-fifty a seat.'

'Didn't I just say, "I hate to think how much that cost?"' Sanders groaned. 'That's a month's salary to me. Shit. How much is your friend getting paid?'

'Chris? I don't know how much he gets a set,' Kelly told her honestly.

'Best guess?'

'Well . . . for a festival like this, and on the main stage? Low six figures.'

'Jesus! *For one night?*'

'For one *hour.*' Kelly corrected her.

Sanders couldn't believe it, and told Kelly as much.

'You said this festival nets the city over a billion in revenue,' Kelly pointed out. 'If the main stage costs a couple million a night in artist fees, that's still a good return on investment.'

They fell into silence as they crunched over the huge numbers in their heads, and then a far more important issue that they could not fully understand.

'You're not religious, are you?' Sanders asked her friend.

Kelly shook his head. 'But I'm spiritual.'

'Right,' the cop acknowledged, 'so you believe you can get . . . I don't want to say a message, but a feeling, a sense from somewhere that you don't know where?'

'Sure. Absolutely.'

'That's how I feel about Iris's death,' Sanders said. 'There's something that keeps picking at me. It's not that we have *anything* to show that someone did something to her, but . . . we don't have proof that they didn't, either. I just don't like it.'

'It doesn't sit right with me either,' Kelly agreed. 'We know that she was at the festival yesterday, and Khan says that she came to his to borrow gear to go hiking, but it just doesn't *feel* right that she would travel that distance alone, and do that after dark. At the very least, I think that somebody abandoned her out there.'

'Someone knows how and why she was out there at that time.' Sanders nodded. 'I'm certain of it.'

Before she could say anything else, her eye was drawn to a black SUV that pulled into the lot. Chris Herbert stepped out of it, an entourage at his back and a bottle of vodka in his hand.

Sanders sneered in distaste. 'Who's that asshole?'

'That's *my* asshole.' Kelly laughed as he opened the door. 'Don't worry, T. I'm gonna find out who it was that took Iris backstage. We can pick up the breadcrumb trail.'

'Not if your friend pukes all over it,' Sanders muttered as Herbert caught sight of Kelly's big frame and headed over. 'Close the door,' she told her friend. 'I don't want to have to be pleasant, or bust him for possession.'

'I'll see you soon.' Kelly smiled, carrying out her wish. Within a half-second, the police officer was driving away.

The DJ grinned at Kelly, took a huge swig of vodka, and yelled: '*Get to the choppaaaaa!*'

It was time to visit Pandora.

28

Kelly climbed aboard the helicopter with Herbert and four of his entourage. The space was small, and the Australian asked Kelly if he would mind leaving his prosthetic arm and leg behind.

'You're a big bastard,' he told his friend. 'And they've got golf buggies at the festival. I can drive you around in one of them.'

Kelly laughed and declined that offer, and the next – a pull from the Aussie's bottle of vodka.

'You're not drinking?' Herbert asked with some surprise.

'I'm not.'

The DJ pulled a face. 'Since when? Why?'

'I guess I'm working.'

'You don't work,' Herbert scoffed good-naturedly. 'You go around the world telling people about how a shark tried to eat you, and then you fuck the good-looking one in the audience.' He laughed, turning to the four others, who were unknown to Kelly. 'I'm telling you that's what he does,' he assured them. 'It's like he's a DJ, but with his gob.'

'And you do it with your *arse*?' Kelly replied grinning, attempting his best Aussie accent.

'We'll make a Skippy out of you yet, mate,' Herbert said proudly. 'Fuck me, did we just move? Are we taking off?'

They were. The bird picked up from the pad with grace, and after a few checks while hovering a man's height from the deck, the pilot was ready to begin their flight.

'Here we go then!' Herbert beamed, spilling vodka. 'Death or glory!'

Kelly couldn't help but smile. He liked Chris. He liked him a lot. The decade following the shark attack had been a roller coaster for Kelly, and he could see Herbert's dramatic, drunk, or drug-fueled behavior for what it was: Chris Herbert was a young man trying to get to grips with life any way he could. He was a thirty-year-old loving Mummy's boy from a middle-class family in Sydney, and he was about to get onstage – alone – at the biggest electronic music festival in the world. Kelly doubted that, as a kid, Herbert had a single pair of eyes on him. In a couple of hours, he'd be the focal point for fifty thousand.

'Excited?' Kelly asked his friend.

'Fuck off,' the DJ replied sheepishly. 'You know I don't like it when you crawl inside my head.'

But that was exactly what Herbert *did* like about their friendship. It was why, in less than two years of knowing each other, and only being in the same physical location a handful of times, the pair had become friends. They were both sensitive guys who wanted to matter in a world that they struggled to understand.

'I'm glad you're here, mate,' Herbert told his friend. 'Now look at that.'

He pointed through the glass of the helicopter's window. Kelly turned, and for a second, his breath caught in his throat.

'Shit,' he mumbled.

Beside him, Herbert put his arm around his friend's wide shoulders. 'Fuckin' Vegas, baby.'

Kelly looked at it in awe.

Casinos grew out of the desert like garish titans risen from jewel-filled tombs. Kelly shook his head. On street level, the Strip was impressive. From the air, the scale of the architects' work could truly be appreciated. Las Vegas was a tribute to the audacious. A testament to those who wouldn't – couldn't – say, 'That can't be done.'

'Sometimes I think this place is the arsehole of the world.' The DJ spoke beside him. 'And sometimes I think it's the fucking crown.'

Kelly didn't know if he'd ever heard his friend speak truer words.

'And how do you feel right now?' he asked him.

The Aussie grinned. 'Like I need to piss.'

Kelly laughed, and pulled his friend into a hug. Around them, the other passengers stared out at the sprawling city, or the mountains that lay beyond them, red and rusty, magnificent and daunting. Had it only been this morning that Kelly was in those dusty canyons?

'You OK, mate?' Herbert asked. 'Not flight sick, are you?'

'I'm fine,' Kelly replied. A vision of Iris's body had passed quickly across his eyes, replaced now by a riot of color. A press of humanity.

Pandora.

'Fuck me,' Herbert whispered, and Kelly felt a tremor of excitement – or possibly fear – pass through the man as he took in the scale of the crowd that he would soon perform in front of. The stages of the festival looked like brightly colored coral reefs, with tens of thousands of ravers pressed about them in dense, moving shoals.

Kelly's phone began to vibrate in his pocket. He didn't want to tear his eyes away from the scene as they descended, but neither did he want to miss a call from Sanders. Instead, he found that it was Amy Morgan who had messaged him. Evidently, she was somewhere in the ground below him. Finally, she'd responded to a message Kelly had sent at Sanders' prompting:

Kelly: 17:35 Hey. Random question but do you know who Iris got the backstage bands from? I think it might have been my friend, lol! You at the festival now?

Amy: 18:42 Hi! Don't know who gave her the bands sorry. Yeah I'm here. Garuda stage. You?

Kelly: 18:42 Awesome. I'm about to land. Ah that's a shame. I thought it would be funny if she had been with my friends.

Amy: 1842. You're flying?????!!!!! OMG I HATE YOU! :p

Kelly was about to put his phone away when it buzzed again.

Amy: 18:43 Oh and is your friend you're talking about SNARL? Because we saw her on his Insta-story. If you see her please tell her she owes Adam and me for the camping LMAO

Kelly swallowed, and texted back.

Kelly: 18:44 I will. Be safe.

He turned to Herbert. 'Do you know Snarl?'

A look of distaste passed over the DJ's face. 'Yeah. Fucking Pom.' He spat as Kelly noted the slang term.

'He's a Brit? Tell me a bit about him. I haven't seen him perform.'

'Count yourself lucky then, mate.' Herbert snorted derisively. 'He's one of those dickheads who copied Deadmau5 and put a bucket on his head. He looks like such a cunt that people forget how shit his music is. I suppose it's marketing genius, really. Or he's just a cunt. Probably that, actually.'

'Could you introduce me?'

Herbert laughed, and then pulled a face. 'You're serious?' Kelly was. 'Go on then, you beautiful bastard. Can't say no to you, can I?'

Before Kelly could reply, the helicopter touched down with a gentle bump, and the cabin's other occupants cheered.

His morning had started beside an ocean, and taken him to death in a dusty canyon. Finally Kelly was at the festival, and he knew in his heart that the key to Iris's death lay here. One way or another, Kelly would find it.

29

Kelly and Herbert were taken from the helicopter via golf cart to the festival's artist area, a collection of trailers, awnings, and semi-permanent bathroom units. The party was in full swing for those with passes to the exclusive area, and Kelly recognized a half-dozen faces, though most big acts tended to enjoy the sanctity of their trailers more than the open air, which was still fierce with heat despite the sun dipping towards the horizon.

'Take me to Snarl's trailer,' Herbert told the artist liaison behind the wheel, an awestruck kid barely into his twenties.

'He's onstage right now, Mr Herbert.'

'So?'

The kid looked pained. 'He said that no one's to go into his trailer when he's not there. He locked it.'

'But you'll have a spare key in the office, won't you, mate?' Herbert grinned knowingly.

'I guess . . .'

'And you wouldn't want Snarl's mates sitting on his doorstep in the heat, would you? Not when I've got my own set later.'

'We have a trailer ready for you . . .' the kid tried meekly.

Herbert seemed to shake his head and nod at the same time. 'Yeah, nah, mate. Let's just pick up the key from the office, yeah? Good lad.'

A few minutes later, and Kelly was following Herbert through Snarl's trailer door. The artist liaison looked nervously from the Australian to the bottles of liquor and champagne nestled snugly into buckets of ice.

'Don't worry, mate, we won't touch his stuff,' Herbert promised.

'What you wanna drink?' h3e then asked Kelly as the kid exited the trailer.

'I'm good,' Kelly said honestly, smiling as Herbert took a bottle of champagne from a bucket, and popped the top.

'Not a bad rider, this.' The DJ shrugged as he referred to the name given to an artist's legally binding wish list of creature comforts. 'You ever heard what Slayer had on theirs?'

Kelly shook his head. He was a fan of Slayer's music, but Herbert worshipped the thrash metal band on a whole other level.

'Fucking legends, they are.' The Aussie grinned. 'Few years ago they came up with a great one.' He went on to list the items on that rider from memory, the demands including fifty thousand live bees, two shoe boxes to hide Grammy awards (Grammys not be written on the boxes), and a reliquary containing the finger bones of St George.

'And what's on your rider?' Kelly asked his friend.

'Booze.' Herbert grinned. 'Oh, and an iPhone charger.'

They sat opposite each other in a pair of comfortable armchairs as they waited for Snarl to arrive. Through the trailer's walls came the constant buzz of bass. Herbert spotted a mirror lying on a table that was dusted with powder and racked up his own line, Kelly declining to partake. The DJ had just snorted his way along it when the door opened, and an angry man stood on the threshold.

'What the fuck are you doing in my trailer?'

The words emerged from a reedy, spotty-faced man with a head that reminded Kelly of a peanut; the question died on the man's lips as he recognized Herbert bent over the mirror. When he saw the bulk of Kelly in the armchair, the protest choked off altogether.

'Oh. All right, mate,' he said instead to Herbert. Kelly recognized his accent as coming from the north of England.

'All right, Sam. Come in,' the Aussie offered to the man in whose trailer he'd made himself at home. 'Want a line?'

The younger man stepped through the doorway and didn't accept until Herbert had introduced Kelly as a good friend. Then the Aussie began chopping up a thick line for Snarl, real name Sam Thomas, and winked at Kelly as the Brit made it disappear up his right nostril. Kelly returned the gesture – he knew that Thomas would be a lot more talkative with that drug running rampant in his brain.

'Where's the rest of your crew?' Herbert asked Thomas as the man blinked harshly.

'Breaking down our gear,' he replied. 'Fuck me, that's strong stuff. Where did you get that? Everything I've had in Vegas is shit.'

'I get it through someone that he put me onto.' Herbert pointed to Kelly. It was no lie, a fact that sat uncomfortably with the man who had wanted more than anything to become an officer of the law.

'Can you sort us out?' Thomas asked, clearly feeling the buzz of the drug pushing through every part of his body. 'Fuck me, this is good.'

Kelly nodded, then looked to Herbert.

'I'm gonna go take a shit,' said the tattooed DJ. Kelly had asked him earlier if he could arrange for him to speak to Snarl alone. 'Coke always fucks my guts. Back in a bit.'

The trailer door closed behind him.

'So how do you know Chris then?' Sam spoke quickly, eager to run his gums now that the powerful drug was at work. 'You don't sound Australian?'

'I'm from California,' Kelly replied, before dipping into lies. 'And I met him through a buddy of ours. I think you know her actually,' he added, as friendly and offhand as possible. 'Iris Manning?'

The name struck Thomas immediately. Kelly noticed that the man's smile slipped a little.

'Yeah,' he managed after a moment. 'Yeah, I know her. Kind of.'

'How's that?'

'Oh, we got introduced to each other.' He shrugged; then he rubbed at his nose. 'You got any more of that stuff, mate?'

107

Kelly nodded, but didn't move to produce it. Instead, he took in the man who was now struggling to stand still. Kelly knew what was happening behind the Englishman's shifting eyes. Anxiety was hitting him, and not simply because his brain was crying out for more cocaine. Something about the memory of Iris Manning was making him uncomfortable. Kelly took what he knew about the girl, threw it up in the air, and took a swing.

'She fucked you over too, huh?' Kelly grinned, man to man. 'Bro, she did that to me.'

'She did?' Thomas asked, suddenly less fidgety. Kelly noticed then how the Englishman took in his big frame and good looks. Suddenly, Thomas wanted to talk about the girl; and it had less to do with drugs, and more to do with the insecurities of a man far from home, and far out of his comfort zone – there was a reason that Sam Thomas wore a costume onstage, and Kelly guessed that it was to give the meek-looking man the confidence to stand in front of thousands of people.

'I'm not built like you,' Thomas confessed, as if it needed saying. 'I don't find talking to chicks easy, even since Snarl took off. I mean, meeting them, yeah, that's a piece of piss, but talking to them's hard.'

Kelly tapped his prosthetic arm and leg. 'I feel you, bro. Drink and coke help though.' He smiled. 'Look under the mirror,' he added and Thomas grinned when he saw the baggy of powder that Herbert had left there – the new friendship between Kelly and Thomas was now cemented.

'How did you meet?' Kelly asked once the man had more powder up his nose.

'Same as I meet half these girls.' Thomas shrugged. 'Well, all of them, really,' he added with a little acid. 'I sent a talent scout into the crowd with some spare backstage bands. Got him to bring them back here for this.' He gestured towards the blow and the booze.

'You're a big act,' Kelly told the man. 'That must be enough.'

Thomas shook his head. 'Wasn't for her. I gave it my best shot, but she ditched.'

'So you guys didn't . . .'

'I wish.'

Kelly said nothing. Sam began chopping up another line.

'You know when she left?' Kelly asked. 'Who she left with?'

Thomas stood up straight, suddenly nervous. 'You're not her boyfriend, are you?'

Kelly had to tell him that he wasn't three times, and punctuate each denial with laughter, before the DJ would believe him.

The Brit snorted. 'I've had that shit before. Girls aren't loyal, man. I've seen some shit.'

Kelly didn't doubt it. He looked at his watch. He figured that at any moment Thomas's friends and tour crew would be arriving. He had a few moments to ask the final question he wanted answered, but first, he took in the DJ, who was now barely able to stand still. Sam Thomas had a career that millions of people wanted. He was touring the world, and his music made people's lives better, no matter what Herbert said. But Kelly could see that, despite the big paychecks and adoration, Thomas was still the insecure child he had been when growing up skinny and spotty. He likely felt as invisible now as he did then, and that was something that Kelly could understand. Despite his frame, there had been times after the shark attack that Kelly felt as though he would never be wanted. Kelly felt through the DJ's words that, although Thomas craved attention, he also resented the fact that he only seemed to get it by being the costume-wearing headliner, and not for being Sam Thomas.

'You made a lot of people's day today,' Kelly told the man. 'Really. They'll remember this for a long time. You should too, bro. Don't get too fucked up tonight.'

Kelly stood and put out his hand. It was time for him to leave.

'You can stay if you want?' Thomas offered, perhaps recognizing in Kelly a person who enjoyed company for what it was, regardless of stature.

'I better find Chris,' the American replied, shaking the man's hand. 'It was good to meet you, Sam. Oh, and before I go, if you don't mind, I just got one thing to ask . . .'

Kelly got the answer to it, and he knew that he was one step closer.

But closer to *what*, he had no idea.

30

Kelly stepped out the trailer into a rumble of bass and the oven of the desert. It took him all of two seconds to spot Herbert, who was holding court to half a dozen people beneath an awning of camouflage netting, where misted spray was fanned over those who chose to relax in the outdoors, rather than in the air-conditioned cocoons of their trailers.

Kelly decided to use the moment of quiet – if it could be called that – and phoned Sanders.

'What's up?' she answered. Kelly wondered if he heard a little irritation in her voice.

'I spoke to the DJ that gave Iris the backstage band. He said that she ditched out of the festival not long after dark. Doesn't know why.'

'Alibi?'

'His tour crew and others. They left here after midnight. Flew back into the city. They're staying at Encore, so if it ever came down to it, there would be security camera footage to prove that one way or the other.'

It was hard to tell with the background noise, but shielding his ears, Kelly was almost sure that he heard the detective laugh. When she spoke, he was certain of it.

'Kelly, unless you provide a casino with an airtight warrant they will never show you shit. And where *we're* at? Seems like we're just following a trail that's going to end up with a drugged-up girl wandering into a canyon . . .

'Look,' Sanders added a moment later, 'sometimes things are how they first appear. Maybe this is what it looked like. What you just found has given us some proof that she could have easily gotten to the canyon that night.'

'Yeah, sure, but why, and how?'

Sanders had no answer for that. 'I'm gonna call the coroner's office,' she said instead. 'See if they've fit her in tonight.'

The line went dead. Kelly took a moment to look around at his surroundings and the sky, where a struggling sunset was painting the mountains pink and orange. Kelly soaked it up until Sanders called him back. At that moment, the beauty of the landscape took a backseat to urgency.

'We've got a problem,' she told him, not waiting for Kelly to speak. 'The autopsy's not tonight.'

'They're busy?'

'Maybe. But listen, Kelly. It's not tomorrow either. They've got the procedure down for *Monday morning.*'

Kelly filled in the gaps. 'The day after the festival ends.'

'Right. This is some bullshit. The city is playing it safe just in case this does come up looking bad on their money party.'

'Can they do that?'

'No luck contacting her next of kin as yet, so who's gonna complain?'

Kelly knew who from her tone, and told her so.

'Right,' Sanders agreed. 'But there's only so much I can do.'

The answer came to Kelly. It was obvious. 'We need to find her parents.'

'We do. And look, Kelly, you're not going to like this, but "the mountain-lion attack" is leading news. They haven't named Iris, obviously, but the LVPD seem pretty happy just taking the party line on this right now.'

Kelly fought hard to resist the urge to kick the nearest trash can. He knew exactly what sensationalist reporting could do to animals. Whatever the cause of Iris's death, innocent animals would now pay the price.

'That's fucking bullshit,' he growled, the tone so unfamiliar to Sanders that it took a moment for her to reply. When she did, her voice was neutral, but firm.

'Well, that's how it is, Kelly. Best way for us to change that is to give them something else to report, right?'

Kelly took a deep breath.

Then he took another five.

'Yeah. Yeah, you're right. OK.' He thought for a second. 'How about this . . . Snarl said that Iris came back to his trailer to party and do drugs. If we're going to be waiting that long for toxicology and the autopsy, maybe there's some sign of them in her personal effects? Empty baggies? Powder on a credit card?'

'I asked the coroner's office to email her list of effects,' Sanders told him. 'A bracelet, a packet of Marlboro Light cigarettes, two hundred and five dollars, a receipt for a coffee, another for a tub of Combat Combover pomade, a stick of lip balm . . .'

Sanders continued, and Kelly's heart began to beat faster.

'Read it again,' he asked her when she finished.

She did.

'You noticed something?' Sanders asked expectantly.

He had. But not what was *on* the list.

What wasn't.

'The backstage bands on Iris's wrist,' Kelly told the detective. 'They're not there.'

31

Kelly and Sanders went over the reasons that the wristbands from Iris's severed arm might not have found their way onto the list of her personal effects. There were many possibilities – most obviously simple human or computer error – but given how things were stacking up against them, Sanders was not inclined to believe that it was a case of bad luck.

'They tie her to the festival,' she told Kelly. 'And someone doesn't want that tie to be on public record.'

'But there are the pictures of her online?' he put in. 'And now Snarl confirms that she was here with him.'

'Only because you found those things,' the detective told her friend. 'Where would the investigation stand now if you hadn't found the picture, then met with her friends? Think about it, Kelly: it would just be a dead girl on a slab waiting for an autopsy in two days' time. We wouldn't even know her name.'

Kelly let that truth sink in. 'Snarl gave me a name, too,' he told Sanders, explaining who and why.

'You want to talk to them alone?' she asked.

Kelly did, but Sanders was the one with a badge. 'Do you think that's best?'

'I do. I can stay close by, just in case, but I think you'll get more out of them if it's off the books. I've got a feeling that once they see a badge these people are gonna circle the wagons, and it could be days before we get someone to talk, if ever.'

'The traffic sucks getting out of here,' he told his friend before checking his watch. 'Herbert goes onstage soon. His set's an hour long. I'll be quicker getting back if I wait for him and get the chopper.'

Sanders agreed. 'I need to talk to the captain, anyway. At the very least I want the autopsy moved up. This is just stupid. Call me when you land?'

'Will do. Good luck, T.'

'You too. Enjoy the show – I guess. That's one good thing about the dead, Kelly. They don't mind if you turn up a little late.'

But DJ Chris Herbert did.

'Oi, you peg-legged bastard!' the Aussie called out as he caught sight of Kelly on the phone. 'Come on! It's time for me fucking show!'

32

Kelly accompanied Herbert all the way to the back of the festival's main stage, a semi-permanent building that resembled the workings of a movie studio as much an outdoor music experience. Coils of thick cable ran across the floor like hungry anacondas, and an army of stagehands shuffled through the belly of the monster like the crew of a battleship, their faces obscured behind bandannas and dust masks. Huge cylinders taller than Kelly housed CO_2 for the cannons that would blast it over the head of the crowd, and in other areas strict no-entry signs marked off the danger points where Fourth of July levels of fireworks would be blasted into the air at the end of each day. The closing of the festival was a spectacle in itself.

'This is fucking nuts,' Kelly thought he heard Herbert say as the DJ onstage dropped a beat so heavy that the entire structure shook, and the unseen crowd roared with a noise that matched the engines of a passenger jet at takeoff.

Kelly was about to ask his friend if he was nervous, but thought better of it – who wouldn't be? Fifty thousand people were about to set their eyes on him, and from the electricity in the air there was no doubt that the DJ preceding Herbert had rocked the crowd, and that the Aussie would have a tough act to follow.

'I need a drink,' Herbert said suddenly, and Kelly saw that the man had been shocked by adrenaline into sobriety. 'Seen any around?'

Kelly had, but instead of telling his friend that, he put the flesh of his right hand onto the man's shoulder. 'You don't need a drink, bro. You're good.'

Herbert looked at Kelly as though he was an idiot. 'Mate, there're fifty thousand people out there and I'm about to shit my fucking pants. I need a drink.'

'No. You're good.' And with that, Kelly pulled his friend into a tight bear hug. 'You don't need a drink, but those people in the crowd need *you*, bro. Get up those fucking stairs and give them an amazing show. I'm proud of you.'

'Fucking hell, let me breathe, mate.' Herbert laughed, his nerves receding, if only by a little. 'You really think I can smash this?'

'I know you can.'

Herbert laughed, his bravado back, the mask of cocky indifference firmly in place. 'Only joking, you dickhead, I know I can. I'm fucking CR1Z.'

And with that he scampered up the stairs and out of sight. A few seconds later, Kelly heard his voice boom out over the stage's hundreds of speakers.

'My name is CR1Z from Sydney, Australia! And I came here to fuckin' party with you guys tonight!'

The crowd screamed. Kelly smiled. For an hour at least, he could do what he had come to Vegas to do.

He headed out of backstage, and made his way towards the crowd.

33

The next hour passed in moments. At the front of the stage, Kelly was separated from the ocean of the crowd by just a thin barrier, and yet he felt as though he was in the center of the mass, connected to everyone through the beat that passed through the towers of speakers and into every cell of his body. There was something tribal and primal about that beat. A connection between friends, family, and strangers alike. There were people from all walks of life in the throng. All nationalities. All races. All ages. Here they were under one banner. United in one purpose: to have a good fucking time.

Peace. Love. Unity. Respect.

It was the motto of the festival and the raver, and Kelly saw it with his own eyes. Despite the crush and the heat, there were no fights. No angry shouts. Instead, ravers shared water, and made room for the shortest to get a view of the stage, or even lifted them onto their shoulders. It was a rolling tide of happiness, a sea of people united no matter their differences.

Kelly was bursting with pride as he watched his friend lead the crowd on a journey. Kelly knew Herbert's story well, and felt nothing but happiness for him. *This* was Herbert's dream. From his early teens he had wanted to be a musician and a DJ, and here he was, playing on the main stage of the biggest electronic music festival on earth. No matter what else was to come, this moment could never be taken away from him. Kelly knew that Chris felt as though he had been born for this, and now he had achieved that purpose.

And what of Kelly's purpose?

He didn't want to think about it in that moment, but it – the demons - crawled up on him like an assassin, whispering in his ear that he would never know the sense of achievement that Herbert was now feeling. That he could never fulfill his dream as the Australian was doing.

And why?

Kelly didn't want to think about it.

Instead he cheered out loud, hoping the noise would drown his thoughts. He danced, hoping the rhythm of the bass would beat his negative emotions into submission, as it had done so many times before. Hadn't that been how he had come to find dance music in the first place? Desperate for escape. Desperate for peace, love, unity, and respect from the one person who would not give it to him.

Himself.

Suddenly, Kelly felt a pang of hunger. Heard a whisper of a chemical promise which swore to him that it could make the feeling go away. That it could heal the hurt.

It had worked before, hadn't it?

No, Kelly told himself. No, it had not.

He was saved from further aching thought as fireworks began to arc into the air. It was the climax of Herbert's set, and not even the pessimistic voice on Kelly's shoulder could compete with the exploding beauty of the fireworks as they crisscrossed paths with lasers and floodlights. It was sensory overload, synesthesia coupled with a flood of emotion as the final track of Herbert's set peaked, and the Aussie got onto the microphone with a note in his voice that Kelly recognized as pure joy. As only a good friend could, Kelly knew that his boy was holding back tears.

'Pandora! I fucking love you!'

The set was over and, with it, Kelly's escape.

The dead were waiting.

34

In the cabin of the helicopter, Kelly was speechless. Where the flight out to the festival had taken his breath away, the flight back to Vegas threatened to stop his heart.

That moment came as the chopper climbed into the air, the festival revealing itself below as a battleground between alien spaceships, the darkness split by lasers and flashing lights in every color imaginable. Kelly had traveled the world and challenged himself to experience as much as he could on the planet, but he couldn't think of a time when he had been so stunned by the sheer scale and creativity of what he was seeing with his own eyes.

'Amazing,' he finally murmured, wondering at how many minds, and how many sets of hands, had gone into conceiving such a spectacle and then making it a reality.

Herbert was silent beside him, a look of serene calm having overtaken him after his initial twenty minutes of bouncing off the walls when he came offstage. They were the only two occupants in the helicopter's cabin; Herbert's other friends had decided to stay at the festival when the DJ had told them all that he was 'fucking ball-bagged, and going straight to bed. The set took it all out of me.'

That, Kelly thought to himself with a smile, *and the fact that he probably hasn't been to bed in days.*

Kelly looked back to the ground, where the highway was marked by a string of red lights, the traffic to and from the festival equally painful.

Not wanting to disturb his friend, Kelly let his own mind wander. Pandora was behind him now and, with a feeling of unease, he wondered if he would make it back to the festival – or, rather, if he would even want to. Seeing his friend on the main stage had been a moment that would be hard to equal, but more than that, Kelly knew that he would itch until a reason – a real reason – could be produced to explain why Iris had come to be in that canyon. Right now all that he and Sanders had were questions, a city that seemed happy to turn a blind eye, and a name.

Then, as they landed at the heliport, and Kelly turned his phone off flight-safe mode, he discovered that they didn't even have as little as that.

35

Kelly caught a ride with Herbert to the parking lot at McCarran where he had left his Tesla earlier that afternoon. After a hug and a promise that they would see each other again before they left town, Herbert went on his way to his suite at the Cosmopolitan, and Kelly drove himself to the Grand. After valeting the car, he dodged drunk gamblers and horny cougars as he made his way to an Asian restaurant at the casino's center.

It was easy enough to spot the person he was meeting. Sanders sat alone with a face of fury.

'Is it that bad?'

'They took the case from me and handed it off to a junior detective so that he could put a bow on it,' she spat.

'Who's they?'

'What does it matter?' Sanders shot back – but then instantly regretted the tone, and castigated herself a lot more harshly than Kelly ever would have. 'Sorry, Josh. I just . . . I don't know. I hate to fucking lose.'

'We haven't lost.'

'No,' Sanders agreed, her voice like iron. 'We haven't. Look, before, I had a feeling in my gut that something was off, and I wanted to find out what it was, but now I want to curb-stomp anyone who tries to fuck with us on this.'

Kelly knew that his friend was passionate, but even so . . .

'I think you should eat,' he said, half-smiling.

Sanders laughed. 'If you'd made a period joke about this I'd have beaten the shit out of you. But yeah, I already ordered. Got you a vegetable pad thai? That work? They do a great one here.'

'Oh, that works,' Kelly agreed. 'Feels like a long time since I ate.'

'I'm not used to seeing you without food in your mouth,' Sanders agreed. 'Sometimes I think you ate your own limbs.'

Kelly laughed. 'Framing Jaws isn't such a bad idea,' he acknowledged. 'And neither's framing a mountain lion.'

Sanders pulled a face. 'I think *framing's* a bit strong a term, Kelly. I mean, do you doubt something tried to – *did* – eat her?'

He didn't.

'What I don't like,' Sanders went on, 'and what I've never liked, is how she got out there. Now, before you beat me with your PETA stick, I'm just saying that I'm very open-minded to the idea that a cougar *did* kill her – no, quiet, Josh, I'm talking – but that doesn't really matter to me at the moment, because I don't have a satisfying reason as to *why* she was out there. OK, go on. Your turn to speak.'

Kelly did, but only after a few moments. 'I suppose it could have done,' he finally said. 'A mountain lion could have killed her, I mean. I've been so worried about how overblown a reaction to that would be that I haven't really considered it.'

'Well, you should,' Sanders urged gently. 'We need to think about these things.'

'We do,' Kelly agreed. 'But I don't think it was a mountain lion that took her wristbands away before they could be logged with her personal items, and I don't think it was a lion that scheduled her autopsy to coincide conveniently with the end of the festival.'

'You know what?' Sanders shook her head. 'It wasn't a cat that told me to pass off the case to a junior detective, either.'

'So what do we do?'

That answer had to wait as their food was brought out. Kelly had to admit that his friend had chosen extremely well.

Sanders spoke as she finished a mouthful. 'There's another big thing missing.'

'Her car?' Kelly guessed.

The detective nodded. 'I brought that up, and I got told that maybe she walked.'

'It's a minimum of twenty miles!'

'Exactly, but when I told them about her using drugs at the festival, they just used that as proof that she wasn't acting in sound mind.'

Kelly put down his fork. 'That's ridiculous, Tonya. Either she drove, and someone has taken the car, or someone took her there.'

'I'm not disagreeing with you, Kelly.'

They lapsed into silence then, chewing over their thoughts as well as their dinner. Only when the plates were near empty did Sanders ask, 'So, are you enjoying it?'

Kelly looked at his dish. 'It's a bomb pad thai.'

Sanders scoffed. 'You know what I mean.'

Kelly did – being a detective, no matter how unofficial.

He nodded. Despite the tragedy, he really was. He told his friend as much, before asking: 'Is it always like this, though?'

'If you mean obstacles and roadblocks, then yeah, it's always like this. Unfortunately, you don't get many lay-ups in this business.'

Kelly breathed out heavily, and sat back into his chair, checking his watch.

'How long?' Sanders asked.

'Twenty minutes.'

With permission of the police department or not, the pair was not about to give up on the chase.

Josh Kelly was about to tackle an obstacle his way.

36

It was a short walk through the Grand Casino to Rusa, the nightclub that was housed within its walls. Over the last decade, the club had become as much of a pull as the casino's slots, a quick search on Kelly's phone leading him to an article on Forbes.com, which estimated that the club netted its owners a hundred million dollars a year.

The night was young, but already a healthy line was building inside of the casino, snaking its way towards Rusa's doors. Many of the clubbers appeared to have come straight from Pandora, but plenty of others would have been tourists to Vegas who knew nothing of the festival's existence. Like taking in a show or the Bellagio's fountains, attending a club in Vegas had become a staple of the town's experience.

Kelly looked at the line, and sighed. Like the pool party he had attended that afternoon, many of the people in line were male. Kelly had no desire to stand with them, and walked straight for the roped-off section at the entrance, where a half-dozen suited bouncers stood with impatient stares.

'Back of the line,' the first said to Kelly.

Kelly smiled patiently. 'I'm looking for David Vang.'

'Don't know him. Back of the line.'

'He's a promoter here.'

'No. Don't know him. Get to the back of the line or I can just blacklist you.'

'Look,' Kelly tried, 'I got given his name by DJ Snarl. He said he was the guy I needed to talk with to get a table here. I'm looking to spend about ten K.'

The mention of DJ Snarl caught the bouncer's attention. The mention of Kelly buying a table flipped his attitude on its head.

'Sorry, sir, yeah. Yeah, I forgot that he's working tonight. Let me go get him for you. I'll be right back. I got you.'

Kelly tried not to laugh as the bouncer disappeared inside of the club. Doubtless he would be telling the club promoter, Vang, that he had convinced a guy to buy a table. As a promoter, Vang would get a cut of whatever business he brought into Rusa, and now the bouncer would be negotiating his own slice of that share. After five minutes, both bouncer and promoter appeared together. Vang was a short Asian-American with a flow of jet-black hair, and a huge smile on his face as if Kelly were his long-lost brother.

'What's up, bro? I hear you'd like to get a table? Don't worry – I got you. My name's David.'

'Kelly.' The bigger man smiled, shaking his hand, and not letting go.

'We're going to go for a little walk and talk.' Kelly, still smiling, increased his grip strength before Vang could protest. 'Don't make a scene. Just come for a walk with me, and talk.'

Vang looked up at the man who was a foot taller than him. Kelly saw anger in his eyes. He knew that he was about to call back to the bouncers, and so he played his ace.

'Your drugs are inside of a dead girl.'

37

Kelly led Vang away from the eyes of the bouncers, and into an alcove in one of the casino's busy passages. With the number of guests moving to and fro, and given what he had just been told about his connection to a dead girl, Vang didn't notice the woman who stood opposite them in the corridor, headphones in her ears, her eyes casually looking at the phone in her hand, which had an open line to Kelly – it had been kept that way since they had split in the restaurant.

'Look, sir,' Vang began, believing quite reasonably that the man towering over him was a cop. 'I haven't done anything wrong.'

'Sure you have,' Kelly replied, using the heavy fiber of his left fist to graze against the man's ribs. 'But if you tell me what I want to know, there's no need for anybody to know we had this talk, understood?'

Vang nodded his compliance. Kelly noticed that he was shaking.

'Stop that,' he growled, not wanting to draw any more attention than his appearance already did. 'Control yourself.'

Vang did his best, but his best wasn't much good.

Kelly shook his head in frustration. He'd taken an instant dislike to Vang. It was the way he was all bright and smiley because he thought Kelly was about to blow ten racks on a table, the big man decided. He wondered if Vang would have even acknowledged him if he was in the general admission line. *Maybe,* Kelly thought to himself, *if he thought he could get a shout-out through my social media.*

He saw that Vang had finally found some kind of control over his nerves. 'You arrange girls for the DJs,' Kelly stated simply, anxious to be done. 'You bring them to party, and you supply the drugs.'

Nothing that he said was a question, but Vang nodded anyway.

'Promotion work sucks, man,' he pleaded. 'I get paid shit, so I hustle a little on the side. I don't deal to anybody outside of the industry, though. It's just DJs. People I know.'

'Is Iris Manning one of those people?'

For a moment, Vang looked as if he was trying to swallow an orange. 'Fuck . . . Iris is . . .?'

Kelly said nothing. Looming over the shorter man was talk enough.

'I was with her last night,' Vang confessed. 'Snarl asked me to hook him up with some girls, so I hit up the ones I knew to see if any were at the festival. Iris was.'

'You gave her drugs?'

'I gave her *more* drugs,' Vang admitted. 'She was already rolling. She just wanted some coke to straighten out.'

'That was all you gave her?'

132

Vang nodded quickly.

'How much?'

'Only a gram, man. Not enough to kill her. Shit.'

Kelly thought over what he was being told. 'You use your own stuff?'

He did.

'You give her the same stuff that you gave the DJs?'

He had.

Kelly chewed that over. If Vang's drugs were bad, there'd be a lot more casualties, so why were guys like Snarl walking around the next day?

'I got told she left with you.'

Vang nodded reluctantly. 'She did.'

'Whose car?'

'Mine.'

'Where was hers?'

'At her place, I guess? That's where I left her.'

'Why did you leave the festival early?'

'She insisted on it, man. I don't know why. She took off on, like, a call for a couple of minutes, and when she came back she said she wanted to go back to Vegas.'

Kelly snorted at that. 'You drove her because you figured you'd get laid, huh?'

Vang's sour face said that that was the truth. 'What's this about, man?' he asked after a moment. 'Is she really dead?'

Kelly decided that silence was his ally. Nature abhors a vacuum, and Vang tried to fill the quiet in their conversation by hurling denials and accusations.

'Look, she messed me around a bit last night, man, but it's Vegas, that shit happens. I don't take it personally, OK? But look, some other people do.'

Kelly leaned in closer. 'Like who?'

Vang scratched at his wrist. 'You know where she works, right? What she does?'

'Bottle service at Rusa.'

The promoter nodded emphatically. 'Iris's good at getting under people's skin, man. Just last week, she was throwing fists backstage.'

Kelly raised his gaze. It was all he could do not to look across to Sanders on the other side of the passageway. 'She had a fight?'

Vang nodded so hard Kelly thought he could hear the man's spine crack. 'A fucking big one.'

'With who?'

It took a little pressure from carbon knuckles into Vang's ribs before he'd tell. A little promise of violence. But, finally, Kelly had found a person with real reason to do Iris harm.

And she was inside Rusa.

38

Vang led Kelly towards the front entrance of Rusa. The promise of arresting him in connection with Iris's death was enough to shake him into compliance, the promoter either too dumb or too scared to ask to see Kelly's badge. If he had, Sanders was on scene to add a little more pressure, but now that he was heading inside of the club, Kelly was glad that a shield hadn't been needed – Rusa was as corporate as it got, and progress would stop if the club realized that Kelly didn't have a shield, let alone a warrant.

'Is there not another way in?' Kelly asked, looking at where the thick snake of clubbers waited for their moment to enter the club. Kelly was no superstar, but there was always the chance that someone would recognize him from his documentary work or social media, and ask for a photo. It always came at the most inopportune time, like a date, or running late to catch a flight, and Kelly hoped he wasn't sending out a vibe to the universe that would see him stopped before he made it through Rusa's front door, with all pretense that he was a cop blown out the window.

'This is the best way,' Vang insisted.

'I can't get searched.' Kelly told him, seeing the bouncers waving metal-detecting wands over those who had reached the head of the line. 'My gun,' he added, and Vang nodded slowly.

'Don't worry, I got it. Hey, Derek,' he called to the bouncer who had initially met Kelly with such indifference.

The man came over, and Kelly caught Vang's hushed words.

'Turn the wand off. He's good.'

The bouncer nodded, then ran through the motions of scanning Kelly. Kelly had no gun, but the last thing he wanted was the attention that came from baring his prosthetic limbs in front of a crowd. For the people who had stood in line for over an hour, the fake limbs of Josh Kelly would rival Cirque du Soleil as entertainment.

'You're all good,' the bouncer announced. 'Have a great night, sir.'

'Thanks.'

Kelly followed on with Vang. There were a couple more suited men with slick hair and clipboards to negotiate, but they were all smiles and handshakes when Vang introduced Kelly as a 'real good friend of the club.' Kelly wondered what being 'a great friend' of the club would get him. A blowjob, maybe. When it came to selling tables, there seemed no limit to customer satisfaction.

'Here,' Vang told Kelly once they were inside the corridor that led to the dance floor and tables. 'Put this on your wrist.'

It was an Access All Areas band, something given to staff rather than the well-spending punters. Kelly knew from experience that some guys who spent crazy amounts of money and had the best table in the house would be green with envy of the few friends the DJ had brought along to accompany them in the DJ box – there was always *the next thing* that people had to have.

Vang was about to say something else when the words died on his lips, and he tried to twist them into a happy smile. Instead, the promoter ended up looking as though he'd just drunk some vinegar.

Kelly half turned and found that there was a woman beside him. She was Latina, her suit tailored to a physique that Kelly reckoned had been built on the track and honed in the cross-fit gym. The woman's plump lips gave Kelly a professional smile, and then her almond eyes narrowed as she took in the band on his wrist.

'Arabella Robins,' she introduced herself to Kelly, ignoring Vang. 'I'm the manager.'

'Josh Kelly,' he replied, appreciating the shake from a hand that was as gym-worn as his. 'Great-looking club you have here.'

Robins's head twitched in amusement that Kelly sensed was at his expense.

It was. 'If you like the corridors you'll love the dance floor. So who are you here with?'

Kelly decided to let Vang do the talking.

'He's with me.'

'Oh.' The manager smiled helpfully. 'Then there must have been a mix-up with the wristbands. I can take care of that for you.'

Kelly said nothing.

But then, neither did Vang.

The woman frowned. 'What's up?'

Kelly looked the promoter's way. One quick glance at the wide-eyed man was enough to know that Vang had become utterly useless. Kelly knew that further progress rested on his own shoulders, and so, before Vang could even begin to stutter a reason, Kelly turned to Arabella Robins, and looked her straight in the eyes.

'One of your employees is dead.'

That got her attention.

39

'One of your employees is dead,' Kelly told the club's manager, 'and I'm trying to find out why.'

He watched her face as she took the news. The club's corridor was washed in purple lighting that caught in the woman's widening eyes. Kelly saw her jaw twitch, and her shoulders tighten.

'Who?' she asked after a moment.

'Iris Manning.'

Robins balled a fist, and put it to her mouth. The display of grief lasted for less than three seconds, and then it was gone.

'Wait in my office,' she told Vang, who scurried away from Kelly without a backwards glance. Then the club manager pushed open a door, and gestured for Kelly to lead on. He did, moving into a large storeroom where boxes of electrical supplies and speakers stood in neatly ordered rows.

The room was well lit, and Kelly found himself under scrutiny. He could see Robins taking in his surf-styled hair, his stubbled face, and of course his prosthetic arm.

'You don't look like a cop.'

Kelly saw value in the truth. 'I'm not.'

The club manager thought about that for a moment. Already Kelly had the impression that she was a person who considered her words and moves before acting. She was taking in what was in front of her, assessing, then executing. Kelly had seen the same behavior in high performers the world over. They were often at his speaking engagements, either as the CEOs of hugely successful companies, or as the keynote speakers that would take the stage after him for a conference's main event.

Robins broke her silence. 'Iris Manning is dead?' Kelly nodded. 'And you're not a cop?' Kelly nodded again. 'Then I'm going to have to ask you to leave the premises, and not to speak to any more of our employees. Can we agree to that?'

This time, it was Kelly who bided his time before answering. 'You're not curious about why I'm here?'

'I'm curious about why the police *aren't*.'

Kelly nodded. 'I can understand that. Will you allow me to tell you why?'

'Go ahead. But what I said still stands.'

'Fair enough. There's a detective waiting in the casino for the answers I came in here to find,' Kelly went on, 'with the help of the club, not working against it. If she comes in, and brings the law, everything's official and it's a paperwork mountain. If I'm here, it's just a couple of friends talking. That's all. No papers. Just talk.'

Kelly then stood in silence as the club's manager chewed over what he'd said. Sanders had impressed upon him that discretion was a prized commodity in Vegas. No matter the reason, it didn't ever look good to have law enforcement on club property. Despite the image that they put out as hedonistic party places, the clubs were extremely strict on any violation of the law by their customers, and, in turn, their parent companies came down hard on them – and the club's management – if they were seen to have contributed to, or even simply overlooked, something that reflected badly on the club and its owners.

'I appreciate your discretion,' the woman told him after a moment. 'Is there a particular friend you want to talk to?'

There was.

Robins folded her arms. 'The fight last week?' Kelly nodded. 'It was nothing. Girls being girls. There's a lot of stress comes with working in a place like this. A lot of money getting thrown around. Guys are grabby. And it's hard to sleep well when you work all night. It really was nothing,' she concluded.

'Even so, if it's OK with you, I'd like to talk with her.' Kelly didn't need to say what the alternative was – an interview at the station with a detective.

Robins looked straight into Kelly's eyes. She had to tilt her head back to do it, but the posture somehow made her look more powerful, not less. Kelly knew that he was being judged for the truth.

He was not found wanting.

'OK,' she told him simply. 'A talk between friends.'

40

Robins led Kelly out of the room, but surprised him by heading in the opposite direction to the dance floor, where he had expected to find his 'friend.'

'We've got a night swim,' Robins explained without his asking. 'There's a pool that opens up on the other side of the main stage, and our headline act will play out there tonight.'

Kelly had attended night swims before. They were essentially pool parties after dark, but so long as they were suitably dressed, clubbers could also make use of the club itself. Such nights had become extremely popular in recent years; Herbert had explained the phenomenon once with simple reasoning: 'You can get away with a lot more when it's dark.'

Kelly followed Robins out of the air-conditioned corridor and through a set of locked glass doors, emerging in a staff-only area set off to the side of the pool. Immediately, Kelly was assaulted by the noise and heat. Despite the sun having set a couple of hours ago, it was still hot enough for Kelly to feel the urge to jump into the pool, which was half full with partygoers. He smiled at that thought. Kelly had come to Rusa with a purpose, but even if that purpose was partying he wouldn't be getting into the water. Not too many people were leaving it to take bathroom breaks, and more than a few would be fucking in there. Kelly'd seen a few floating condoms in his time.

'Good travel advice,' Herbert had told him. 'In Mexico, don't drink the water. In Vegas, don't get in it.'

Robins led Kelly past a couple of bouncers and towards the far end of the pool. The place was yet to really get going, and a warm-up DJ was playing a more relaxed style of house than Kelly had heard so far that day. When the crowds arrived from the festival, and the headline acts with them, that's when the bigger beats would be unleashed. Until then, it was the job of the lesser-known DJ behind the decks to keep the crowd moving, having fun, but most importantly – spending.

'What's the cost here tonight?' Kelly asked, his voice raised against the music.

'Tables start at two, bungalows at ten,' the club manager told him, meaning the minimum-spend agreements per table, before tax and gratuity would be added.

And it was to the bungalows that Robins now led them, the units set back from the pool and raised so that their occupants had an unobstructed view over the entire party. In front of each bungalow was a walkway and private 'dance floor,' and Kelly noticed that over half of the expensive suites currently had their curtains closed.

Robins tracked his gaze. 'They're all reserved for later,' she explained, the compulsion to explain born of constantly balancing books and the expectations of those above her.

'In here.' She motioned, and Kelly followed her through the curtains and inside one of the bungalows. It was empty except for the tables and sofas that would soon play host to bottles and big spending bottle poppers. 'Wait here please.'

She left the bungalow then, but not Kelly's thoughts.

Robins wasn't the most outwardly attractive woman Kelly had seen that day, but something about the club manager's demeanor had stuck into his flesh like hooks. It was her confidence, he decided. The way that the operation of the club was unquestionably in her control. Kelly was born and raised in California, and he was used to seeing beautiful people. What he was less used to seeing was a beautiful mind to go with it.

Kelly passed a hand through his hair, and reminded himself that he was here to do a job. He wondered how first responders could do it. How did they separate the flesh and blood that they saw in murders and in traffic accidents from the flesh and blood that they lay beside at night? They were a special breed, Kelly recognized, and one that his country was lucky to have. Maybe, for the first time in his life, he understood – if only slightly – why many struggled outside of their uniformed shifts, and why first responders suffered some of the highest divorce rates of any profession.

Kelly sighed. As an LAPD recruit, he had never worried about such things. He'd been madly in love with not only his new profession, but his girlfriend of three years. No matter the odds, Kelly had known that they would be the ones to beat the odds. They would be the exception that proved the rule.

A lot had changed in ten years.

Kelly was saved from further thought as the curtain was pulled back and Robins reappeared. She was followed by a tall girl dressed in a bikini that carried Rusa's logo, white sneakers on her feet and a Rusa emblazoned fanny pack at her waist. She was a bottle-service girl at the club, and, like her fellow employees, she had been chosen for the position because she was beautiful, confident, and could put just the right pressure on a guy to make him spend his life savings in return for the promise of a phone number.

'Josh,' Kelly introduced himself. 'Do you know what this is about?'

'Stephanie. And no, I don't.'

Kelly smiled sadly. Then he looked at Robins. 'I think you'd better close the curtain.'

41

After Kelly had broken the news of Iris's death, Stephanie Wilson took a seat on one of the bungalow's sofas. Robins was beside her, an arm over the girl's shoulders. There were no tears, simply shock.

'I feel bad,' Stephanie finally confided after a moment.

'It's a big shock,' Kelly told her. 'Take your time.'

But the girl shook her head. 'No. I mean, I feel bad because I don't feel bad,' she admitted. 'Fuck. That's awful, I know, but . . . I just don't.'

'These things take time to process,' the club manager said in a calm, reassuring voice. 'Once we get done talking, you can go home, and let things sink in.'

Stephanie shook her head. 'No way, Arabella. Sorry, no offense to Iris, but I'm OK. I'm not losing out on money because of this. No offense, but I'm not.'

Kelly looked at Robins. He could see that she was weighing up her next words.

'We can't have this news getting out,' she said eventually.

'I know.' Stephanie nodded pragmatically. 'It'll kill the vibe. But look, Arabella, I'm fine. I just want to get back to work. I'll keep my mouth shut about it, but I wanna grind and make my money tonight. This is one of the best weeks of the year.'

After a moment, Robins nodded her consent. 'I've gotta step out for a minute,' she told them before fixing her eyes on Kelly. 'Please stay here until I'm back.'

'Sure.'

She left, and Kelly turned to Stephanie. She really did look fine. Maybe even angry, an emotion that Kelly put down to the prospect of losing money.

'You must think I'm a bitch,' the girl said, following her words up with a chuckle of sad laughter. 'I know it looks bad, but I wasn't friends with Iris, and me going home isn't going to bring her back, is it? I need to make my money.'

'I get it,' Kelly replied. 'Really I do.'

'I've got a kid. I can make a couple of grand tonight if I hustle. I'd be a shitty mom if I went home.'

Kelly raised his hands. 'Look, I totally get it. Really.'

'OK,' she allowed. 'I just don't like feeling that people are judging me.'

'I'm just here to talk,' Kelly promised. 'Mind if I sit?'

'Of course not.'

Kelly took a seat on the sofa opposite the bottle-service girl. For the first time, she took real notice of his arm.

'Were you in the army or something?'

Kelly gave her the CliffsNotes of how he had come to be wearing a prosthetic. He knew that sharing something personal from his own life would make Stephanie more likely to open up about her own. At the beginning of many of Kelly's talks, the audience members would be

147

nervous and tongue-tied about introducing themselves, and saying a little about where they'd come from. By the end, they'd be telling Kelly secrets that they'd kept inside for decades.

Stephanie shook her head as Kelly finished his story. 'That's crazy,' she told him as the rumble of bass droned through the thick curtain. 'So you're a friend of Iris's?'

'No. I'm helping the police look into what happened to her. That's why I came to talk to you, so we can keep it all off the record.'

Stephanie frowned. 'Why me?'

Kelly let silence do the talking.

It worked.

'It was just a few punches . . .'

'Can you tell me why?'

'Sure.' She gave a single cough of dark laughter. 'Because she was a cunt.'

Kelly said nothing.

'Do you know why I worry about getting judged?' she asked, not waiting for Kelly's answer. 'Because of girls like Iris. She was a fucking bitch, dude, and honestly, I'm not sorry that she's dead. It sounds shitty to say it but it's the truth. I'm not sorry.'

'What was she doing that reflected badly on you?' Kelly asked, leaning forwards.

'Not just on me.' Stephanie tutted. 'On all women. She doesn't – didn't – have any respect for anyone. She's a total gold digger.'

'Is that why you guys had a fight?'

'Hell no. If I was fighting with every gold digger it would be like the UFC in here. The fight was because she screwed my friend over.'

'What happened?'

Stephanie's face curdled as she looked away and recalled that night. 'She'd been leading one of my friends on for months. I tried to tell him, but he was in love with her. And then, as soon as he lost his job, she just goes and dumps him. The same day, just like that.' She snapped her fingers. 'She was a total fucking user.'

It all sounded familiar to Kelly. 'Your friend's Blake Mathews, right? He was the resident DJ here?'

'That's right,' Stephanie replied, a little surprised. 'You know him?'

Kelly said that he'd heard of their relationship, but left out that he'd met the man himself.

'Blake was working so hard to clean himself up,' Stephanie insisted. 'It's not easy living in Vegas, especially as a DJ. Blake made some mistakes but he was going totally clean to show Iris that he could do it. The sad thing is, she didn't care. It wasn't the drink and drugs that made her finish things with him. It was Blake losing his status.'

Kelly chewed over what the girl was saying. He had noticed Blake's shaking hands in his apartment. Kelly had put that down to nerves, but it now seemed clear that it was a symptom of Blake's detoxifying from drug and alcohol abuse. Thinking back to the apartment, Kelly couldn't remember seeing a single bottle of liquor or beer in the place.

'Iris just saw Blake as a chauffeur and a PA,' Stephanie went on, her anger setting her on a roll. 'She'd call him up whenever she needed something doing, and he'd come running. I told him not to – a lot of us did, because we really like the guy, he's so sweet – but he wouldn't listen. Blake was in love, and Iris took advantage of that. Last week I heard her bragging that all she had to do was click her fingers and he'd do anything for her. That was too much. Fuck that bitch. It was too much.'

'So you hit her out of loyalty?'

Stephanie nodded emphatically; she looked ready for war. 'I did. And the only reason I'm sorry about her dying is that I won't ever get the chance to do it again.'

42

Kelly thought it best that he give Stephanie a moment to cool off. Her thin jaw was clenched tightly, her manicured hands balled. Kelly had no doubt that if Iris were alive and in the bungalow with them, then fists would be flying once more.

'When was the last time you saw Iris?' he asked when he saw her anger drop from boiling to simmering.

Stephanie shrugged. 'Sometime last week. After the fight. They've kept us working at opposite ends of the club, but I heard she came in last night.'

That news made Kelly sit up. 'Really? Do you know when?'

'Not specifically. I just heard one of the girls bitching because she'd come in late and left early,' Stephanie said contemptuously. 'Working off her own rules, as usual.'

Kelly cast his eyes over her. She didn't look like a killer to him, but he acknowledged to himself that he had no idea what a killer looked like. Just because he had grown up thinking that beautiful women meant good times didn't mean that they weren't capable of doing anything that any other person had the capacity for. Equality went both ways. Kelly firmly believed that women deserved parity, but if that were the case, he had to admit that the level playing field encompassed possible guilt. Kelly couldn't let the way he'd been raised and conditioned affect his judgment, and he needed to keep an open mind that *anyone* was capable of *anything,* good or bad.

But his *gut.* His gut said that – though she was clearly no fan of Iris's, to say the least – Stephanie was not a murderer, or complicit in how Iris had come to be found dead in Sloan Canyon.

He told her as much.

'I doubt I'm the only person that hated her,' the girl replied.

'Do you know of anyone who would want to do her harm?'

'*That* kind of harm? No. But look, she was making some choices that . . . that maybe make that kind of thing more likely to happen.'

Kelly was puzzled. 'How do you mean?'

Stephanie looked uncomfortable as she told him. 'There was a girl that used to work here – Josie Amendola. She left pretty quick but I heard that her and Iris stayed in touch, and that Iris was following in Josie's footsteps.'

The tone of her voice told Kelly that those footsteps were not on a good path to follow, but before he could ask why, the bungalow's curtain was sharply pulled back – it was the club's manager.

And she had company.

43

As the bungalow's curtain was pulled back the thump of bass grew louder, and the night swim's colored lights washed over the two people standing on the threshold, bathing them in shifting hues of purple, green, red, and blue. One of the figures was the athletic shape of Arabella Robins, the club's manager. The other was a suited man every inch as tall as Kelly. He had a shaved head and long arms, and a smile on a face that was lightly covered in a blond beard.

Kelly stood up. As the new man stepped closer, Kelly saw that his smile was strained. As he came closer still, and put out his hand, Kelly could see that his blue eyes were rimmed with red.

The man had been crying.

'Sven Niklas,' he introduced himself, his words accented. 'I'm the owner of Rusa.'

He was Swedish, Kelly guessed. Swedish, and grieving.

'Josh Kelly.'

The club's owner looked from Kelly to Stephanie, who was now getting to her feet.

'Stephanie has been helpful?'

'Very.'

The man surprised Kelly by pulling the bottle-service girl to him and hugging her tightly. 'Arabella says you want to work tonight? Are you sure?' he asked her.

'I'm sure.'

'OK. But the news . . .'

'I won't say anything.'

Niklas hugged her again. 'Thank you. Come find me if you need to talk.' He waited until Stephanie had stepped out and closed the curtain before he spoke again. 'We're family at Rusa,' he explained to Kelly.

Kelly wasn't sure what was going to come next. He expected an offer of help, or to be told to leave. What he didn't expect was to receive his own hug.

As Niklas squeezed him tight, Kelly thought he heard the man choke back a sob of grief. When they stood apart, Kelly was certain of it. The Swede's eyes were wet.

'I just can't believe she's fucking gone, man.' He shook his head. 'I can't fucking believe it.'

Kelly was about to open his mouth to offer his condolences, but he thought better of it. He could see that Niklas wanted to speak. To be heard.

'Iris was with us for two years, man. She was such a great girl. So funny. So sweet. Everybody here loved her.'

That was a different hymn sheet from the one that Stephanie was singing from, and Kelly wondered if – like many bosses – Niklas was simply disconnected from his work force, and chose to think the best of the people that worked for him.

'You didn't ever have trouble with her?' Kelly finally decided to ask.

The tall man shook his head. 'She was one of my go-to's. She was a trouper, man.' He let out a deep exhalation then, and pulled down the corners of his suit jacket. 'Josh. Josh, man, I want to thank you. I want to thank you for breaking this hard news but I also want to thank you for your discretion.

'Arabella's told me how you came here so that Rusa could . . . Look, I don't want it to sound distasteful, OK? But we all know how the world works. It can be a shit place, and you've helped stop something that is already a tragedy affecting Rusa in a negative light, and I appreciate that. I really do.'

Kelly's motivations for keeping things discreet had everything to do with the dead girl's interests and nothing to do with the club, but he put out his hand anyway. 'You're welcome, Mr Niklas. I know what the media are like, and I don't think sensational headlines or reporters trawling for a story help anybody.'

'Sven,' the club owner insisted. 'And you're right, Josh, they don't. But, look, OK? Arabella says you're helping the police with their investigation?' Kelly nodded. 'Iris was part of the family here, so if there's anything we can do to help, you call me.'

Niklas took a metallic business card and put it into Kelly's hand. 'You need rooms at the casino, cars, anything you can think of, you call me OK? That's my personal number, man, and I'll be available twenty-four seven. What's yours?'

Kelly told him, and both the club's owner and manager took it down.

'You're a private investigator?' Niklas then asked.

Kelly thought on it a moment before answering. 'Just someone trying to help. The professionals are on this case, but, well . . . I just want to help the best I can.'

Niklas nodded solemnly for a moment. 'Can I ask how she died?'

Kelly gave a sad shrug of his shoulders. 'They don't know yet.'

For a moment, the bungalow was silent except for the drone of the bass outside. Then, suddenly, Niklas began to shake as if he'd been pulled from a frozen lake. Robins came quickly to his side, and helped move him to one of the bungalow's sofas. At first Kelly was panicked that the man was having some kind of seizure, but then, as the tears came, he saw it was grief that had taken hold of the club's owner.

'Jesus fuck.' The Swede shook. 'I can't believe it. I can't believe she's dead.'

'I can leave . . .' Kelly offered, but Niklas shook his head almost violently.

'Please stay. Please. I have to talk to you about something . . . and it sounds so . . . disgusting.'

Kelly braced himself for what he was about to hear. Las Vegas. A club owner. A beautiful girl. He thought he knew where this was going.

But he was wrong. If lust was on the club owner's mind, then it was a fetish for business.

'The festival . . .' Niklas tried to begin. 'This news . . . it's tragic . . .'

Kelly got the gist quickly, and decided that he liked the man enough to spare him having to drag out his words. 'The show must gone on,' he told Rusa's owner.

Niklas rubbed his hands across his shaved head, and looked up at the ceiling. 'Yes. Fuck. It does,' he confessed as if to God. 'I'm sure you think I am the biggest bastard for saying it, but yes. This club, Josh, this is mine, but the festival? It's for Vegas. *Work* for so many people. *Memories* for so many people.'

'I understand,' Kelly told the man. And he did. Like the media reports that were putting bullseyes onto wild life, Kelly didn't want to see accusations and speculation of something like a serial killer cast around at an event that he loved. 'I came to town for the festival,' he enlightened them. 'That music got me through dark times. I'm not trying to slander anything, or anyone. I just want to know what happened to Iris.'

Niklas got to his feet. The shaking was gone, but he looked a wreck. 'And so do we, Josh. We will help you however we can. Whatever the police need. But we must be discreet. Please, Josh. Let us all do it for Iris.'

The club owner put out his hand. Kelly took it.

And then, as Kelly turned to thank the woman beside him, Sven Niklas ran.

44

Kelly made no move to follow the club owner as he made his way quickly to the back of the bungalow, and to the private toilet. Even with the sound of the bass he could hear him retching.

'He's really upset,' Robins told Kelly, as if it needed saying.

'Is he that close to all his employees?'

'Rusa is Sven, and Sven is Rusa,' his manager explained. 'He really does believe it's a family.'

The sound of retching stopped, but there was no sign of the club's owner emerging.

'Iris was here last night,' Kelly said as a matter of fact, and Robins made no attempt to say otherwise. 'Was she working bottle service?'

Robins nodded. 'She wasn't scheduled but she was requested. We get that sometimes from regular high rollers.'

'Can you tell me who he is?'

'I can do you one better. Follow me.' She held back the curtain, and felt Kelly's hesitation. 'Don't worry about Sven. Some peace is probably the best thing for him.'

And so Kelly stepped out to the front of the bungalow. The pool was beginning to fill with clubbers, and a couple of groups were being shown into their bungalows by bikini-wearing hostesses with smiles as big as their chests. Kelly could see that Robins was watching them – appraising them – looking for anything out of sync in the well-oiled money machine.

'He flew in the day before the festival on his own jet,' Robins explained of the high roller as they walked. 'He has one of the best VIP suites at the festival, but he only goes for a few hours each day.'

'Where did he come in from?'

'The Caribbean. He lives between there and New York, but he spends a lot of time with us.'

'He has a place here too?' Kelly asked, wondering at the lifestyles of the rich and famous.

Robins shook her head. 'He's a great friend of Rusa, and that makes him a great friend of the casino. He's comped a suite on all of his stays.'

'Even during festival week?'

'That's right.'

Kelly took a moment to let that sink in – it was standard practice for casinos to comp accommodation to high rollers, whether they were gamblers or bottle poppers, but to do it during such a busy week meant that the man was a highly treasured customer.

'Wait here a moment,' Robins then told Kelly, stopping him short of a bungalow that was home to a dozen dancing clubbers, all of them attractive women. At the front of the

VIP section, leaning against the railings and watching over the party as though it was his domain, was an Asian man that Kelly put in his early forties. The man wore a black tee and black shorts, and everything about his manner and the position of his table in the club cried money and confidence. When Robins appeared by the man's side he greeted her like an old friend, and after a few questions in his ear, Kelly saw that he gave Robins a solitary nod.

The club manager turned to Kelly, and waved him over.

He was about to meet the big fish in Rusa's pool.

45

Kelly's appearance drew excited looks from the girls in the man's bungalow as he approached, but Kelly knew that that was as much as he could hope for from them – if they wanted their night on somebody else's dime, then it wasn't a good idea to start giving other men their attention. Kelly had once found himself in an altercation because a businessman from San Diego who had flown out a dozen California girls to Vegas with him on a private jet had lost his shit when they started talking to other guys at the club. They'd taken his 'kind offer' at face value, not seeing the strings attached. That these girls in the bungalow knew better told Kelly that they were locals, and used to the game. Still, a couple brushed by Kelly a little closer than they needed to as he made his way to Robins, and the high roller that was paying for their entertainment.

'This is Sam Chao,' Robins announced above the music. 'He's been a great friend of the club for a long time.'

That was a ringing endorsement, and if the words didn't tell Kelly not to overstep, then Robins's look did.

'Josh Kelly,' he introduced himself, shaking the man's hand. 'If you don't mind, it would really help me out if I could ask you a couple of questions about Iris Manning. She was here last night.'

But it was Chao who began with the questions.

'Your arm,' he said, 'what manufacturer is that? Calthetic?' Kelly was taken aback, and Chao could see it. 'I've been buying up a lot of shares in life enhancement,' he explained. 'It's the next medical revolution. If you have any money lying around, put it into the companies that are making life longer and better. You'll make your grandchildren rich.'

Kelly half smiled. 'I'll need kids first.'

Chao narrowed his eyes slightly. With the sound of the music, he had to lean towards Kelly to be heard, so it wasn't possible for the taller man to read Chao's face, and to see if he was joking. 'Did you lose your testicles?' he shouted into Kelly's ear. 'What was it? A bomb?'

Kelly shook his head. Almost every man he met was curious to know that answer, but only a few had ever asked so brazenly. 'All good down there. Just haven't met the girl.'

Chao laughed at that. 'Then look around!' He gestured to the women all about them. 'I could see them eye-fucking you as you came over.'

Kelly smiled. 'Maybe some other time.'

'I don't blame you. Never meet a woman in a club. Not for children, anyway. So how *did* you lose it?'

'Shark.'

Chao's eyes went wide. 'So you've faced death,' he said with weight.

'I suppose you could say that.'

'You must have fought hard to stay alive.'

For a moment Kelly pictured his body pinned to the surfboard. How the shark had shaken him like a toy. He'd wanted to fight, but against the creature's power he'd been useless. No, Kelly's real fight had come later, and, sometimes, it had been one he'd wanted to lose.

'Would you live forever if you could?' Chao asked suddenly, breaking Kelly from those thoughts.

'Live forever? I don't know. I've never really thought about it.'

'Everyone's thought about it!' Chao exclaimed, gripping the flesh of Kelly's upper arm. 'Come on.'

The taller man shrugged his thick shoulder. 'I really don't know. Maybe yes, I guess . . .'

Chao shook his head. 'Everybody wants to be bigger, faster, wealthier, healthier. The way life is right now, you gain some of this as you get older, but other things you lose. Look at those guys over there.' Chao pointed to a trio of chiseled guys barely into their twenties. 'They have the health. But the wealth? They're in general admission. They don't even have a few thousand for a table. They probably won't see money until they're older, if ever. How many young guys you see driving Ferraris?'

Kelly smiled. 'I used to live in Hollywood.'

Chao laughed at that. 'Well, shit. But the rest of the world?'

Kelly got where the man was going. 'You think people will be able to have both through—'

'Augmentations.' Chao nodded. 'Mental and physical. You know that one of Google's founders has invested over a billion into longevity?'

Kelly had read something about it and told Chao as much. What he didn't understand was why the businessman was so interested in talking about it. Maybe Kelly's face gave that away.

'I don't meet many people who have faced death,' Chao admitted. 'I keep my circle' – he looked around him at the beautiful women – 'young. Naïve. Good for not getting bullshitted about business "opportunities" while I try and relax, bad for perspective. I imagine your own worldviews are a little more balanced.'

'I don't know about that.' Kelly grinned, taking in their surroundings. 'This isn't such a bad worldview.'

Chao laughed and shrugged. 'It's a nice distraction. I know you've got questions for me though, so how about we make a deal? I'll answer yours, and before I leave town we sit down someplace quieter and I can ask you mine? I'd love to know more from an end user who clearly hasn't let his injuries slow down his life.'

Kelly thought that was some assumption to make, but the truth was that he did get paid handsomely to talk about just such a thing – a better life after his injuries – and if it could help Iris, then donating a few hours of his time was the least he could do. 'Absolutely.'

'Great.' Chao beamed. 'So how can I help?'

'Well, it's about Iris, your server last night,' Kelly began. 'You requested Iris?' he asked, receiving a nod in reply. 'Why her?'

'Because I like her tits and tattoos.' Chao grinned again. 'What other reason does a man need? She served me a couple of years ago and I've requested her every time I've been back to Rusa. Why?'

'I'm trying to piece together when and where she was yesterday.'

'Why?'

'Her family are looking for her,' Kelly lied quickly. 'I've been told that she left early last night, so it would really help if you could tell me when was the last time you saw her?'

'Oh, that's easy.' Chao shrugged as if Kelly had just asked him the time. 'When I got done fucking her.'

46

The club's big spender smiled at Kelly. 'You look shocked.'

'Sorry. I didn't—'

'Look,' Chao cut him off. 'The girls that work here aren't supposed to fuck the club's clients, but look around, man.'

Kelly did. All about him, Rusa's employees were using their sexuality to coax drunk guys into overspending and over-tipping.

'You can't have this atmosphere and not have shit happen,' Chao went on with a shrug. 'Iris is hot, and she liked me.'

'She left here with you?'

Chao shook his head. 'No fucking way. That's not a good look. She met me up at my suite. It's here, in the casino. Five minutes from here to there.'

'Do you know what time she left your suite?'

'Yeah, probably about three.' Chao looked at Kelly for a long moment. 'You know why I'm telling you this stuff, man?' Kelly didn't. 'Arabella told me that Iris is in some kind of trouble, and I like the girl. But she also told me that you're doing things the right way, and I appreciate that.

Someone says the wrong thing and . . . well, you know. Shit sticks even when it shouldn't,' he finished, before quickly changing subjects. 'Arabella also told me you came here for the festival?'

'I did.'

'I've got a section there,' Chao told him. 'Come anytime you want. Just give my name to the VIP staff, and they'll show you to it.'

'I appreciate that.'

'And I appreciate you looking out for Iris. What kind of trouble is she in anyway?'

'The worst kind, I'm afraid.' Kelly spoke before thinking, only realizing his mistake after the words had left his mouth.

Chao blinked hard. 'She's . . .?'

Shit. Kelly cursed himself for letting the extent of the tragedy slip. Accepting that the cat was out the bag, he gave Chao a nod.

The businessman wiped a hand over his face. 'Wow. Fucking wow, man. That sucks . . . How?' he finally asked.

Kelly didn't have an answer for him. 'That's what we're trying to find out.'

'The police are going to want to talk to me,' Chao guessed. 'I was with her last night.'

'I'm working with the police,' Kelly embellished, hoping to make the man feel better. 'They'll know you've already been helpful.'

But Chao was already thinking ahead, and trying to be more helpful still. 'This casino loves me,' he told Kelly. 'I can ask them to get you tapes? The security tapes. You can see where she goes after she leaves my suite, right?'

Remembering what Sanders had said about the casino's begrudging attitude towards handing over tape without a warrant, Kelly hoped that Chao's influence could open doors. 'Thank you. That would be great.'

Chao turned to the table behind him, stacked with ice buckets and liquor. 'You want a drink?'

Kelly shook his head. Chao took a long pull straight from a bottle of Jack, before pouring the rest over the railings, his words almost lost to the music.

'To Iris,' Kelly thought he heard him say. 'To Iris.'

47

Robins was back at their side a moment later.

Chao took her hand. 'Arabella. I'm so sorry to hear the news.'

The club manager's eyes flashed to Kelly. He saw daggers in them before she turned back to Chao, and made a professional and friendly apology for having to take Kelly away. 'I'll be back to see you later to make sure you have everything you need.'

'Come talk to me soon,' Chao made Kelly promise before he shook hands and left.

Arabella Robins was not so gracious.

'You fucking told him?' she hissed as they walked away. 'Shall I get the DJ to make a fucking announcement, too?'

Kelly was shamefaced. He knew he'd fucked up.

'Look—' he tried, but Robins stopped him dead.

'No, *you* look, Mr Kelly. Iris was one of our family here. Now, as much as we appreciate what you're doing for her, you do *not* start telling our employees and our customers about it, do you understand me? From now on, you talk to me, you talk to Sven, or you talk to fucking nobody. Do you understand that?'

'I do.' And he did. He was totally unprepared for this, Kelly realized, and why should he expect any different? He wasn't Sanders. He wasn't a fucking detective.

'I'm sorry,' he told her honestly, and perhaps Robins saw the genuine apology for what it was, because her shoulders softened.

'Look, me too. Sorry. It's just . . . yeah, talk about high fucking stress.' She shook her head, and Kelly wondered about the pressures she must be under – the festival week was the club's busiest of the year, and on top of that, the loss of an employee?

'Sven's gone home for the night,' she told him. 'He's really shaken up.'

'I can't even imagine.'

'I've never seen him like this.'

For a moment, Kelly said nothing. 'Anything I can do to help, just call me.'

'I will. And do you need anything more from me?'

He did. After a couple of questions, and moment of thought, the club's manager was able to provide it.

'And I got you this,' Robins added, pulling a folded piece of paper from her pocket. Kelly looked at it – it was a printout of Iris's emergency contact details. 'We've forwarded them on to the police, too.'

Kelly ran his eyes over the paper's contents. There were two contacts. The first was Blake Mathews, and the address listed was not the apartment where Kelly had visited him earlier – he guessed it hadn't been updated since Blake and Iris's 'break-up.' The second address belonged to Richard and Sandra Manning in Irvine, California.

Robins read the man's mind. 'Their whole world is about to get torn apart.'

Kelly nodded sadly, and folded the paper before placing it in his pocket. 'Thank you for this.'

For a moment, they simply stood, contemplating the end of a young life and the devastating ripples it was about to send out into the world. Behind them, oblivious, hundreds of revelers splashed, danced, kissed, and had the time of their young lives.

'It's fucked up, isn't it?' Robins said.

Kelly knew what she was talking about. The fine line between life and death. The tragedy of things taken for granted. He thought about trying to talk it away, but when it came down to it, what else was there to say?

'Yeah,' he agreed. 'It's fucked up.'

48

Kelly met Sanders in the casino's undercover parking lot, her truck pulled up in the lane behind his Tesla. He climbed in to sit beside her, swearing as he caught his prosthetic on the step.

'God-fucking-damn it . . .'

'Are you OK?' Sanders wasn't used to seeing Kelly lose his temper, no matter how slightly.

'I fucked up in there,' Kelly confessed, and told her how he'd let slip about Iris's death.

'You did well,' the detective insisted. 'I've sent the details of Iris's parents to the OC's sheriff's department, and they're going to break the news to them in the morning.'

'Why not now?' Kelly asked, surprised.

'I asked the same thing,' Sanders admitted. 'But it's already two in the morning, and they don't have a unit to spare right now. And like the sheriff said,' she went on sadly, 'maybe it's not a bad idea to let her parents sleep. It's probably the last night of good rest they'll ever get.'

The truck's cab was quiet as that sank in. Kelly pictured the scene that was to come. How a stranger in uniform would appear on the family's doorstep. How they would have to break the hardest news that it was possible to break – that a loved one had died before their time. That the parents would outlive the person that they had poured all of their love and energy and hope into since the day that she'd been born.

Kelly exhaled loudly. 'This sucks.'

'You doing OK?'

'Yeah. Yeah, but it still fucking sucks.'

Sanders wasn't about to argue that point. Instead she told Kelly that, without the permission of Iris's next of kin, there was no way they could take a look inside of the girl's apartment. Before she could say any more, a car looking for a parking spot began honking at her.

'Go around me you fucking idiot!' Sanders shouted out her window, brandishing her police shield. 'I'm a cop, dick face! Go around!'

The driver did. As the car crawled sheepishly by, Kelly turned to look at his friend. 'Are *you* doing OK?'

Sanders snorted. 'Nothing about this feels right, Kelly. Presuming Chao isn't lying, we know that Iris didn't leave here until three a.m.. That means that she couldn't have gotten to the canyon much earlier than four in the morning. Why? Why would she do that?'

Kelly shook his head. 'I don't think that she would.'

'Exactly,' Sanders agreed, hitting the dash to drive the point home. 'So where do we go from here, Kelly?'

Her friend took something from his pocket, and told her.

49

It was a ten-minute drive to their destination. They rode in convoy, pulling both of their cars to a stop outside of a row of industrial units. The lights of the city were close and vibrant, but this part of town was locked down for the night.

With one exception.

Kelly heard it before he saw it. A muted thump of bass. It reminded him of Camp Pendleton's artillery, which he sometimes caught from his San Clemente balcony. Kelly saw light then, too. Only a little, but enough seeping out through windows that he knew he was in the right place.

It was a deep house party – an after-hours spot – and Arabella Robins had given him the address. Kelly had figured Rusa's manager would be in the know about such spots. These kinds of parties were usually reserved for the locals, rather than tourists, and Kelly had come here to find a girl.

'She'll be there,' Robins had promised him. 'She's always there.'

Kelly looked at the industrial unit. It could have belonged on any dusty lot in an American desert state.

Faceless. Forgettable. A dozen cars parked in front of the roller shutters and barred windows. Kelly walked to the solitary door, and knocked.

It opened a moment later. The sound of the rhythmic bass grew, and Kelly found himself looking at an unlikely bouncer. The man was scrawny, covered in tattoos, and had a shock of purple through his hair.

'What's up?' he asked.

Kelly smiled. 'I'm here for the party.'

The man's eyes narrowed. Kelly knew that he wasn't the kind of guy that people forgot.

'It's my first time,' he pre-empted.

'Friends and family only.' The kid shrugged. 'Sorry, man.'

Robins had warned Kelly to expect that. His first instinct had been to bribe his way in, but Robins had told him that bribes were the surest way of getting the door in his face: 'They're like a community,' she'd said. 'It's about connections and respect.'

And so Kelly brought up a name from his past. A name that commanded a *lot* of respect in Vegas. 'I'm a friend of Danko's,' he told the man, seeing that he'd hit his target. 'A good friend.'

The kid paused for a moment. 'If I called him he'd vouch for you?'

'Of course. We can, if you like?' Kelly added, hoping that the kid would turn him down – it had been a long time since Kelly had talked to Danko, and he was the kind of guy who changed numbers frequently.

'Nah, all good. Twenty for the cover, please. Do you need any K? G? Molly?' Kelly shook his head, peeled a note from a roll, and handed it over. He stepped inside, and the kid locked the door behind him. 'Just through here.'

'Through here' was through another set of doors and noise-dampening curtains that had been draped behind them. Then Kelly stepped into a room full of beats and purple lighting, the small industrial unit packed with what Kelly guessed was about fifty people, dancing and swaying to the sounds of the DJ in front of them. The walls of the place were graffitied, and a makeshift bar stood off in a corner. Kelly walked to it, and paid for a water. After he insisted the girl behind the bar keep the change, he asked: 'I'm looking for my friend Josie? Josie Amendola?'

As Kelly had hoped, she saw no reason not to point Josie out – everyone coming into the party had to be vouched for, so there was a level of trust in the place that didn't exist inside a regular club. Kelly also noticed that no one was recording or taking photos on their phones. Little wonder that Robins had warned him that he might see a celebrity or two in the mix.

But it was Josie that Kelly was looking for, the former employee of Rusa whose footsteps Iris has supposedly followed in. Followed where, Kelly now hoped to find out.

She was sitting on a sofa with a guy and a girl. None were older than their mid-twenties, and all had the wide pupils of someone 'on a roll,' as peaking on MDMA was known to those that did it. Josie was short and dark, a corset top pushing her chest up to her chin, a thin strip of skirt the only modesty below her waist.

176

'Are you Josie?'

She nodded and smiled flirtatiously. Why wouldn't she? She was rolling, and that was euphoria in itself. Now there was a tall, good-looking guy asking after her.

'Do I know you?'

'Not yet.' Kelly flashed his teeth. 'Josh Kelly.'

'I'm Josie. Are you here with DJ Hanzel? He goes so deep.'

'No, I'm just here by myself. Did you go to the festival today?'

Josie had, and for a moment, Kelly endeared himself to her by talking about his experience out there. She was jealous that he'd seen the place by helicopter, and loved that he was a friend of the headliner, CR1Z.

'Are you a DJ?'

Kelly shook his head.

'So what do you do?'

Kelly told her about his documentaries and conservation work. Josie was enraptured. After ten minutes of the conversation, he decided that it was time to mine for the information that he'd come for.

'I was at Rusa tonight,' he told the girl as she began to press up against him.

'I used to work there!'

'I know! That's where I heard about you. I asked a friend of mine where I could find a place like this,' he shared before adding, 'Iris Manning told me that I should come here and ask for you.'

Kelly saw instantly that he'd chosen the wrong words. Josie's face curdled.

'She said that *we're* friends?'

Kelly shrugged and smiled. 'Well, maybe I assumed that. It's been a long day,' he tried to joke.

'Well, we're not,' Josie said simply, and emphatically. 'I got her a job and she bailed on it. Made me look fucking stupid.'

'Oh, shit. What job was that?'

'Webcams,' Josie answered unashamedly. 'It's basically the same as bottle service, except you get to work from home sometimes.'

Kelly wasn't sure about that, but he knew there was great money to be made from girls who were willing to strip in front of cameras. Sin City had always been well known for its strip clubs, and now it was home to dozens of centers where girls would come in to work on flexible hours. It was a global enterprise, and where better to situate it than in a city where thousands of girls were already working in the 'sex trade?'

'I doubt you've ever had to use one of those sites,' Josie said to the handsome man beside her.

Kelly answered honestly that he hadn't. 'But that doesn't mean that I'm against it,' he added.

Josie shrugged, and Kelly could see a woman totally at peace with her choices in life. He admired her for that.

'I got Iris a job there and she dropped out after, like, her third performance.' Josie shook her head. 'She just didn't show up. So unprofessional.'

'Do you know when this was?' Kelly asked, thinking of her dead body, and how that could have been the reason.

It wasn't. 'Couple of weeks ago,' Josie informed him. 'Why?'

Kelly shrugged. 'I guess I didn't know her as well as I thought.'

A grin crept over Josie's face. She thought she was looking at a jilted lover, and put her hand onto the flesh of Kelly's thigh. 'Forget about her. She was just a gold digger. She dropped out because some guy online offered to be her sugar daddy. You don't want to be with a girl like that,' she told him, working her hand up his leg, 'you want an independent girl.'

'She had . . . a sugar daddy?'

Josie began to dig her nails into his skin. 'She sent me a picture of the car he bought her – she was bragging, the dumb bitch.'

'Do you have it?'

'Let it go, Josh. You're way too hot for her anyway.'

'Thank you. I would . . . I would like to see it if you have it though?'

Josie grinned at that, and ran a hand through his hair. 'You guys and your fucking jealousy. I don't have the photo, baby. I deleted it and I don't back up.

'Now,' she asked him, 'do you want to dance, or shall we go someplace and fuck?'

50

Sanders was leaning back against the bumper of her truck when Kelly came out of the industrial unit, and made his way over to her, the slight roll of his gait emphasized by his tall silhouette.

'Why are you smiling?' the detective asked him, sniffing the air. 'You smell like whore.'

Kelly laughed. 'Nothing like that,' he protested, but Sanders was having none of it.

'You went deep undercover, huh?'

'*No.*'

'Then why are you smiling? Did you take something?'

Kelly shook his head.

'Then why the stupid grin?'

Why? Because, as he had walked out of the party, Kelly had seen his 'partner' waiting for him outside. This was what Kelly had been wanting his whole life. A crime to solve. A team to crack it with. All that was left was delivering justice to the bad guys.

But how the fuck to do that?

His smile slipped.

'Iris had a sugar daddy,' he told his friend.

Sanders rolled her eyes. 'What pretty girl doesn't in this town? Shit. I remember when women had self-respect.'

Kelly was certain that they still did – the woman in front of him was proof of that – but he let Sanders go on her rant regardless. Sometimes, she just needed to vent her spleen, and Kelly couldn't blame her for that. Tonya Sanders had been a pretty girl, and a stunning woman. All her life she'd had interest and suitors, and then, when a bullet chewed up her face, she'd suddenly started to draw stares for a different reason. The interest was of a different kind, and the suitors stopped calling. Society's reaction to Sanders told her that her worth had only been skin-deep. That she was deserving of the attention when she was beautiful, but not when she was scarred. Kelly knew that the worth of Tonya Sanders was in her intellect and soul, but it could be hard to convince her of that when she saw people's treatment of her as proof that she had changed. As a consequence of that behavior, Sanders was now fiercely against those parts of society that placed skin-deep beauty above all else, and the culture of sugar daddies was the pinnacle of such shallow attention.

Sugar daddies – or 'sponsors', depending on whom you talked to – were guys with too much money who lavished it on young, pretty girls. The arrangement wasn't necessarily one of cash for sex, though most of the people Kelly had come across in such 'relationships' were sleeping with each other. Sometimes, the girl would have a boyfriend that the sugar daddy would be fully aware of. Sometimes he'd buy her cars, or pay her rent. Sometimes it would just be the occasional piece of jewelry, or some cash to go shopping. The rules varied as much as the age of the men and the

background of the girls, but there was always constants –
the guy had money. The girl had looks.

'I fucking hate this town,' Sanders finished, and Kelly
was surprised that she didn't spit into the dry dirt.

'You love it,' he reminded her with a smile. Why else
would she still be here after forty-five years?

'Maybe just a little. But this sugar-daddy stuff makes
me sick, Kelly.'

Kelly wasn't about to argue with that. Nothing about
the behavior sat well with him. As a man, he felt disgusted
by it. But then again, Kelly conceded, maybe it was easy
for him to say that when he was six foot three, tanned
and handsome. He knew that there were guys out there
– successful, lonely guys – who just wanted what a lot of
men want at some point in their life: the company of an
attractive woman.

'I just don't get how the guys can be OK with it,'
he admitted to Sanders. 'You know, spending time with
someone that you *know* is only there because of the material
shit you're giving them.'

'I'm sure you've met a few,' Sanders said. 'Why don't
you ask them?'

'I have.'

'And?'

And Kelly hadn't liked the answer he'd heard – that the
guys were OK with it. He didn't know if that made them
suckers, manipulators, or both. The girls were a trophy in
their cabinet: that was it. A replaceable part. Something to
boast—

'Wait!' Kelly broke out suddenly. 'These guys do it to boast, right? Well, from what we know about Iris, she wasn't the type to keep quiet about things either. If someone bought her a new car, and she was boastful enough to send pictures of it to people, then maybe there are some online, too?'

He looked through her profile, and it took less than two minutes to find Iris posed in front of a shiny white BMW 1 Series. There was no concrete way to tell if it was the car that had been bought for her, but the hashtag of #NewWhip told Sanders and Kelly that this was likely the gift from the sugar daddy.

'Too great a coincidence for it not to be,' the detective agreed. 'If only we could see the plates.' They were out of the shot, but it was something nonetheless. 'I'll put the call out. See if anyone's reported one abandoned or burned out.'

Kelly knew that that was the best they could hope for. In a city like Vegas there would be hundreds – maybe thousands – of white BMWs. They couldn't hope to check them all in the limited time frame that they had, and with Sanders having already been moved off the case.

'Are you even on the clock now?' Kelly asked.

The cop shot him a look – *What do you think?* She snorted. 'Need a sugar daddy myself.'

'You know they have apps for finding them now?' Kelly said. 'To make it easier to find daddies, and vice versa. There are even apps where guys can find hot girls to go travel with them. The girls get their Instagram pictures taken on the beach, and the guys get, well . . .'

Kelly regretted divulging that information a moment later, as Sanders spent the next sixty seconds crucifying humanity, but there had been a point behind what he was saying. 'Maybe Iris is on some of those sites.'

'Maybe,' Sanders allowed. 'But how does that help us? We're not getting a look into anything private without her next of kin or a murder investigation. Not her apartment, not her skanky profiles.'

Kelly was a little shocked by Sanders's tone, and her words. 'Tonya . . . easy. Iris *is* the victim here.'

The fifteen-year cop snorted out a laugh at that. 'Oh to be young and innocent.'

Kelly felt her judgment, and didn't enjoy the sensation. 'What does that mean?'

'It means that you don't have to like a vic to solve their case,' Sanders replied, deadpan. 'Honestly, Kelly, this girl sounds like a fucking bitch – everything that I despise – but I'm still gonna work my ass off to find out how she ended up in that canyon, and why.'

Kelly nodded. 'Because you *do* care.'

Sanders laughed, and shook her head. 'Because it's my job, Kelly. And I don't fucking lose.'

Kelly looked into his friend's eyes. Before he could tell her what was on his mind, his cell began to vibrate.

It was an unknown number. Kelly took it on speaker so that Sanders could hear. 'Hello?'

'Kelly?'

'Yeah.'

'This is Arabella Robins. I need to talk. *Now.*'

51

It wasn't much longer than a couple of hours ago that Kelly had been in the Grand Casino, and now he was back, dropping his car with the valet before heading towards the hotel check-in. Vegas supposedly never slept, but from looking around, Kelly could see that the place was currently hitting snooze. A skeleton staff was operating the floor and desks in these early hours, and though Kelly could see a few diehards on the casino's tables and yanking levers on the machines, for the most part the place was empty. Occasionally a group of girls would appear heading home with their heels in their hands and drunken smiles on their faces, and a couple of guys wandered the floors in the hope of not going to bed alone. Kelly knew that this was the hour where bad decisions would be made: a tattoo; a wedding; a pregnancy. On one drunken weekend when Kelly's brother returned from Iraq, he and a buddy had tried to marry a pair of Swedish nannies. Fortunately for all it had been dawn, and even Sin City's ministers had to take a break at some point.

'Here to check in, sir?' a young attendant asked Kelly with a corporate smile.

'Actually, I'm here to pick up a key card. It's been left for me by Arabella Robins, the manager of Rusa.'

'Oh, certainly, sir,' the girl replied, perking up. 'Are you a DJ?'

'I'm not that cool, I'm afraid,' Kelly apologized, taking the offered card.

Her smile slipped from excited to tired professional. 'Here you are, sir, suite one hundred and ten on the executive floor. Elevators are over there on your right. Have a great stay.'

'Thank you.'

The only luggage Kelly had on him was his wallet, but the attendant hadn't batted an eyelid. It wasn't unusual in Vegas for people to check in at all hours and in all kinds of states. Friends shared rooms, then lost keys, and had to find another bed for the night. Sometimes, for the drunk, a room at hand seemed preferable to the journey to the other end of the Strip. Sometimes it was the promise of company that compelled the last-ditch check-in, and to hell with the price.

For Kelly, however, it was a meeting with Arabella Robins, the club's manager. She had something to tell him that she was only comfortable talking about in person. Given what Kelly was learning about Iris, and the 'business first at all costs' attitude of the casinos and Rusa, he understood why she would want to have any conversation in private, away from possible eavesdroppers or recording devices.

Kelly had told Sanders he would meet her back at her house once he was done talking with Robins. He and the detective needed to sleep sometime, and nothing they had uncovered so far led either to believe that Iris's death suggested serial killer. As Sanders told him, 'Time's a factor, but we can't run on fumes.'

'I'll be back by dawn,' Kelly had promised.

But when the suite's door opened, Kelly knew that it was a promise he was not going to keep.

52

Kelly stood at the door of the suite and looked at Arabella Robins. She was barefoot in yoga pants and a sports bra, her wet hair tied back into a ponytail, dark skin shining and scented.

'What?' she asked Kelly.

She knew what, he was sure. Kelly was a sucker for active, athletic women, and here was a beautiful one fresh out of the shower. If he'd come to Vegas to play cards, Kelly'd be broke already. His poker face sucked, and so he tried honesty.

'You look good.'

Robins knew it. 'Thanks. Come in. You want a drink? I can get something brought up if it's not in the fridge.'

'Just a water, thanks.'

Kelly looked around the suite. It was on the tower's corner, and had beautiful views of the Strip in both directions. The floor's number was one, but the executive levels of the casino didn't begin until they were above the standard guest rooms. As with everything, the best came with a bigger price tag. 'Beautiful. Do you live here?'

The suite was a good size but it was spartan, empty of any personal touches.

'This week gets so crazy that it's easier just to stay here,' the club manager explained. 'I do the same over Labor Day weekend, Christmas, and New Year. My house is on the west side of the city.'

Kelly could picture the woman in the same kind of gated community as Zakhir Khan, the 'drug dealer' who had turned out to be an internet marketer – a well-paid one.

'Must have been a crazy night,' he offered.

Robins nodded as she handed him a bottle of water. Kelly felt as though she was standing a little closer than she needed to, but her eyes betrayed nothing but business. 'I've filled in for Sven before, but not under these circumstances. It was a rough night.' She breathed out. 'I hate to leave until everyone's out, but I just needed to get a workout in, and clear my head.'

Kelly looked at the woman's toned arms and shoulders. They were still flushed with blood.

'You work out,' she said as a statement, and Kelly nodded.

'Especially after a bad day, but I like to surf if I can. That's what clears *my* head.'

'I've never tried that.' Robins's eyes teased. 'I'm scared of sharks.'

Kelly laughed. 'How did you know?'

'Chao told me. He really liked you.'

'He seemed like a clever guy.'

'He is. Self-made man. Net worth of a hundred million at forty-three years old.'

189

'That's impressive.'

Robins agreed, and Kelly could see that the story of financial success lit a fire in the woman's eyes. 'So tell me about the shark,' she pressed him, and Kelly did.

'I bet the girls love your scars.' She smirked. 'And I'm right to be scared of sharks. You're the proof.'

'Are you scared of cars?' Kelly asked her.

Robins frowned. 'No?'

'There were forty thousand motor deaths in this country last year. You want to guess how many deaths from sharks?'

She shrugged her athletic shoulders. 'Ten?'

Kelly smiled. 'Zero.'

'Bullshit!'

'I swear!'

Robins narrowed her eyes. 'How about from motor sharks?'

Kelly laughed. 'I'd have to check that, but I think it's zero.'

'I don't believe you.'

'I'm telling you,' Kelly said passionately, enjoying the opportunity to convert someone into experiencing the ocean. 'Not *one*. We can look it up if you like?'

'No. No, I believe you. That's crazy, though. Why am I so scared of them, then?'

'It's right to be respectful of sharks,' Kelly pointed out. 'But there's a difference between respect and fear. The fear comes from how we portray them. Sharks just have a really bad rep, and people don't understand the animals enough to know different.'

'But you're trying to change that.' Robins smiled confidently. 'I googled you. Wasn't hard. I had your name and I knew about your . . . accident. Like you said, it's not common.'

'I told you that I wasn't a cop,' Kelly defended himself.

'I know.' She smiled, leaning in a little closer. 'And that makes me feel all right about doing this.'

She kissed him.

Hard.

Without thinking, Kelly took a handful of her hair, pulling her tight to him as he kissed her back with even more force, Arabella gasping as she fumbled for his belt.

Moments later, she got to see the scars.

53

Kelly awoke a few hours later. His moment with Robins had been raw and passionate, with no thought to drawing the suite's blinds. Kelly regretted that decision now as the harsh light of the desert poured into the room, but he regretted it a lot less when he saw the naked figure beside him, Robins on her front, her head turned away from him.

Kelly mouthed 'Wow' as he took in the beauty of the woman. She was athletic and curved, but Kelly's attraction to her had sprung from a place far deeper than Robins's smooth, dark skin. She was a go-getter. A boss. In the PowerPoint world that was the guest-speaker circuit, Kelly had noticed how fond people were of shortening strategies, rules, and the most ridiculous things into acronyms. One night at a hotel bar, a few drinks down with another speaker, Kelly had joked that what he looked for in a woman were the three Cs: confidence, competence, character.

'What about curves?' his companion had asked.

'OK.' Kelly'd grinned. 'Four Cs.'

Kelly looked at the prosthetic limbs that were still on his body, testament to how tired he'd been after a day of heat, and questions that hadn't come with enough answers.

Kelly'd come to the Grand Casino hoping to get more of those, but Robins's reasons for calling him to the suite had been based on desire, not death.

Kelly wondered at that. People had different reactions to grief, he knew. Clearly Robins fell into the category that felt that the best way to deal with death was to do something life-affirming. Kelly knew that when a younger person died the emotional fallout was very different than if it had been an older individual. It was a terrifying reality check that the end could come for anyone, at any moment. Death didn't give a shit about what was in your bank account, or how many Instagram followers you had. Less than two days ago Iris had been young and popular, that much was certain. Now she was cold and dead in the city's morgue, awaiting an autopsy that Sanders had tried in vain to bring forward.

It was the final day of the festival, Kelly realized. It would finish at midnight with a huge fireworks display, and then the revelers would slip away from Vegas. Witnesses. Maybe suspects. The odds were that they would be gone from the town, and with them the best chance of discovering why Iris's body had come to be found in Sloan Canyon.

It was for that reason that Kelly woke Robins. He needed to get back to Sanders, and he wasn't the kind of guy who tried to slip out after sex like a ninja.

'Hey.' He smiled as she opened her eyes.

Robins gave him a weak one back, but it was born of tiredness, not shame. She made no move to cover herself with a sheet. Instead, she cast an appraising eye over Kelly, and liked what she saw. 'Damn, you look good. I'm glad that shark didn't get more of you.'

Kelly knew then that he wasn't leaving the bed just yet. Robins moved her hand, and made sure of it.

'Wait,' she said as he tried to kiss her, grinning at him as she rolled across to pick up the phone from its stand. 'Room service? Hi. Yeah. Just bring one of everything on the breakfast menu please. Thanks.

'What?' she asked Kelly, seeing his look. 'I'm about to build an appetite.'

'I have to go soon,' he told her, but with his eyes on her body, the words convinced nobody.

When it was over, Kelly and Robins lay with their eyes gazing up at the ceiling. There was no touching, no kissing, just two people comfortable in their nakedness, and in their choices.

'You sweat a lot,' Robins teased, a smile playing at the corner of her mouth. 'I thought you said you worked out?'

Kelly took a bead of sweat from his chest and put it on the tip of Robins's nose.

She didn't flinch. '*That's* supposed to bother me after what you just did?'

Kelly laughed with her. '*We* did.' He grinned, but the truth was that Robins had been firmly in the driver's seat. Kelly didn't know how Robins managed her work force, but in the bedroom, the woman ruled with an iron . . .

'What are you smiling at?'

He told her.

'You're such a child.'

Kelly knew that the words were well meant and he took them that way. There was so much to be serious about in the world that it was nice to act a fool sometimes. He watched Robins then as she climbed from the bed and walked to the bathroom. Almost every instinct in his body cried at him to pull her back onto the bed, and the few that didn't told him to follow her into the bathroom. When he saw that the door was left open, he took the sound of the running shower as an invitation.

She was already under the water when he walked in. 'Can you come in with those?' she asked as she looked at his arm and leg.

He laughed. 'What do you think I do when it rains?'

'You live in California.'

'Touché.'

'Get in here.'

Kelly didn't wait to be told twice. The cubicle was huge, but Kelly pressed his flesh against Robins's.

'At least I won't need to go to the gym today.' The woman smiled over her shoulder as Kelly massaged them, soap and suds running down her back.

'When does your day start?' he asked, thinking that his own would begin when Sanders called. Selfishly, he hoped that that wasn't happening anytime soon.

'Honestly, I'm not sure. If Sven needs more time, I'll have to pick up the slack.'

Kelly felt for the woman who had so much on her plate, though he had a feeling that she wouldn't have it any other way. He told her as much.

'You ever heard of Red Rock, Arizona?' Robins asked. Kelly had not. 'Exactly. It's eighty miles from Phoenix, population two thousand.'

Her tone suggested she'd gotten out of there as fast as she could. Kelly asked how.

'I got track and academic scholarships for ASU,' she explained. 'My parents weren't able to afford it but I knew college was my way out. Don't get me wrong, I know I could have just come to somewhere like this without the education, but . . . I didn't want that life.'

Kelly looked around the expensive bathroom, thought of the views from the suite's windows, and about the power and responsibility that came with running one of the biggest and best clubs in Las Vegas. There were different ways to come to life's finer things, and Arabella Robins had chosen hard work and education.

'When did you start working with Rusa?'

'I met Sven before Rusa was a thing,' Robins explained. 'I came straight to Vegas when I finished my MBA. I worked a couple of jobs, mostly just to get my ear to the street, and I heard about a new guy in town who'd operated a string of clubs in Europe.'

'Sven has clubs there?'

'He had three, but he sold up because he saw the boom that was coming out here. I saw it too, but I didn't have the capital and experience that he did, and so I hitched my wagon to his.'

'Just like that?'

'Nothing's ever "just like that," but Sven recognized I was as hungry and hard-working as he was. I started as an assistant, and earned my way to manager. I think that if you're a woman and you show up like that in Vegas, and work your ass off, you stand out more because so many girls are looking to get handouts.'

'*Pretty* girls,' Kelly pointed out. Robins was as beautiful as any of the bottle-service girls that worked for her.

'I'm not saying some of those girls don't work hard,' the club's manager went on, 'because some really do, but I didn't want to make my money by looking pretty in lingerie. I want my own fucking clubs, Josh. I've got dreams that most people would laugh at.'

'I wouldn't,' Kelly told her honestly.

'No,' she agreed. 'I got that vibe from you. Sven has it too. If I told him I was going to build a rocket and go to Mars, he'd be the first to buy a ticket. You find people like that out here. There's a lot of douchebags and a lot of sponges, but if you look hard enough you find great people with real fire.'

Kelly closed his eyes as Robins's fingers worked around his neck, and her chest brushed against his back. 'LA's the same,' he told her. 'You meet the best and the worst people.'

Robins turned him around, then. Kelly looked down at her. He saw passion in her feline eyes. He saw danger in them too.

Kelly liked it.

'Can we do this again?'

She dug her nails into his back, and smiled as she raked them along his flesh.

'Like you had a choice.'

54

Kelly stepped out of the elevator with a smile on his face. The casino was coming alive, gaggles of tourists and gamblers making their way onto the floor, but among their number Kelly noticed a few with their heads hanging down moving *towards* the elevators – last night's diehards who had survived way past the sunrise. Kelly saw one heading towards him, and he held the elevator doors open. 'Good night, huh?'

The young man's answer was short, but said it all. 'Bro . . .'

Kelly chuckled to himself as he weaved through the pedestrian traffic in the direction of the valet. He felt surprisingly fresh after only a couple of hours' sleep, and he knew that Arabella Robins was partly responsible for that. The strong coffee that had come with breakfast was too. As Kelly was getting dressed, Rusa's manager had offered to have the concierge bring him clothes from the casino's stores, but Kelly was planning on heading straight to Sanders's home to pick up a fresh set before they headed out for the day – wherever that would be.

Kelly handed his ticket to the valet. Already the day was getting hot, but that wasn't the reason that Kelly now felt uncomfortable. Robins had been a distraction, but the truth of the past twenty-four hours began to settle onto Kelly – he'd seen a body and chased a ghost, but where was he? What had he actually achieved?

You got her next-of-kin details. You can be proud of that.

But was that really something to be proud of? Kelly pictured how – likely when he'd been in bed with Robins – Iris's parents would have been receiving the worst news that it was possible for them to hear. Nothing would ever be the same for them. At best, they would emotionally survive the rest of their lives. Tolerate it. But their reason would be gone. Their light would be extinguished. It was a nightmare that no person should have to suffer, but for Richard and Sandra Manning, it was about to become a grim reality.

Kelly swore under his breath. When he'd signed up for the LAPD he knew that being a cop would be hard – one of the toughest jobs imaginable – but this was his first real insight into that life. He felt more respect than ever for those who carried a badge, and, in the same moment, he had more of a window onto the burden that his friend Tonya Sanders carried. Her life was hard before she was shot. Was it any wonder that she struggled with the additional burden of her injuries, both emotionally and physically?

Kelly shook his head. *No. Tonya came through it because she* already *knew suffering. That gave her the strength to get through it.*

Sanders would say different. She would say that it was the ear and heart of a stranger who'd helped guide her from the darkness. She could say it, but Kelly would never hear it.

His Tesla pulled up in front of him, and Kelly snapped from his thoughts as he handed the valet a twenty and climbed inside. He needed music. Something uplifting. Something life-affirming. He quickly connected his phone to the car's Bluetooth, and asked Siri to play his trance playlist. Within a minute Kelly was on the Strip, his music loud enough that he couldn't think. It was just what he needed, and as the vocalist sang about her own saving light, Kelly wondered about his. How music had changed – maybe saved – his life.

I need to get Tonya to the festival. He smiled to himself. *She just needs that first taste.*

But when Sanders called a moment later, she wasn't in the mood to talk music; they had a problem.

A big problem.

'There's no problem too big,' Kelly told her, energized and overflowing with positivity from the music. 'Whatever it is, partner, we can solve it.'

The detective's voice was more measured. 'We're not partners, Kelly,' she said gently. 'And we can't raise the dead.'

55

Sanders didn't need to give Kelly a name of who had died. Instead she gave him an address – one that he'd visited less than a day ago. An apartment, on the north side of the city.

Kelly pulled his Tesla into the wide parking lot. It was mid-morning, and asphalt was shimmering with haze. Kelly took in the other vehicles present. Last time he was here there'd been a half-dozen cars and trucks. Today there was an ambulance and a squad car to go with them. The fact that there were no sirens or lights told Kelly a lot – the dead could wait.

Kelly's eyes were caught by sunlight reflecting from bright alloy wheels. They belonged to a black Audi. It was owned by Blake Mathews.

At least, it had been.

'He's dead,' Sanders confirmed as Kelly joined her.

Kelly didn't speak at first. He looked from Sanders to Blake's apartment, seeing the uniformed personnel – cops and EMTs – moving in and out the building as they went about their business and secured the scene.

'Why aren't you in there?' he asked eventually.

Sanders looked at the apartment. 'It doesn't belong to me.' 'It' being the scene and the case. 'Besides, I took the day off.'

Kelly's head snapped around. '*Vacation?* Today?'

'Keep your panties on, Kelly,' Sanders said with an edge of irritation. 'Did you want to keep looking into Iris or not? I had vacation booked in for you before Iris came in on my watch, but they took her off me, remember? The department would have shunted me onto something else today if I'd have gone in. The only way I could have stayed free to keep digging was to take vacation.'

Kelly understood the reasoning, but then something about Sanders's wording struck him. 'What do you mean *could have*?'

Sanders looked at him patiently. 'This was a suicide, Kelly. Blake Mathews killed himself.'

Kelly was staggered. 'What? Why?'

Sanders shrugged. She'd seen a lot of tragedy. Her words were simple, but said all that needed saying.

'Because he killed Iris.'

56

The sun beat down on Kelly as he absorbed the news of Blake Mathews's death, and of his apparent crime. Kelly didn't know the guy, but he found it hard to reconcile the fact that a person he had spoken to less than a day ago was now dead. What had been a living, breathing, functioning person was now a husk. A carcass. Mathews's time in life was over, but not his part of it. The young man's legacy would be the tragedy of his family. The work, and tales of the police, ambulance crews, and morticians that were pulled into his savage death. He would live on in memory, and maybe nightmare. If what Sanders said was true, then he would live on an infamy, the jilted lover who killed from passion: a story as old as time.

'How did he . . .'

'Hanged himself. You don't want to go in there.'

'You did?'

'Told them I could help confirm his identity.' Her grim look told Kelly that it hadn't been a pleasant task. 'People make a lot of mess when they hang. Pull some creepy faces.'

Kelly swallowed at that, but he didn't blame Sanders for saying it. People had to find their own ways of confronting violent death, and reconcile themselves to the idea that every person was a bag of meat that would leave the world as a mess for someone else to clean up. If Sanders needed to crack dark jokes or paint dark pictures, then Kelly would shut up and provide the audience.

'I didn't think he'd killed her.' She shook her head. 'I really didn't.'

For a moment, Kelly said nothing. 'How'd you know to get down here?'

'You want to be a good detective, you make friends with the people who have an ear to the street,' she explained. 'The ambulance crews, patrols, dispatchers. Before I left the station last night I gave them a list of every name we talked to. If anything about them came up, they would give me a call. Happens more often than you'd think. Trouble follows trouble.'

Kelly looked around at where they were and frowned – with the noise of AC units and fans, he didn't expect that anyone except maybe the most immediate neighbors could hear the goings-on inside Mathews's apartment. 'Who called it in? If he hanged himself, it's not like he'd make a lot of noise.'

'You'd be surprised how much noise a person can make when they hang, Kelly. With old-school execution, they'd have a big drop that basically snapped the person's neck so that they didn't wriggle and kick too much on the end of it. Now, when people take their own life, you're talking maybe a foot and a half of drop. It's a slow death, and a lot of them start kicking out. Sometimes, it seems pretty clear they changed their mind, and were trying to get their feet up onto something.'

'Jesus . . .'

'Yeah.'

'You think that's what happened with . . . him? He changed his mind?'

Sanders shook her head. 'I thought you'd appreciate this,' she told Kelly as she pulled out her phone. 'The guy wrote his suicide note on Facebook. People started to see it and called nine one one, but by the time anyone got here he was dead. Look.'

She handed him the phone.

Kelly looked at the Facebook post, and then read it out loud. '*I can't live with the guilt of the mistake that I made. I killed the person I loved most. I don't deserve to go on. Goodbye.*'

Kelly lowered the phone.

'What?' Sanders asked. In the past twenty-four hours she'd come to see a new set of expressions on her friend's face, and this was one of them – something was up. 'Tell me what it is?'

'This note,' Kelly said, figuring it out himself as he went along, 'it's a personal thing, right? An admission of guilt that you fucked up. It's the guy's last chance to beg for forgiveness and absolution in the eyes of his friends and family.'

Sanders shrugged her shoulders. 'Sure.'

'So why, then,' Kelly asked, 'is it posted on his professional page, and not his personal one?'

57

Sanders didn't have an answer for Kelly – she had a question.

'What's the difference?'

Kelly showed her the phone. 'This is a professional Facebook page,' he explained. 'You see how the layout is different? And then up here it shows his username, @ blakemathewsdj, rather than just his name. It's a page that you have an audience with, rather than a connection to friends and family. Think of it as the difference between a phone line into an office and the cell that you use with your loved ones.'

'OK. I get it.' Sanders frowned as she looked at the phone that Kelly shielded from the sunlight. 'He looks so happy there,' she sighed, seeing the profile picture of Mathews in a DJ box, headphones around his neck and a huge smile on his face.

Kelly looked at the date of the photo. 'Three months ago. I guess a lot can change in a short time.'

Both of them knew something about that: life-changing moments that had taken place in seconds.

'Anyone can see a professional page?' Sanders guessed. Kelly nodded. 'So maybe he put it up there so that the world could see? He wanted everyone to know.'

Kelly's gut told him that wasn't the case. 'You saw him,' he said to Sanders, 'the guy looked like he'd come straight out of an emo band. How long were the posts he wrote about Iris? The ones that put him on your radar in the first place? They were from his personal account, but he'd made them public, right? So that's his precedent.'

'They were pretty long.' Sanders nodded. 'Half sappy poetry, half "fuck you."'

Kelly's conviction grew. 'So he pours out love and hate for pages, but wraps up his life in a couple of sentences? I don't see it.'

Sanders shrugged, and gestured towards the apartment. 'Proof's in there.'

'Proof that he's dead. Not proof that he killed Iris.'

For a moment, the pair stood in silence. In the background there was the chatter of the first responders and the sound of the occasional car that slowed to gawk at the scene, but neither the detective or the amateur made a sound until Sanders let out a long sigh that was cut through with frustration and anger.

'You're right,' she admitted. 'Sometimes it's about the gut, and my instinct says that something's not right. It said it yesterday and it's saying it now.

'I don't think this kid killed Iris Manning, Kelly.'

The statement hung in the air.

'So who did?'

58

'Who or *what*,' Sanders corrected him.

The question sat heavily between the pair until a detective arrived on the scene. Her name was Chaz Riggins, and Kelly put the officer to be in her late thirties, her suit fresh and collar starched. Ex-military, Kelly reckoned. Riggins smiled a hello as she was introduced to Kelly, but he could see that there were questions behind his eyes – why was he here? And for that matter. . . why was Sanders?

'We interviewed Mathews yesterday,' Sanders explained.

Riggins pulled a face at that. 'Weren't you on the mountain-lion case?'

Kelly bristled at that but Sanders nodded. 'We came here because I needed next of kin, and your body is her ex.'

'So I guess it *wasn't* a mountain lion, huh?' Riggins grunted, granting the cat a pardon. 'We should speak to the captain, then. If this ties in with your vic yesterday, then this is your crime scene.'

'I wish.' Sanders exhaled. 'Captain passed that case off to Brovetski.'

'You kidding me?'

Sanders wasn't.

'He's the captain's pet,' Riggins grunted. 'He probably thought he was doing him a favor giving him an interesting case. Get his face on the TV.'

Sanders wasn't so sure. She felt as though the case had been passed off for the city's benefit, not Brovetski's, but she didn't know Riggins well enough to tell her that. Sanders didn't have a lot of friends in the department. Not close ones, anyway. The emotional guard that she kept had seen to that.

'You want this scene?' Riggins asked.

Sanders gave a solid, emphatic nod. 'I do.'

'Then I'll call the captain. Sounds better when someone's trying to hand the case off, rather than asking for it.'

'Thanks, Chaz.'

'Easy day,' the younger cop said before walking away. At that moment, a white van pulled into the lot.

Sanders smiled darkly when she saw it. 'The Grim Reaper's arrived.'

59

The coroner was a tall and skeletal figure with a nose as hooked as the Reaper's scythe. For a moment, Kelly entertained the thought that the man could be profiteering from his own night's work, but he was snapped from his imagination by a slight shove from Sanders – she wanted to talk to the man.

They had to wait a while for that to happen. It was still Riggins's scene, and when she returned from her phone call in the car, it didn't seem like things would be changing.

'Captain says the admission of guilt in the suicide note is bullshit,' Riggins explained. 'He said Mathews has a history of being a loser, and he's trying to claim attention for himself.'

Kelly wondered aloud how the captain had become such good friends with the deceased.

'Does he know I'm here?' Sanders asked Riggins, who shook her head.

'Thank you,' Sanders told her. 'But look, maybe what the captain's saying actually makes some sense? We know that Mathews was obsessed with Iris, but in a loving way, not a creepy one. Kelly, you were here. Did that man look like he'd killed her?'

Kelly sighed, picturing how Blake had broken down, his heart seemingly ripped from his thin chest. 'No,' he admitted. 'If he knew about her death before we told him, then that was the greatest bit of acting I've ever seen.'

'And we can't discount that possibility,' Sanders acknowledged. 'But look, maybe the captain's nailed it. Think about it. You're a failed DJ and the love of your life is found dead. What bigger way to go out than claiming you killed her during the festival? Mathews was never going to be a headliner at the show, but now he can be front page on the national papers instead, and who's gonna be talking about any other DJ?'

Kelly thought it over. Riggins shrugged, a gesture that Kelly took to mean that she could buy that theory. 'I suppose it could be that,' Kelly finally said.

It was at that moment that the coroner emerged, and beckoned Riggins over. She went inside of her scene, leaving Kelly and Sanders alone.

'So Iris winds up dead in Sloan Canyon,' Kelly thought aloud, 'and the grief for Mathews is so much that he kills himself. He sees the chance to go out with the fame he always wanted, and so he claims to have been responsible for killing her, before taking his own life.'

'Maybe,' Sanders said, her lips pouting a little as she thought it over. 'What else you got, Kelly?'

Kelly could see that she had something herself but, like the teacher she was at heart, Sanders wanted him to work out the answers himself – at least, the *possible* answers.

'I get why he would be heartbroken and why he would want to get the fame he probably felt he was denied,'

211

Kelly told her, 'but I don't know if the guy we talked to yesterday would want that by claiming to have hurt the woman he loved. It just doesn't sit right with me. From what I heard at Rusa, he worshipped Iris. Would he want to be remembered as the man that killed her?'

'Maybe. Some of the shit he wrote online was pretty . . . intense.'

But Kelly wasn't convinced. 'That's just emo talk. It's no different to rappers saying they're drug dealers and shooters. How many of them actually walk the walk? Words can just be words.'

Sanders could see that there was more. 'Go on?'

Kelly flexed his shoulders. There was something that had been bothering him – bothering him deeply – since Sanders had first shown him the suicide post.

'Mathews's note went online at oh eight forty-three,' he told her, the time and the message's contents now seared into his mind. 'What time was the first nine one one call?'

Sanders flipped open her notepad to the information she had gathered earlier that morning from the dispatcher. 'Oh eight forty-five.'

'Two minutes from the note going online to someone seeing it and calling the police.'

'Why's that important? He'd want people to see it, wouldn't he?'

'Sure,' Kelly agreed. 'And that time of day is one of the busiest for traffic – not just on the roads, but internet traffic. Social media is an addiction for a lot of people, and just like they cram in a last cigarette before a shift, people want to hit refresh and check their feeds, even on weekends. It's ingrained habit.'

'Where are you going with this, Kelly?'

'That note went up at a time of day when it was bound to be seen,' he told her. 'And not just seen, but acted upon. Think about it. Two minutes from posting to the police being called. How long does it take to die from hanging?'

Sanders had no idea, but Google did: 'About two minutes.'

'Right,' Kelly said enthusiastically. 'So think about it. He's got to upload the post, and then get himself onto the chair or whatever, and into the noose. Let's say that takes thirty seconds. That means he's ninety seconds into hanging when the nine one one call comes in. If there was a police car in the area, they could have got there in around, say, three minutes.'

'He's still dead by then.'

'But dead enough that they can't resuscitate him?'

'I guess not.'

'So if you *really* want to kill yourself, why take that risk of being found?'

Sanders shrugged. 'Maybe he wanted to be rescued? I don't know. I doubt he thought it through as much as you, Kelly. The man was clearly distraught when we saw him, and we can't rule out that he killed her, even if our guts say that he didn't.'

But Kelly shook his head. She'd missed his point. 'Facebook professional pages have the ability to schedule posts *ahead* of time. Personal ones don't. That's why the pro one was used. The post could have been scheduled so that by the time it was seen, Mathews was already dead.'

'Shit . . .' Sanders muttered, running a hand over her scarred jaw. 'Someone else could have set it.'

60

'Think about it,' Kelly said, 'if you were staging a suicide for someone to take the wrap for a death, you need that body to be found. Mathews was a loner, and maybe he would have been dead in there for days – weeks – before anyone found him. An online suicide note changes that!'

'Whoa, Kelly.' The detective raised her hands. 'I think you're getting ahead of yourself now.'

But her friend was on a roll and wouldn't stop. 'Neither of us likes how Iris was found, right? It just doesn't make sense. And then this guy just cops to killing her?'

'Maybe he did.'

'Come on, Tonya, you know – you *know* – he didn't. Maybe he did kill himself, but that note could have been written by anyone that got a hold of his phone. He was hanging right there. They could have used his thumbprint to unlock it, scheduled the post, and given themselves plenty of time to get clear.'

'And why would they do that?' Sanders asked the animated man in front of her.

Kelly stopped moving. 'I don't know.'

'Right,' Sanders tried to calm him. 'We really don't know. Theories are great, Kelly, but evidence is king, and right now the evidence says that Blake Mathews killed Iris and then killed himself.'

Kelly snorted. 'Don't forget the Captain Wolford's fucking mountain lion.'

'I haven't. For obvious reasons, the city would rather keep these two things separate – at least for now – but hear me out for a moment, Kelly. Mathews *could* have killed Iris. He had the motive, for sure. Now, a mountain lion chewed her up, no doubt, but that could all be post-mortem. We just won't know until the autopsy tomorrow.'

'I don't like this.' Kelly shook his head. 'Any of this.'

'Neither do I,' the detective agreed, her next comment stalling as the spectral shape of the coroner left Mathews's apartment, and walked towards his white van.

Sanders moved to intercept him. Kelly followed.

'Detective Sanders,' the coroner greeted her. 'Are you also working this case?'

'Ties into one of mine. Got a couple of questions if you don't mind? Rapid fire,' she added as she saw the man look painfully at the sun.

'Go ahead.'

'How long does it take to die from hanging?' she asked first, getting the same answer that she'd received from Google.

'Is there an estimated time of death?'

The man nodded, his hooked nose cutting through the air. 'Two to three hours ago judging by core temp and the lack of rigor in his face. That was hard to tell though,' he added, 'as it looks like he had Botox.'

Sanders shook her head. 'Vegas.'

'I can't say that I see the attraction to the practice. Anything else?'

'We were told he was a heavy drink and drug abuser trying to get clean. I suppose that will all come out in the autopsy?'

'It will. Long-term use I'll be able to see in the tissue. Short-term, blood and stomach contents. If what you say is true, then it's sadly common with suicides. Quite often, when addicts try to get clean they act irrationally and are prone to mood swings. I see a few in the office that have gone out that way.'

Sanders thanked him, and motioned for Kelly to follow her over to her truck. 'Irrational, and mood swings. That fits suicide and murder.'

Kelly couldn't argue with that, but . . . 'I still don't feel it. What does your gut say, Tonya?'

She surprised him by smiling. 'It says I missed breakfast. Follow me, Kelly. I'm buying.'

'You can eat after . . .' He looked at the building that housed Mathews's body.

'Where we're going, I could eat if I saw my *own* body. Let's go.'

61

Kelly followed Sanders's truck to a strip mall ten minutes away, and parked in front of a diner.

Kelly wasn't sure that he could eat, and it had nothing to do with the food that he'd put away with Robins a couple of hours ago – his mind was flooded with questions and theories, and few answers. That level of confusion didn't leave him much of an appetite.

He climbed out of his car and looked into the cab of Sanders's truck. She was on the phone, and didn't look happy.

Why would she be? Kelly asked himself. The fallout from Iris's death was unraveling in every direction except those that were helpful.

A moment later, Sanders stepped down from the truck and slammed her door with such force that a passer-by looked her way and scowled. For a moment, Kelly worried that Sanders would overreact to the stare. Instead she shook the phone in her hand, but she couldn't strangle bad news.

'The OC's sheriff's department. Mrs Manning got the news, and when she did she fainted and hit her head against the doorframe. They had to take her into the hospital.'

'*Hospital?*'

'A precaution. They told me that if they don't take her, their department could get dry-fucked by lawyers. They've managed to contact her husband, and he's on his way to the hospital. Bottom line,' Sanders finished with a grimace, 'is that her parents aren't making it here today.'

Kelly put the pieces together. 'No parents, no next-of-kin permission to get into Iris's place.'

'Or her phone, email, or any of that stuff,' Sanders confirmed. 'We're locked out.'

'We can't get it remotely?'

Sanders shook her head. 'First things first. They've got to ID her body, and I'm not about to FaceTime them for that.'

'We could ask someone from the club to do it?'

'We could, but that won't help with the pile of legal papers that come after it. We need all of that signed off before we can start breaking and entering into Iris's life. At least, the parts that have locks.'

'Fuck it.' Sanders shrugged. 'Let's eat.'

They were shown to their table by an aging server who tried and failed not to look at Sanders's scar and Kelly's arm. Like all of the staff, she wore teddy-bear-patterned pajamas and a 'been up since 3 a.m.' smile.

Once their order was in, Kelly looked over his shoulder to see that they were out of earshot. The breakfast rush had been and gone, and only a couple of tables were occupied. 'I was thinking about our conversation yesterday afternoon . . .'

'With Mathews?'

Kelly shook his head. 'Khan. Something he said . . . That Iris was going hiking.'

Sanders thought on that for a moment. 'Coincidence?'

'Would have to be a big one.'

'Yeah. What're the chances she says that she's going hiking, then goes to the festival, then to Rusa, and then somehow, after three a.m., she ends up dead on a hiking trail?'

'It doesn't make sense.'

'None of this does.' Sanders exhaled. 'I swear I'd rather get shot in the face again than deal with the grinding gears in my head right now.'

Kelly stretched out on his side of the booth, and looked out the window. His stumps were rubbing raw from being on the go, but he tried to put the discomfort out of his mind as best as he could. 'As far as we know,' he said, 'Chao is the last person who saw Iris alive. She left his suite at three a.m., and the next definite time we have for her is when the hikers found her body, at . . .'

'Just after nine.'

'OK, so six hours unaccounted for, and in that time she dies. Does it seem a bit odd to you that the prime suspects for it are a mountain lion, and a guy that just so happens to kill himself?'

'It does. But I don't binge-watch as much Netflix as you, Kelly, so I'm not looking for conspiracy in everything that's out of place. Sometimes crazy shit just happens.'

'I'll give you that,' Kelly told his friend. 'But we evolved to have gut feelings for a reason. Think about it.

Every bad decision you made. When you look back on them, what was your gut telling you at the time?'

Sanders gave a shallow nod to say that she conceded the point. 'Usually my gut told me to do the opposite, and I can see that you're dying to tell me the science behind it, but again, Kelly, this is *theory*. We need *evidence*.'

'You're right,' he agreed, and pulled out his phone. Sanders watched as he rapidly typed out a text message and sent it.

'That was to the club's manager asking for an update,' Kelly explained. 'I've been requesting the casino's tapes so that we can track Iris's moves after she left Chao's suite.'

'That would be great, but I told you how clammed up the casinos are without a warrant. I'm sure you gave it your best, but they're not going to change their operating procedures because a one-legged Don Juan is in town.'

Kelly grinned and flexed the fingers on his animatronic arm. 'It's the one arm that matters.'

'Gross!' Sanders scowled, pretending to be offended. 'And I hope you washed that thing.' She laughed. 'Shit, that reminds me: I brought you a fresh set of clothes. They're in the truck.'

'You're a star.'

'No question. But look, Kelly, and don't take this the wrong way. When I first asked you to help on this it was because there were a few twists and turns that just didn't look right. Now the whole case is a bowl of spaghetti. Somebody else's bowl, by the way. Brovetski is a good cop, but . . .'

They paused in their conversation as their server brought coffee. Sanders put in cream and sugar before continuing. Kelly took his black.

'It's my day off,' Sanders started again. 'What am I gonna do? Come to the festival with you, or bash my head against a wall with this case?'

The choice was obvious. 'When I played football,' Kelly began, 'I used to want to leave it all out on the field. If we lost, we lost, but if I didn't give it everything . . .'

Sanders met his eye. She felt the same way. Neither of them were quitters. That was how they were still standing, despite the tests they'd faced their lives.

'Have you ever dealt with Rusa before?' Kelly asked, letting his mind probe the corners of 'their case.'

'No. But I did some asking when I called in to the dispatcher. She put me onto the desk sergeant, a real experienced guy, twenty years on the street. He said there was never trouble, but a couple of rumors said that there were mob ties to Rusa.' Sanders didn't look impressed at that hearsay.

Kelly wasn't either. 'More so than any other casino or venture in Vegas?'

'Doesn't sound like it. And a rumor is all it was. I'll look into it, though. Not like we're drowning in leads.'

Kelly nodded at that sad truth.

'I gotta use the bathroom.' Sanders stood up. 'If my pancakes arrive, don't fucking touch them.'

Kelly laughed as his friend left for the bathroom. Then he did what most people do when left alone, and looked at his phone. He opened his Instagram app, seeing thirty new messages. Kelly flicked through them. Most were from people who had read, seen, or listened to Kelly's inspirational story, and were thanking him for helping them overcome obstacles in their own lives. A few were telling Kelly that they would love to fuck his brains out. A final couple were from lovers of hunting, and their offer was to blow Kelly's brains out. One even went so far as to promise to mount Kelly's head beside those of the animals that he cared so much about.

Kelly snorted, and put his phone down. He'd seen these things before. Angry hunters claimed Kelly threatened their way of life, but what Kelly thought he threatened was their grip on their definition of masculinity. Sometimes Kelly would engage with such people – he'd even managed to have a civilized conversation with some – but today wasn't the day for that.

'You were a long time,' Kelly joked as his friend returned.

'Get some of my best thinking done on the toilet. Don't you?'

Kelly couldn't argue with her. He could see that she'd thought of something. 'So what's the master plan?' he asked.

'Pancakes,' the cop said, spotting her order coming out of the kitchen. 'And then we pay another visit to Zakhir Khan.'

62

Kelly left his car at the strip mall and rolled with Sanders to the western side of the city. Despite what he'd said earlier, Kelly hadn't been able to resist Sanders's pancakes. He'd used his prosthetic arm to steal food from her plate, impervious to the jabbing attacks of her fork. When it came time for the check, Sanders had needed to call the server back – she'd made a mistake, and significantly undercharged them.

'That's a thank you for your service,' the woman had said.

Sanders and Kelly had shared a look. Quite often their wounds were mistaken for those of war, and they told their server as much.

'Y'all are so humble,' the woman had gushed.

'Pays to be a freak,' Sanders had joked darkly to Kelly, leaving a large tip on the table.

Kelly held open the door. 'Why do you want to go back to talk to Khan?'

'Because he said that Iris was going hiking. Why would he say that?'

In search of that answer they made their way to Khan's gated community. The guard was the same veteran who had been on their shift during their last visit, and waved them through without Sanders needing to roll down her window and show her badge.

As they made their way along the street to Khan's home, Kelly's eyes picked out a knot of people on the sidewalk. 'They're outside Khan's house,' he told his friend.

He was right. There were four of them, young and tired and dressed for the festival – *yesterday's* festival.

'You our Uber?' one of them asked as Kelly opened his door. The big man could see a sarcastic reply forming on Sanders's lips, and killed it with a look.

'Drive to the end of the block,' Kelly told her quietly as he stepped out. 'Leave me here.'

'What? Why?'

'Do you trust me?'

Sanders narrowed her eyes, and drove away.

Alone, Kelly walked to the four young people on the pavement. 'Long night, was it?' He smiled.

'Bro, so sick. Some of them are still goin' but we gotta sleep. We wanna make it back to the festival later.'

'You don't wanna miss the finale,' Kelly agreed.

'Bro,' another of the crew asked, 'what happened to your arm?'

'Bro, don't ask him that!' his friend chided, turning to Kelly. 'I'm sorry, man.'

'All good,' Kelly told them. 'A shark took it.'

'No fucking way!'

Kelly fielded a minute of Q & A before he saw his opportunity. 'Got my leg too,' he said. 'It's really fucking hurting actually.'

Those words were all that were needed for the polite youngsters to spring into action, and to help Kelly to the door of Khan's home. One of them pushed it open as he labored towards it. 'Thanks. My phone died so I couldn't call ahead.'

'No worries, bro. All good.'

'You're Zakhir's friends?'

'They are,' said the guy holding open the door. 'I'm his cousin. I live here, but . . .' He shot a quick look at one of the girls sitting on the pavement, and winked at Kelly.

'Nice,' Kelly said quietly.

The young lad winked again, and gave Kelly a private fist bump as he stepped through the door. 'Have fun.'

Kelly had just been legally invited into Zakhir Khan's home.

63

Kelly let the thump of bass be his guide. He passed a bank of a half-dozen computers and monitors before walking into an open-plan kitchen and living area that was deserted except for dozens of empty bottles and plates that were dusted with powder. There was the smell of orange vape in the air, and lingering fingers of smoke caressed the ceiling. Kelly looked to his left, and saw a wide staircase leading down to a basement.

He followed it.

The basement's lights were turned off, but that didn't mean that it was dark – green and red flashes danced along the carpet and walls like a million fluttering insects. Four sofas were ranged around the edges of the room, forming a dance floor in the middle. It was empty, but a half-dozen people occupied the sofas, and drink and drugs occupied the spaces between them. Music was playing but it was low tempo, the emphasis on melodies and riffs, the kind of music that a person needs in their life when the party's over and the roll is gone.

Kelly saw a few heads turn his way. A couple of hands went up in greeting. Kelly returned the gesture; then he looked around – there was no sign of Khan. When Kelly turned back for the stairs, he realized why.

The man was behind him.

And there was a rifle in his hand.

227

64

Kelly looked at the deadly piece of metal in Khan's hand. It was an AR-15, a semi-automatic rifle, held down by the man's side. Khan's eyes and face were angry.

'What the fuck are you doing in my house, bro?' he demanded. 'I gave you some water. I thought we were cool.'

Kelly didn't have time to think of how crazy those words sounded. Instead, he slowly lifted his hands. 'I just want to talk.'

Khan shook his head, but made no move to raise the weapon. 'Bro, you can't just come into someone's house without a warrant.'

'I was let in,' Kelly told him honestly. 'And I'm not a cop.'

The whole scene was playing out on the corner of the staircase, out of sight of the others, who would never hear the words thanks to the basement's speakers.

'Can we talk?' Kelly asked.

'Do you have a gun?'

'No.'

'Well, I do, so don't fuck around, bro. This is not cool.'

Khan walked away from the stairs but kept his eyes on Kelly. Feeling it was sensible, the taller man kept his hands plainly visible. He wondered what drugs were in Khan's system right now, and how they were affecting him.

'Sit on the couch,' Khan ordered. Kelly did as he was told. Then he watched, stunned, as Khan burst into a high-pitched laugh.

'Bro! That was fucking crazy, hahaha! I didn't know what was going on, man! I was upstairs and I saw you pass through from the stairs, and I'm like – oh shit! – so I got my gun and I'm like, fuck, what if I have to kill this dude? Shit! Bro! Hahahaha!'

'I'm glad you didn't.'

'Yeah, but can you imagine it though? Holy shit! Everyone downstairs would have freaked the fuck out! Like, ohhhh shiiiiit! Check out that guy's brains!'

Kelly said nothing. He was on the verge of freaking the fuck out himself, his heartbeat only beginning to drop as Khan placed the weapon on an armchair.

'So what's up?' the gunslinger asked casually.

It took Kelly a moment to recover. Khan seemed totally at peace, wholly at odds with the rifle that sat beside him.

'Can't we put that away?' Kelly tried.

Khan giggled. 'No, bro. You still came in my house without permission. I've got guests here that are my responsibility. I gotta look out for them. I would have shot you if you were here to fuck shit up, I swear. I go to the range with my boy who was in the army, so I know how to use it.'

Kelly didn't doubt it. 'I'm just here to talk?'

'About what? And where's your partner? She's not gonna come around the back and try ambush me, is she? You need to be honest, bro. I'm trying to be cool with you.'

'She's not,' Kelly promised, before telling him the nature of their relationship. 'But she wants answers. The police want answers. So it was either them coming, or me.'

Khan seemed to appreciate that. 'OK,' he said. 'So what's up?'

Kelly looked at the man. If he was capable of violence – murder – would he have hesitated to shoot Kelly? Would he have put his gun down, and calmly taken a seat?

'They want to know where you've been for the past three days,' Kelly explained. 'And if you were with people.'

'You mean like alibis?' Khan giggled; the man was no idiot. 'Bro, I've been partying here or at the festival. I've got anywhere from like a half-dozen to a hundred thousand alibis at a time.'

Kelly had suggested to Sanders that that might be the case, but there was something that had bothered them both. 'You said that Iris went hiking?'

Khan shook his head. 'No I didn't.'

'You did, Zakhir.' Kelly spoke evenly. 'It's in the detective's notebook, and that's a legal document. You said that she came here the night before the festival. You said that she came to borrow some gear from you, because she was going hiking.'

It hit Khan a moment later. 'Oh, shit! Shit! I got it now.' He giggled. 'Oh, bro, my bad! Did I really say hiking? Bro! I meant to say *camping*.'

'Camping?'

'Yeah, bro, out at the festival. They got a campsite. Iris didn't have stuff so I gave her a sleeping bag, headlamp, all that kinda shit.'

Kelly felt a little deflated inside. Then something in his memory shouted that it wanted to be heard. 'Take a look at this,' he said to Khan, remembering what he had been told at the pool party. 'Do you know these guys with Iris?' He showed them the picture that he had discovered of Iris at the festival. The picture that had started the case rolling . . .

Off a cliff, Kelly thought to himself.

'Yeah, I know them, bro,' Khan confirmed. 'That's Amy, and that's . . . er . . .'

'Adam.'

'Yeah. Amy and Adam.'

'How do you know them?'

'How do you think? Raving, bro. Vegas is a small town once you get to know it, and the EDM community isn't big either. Not the core of it, anyway. Those guys have been here to party a few times. I liked them. They were cool.'

'Did you know they were friends of Iris's?'

'Who isn't?'

Kelly flicked his eyes to the rifle. He was no longer nervous that Khan would be using it, but something about the implied violence made him think. That, and what Khan had said about Vegas and the EDM community being smaller than people thought.

231

'You obviously know the scene well,' he said to him. 'How about Sven Niklas? Is he a friend? Do you know much about him?'

'I know *of* him. I don't think he really has many friends.'

'No?'

'None that I know, anyway.'

'I heard he was some kind of criminal,' Kelly tried to say casually.

There was nothing casual about Khan's laugh. 'What! Who told you that?'

'Just a rumor I heard.'

'Probably started by an old white dude.' The young man laughed again. 'Bro, it's like I told you yesterday. Every time some old white dude sees a young guy with money that he's made in an industry that the old guy doesn't understand, old white dude assumes it's drugs or crime or some shit. Did you see the Senate hearing with Zuckerberg? Zuckerberg's trying to explain how Facebook works in terms of data and marketing, and those old assholes are questioning him like he's a thief. It was painful to watch, like trying to explain to your grandma how to use email. Dude, seriously.'

Kelly let the rant run its course, but he asked one more time because he knew that's what Sanders would do. 'So as far as you know, Sven Niklas has no criminal ties?'

'As far as I know Sven Niklas is a pussy cat,' Khan told him firmly. 'Oh, yo!' he piped up, triggered by the thought of cats. 'You hear that someone got killed by a mountain lion?'

Kelly got to his feet and tried to muster a smile. 'I did,' he said, fighting to keep the images of Iris's torn body from his mind. 'I did.'

The 'interview' was over.

65

Kelly walked into the sunshine outside of Khan's home. There was no sign of the kids who had been waiting on their Uber, but Sanders's truck was a couple of hundred yards down the dead straight street. As soon as Kelly waved his hand, Sanders pulled from the sidewalk and headed towards him.

'What did he say?' the cop asked as he closed the passenger door behind him.

Kelly brought her up to speed, leaving out the fact that at first it had been Khan doing the questioning, and that he'd had a firearm in his hand. Kelly had the feeling that Sanders would put her shoulder to the man's door and beat his ass if her friend so much as hinted that he'd been threatened. Looking back on it, Kelly knew that the man had acted reasonably, considering that there was a stranger in his house. *Well, with the exception of handling a rifle while on drugs.*

'Why are you smiling?' Sanders asked him, and Kelly was saved from the truth because his phone vibrated – a message from Robins.

'She says to meet us at the VIP entrance of the Grand. How long will that take us?'

The cop told him. Kelly sent a reply.

'Did she say what it's about?'

Kelly shook his head. 'No. I get the feeling that anything she gives us will be in person, and off the record.'

Sanders smiled at that. 'I'm not chauffeuring you to your booty calls, motherfucker.'

Kelly assured her that it was business.

'Right,' Sanders snorted, before getting back on track. 'So Khan says Sven Niklas is a pussy cat, huh?'

'Yeah. Khan said it's people throwing shade because they don't understand the club industry. They can't see how someone can make that much money from dance music.'

'I get that,' Sanders allowed. 'I find it hard to believe these DJs are getting millions to press play.'

'People pay to be entertained, T. You know what the average annual salary of an NFL player is?' Kelly asked. 'Over two million. That's an average including everyone on the active roster. In the NBA it's higher than that.'

Sanders looked at him. 'Why do you know this stuff?'

Kelly sat back in his chair and tried to stretch out in the cab – his stump was raw and painful. 'I've got a friend in LA that I met on the speaking circuit. He has a charity that brings veterans and former pro-athletes together in Hollywood. They go through a lot of the same things when they get out. Losing their team, their identity, that kind of thing. Doesn't matter if they were a marine making forty thousand a year or a guy that got a forty-million-dollar contract when he was drafted into the league.'

'I guess if you got problems you got problems,' Sanders agreed.

'Right. It's easy for people to think a big bank balance solves all your problems, but it's rarely the case.'

'How much you think a guy like Sven Niklas is worth?'

'I don't know,' Kelly admitted. 'But I can look.' He took his phone and searched for 'Sven Niklas net worth.' 'I don't see any estimates,' he told his friend. 'But he bought a home for seventeen million, so I think it's safe to say he'd doing all right.'

'I don't know how you can look at a phone in a moving vehicle,' Sanders told him. 'It would make me sick.'

Kelly looked at her with a grin on his face. 'Sicker than thinking about a seventeen-million-dollar house?'

She pulled a face. Kelly chuckled and looked back at his phone. They had time to kill, and he had an itch to scratch. Unlike Blake Mathews and Zakhir Khan, Rusa's owner had the kind of profile that meant parts of his life made its way online whether he wanted it to or not. If his purchase of a home was documented, then what else could be?

Kelly was ten pages deep into the search results when he found it:

'Holy shit.'

'What?'

'There's something here from two thousand nine. It claims that Niklas has ties to organized crime in Sweden.'

'Get out! What? How the hell did you find that?'

'It's a blog post on a dance music site,' Kelly told her, suddenly deflated. 'It's not a news site, and I'm trying more specific searches, but I can't find any bona fide news outlets carrying the same story.'

'So?'

'So someone can write anything on a blog. There's no accountability. No code of conduct or ethics like the mainstream media.'

'You watch the news, right?' Sanders asked him. 'You think we still have one of those?'

Kelly didn't answer. Instead he kept scrolling and searching. He found nothing. Just the single short post of four paragraphs that claimed Sven Niklas had used dirty money to buy his few clubs. There was no supporting evidence.

'Probably just someone with an axe to grind,' Kelly said as he put his phone away. They were arriving at the VIP entrance at the rear of the Grand, and Arabella Robins was waiting for them.

She walked to the door before Kelly could open it. Instead, he wound down his window.

The club manager's message was clear. 'No cops,' she apologized after flashing a corporate smile.

Kelly looked at Sanders. The detective snorted. 'Keep it professional.'

Kelly winked, and followed Arabella Robins inside of the Grand.

66

Robins was all business as she led Kelly into the heart of the casino. 'Any progress?'

Kelly shook his head, and kept his mouth shut about the death of Rusa's former resident DJ.

If Robins was aware of it she didn't let on. After a short walk into the guts of the casino she stopped at a door and entered an eight-digit PIN number, followed by a swipe of her access card.

'I hope this will help,' she told Kelly as she led him into the casino's security center.

A familiar figure was waiting amongst the banks of screens being viewed by sharp-eyed security staff.

'Josh, man, thanks for coming,' Sven Niklas greeted Kelly, shaking his hand. Kelly took in the sight of Rusa's owner, and thought that he saw make-up below his eyes. After seeing Niklas's visceral reaction to Iris's death the night before, he doubted that the man had slept much since then. 'How are things going?' the Swede asked.

Kelly kept his answer ambiguous – they were doing everything they could to piece together Iris's last day, and her parents had been informed thanks to the details Rusa had provided.

'Fuck, man, her parents.' Sven shook his head, and for a moment Kelly worried that he was about to burst into tears. It was touch and go for a moment, but after a few calming breaths and a steadying hand on Kelly's shoulder, the club's owner was good to go on.

'Rusa's going to look after her mom and dad, Josh. I'm telling you. Whatever they need for the rest of their lives, we're going to get it to them.'

They all knew the one thing that parents truly needed was their children alive and well. Robins seemed to realize that such a thought could strike Niklas and start the waterworks, so: 'Shall we get started?' she suggested, pre-empting it.

Niklas nodded and gestured for Kelly to follow. In the corner of the room, a computer monitor was showing unchanging footage of a hotel corridor.

Niklas turned to Kelly. 'So look, man, Arabella and I think we've put two and two together. We heard on the news that a woman was killed outside of town by a . . . by a . . .'

Niklas couldn't finish the sentence, and so Kelly gave the most shallow of nods. 'I'm sorry.'

'Fuck, man, fuck,' the Swede cursed softly. 'That's so . . . that's fucking . . .'

Arabella Robins stepped forwards. 'What Sven is saying is that if we can help you to find out why she was out there, then we want to do that.'

Niklas nodded at the words. 'Like, what the fuck was she doing out there, man?'

'That's what we're trying to find out,' Kelly assured him.

'Well, maybe this will help,' Robins said, pointing to the screen. 'Sven and I have had to call in favors to get this, Josh. We appreciate that you're not police, but we think that if we can show it to you, you can guide them in the right direction. We can't allow you to make copies or take images of what you see on the screen. If the police want it, they can try and get it through the casino and the lawyers, but Sven and I have very little sway over them.'

'They're callous bastards,' the Swede put in.

'They're looking out for the casino,' Robins explained a little more diplomatically. 'And we want to look out for Iris.'

Kelly had no doubt that they did. He saw real grief in the tall man's eyes. In Robins's, he saw determination. A mindset that could not conceive of defeat, whether it was in business, or in unraveling the mystery of how Iris Manning had come to be in that canyon. 'Thank you,' he told them.

And then he watched the tape.

It had been edited to follow Iris's journey. She left the room that must have been Chao's suite just after 3 a.m., as the high roller had said. Then Kelly saw her walk to an elevator, take it down, walk across the casino floor, and head for one of the casino's smaller exits.

'This is where we lose her,' Niklas said with sorrow.

The final footage was of Iris walking out the hotel and onto the Strip. Kelly saw her cross the lanes on a marked crossing, and then, as traffic resumed its flow, Iris was lost behind the vehicles.

'That's all the security team here could find of her.'

Kelly recited what they had seen. He hoped that by doing so it would imprint more deeply in his mind. 'So Iris is let into Chao's suite at oh one forty-seven. She leaves at oh three oh three. She's out the door of the casino at oh three oh eight. We didn't see her talk to anybody on her way out, and there're no signs that anyone followed her.'

The other two nodded. Kelly thought for a moment. 'What time did Chao leave his suite?'

Niklas had thought ahead on that himself. 'Not until noon.'

'She doesn't go back there?'

Both Niklas and Robins shook their heads.

'This is the only footage of her in the casino after she leaves Rusa,' Robins explained. 'The casino's pretty quiet in the mornings, and the team here are really thorough.'

A silence descended.

'We need to find the person she was with,' Niklas said after a heavy sigh. 'The person that left her alone in the mountains.'

The statement struck Kelly. 'How do you know that she wasn't alone?'

Sven Niklas looked at Kelly as though he were simple. 'Somebody must have driven her there. Her car's here, man.

'Her car's here, at the casino.'

67

Robins led Kelly through the casino to where Iris's white BMW had been parked for two nights. Security had searched for it at Robins's behest, and Kelly chided himself for not having the same forward thinking. Niklas had apologized that he could not accompany them, but he had a full plate – despite the tragedy it was still the final day of the festival week, and one of the busiest days of his year.

As they walked side by side, Kelly tried not to steal glances at the woman he had been intimate with that morning.

Robins paused to get a coffee from one of the casino's cafés. 'Thanks for keeping it professional,' she said. 'People talk if—'

'I get it,' Kelly cut her off with a smile.

'Good,' she told him with just a little flame appearing in her eyes. 'Because I don't want you thinking I'm not interested.'

'Time and a place,' Kelly replied as they fell back into step. He looked around then, seeing grandmas pulling on the levers of slot machines, and groups of younger customers sitting at bars with Bloody Marys in front of them, a recharge before the next round of hedonism.

'Something's bothering you.' Robins spoke up, her eyes tightening a little. 'Something outside the obvious, anyway.'

Kelly's look asked the question: How did she know?

'Well, for a start you're not talking much,' Robins told him, flashing white teeth, 'and you were looking at Sven differently.'

Kelly silently cursed at himself. 'I was?'

She nodded. 'Yesterday you were beyond apologetic, and empathetic with the guy. Today you were a little more standoffish. What gives?'

Kelly didn't look as though he wanted to reply, so Robins poked him in the ribs.

'Oh, so I'm good enough to bang but not good enough to talk to?' she teased.

Kelly shook his head. 'It's silly. Just something I read on the internet,' he admitted, telling her about the blog post accusing Niklas of buying his first club with dirty money.

Robins didn't quite spit out her coffee, but she came close.

'Do you know why Sven got into the club game?' she asked when she recovered. 'He was a goofy kid. Tall and gangly. I've seen the pictures, and . . . yeah. He didn't get much attention from women, but Sven's smart. He knew that if he got into clubs, then they'd come to him.'

Kelly didn't see what that had to do with dirty money.

'I'm getting to that. So at twenty-one, Sven starts promoting his own nights that he'd put on at venues he'd hire. They started getting a good reputation, and in two thousand three Sven got approached by a guy called Dave Taylor, a British club promoter who was looking to expand. Taylor had the money, Sven had the talent, and so the two of them opened up their own club.'

Kelly could guess where the story was going. 'So it was Taylor that was dirty?'

Robins nodded. 'He got busted in two thousand eight as part of a coke-smuggling group. Sven was actually investigated but totally cleared, but some of the money that Taylor put into their businesses was probably dirty. They had three clubs at this point, one in London, two in Sweden.'

'Did he lose them?'

'He sold up what was his,' Robins confirmed. 'But it was all great timing on his part. Sven saw the opportunity that was coming out here, so things couldn't have gone better for him. He had an easy way of getting out of the partnerships he was in with Taylor, and he brought his side of things over here.'

'And that's when you joined him?' Kelly asked, thinking back to their conversation in bed.

It was. 'Sven is one of the big reasons that we have dance music in Vegas. He helped establish it here. That's why Pandora's owner let him buy a stake in the festival.'

'He's one of the festival's owners?' Kelly asked, trying to hide his interest.

'Yeah, and one day I will be,' she replied and, for a second, Kelly could see her visualizing the future, her ambition clear. 'Look,' she came back, 'Sven is a super-clever guy. He knows there are those rumors about him having ties to crime, and, honestly, I think he loves them. In business it's good to be seen to have an edge. Doesn't hurt with women, either,' she finished with a smile.

Kelly couldn't argue with those assumptions. They reached a set of double doors that led into one of the casino's parking garages. As Kelly held the door for Robins, he felt as though he'd just opened an oven to check on his dinner, the heat blasting. He saw Robins smile.

'What?' he asked her.

'You grow up soft in California,' the Arizona native teased, leading him through the half-filled garage. 'It's over here.'

They came to Iris's white BMW. Parked undercover, it was free of desert dust. Clean enough that Kelly didn't think it had been out into the canyons anytime recently.

'It hasn't moved since Iris came into work on Friday,' Robins confirmed.

That was day one of the festival. Later that night, Iris Manning had come to 'rest' in the canyon. It didn't appear to Kelly that her vehicle had been a part of that. At least, not directly.

He thought of the man that had bought it for her. The mysterious 'sugar daddy.'

'You look like you drank vinegar,' Robins told him. 'What's up?'

Kelly kept it to himself. 'The casino across the Strip,' he said instead. 'Where Iris went at the end of the footage. Do you think you could pull strings with them so that we could pick up her trail?'

Rusa's manager shook her head. 'You'll need the police and lawyers for that, Josh. It's the age of ass-covering. People don't go out on a limb any more.'

But she had done.

'Thank you for doing this,' he told her.

Robins saw that there was more in Kelly's eyes than simple gratitude. 'There're cameras,' she warned with a sly smile.

'Tonight then. When you get off work?'

Robins's eyes told him yes. She was as anxious as him to pick up where they'd left off.

But first Kelly had a trail to follow. A cold one. He looked once more at Iris's car, and knew where it led.

It was time to meet the sugar daddy.

68

The real-estate development was in Henderson, a fleet of trucks lining the street outside. There were four homes under construction, an army of workers busy around the timber frames like ants on a skeleton. Kelly stood beside Sanders as she took it in.

'You know this city was founded in 1905?' she asked her friend, turning to look at the Strip in the distance. 'Less than a hundred and twenty years to put all this up.'

'People can do a lot when they put their minds to it.'

They both knew the truth in that, but it was the darker accomplishments of human hands and minds that had brought them here.

Sanders had run the plates on Iris's vehicle. They'd come back with a name – the car belonged to Gavin Brown, and a little digging uncovered that he was a real-estate developer in the city. The pair's first port of call had been to an office in Paradise, but a heavy-chested young secretary had told them that Mr Brown was at a site – money doesn't sleep, or take Sundays off. Sanders had presented herself as someone with a business opportunity rather than a badge, and that had gained them the man's location – with luck, they hoped that he wouldn't be forewarned of their arrival.

'I'm guessing that's his car.' She pointed towards a murdered-out Range Rover, the four-by-four machine black from the wheels to the windows.

Kelly wasn't the world's biggest car nut but even he found it hard not to be seduced by the machine. 'I love it,' he said simply.

Sanders let a sly grin creep onto her face. 'Of course you do. You're white.'

He laughed, but Sanders wasn't done. 'You should take a crack at the guy. If he goes both ways, maybe he's feeling generous. Could get yourself a new whip from Mr Sugar Daddy.'

Kelly pulled a face. 'I don't take charity.'

'Sure, sure. Come on. Let's go find this douche-bag.'

Kelly thought about saying something to Sanders about making presumptions, but the fact was he couldn't deny that there was an uncomfortable feeling in his stomach about the person they were about to meet. Buying favors of any kind was not something Kelly supported. When they were for the attention of the other sex . . .

'We're looking for Mr Brown,' Sanders said to the nearest pair of construction workers, but Kelly knew damn well that she'd already spotted him – Brown was the only white guy on the site. The other men were Hispanic, decked out in solid boots and dusty gear. Brown wore khakis and a dark blue polo.

'I'm Gavin Brown,' the man greeted them, his eyes narrowing slightly as he took in the strangers on his site. Brown was a few inches below six feet tall, fit-looking, with a salt-and-pepper beard. The paperwork tied to Iris's BMW said that he was forty-five years old.

'Mr Brown,' Sanders said, ignoring the man's eyes looking at her disfigurement, 'my name's Detective Tonya Sanders.'

'Please, call me Gavin.'

He looked at Kelly, awaiting his own introduction.

None came.

Sanders spoke for him. 'He's a ride-along.'

Brown pulled a puzzled face. 'OK . . . What's this about?'

'You're the owner of a BMW that's been parked illegally,' Sanders informed him.

The real-estate developer crossed his arms and laughed. Behind the man, Kelly saw the construction workers shooting curious looks towards the conversation.

'They send a detective for an illegally parked car?'

'Budget cuts,' Sanders said, knowing that the lie was obvious and not giving a shit anyway. 'And I have a special interest in this car.'

'That right?' Brown frowned. 'And why's that?'

Sanders looked straight through him. 'Because the last girl to drive it's dead.'

The words hit Brown like a punch in the gut. The cocky smile and confidence were gone in an instant. His eyes went wider, his arms unfolding and dropping slowly to his side. 'Iris's . . .'

'Dead,' Sanders said again, as if she were telling him the time. 'We ran the plates of the car she was known to be using, and they came back in your name.'

Brown blinked a few times before answering. He had the expensive car and material wealth, but death rocked him just like any other person. 'I gave that car to her a couple of weeks ago,' he finally uttered. 'I signed the title over to her but I guess the DMV still haven't processed the paperwork.'

Sanders wrote something in her notebook. 'So you admit that you gave her the car?'

'Is that a crime?'

It was to Sanders. 'Why?'

'Why what? Why did I give it to her? It was a gift.'

'Why?'

Brown's eyes shifted quickly. He knew that they *knew* why. The looks on Kelly and Sanders's faces were nothing if not judgmental.

'Mr Brown,' Sanders began to explain, putting away her notebook, 'I've got a dead girl and little patience. Work with me now – quickly – and I'll extend some of that patience your way. Try to dance around my questions, and I'll make sure everyone knows that you were generous enough to buy a young girl a new car. That is a wedding band on your finger, right?'

Brown ground his teeth so hard that Kelly swore he could hear it.

'Giving people gifts isn't a crime,' the man tried.

Sanders shook her head in mock disappointment, and began to turn on her heel. 'All right. No problem. You need us, we'll be at your house, talking to your wife.'

'Wait, fucking damn it,' Brown spat. 'Look, what do you want from me?'

250

Sanders looked into the man's panicked eyes. There was nothing but fiery judgment in her own. 'Answers,' she told him straight. 'What were you paying Iris for with that car? You trying to buy a young girl's love?'

Brown coughed out a laugh. Under attack, his ego was fighting back. 'Love? I guess you must not have talked to too many people about her.'

'Just speak up,' Kelly said, losing patience.

'Iris was an escort.' Brown smiled, stressing the revelation as if it absolved him of all blame and heaped it onto the girl. 'And there's nothing illegal about that in the state of Nevada, by the way!'

'You're saying you paid for her time, not sex?' Sanders grunted, not believing a word of it. 'I know how the escort racket works, Mr Brown. You pay for her time and then anything sexual that comes after it just happens to be a coincidence between consenting adults.'

'I didn't do anything illegal,' he said again. 'Please, my wife can't know. I didn't ever have sex with Iris, I swear. It was more of a . . . a . . . it was a show.'

Sanders sent him a sharp look. 'A show?'

'This is *Vegas*,' Brown said in his defense, 'everything's a goddamn sex show here. I just wanted mine to be private. I got Iris and another girl to meet me,' he revealed with a tired exhalation of breath.

'You made them perform sex acts on each other?' Sanders asked, barely hiding her disgust.

'No!' Brown denied. 'It was nothing like that. I just . . . I . . .'

'*Spit it out.*'

The older man let out another deep sigh and looked at Kelly. 'You're a good-looking guy,' he said, 'and I bet you don't find it hard to meet girls.'

The taller man folded his arms. 'What's your point?'

'My point is, that's what it's like when you drive an expensive car and have a fuck ton of money. *There's no challenge in getting girls*. After a while, you kind of start to resent them because you know that all they want is your wallet, and so . . . I made a game out of it.'

Sanders looked pissed, but she kept her voice level. 'What game?'

'Mind games, really,' Brown admitted. 'I'd invite a couple of escorts over, then watch them throw each other under the bus just to try and win a little favor with me. It was pathetic, seeing how they'd act over a few hundred dollars.'

Kelly shook his head. 'So the whole thing's a power trip to you?'

Brown looked back at him as if the answer was obvious. 'That's what sex is, man. A power trip.'

Kelly and Sanders didn't have the time or the inclination to debate otherwise.

'Who was the other girl?' Sanders asked.

Brown chewed his lip for a long time before answering. It took a half-turn towards leaving to make him think of his wife and spill his guts. 'Jane Whittaker. That's her real name. She goes by Jenny Whit for work.'

'You buy her a car too?' Sanders asked, contempt dripping from every word.

Brown shook his head. 'Just Iris.'

'Why?'

'I guess because she wouldn't admit to who she was. *What* she was.'

'I'm losing patience,' the cop told him. 'What do you mean?'

'I mean she wanted paying in "gifts". That's why I got her the car. I guess it made it easier for her to look at herself in the mirror. She could pretend that I was a boyfriend,' the man snorted, 'and that she was something more than just a whore.'

No one was prepared for what happened next.

A fist flew, and a jaw cracked. Within a split second of uttering his insult, Brown lay on the floor like a crumpled pile of laundry.

Kelly turned to Sanders. She looked back at him with wide eyes. Finally, one of them spoke.

'*What have you done?*'

69

The words belonged to Kelly.

The punch belonged to Sanders.

Kelly looked from her to the man on the ground – Brown lay in the dirt alongside his morals. He was groaning now, and Kelly could see that the man's army of construction workers had stopped in their tracks, and were staring in stunned silence. What had been a busy construction site was now as quiet as the grave. Kelly prayed that it wouldn't become the final resting place of the detective's career.

'Jesus, Tonya,' he breathed out. For a moment he thought about helping the bewildered man to his feet, but when Sanders turned and walked from the site, Kelly hurried after her. 'Tonya!' he said urgently. 'Tonya, hold up. Wait.'

She wouldn't. Instead she opened the door of her truck and climbed inside. Kelly took hold of the frame before she could shut it. The metal was hot, but then so was her gaze.

'Tonya,' he tried. 'Talk to me.'

Sanders's eyes pierced Kelly's own to his core, the flame in them fueled from hurt and pain that was buried deep inside of her. Kelly knew in that moment that it had taken every fiber of her control to walk away, and not to fall on the man with a flurry of kicks and punches.

'Fuck that pig,' she growled. 'Fuck him, Kelly. I know I fucked up, but fuck him.' Kelly said nothing as the cop's anger scorched her skin, her hands gripping the steering wheel as though it was Brown's throat. 'He thinks it's all a game,' she accused with hate in her voice. 'He thinks women are just there for his amusement. Do you see him laughing now, Kelly? *Is he laughing?*'

Kelly turned and looked. Shaky on his feet, Brown was being helped to sit on a pile of timber beside the skeleton of his building. 'No,' he told her. 'He's definitely not laughing.'

Sanders looked as if she wanted to spit. Kelly could see that she wanted to say more. The words were caught inside of her throat by the hooks of her pride – by her *hurt* – but Kelly could make a guess at what they would be: guys like Brown saw woman as skin-deep objects for their entertainment. They were the guys who had chased Sanders when her looks had been 'perfect,' and had turned their backs or made jokes about her after the bullet had ploughed up her face. They were the people who had driven Sanders to close herself off from the world, and even from her loved ones. They were the people who had pushed her to the edge, and to the certainty that she would take her own life. When Kelly thought about that, how could Sanders *not* hit him?

'We can go back and do it again if you like?' he told his friend honestly, and maybe Sanders knew that he meant every word because she laughed then, harsh and bitter at first, but softening as she took in her steady friend beside her. Sanders knew that Kelly was there for her no matter what, and that knowledge fell like a smothering blanket on top of the fires of her rage.

255

She shook her head. 'I'm done with him.'

But that would not be the end of the matter, and they both knew it.

'Let's go get your car, partner,' Sanders said with love and sadness. 'I don't think that we're going to be riding with each other for much longer.'

70

An hour later, things seemed so calm. So distant.

The view from the hotel room was magnificent, the Strip pulling away into the distance in its parade of pomp and self-importance.

Kelly drank in the vista. He was newly checked-in and alone, but he wouldn't be that way for long. After Sanders had taken him to collect his car and then headed to the station to face the music, Kelly had taken a room at the Wynn, and made a phone call to arrange his 'date.' Now he was waiting. Waiting and thinking.

Tonya, why did you have to hit him?

Kelly knew why, of course. He also knew that there was no way Sanders would escape a shit storm for her actions.

'Maybe he'll forget your name?' he'd said hopefully as she'd driven them from the site.

'And why would he need that?' she'd replied gently, before playing out how Gavin Brown's complaint would go with icy sarcasm: 'Hi, I got punched in the face by one of your detectives. Which one? Oh, I'm not sure of the name because I never really pay attention when women speak, but she had a huge scar on her face. Oh, you do know her? Great. Yeah, I'd like her arrested, please.'

Kelly tried to lighten the mood. 'It was a hell of a punch, though.'

Sanders fought a smile. 'Fuck yeah, it was.'

'Where'd you learn to hit like that?'

'You don't know everything about me, Kelly.' His friend grinned slyly. 'But now you know to watch your mouth.'

Kelly laughed. 'Yes, ma'am.'

It had been a quick farewell outside the diner where Kelly'd left his Tesla.

'I'll go in, get fired, and get out,' Sanders had told him, putting on a brave face. 'I'll be back. I'm not done with this case.'

'You really think you'll get fired?'

Sanders shrugged. 'Maybe in a year or two, once the lawyers have fed. They'll suspend me today, though. Maybe I should just fall on my sword and resign. Save the city some money.'

'Fuck the city,' Kelly told her firmly. 'Put yourself first this time, T. That guy deserved it.'

'Yeah, well, that doesn't really matter, does it? I broke the law. Good luck with your date, Kelly. I'll call you when they get done with me.'

There had been no hug – Kelly knew Tonya well enough to read her mood, and this wasn't the time for touchy feely – and so he'd simply smiled and waved her off as she pulled her truck out of the lot and went to face the music. Then Kelly had headed out to the Wynn.

His thoughts were broken by a knock at the hotel room's door. Kelly opened it.

Her name was Jane Whittaker. The brunette was pint-sized, lithe, and pretty; her lips were plumped out from fillers, her chest by a surgeon.

'You're Josh?'

'I am. Come in.'

She did; then she set to work on her phone. 'I just have to let them know I've arrived.'

Them: the woman that Kelly had spoken to on the phone after he had searched online for Jenny Whit. It was the name Jane went by for her escort work, given to them before Sanders had rocked Gavin Brown with her punch.

'All good?' Kelly asked as the woman put away her phone.

Jane smiled. 'It's three hundred dollars for the call-out. You pay me that now, and then we can start talking about the rest.'

'It's on the counter.'

The woman moved across the room and opened up the envelope that Kelly pointed to, and counted out the hundred-dollar bills inside it. 'There's five hundred here?'

Kelly nodded. *That's right*. Jane smiled, and slipped it inside of her bag. 'I'm surprised a guy like you has to call a girl like me. You're a hunk.' She took in the sight of him properly then, her eyes coming to rest on his prosthetic arm. 'You get hit down there, too?' she asked gently, her bright eyes kind. 'I've helped out a few guys with things like that. You're a veteran, right?'

'I'm not,' Kelly said. 'And I'm all good down there.'

Jane grinned at that. 'Sit on the bed,' she told him, and Kelly did as he was told. She came over and sat on his knee, her young face a few inches from his, her chest pushing against his own. 'So what did you have in mind?'

'How long do I have?'

'I'm not watching the clock with you,' she promised, tracing a finger along the back of his muscular arm. 'Sometimes this life has its perks.'

'What if I don't want to . . .'

'You want to watch me, huh?' Jane asked softly, her finger now following the line of Kelly's jaw. 'I have things in my bag. Do you want to see them?'

'Maybe some other time,' he told her gently.

She pulled away a little at that point. Not even an inch. Just enough for Kelly to know that she was now somewhat on edge.

'I just want to talk to you . . .' Kelly told her, and he knew that it wasn't unusual for lonely guys simply to want a pretty woman to chat to, and those first words did nothing to send Jane to the door. It was the next three that did it:

'. . . about Iris Manning.'

Jane was on her feet a moment later. She said nothing, simply grabbing her bag, and moving to the exit. Only when she was at the door did Kelly speak again.

'There's a thousand by your feet,' he told her evenly, and he saw Jane's eyes shoot to an envelope that was resting comfortably against the skirting. 'I just want to ask you a few things, that's all.' It was Kelly's own money and, despite Sanders's protesting, he was happy to spend it if it helped bring them closer to unraveling the mystery around Iris's death.

For a moment, Jane did nothing. Then she bent down, opened the envelope, and leafed through the money. 'You think you can play games with people's time and livelihoods?' she asked, surprising him.

Kelly said nothing.

'I don't know if this is a game to you, or some shit, but this is *my life*. This is how I make my money. You fucking guys, you call me out and ask for drugs. You call me out and ask for questions. It's the honest ones that actually want to fuck me who I have more respect for. The rest of you think that you're helping me out, like I need a fucking hero.' She fixed Kelly with a hard stare, and pointed at her heart. 'I'm my own hero.'

Kelly held his peace. The truth was that some of Jane's words had landed blows. Hearing the escort talk, Kelly was forced to plead guilty to the charge of thinking he was the hero in this situation – deep down, he admitted, he really did think he was helping Jane. He really did think he was a knight in shining armor, here to help the girl trapped in the tower. He hadn't really stopped to consider that the life of an escort was one that could be chosen freely, rather than through force, or forced circumstance.

'I can play games too,' the woman told him. 'You want to talk to me? You want to ask questions? You can have three.'

'I have more money,' Kelly promised as she pocketed the cash.

'No.' Jane shook her head. 'This is *my* game. Three questions and I'm done. And you stay on the fucking bed,' she insisted, staying close to the door herself.

Kelly wanted time to think, but he could tell that the woman was about to begin a countdown, and so he asked the first question that came to the tip of his tongue. 'Was Iris working as an independent escort?'

Jane nodded. The distinction was important – it meant that Iris didn't have a pimp. No one to call, as Kelly had done, to book a girl like Jane. No one whom the escort would check in with for security. 'When was the last time you heard from her?' Kelly asked.

'Friday.'

'Why?'

'She wanted to set something up with the two of us and a regular client.'

Brown, Kelly thought to himself.

'Was she with a client this Friday?' Kelly asked, knowing that he was out of questions.

Perhaps Jane saw something in his look, because she showed pity and answered. 'I don't know,' she told him, 'and now I've got to go.'

'Wait, please,' Kelly almost begged. He didn't move from his bed, but his eyes showed urgency. 'You said that guys ask you for drugs?' he tried, hoping that she wouldn't startle at his questions and bolt out the door.

Jane took in the man's calm manner, and found some reassurance in it. 'I did,' she said after a moment.

'I've got a lot more money in the safe,' Kelly promised. 'I'll take whatever you've got.'

71

Kelly looked at the tiny bags of cocaine as if the drug were a lost lover – not the stable kind, but the type of emotionally abusive partner who could take you to the greatest highs and the most soul-crushing lows of your life.

Kelly was alone, but the powder was talking to him. It was telling him to chop it, rack it, and snort it. Kelly tried to tell himself that such thoughts weren't really his own – that they were simply the result of neurological pathways in his mind telling him that he craved it – but he sure as fuck felt as though the hunger was born from his own desire.

One line can't hurt, he told himself. *You've only had a couple of hours' sleep. You need a pick-up, and is this stuff really any worse than coffee? Yeah, it's expensive, but you've got the money. Who are you hurting by using it? You'd actually be helping people. You'll be more alert. You'll be more confident. Maybe the answer to Iris's death and Mathews's suicide is staring you right in the face and you're just too tired to see it? Even if* you *don't want to do coke, you should do it to help* them.

Kelly picked up the nearest baggy and looked at the design on the plastic – he'd seen it in Vegas before. He'd seen it many times before. It was the silhouette of 'Mud Flap Girl,' an iconic design from truck culture that had made it onto the street-level packaging of cocaine.

Kelly opened the packet, and poured some onto the glass top of the room's desk. *It's not like I'd be the first person to do coke in Vegas,* he comforted himself. *You can even see the scratch marks on the desk where other people have racked it up.* Kelly placed the baggy down and took out his wallet, extracting the metallic card that Sven Niklas had handed him at Rusa. It was perfect for what he had in mind.

The coke was rocky, yet to be chopped into powder, and with the miniature avalanche onto glass had come the smell of gasoline. It hit Kelly's nostrils, and he smiled. He had never had bad coke that smelt that way, and instantly his cravings grew stronger.

Kelly picked up the largest rock in his fingers, and inspected it closely – he saw crystals, like diamonds in a rock face. He then put the lump back onto the table, and pulled a clean-looking banknote from his pocket, which he laid over the drug. Then he used the metallic card to 'rake' the note until the cocaine beneath it became a fine powder. He put his index finger into the white, and rubbed it against his thumb. The powder disappeared into his skin, another testament to its purity.

Kelly ran a hand through his hair, and looked at the gram of cut-up powder on the desk. It was strong, and he was tired.

There was nothing left to do but to snort it.

72

Before leaving the hotel, Kelly ensured that the last of the powder was gone from the desk. He didn't know if he would return, but if housekeeping beat him to the place, he didn't want them seeing the residue of his actions left in plain sight. Then, feeling as though he had a new lease on life, Kelly picked up his car from the valet, and turned onto the Strip.

It was a short drive to where Kelly was heading. He felt sharper than he had done since he came to Vegas. There was a rush in his mind and body. A confidence. Not even the setback of Sanders's inevitable suspension could dismiss his optimism. As the cocaine had vanished from the glass top of the desk, Kelly knew that there would be no stopping them from uncovering the reasons why Iris Manning had come to be found dead in Sloan Canyon. He knew in his gut that Blake Mathews was not to blame – he simply *knew it* – and with that same internal conviction he knew that Iris's end hadn't come on a 3 a.m. hike that ended in a mountain-lion attack. That notion was nuts, and Kelly was certain that Sanders would go down guns blazing to prove that, throwing all she could at her superiors before the metaphorical door was slammed in her face.

Her *face*.

Kelly thought back to the construction site, and how Sanders had dropped the real-estate developer with a solid right hook because of his chauvinistic assertions on sex and beauty. Kelly wondered then if *he* should have been the one to throw the punch? 'As a man,' was that what was required? That Kelly should have been the one to deliver violence – or at least threaten it – or would that make him just as much of a sexist as the idiot who had sprawled in the dirt? *It's a complicated world,* Kelly admitted to himself, but one thing that he could be certain of was that he was proud of his friend Sanders. Fiercely proud.

Kelly slowed the Tesla and pulled into the lot of a strip mall north of the Wynn on Las Vegas Boulevard. The single-story structure was the same soulless design found anywhere in the States, with the same tired company signs and the same tired employees working in the spaces below them. Kelly's eyes fell on the darkened windows of the hookah lounge that nestled between a Verizon store and a CVS Pharmacy. The Middle Eastern venture was the reason that he had come to this lot. The reason that he had been here many times before.

Conspicuous because of his build, Kelly climbed out of his car casually and stretched. The stump of his leg was feeling the effect of so much time on the go, but Kelly was no stranger to pain. He'd dealt with phantom limbs, at times fighting burning sensations in a body part that no longer existed. For a while that pain had dominated his life, but one day Kelly had found a way to reframe the problem: *if the brain is so powerful that it can create pain where it doesn't exist,* he had told himself, *then it's powerful enough to make real pain go away, too.*

But before that, there had been drugs.

Pushing his sunglasses onto his head, Kelly pushed open the door to the hookah lounge, and went in search of the man who had them.

73

The inside of the hookah lounge was air-conditioned to the point where it sent a chill through Kelly's body. A dozen tables were surrounded by high-backed booths, and Kelly wondered if it had been a diner in a past life. He looked for the familiar face he wanted to see, but Kelly saw only two groups of twenty-somethings puffing on ornate pipes, and living their lives through their phones.

Kelly walked to the bar.

'Can I help you?' the man behind it asked. He was Turkish, with shocks of white in his close-cropped hair. Kelly reckoned he was maybe fifty, the hint of a gut pushing at his bright white T-shirt.

Kelly recognized the man, and told him how he could help. After receiving a nod, Kelly ordered some hummus – it wasn't just the drugs that were good here.

He walked to a booth near a TV and took a seat. Kelly sat in silent contemplation for a few minutes, thinking about Sanders and how she'd be dealt with by the department, before a plate was set down in front of him. He said his thanks, tore off a piece of pita, and started to eat. After a few mouthfuls Kelly looked up at the TV.

He soon wished that he hadn't, and the bread turned to clay in his mouth.

Another death.

74

The leading story on the news was about the death of an innocent.

Kelly sat stone-faced as the anchor went out to their reporter in the field. She was a young woman, and smiling.

So was the killer.

He had a short beard, and wore a camouflage cap. 'So me and a couple of buddies were out on the mountain to do some target shooting.' He grinned. 'And we saw the lion. It started to come towards us, and we knew that there'd been that girl killed, so we figured we had to kill it in self-defense.'

Kelly wanted to smash the table to pieces. He *knew* that every part of the man's story was bullshit. Like many states, Nevada only authorized the killing of big cats if it was to protect life. Did this man honestly expect people to buy that he'd gone up into that area to shoot tin cans, and that he and his armed friends had felt threatened by a lion? A cat that Kelly doubted would even go within a hundred yards of a group of men?

The reporter's expression said that she bought it just fine. 'You must have been terrified!' she said in awe. 'Look at the size of that thing.'

The camera panned to the dead cougar on the ground. A majestic creature cut down for sport, no more and no less. Kelly's rage began to bubble over, and he reacted the only way that he could without taking out his anger on the lounge's furniture.

Kelly pulled out his phone and searched for the news report. The hunter's name was mentioned; Ray Jarvis was the hero who'd brought down 'the killer lion.' Almost shaking with frustration, Kelly reposted the story on all of his social media, and added a message that he prayed would provoke a reaction.

> *Ray Jarvis obviously thinks that shooting animals makes him a man. Well, I'd like to make him an offer. Get in a cage with me, Ray. Let's see if you have the guts for violence when you're not doing it through a telescopic sight. Get in a ring or a cage with me. You're half a man at best, so I'll leave off my arm and leg to even the odds. Stop hiding behind a rifle, you fucking coward.*

Kelly breathed deeply after he published the posts. He knew that his anger was getting the better of him, but he didn't care. He wanted to smash what little brains the man had out of his ears. He wanted to—

'Josh?'

Kelly turned and looked over his shoulder, but the Eastern European accent had already given away the identity of the man who hailed him: Branimir Danco, a thirty-year-old Albanian drug dealer who looked and dressed like a *GQ* model.

Kelly stood and embraced the man. 'Good to see you, bro,' he told him truthfully.

'You too, man.' Danco smiled, sliding into the opposite side of the booth. 'Been a long time.'

'I haven't been coming to Vegas much,' Kelly confessed. 'I just came in for the festival.'

The Albanian-American pulled a face. 'Then why do you look so pissed off?'

Kelly tried to wave that away. 'Just some bullshit on the news.'

Danco snorted. 'Fuck the news, man. That shit is just set up to make us depressed. It's a scam,' he added, leaning in. 'News companies are *advertising companies*, bro, so to sell advertising space for the highest price they need a lot of viewers. You know how they get that?' he asked passionately. 'By telling stories about good people? No! Bullshit! They make us fear, and they make us hate, and divide us. They make us think that if we don't tune in we're gonna get our heads cut off by terrorists or some shit. Fuck them.'

Kelly couldn't help the smile creeping onto his face. He'd always enjoyed Danco's political and cultural rants. The man was a drug dealer, and Kelly had been his customer, but there had been more to it than that. They'd been friends, and used to hang out regardless of whether there were drugs involved or not.

'How's your family?' Kelly asked.

'Good! Good, man.' Danco said, going on to report on each family member up to the rank of cousin. Kelly was glad of the distraction, and he felt his anger over the

271

lion's death diminish. Instead, he tried to be grateful for the stories that Danco was telling him.

'So what can I do for you?' the Albanian asked after he was done detailing his uncle's new business venture. 'I've still got the best coke and Molly, man. How much you need?'

'None,' Kelly told him honestly.

Danco was one of the main distributors of 'Mud Flap Girl', the coke Kelly had bought and tested from the escort Jane Whittaker. Kelly had wiped the drug from the desk and poured it down the toilet, an action that had given him a sense of empowerment so strong that it rivaled anything the drug could provide.

'You don't use it any more?' Danco asked, and Kelly shook his head. 'Bro, that's fucking awesome! Remember what I told you that time we were at Encore Beach Club?'

Kelly did. 'That I didn't need drugs to have fun.'

'Wrong,' Danco admonished him. 'I said that you were a *great fucking guy*, and you didn't need drugs to have fun. But look, man, I see it a lot. People hit hard shit in life. People have phases. You're not the first guy who tried drugs to get over a problem. Do you think they helped?'

Kelly sat back and let out a sigh. 'I can't say this to many people but . . . yeah, I think they did. They took me to some dark places at times, but those were places I needed to go. I had to confront the things that were there.'

'Monsters under the bed, huh?'

'Something like that. Drugs took me to the edge, and when I saw the edge it made me get my shit together.

272

If I hadn't been pushed out there by drugs, I guess I'd be floating in the middle somewhere. Depressed. No purpose. Just existing.'

Danco nodded at the words. Kelly knew that the man had his own issues from the past – who didn't? – and that the reason Danco had come to be a drug dealer in the first place was to support an immigrant family that he'd become the de facto head of; what other choice was there when his father and uncles had been killed or imprisoned in Albania?

'I'm out the game soon, though,' Danco told Kelly. 'Just selling up what stock I got then moving on.'

'Really?'

'Yeah, bro. I've been getting in on the legal-weed game in California. Man, the money in it! It makes selling coke look like trading baseball cards. Can you believe it though? This weed shit? A few years ago they would have slammed me away for it, and now I'm having meetings at fucking mayors' offices and shaking hands with congressmen because I'm paying so much tax. It's fucked, man.'

Kelly listened patiently as Danco ran on to talk about the hypocrisy of government and their 'war on drugs.' On any other day, Kelly would have loved to dive down into the conversation, but today was different.

'I need to ask you a question,' he told his friend. 'Do you still supply Mud Flap Girl to the escorts?'

'For now,' Danco admitted, frowning a little. 'Why?'

Kelly picked up his phone, opened his photos, and showed Danco a screenshot from Iris's Instagram. 'Do you know her?'

'I recognize her face. What's up?' he asked seriously, assuming the straight back and set shoulders of business.

'She was an escort,' Kelly told him. 'At least, kind of one. She took gifts instead of cash. Worked independently.'

'There're a lot like that,' Danco admitted. 'Halfway between the full thing and a sugar daddy, I guess. I don't get it.'

Kelly asked, 'What part?' The whole concept was hurting his brain, and his heart.

'The gifts, and working alone,' the Albanian explained. 'One leaves a trail, and the other's dangerous. Stupid, really.'

Kelly knew about the trail. It had led them to Brown, and the punch that Sanders had delivered to his face. 'Do you think girls like her are meeting random guys, though?' he asked skeptically.

'Probably not,' Danco allowed. 'But even so, you know what guys can get like. How well do they know these people? If they're working with someone else there are procedures if they don't check in, and all of that. If they're alone. . .' He let the words trail away, and looked dead into Kelly's eyes. 'How important is knowing about her for you?'

Kelly's answer surprised even himself. 'It's everything.'

'You were . . .?'

Kelly shook his head. 'But it is personal,' he told his friend, and it was.

But why?

Kelly had never met Iris Manning, and from everything that he was learning about her lifestyle, it seemed a lot of her choices left much to be desired, and many of her actions left a lot to be desired. So why? Why was it personal?

Kelly *knew* why, but he couldn't tell his friend. 'Do you know something about her?' he asked instead.

Danco nodded. Kelly could see that the Albanian didn't enjoy giving up the information, but he shared it, nonetheless, out of loyalty. 'I've seen her with a customer of mine a few times,' he told Kelly. 'Once on her own, a couple of times with other girls. I deliver to him personally, because he only wants the best.'

Kelly leaned forward. 'Who is he?' he asked, but the Albanian said nothing. 'Please, Bran, who is he?'

The drug dealer sighed. 'I don't know if you want to poke around this guy, Josh.'

There wasn't an ounce of uncertainty in Kelly's voice. 'Bro. Please. Tell me who he is.'

Knowing that it would cause misery, but trapped by his friendship with Kelly, the Albanian uttered a name.

75

Sanders opened the door to her home, her head and shoulders slumped as if she were an inmate heading for death row. It had come as no surprise to her that the real-estate developer Gavin Brown had reported the assault, nor had it come as a surprise when she was placed on administrative leave pending the result of the investigation into the incident. Sanders was suspended in all but name, and she had no doubt that the axe would eventually fall on her second career – Brown had boasted to the police department that he had over a dozen witnesses, not to mention a couple of loose teeth. Sanders could smile at that, at least.

But something bothered her besides the obvious. Besides the very real possibility that she was a forty-five-year-old woman about to lose her job. Maybe she could go back to teaching . . .

Maybe.

Setting aside the likelihood that 'assault' on her record would shut that door too, Sanders didn't really see teaching again as an option. She'd joined the force to help the kids in her class and others like them. Could she honestly say that she'd seen an improvement during her time with a badge?

Hardly. Sanders had seen years when the city suffered a hundred murders and over seven hundred rapes. She'd seen drugs come in and bodies go out. She'd seen every kind of dirt ball and douchebag she could think of.

No, she couldn't go back to teaching.

But was that what was bothering her? What was to come? The next step in a life that had already seen her fall flat on her face?

No. It was what the captain had said, the first part of his statement as unexpected as the second part had been predictable. 'I'll go to bat for you on this charge,' the career man had said. 'Just do me a favor though, OK? Leave the Manning case alone.'

'Why?' Sanders had asked, with reckless disregard for her own career.

The captain tried to look patient, and failed. 'Remember you serve the city, Tonya. *The city*.' Sanders didn't need the rest spelled out: *Las Vegas comes before Iris Manning*.

But why? What could a girl's death do to a city of over half a million?

Sanders pressed the heels of her hands into her eyes. She was beyond frustration. None of it made sense . . .

A dead girl in a canyon that she couldn't have reached until four in the morning – why?

Her festival bracelets disappearing from her personal effects – why?

No car, and no trace of anyone having driven her out to the canyon – why?

'Fuck!' Sanders suddenly screamed across the house. '*Fuckkkkkkkkkkkkk!*'

Frustration had reached boiling point. The cop needed to talk with someone, to work things out, but Sanders had done such a good job of building personal walls that now she couldn't see over them. She only had one confidant – one true friend – but Sanders could see that Kelly was now their best chance of uncovering the truth, whatever that was, and she didn't want to disturb him while he was working his leads. Kelly would contact her when he was ready, Sanders decided, but she wasn't about to sit around like a spare prick until that moment.

Her eyes settled on her laptop.

She flipped it open, and placed her notepad beside it. With no real direction to head in, Sanders began at the beginning, and Iris Manning. She went onto the girl's Facebook page, seeing only the posts Iris had made public. Inevitably, these were of parties, and vacations in the sun.

Sanders clicked on Iris's profile picture, and entered into the gallery that showed dozens of others. Sanders began to scroll through them. The past twelve months were mostly of Iris smiling or pouting provocatively. Before that, they were of Iris hugging and kissing friends. By the time that Sanders had gone as far back as 2016, she found Iris standing between her proud parents. Even in a two-dimensional photo, the love between all three was tangible.

'Shit . . .' Sanders breathed, grief on the part of Iris's parents sitting on her chest like an elephant. There was no worse part to her job than breaking the news to a parent that their child had died before them. Those were the times when Sanders questioned her faith. The times where she had to ask God what it was all about. What meaning there could be in such suffering.

Sanders scrolled again from 2016 to the latest Facebook profile picture: it was a timeline of the obvious change in Iris's personality. From Mommy and Daddy's girl, to Vegas socialite, to a self-absorbed--

Sanders stopped that thought dead and chided herself for it, but . . . evidence was evidence, and every step closer to discovering how Iris had come to die left a bad taste in her mouth.

Sanders shook her head, reminding herself that every revelation only opened up more questions than answers. Almost a day and a half had passed since Sanders had first walked into that rocky canyon, and she was as clueless now as she had been then. More so, in fact, because the apparent suicide of Blake Mathews had kicked up even more dust into Sanders's eyes.

She leaned back into the chair, thinking of Iris, and a life cut short. Whatever her opinion of the girl's morals, no one deserved to be found dead and half-eaten between the rocks – well, maybe a few, Sanders conceded.

That thought led her to trace a finger along the furrow on her face. The bullet had changed her life, and the person who fired it had never been brought to justice. It was just another violent act in a city where many such things went unsolved, or even unreported. There had been days – many days – where Sanders wished that the bullet had killed her. There were other days – many more days – where she wished that she'd killed the motherfucker who fired it.

Sanders often fantasized about that moment: the gunman lying on his back in the dark street, blood leaking as he gasped his final breath.

That man had failed in taking Sanders' *life*, but he had succeeded in taking her future.

A picture of Dez came into Sanders's mind before she could block it. Her fiancé had been everything she ever wanted, a teacher who changed lives for the better by solving math problems, not murders.

Maybe it was the stress, maybe it was weakness, maybe it was simply no longer giving a fuck, but before Sanders could think twice about it she entered her ex-fiancé's name into Facebook, and hit search. A split second later he was on the screen, and he was not alone.

A smiling partner. A beautiful baby.

What had Sanders expected? She knew that when she'd driven Dez from her life that he'd met another woman. She knew that he wanted to be married. That he wanted a family. He had that now, and Sanders had—

No.

No.

She wouldn't feel sorry for herself, not one bit. She hadn't lived through the darkest days to start throwing a fucking pity parade now. She owed it to herself, and she owed it to Kelly, the stranger who had put his own life on hold to help another reclaim theirs.

Sanders closed the webpage. The image of Dez and his family was burned onto her retinas, but she would not let it slow her down. She took her notepad and pen in hand, and began to write:

Blake Mathews – deceased. Suspect?

~~*Zhakir Khan* =~~ *ironclad alibi*

Sam Chao – last person known to be with her

Sven Niklas – criminal past?

Gavin Brown – pig. Used her as escort

Sanders may have been pulled off the case, but now wasn't the time to worry about details like that. Two people were dead, and Sanders wanted answers.

She put the first of her names into the search engine, and set about finding those answers.

76

Kelly stepped out the hookah lounge and into Nevada's evening air. The heat was a little kinder than it had been, a warm bitch slap in the face rather than an all-out assault.

He climbed into his car, swearing softly at the pain in his stump. Kelly tried to push it from his mind, failed, and swung the car out onto Las Vegas Boulevard. Traffic was tough, but Kelly was in no rush. He needed a favor before he could hope to get to his next destination.

'Hey,' Arabella Robins answered her cell. 'I'm glad that you called.'

'You've found something?'

'Oh. No. I just mean it's nice to hear from you.'

Kelly guessed that Robins would only talk that way if she were alone.

'Why don't you come to Rusa tonight?' Robins suggested. 'I can comp you a table, and we can go straight upstairs when I get off.'

Kelly smiled weakly to himself. 'I don't think there's going to be any partying happening tonight. Not on my end, at least.'

'I understand, Josh,' she said, her voice warm with appreciation. 'I think it's really . . . it's really something

282

how you are looking out for Iris. I can't thank you enough. You know that if there's anything we can do for you, you've got it.'

'There is something actually . . .' Kelly said, feeling a little guilty.

'What do you need?'

'Can you get me a reservation at J35?'

'The restaurant?'

'Yeah.' J35 was the flavor of the year in Las Vegas.

There was a heartbeat of delay before Robins replied. 'Sure. I've got a contact there. When do you need it?'

Kelly told her, and then added, 'I only need a table for one.'

'Oh.' A note of relief.

'I really do want to see you later,' Kelly insisted, and that was the truth. Despite the craziness in the air – or probably because of it – he felt the attraction pulling at him from the Grand. She was a seriously impressive woman.

'Tonight then,' Robins promised.

'Tonight.'

Kelly clicked off the line, and pushed on into the heart of Sin City.

77

Sanders rubbed her tired eyes, and then focused them back onto her laptop. In front of her was a press release from a few years back, congratulating Blake Mathews on becoming the new resident DJ of Rusa. The photo of Mathews showed him smiling, healthy, and vibrant. The prose in the piece detailed him as a music-loving kid who had always wanted to become a professional musician. According to the article, Mathews had fallen in love with DJing whilst studying music composition at the University of Nevada, Las Vegas, Sanders's own alma mater. Being in Las Vegas was a fortuitous placement for the young man, and with his great personality and raw talent, Mathews was soon booking shows around the city and in California. Rusa was his first residency.

And his last, Sanders concluded, looking at her notebook. There was little written below the name of the deceased DJ. Just a few keywords that Sanders had jotted as she tried to find an online window into his life and soul: *talented, romantic, musician, local, no record, aged fast.*

Sanders looked at that last note for a moment. By comparing photos, she had seen how rapidly the man's appearance had detcriorated over just a few years. *Drink and drugs will do that.*

Sanders turned the page in her notebook, and jotted down *Sam Chao*. Then she punched the name into Google.

'Fuck you,' she told the search engine as it returned 1,900,000 hits. She began to add keywords like 'Vegas,' but after twenty minutes of fruitless search, Sanders decided that she should go after the low-hanging fruit.

'Sven Niklas. Rusa,' the detective said out loud as she typed. 'Only fifty thousand results, huh? Awesome.'

She started wading, page after page of glowing press reports that described the Swedish man's influence on the Vegas club scene. Only when she found a business magazine's article from 2015 did Sanders discover just how great that influence was – along with a dozen other names, half of which Sanders recognized as local celebrities, Niklas had bought into the 49 per cent of the operating company that ran Pandora, the other 51 per cent remaining with its original owner.

After reading over the names again, Sanders copied and pasted the article into an email to Kelly.

Sven Niklas is a stakeholder in the festival. Explains why he's being so helpful. Trying to keep his baby squeaky clean?

Then the detective got to her weary feet, pacing over to the coffee machine in her kitchen. The pot was going fast, but she needed the fuel. Sanders knew that the truth was out there. Like the gold in Nevada's rock, it just needed digging out with blood, sweat, and tears.

78

J35 was everything that Kelly expected of a high-end restaurant in Vegas. Every item, from the cutlery on the table to the hand towels in the bathroom, was of a quality that matched the price tag. The service didn't just come with a smile, but an aura that made Kelly feel as though he were the Prince of Siam. The food was an American–Asian fusion that almost pushed Kelly's time with Robins into second place as the best experience of his day. For a moment, Kelly nearly forgot why he was sitting within the restaurant's teak walls.

But not quite.

'Can I get the check, please?' Kelly asked his beaming server. Like everything else in the place, she was polished and pristine. In California, Kelly had become accustomed to excellent service at many of his local spots, but J35 made them look amateur.

His server returned a moment later. 'Here you go, sir. Was everything to your taste?'

'Awesome, thank you,' he replied, noticing how the girl's eyes were drawn irresistibly to his phone on the table. He'd left the device open on his Instagram page, and turned in a direction so that his server would see it. At the top of his page was the large number of his followers, social currency in the modern age.

'I was hoping I could grab a quick photo with Chef Michaels?' Kelly asked with his best smile. 'Only if it's no trouble, of course.'

The girl understood the game – Kelly's social media following would merit a moment of the restaurant head's time. The fact that she saw Kelly tack on a very generous tip to the bloated bill didn't hurt either. 'I'll see what I can do, sir.'

Kelly was left alone, and used the moment to cast his eyes over the assembled clientele of the place. There were couples in love, couples seeking love, and couples trying to revive it. Kelly was the only person eating alone, and he couldn't stop a sudden pang of jealousy from hitting him in the chest. A subtle reminder that there had been someone whom he had surprised with dinners and dates. Kelly wasn't short of female attention, but oceans of attention didn't measure up against a drop of pure, joyful love.

Kelly was broken from his sudden melancholy by the arrival of a man at the table. One who drew stares and hushed smiles. He was William Michaels, and his physique reminded Kelly of a ladle standing up on its narrow end.

J35's head chef put out his hand. 'Will. How was your dinner?'

Kelly stood and shook. He had to look down to meet Michaels in the eye and, given what he knew about him, that suited Kelly just fine. 'Pleasure to meet you,' he lied.

And then Kelly did what the bulk of people under forty years old do when they meet a celebrity or public figure: he asked if he could take a selfie.

'Of course!' Michaels agreed, one smile away from free publicity for his establishment.

Kelly thanked him, and lifted the phone so that only he and the chef could see the screen.

'Smile,' Kelly told him.

But Michaels couldn't.

On the screen was a photograph of Iris Manning. Across the image, Kelly had written a simple message.

She's dead.

Let's talk.

79

Sanders pushed her chair back from the desk, and slipped away from her laptop like a rudderless ship cut from its moorings. Apart from the fact that Sven Niklas owned a chunk of the festival's parent company, the last couple of hours of research had turned up nothing.

She needed more coffee.

'Shit.' The pot was empty. 'Goddamn it.' The bag was too.

Sanders looked from the pot to the laptop. She was tired, but time away from the case seemed so . . . wasteful.

'Fuck it.' She swiped her keys from the countertop.

After five minutes behind the wheel, Sanders was beneath the bright lights of a gas station's courtyard. She pushed open the building's door, smiled a greeting to the attendant, and got half of a hello back before the shock at Sanders's disfigurement strangled the woman's words. Sanders tried not to take it personally, and helped herself to the biggest and baddest coffee she could find. As she put her money on the counter, Sanders noticed the attendant looking closely at her own hands. She tried not to take that personally either. The woman wasn't the first person to look away. She wouldn't be the last.

Sanders opened her truck and put her coffee into the cup holder. She was about to climb in when a noise made her turn.

It was the sound of a jet wash. A kid was hosing down his pride and joy, a tricked-out Honda that he'd doubtless drive up and down the Strip until he grew out of puberty.

Sanders watched the kid for a moment, and then something began to scratch at her conscience. A memory first, and then a thought . . .

Sanders got behind the wheel of her truck, and headed north.

80

William Michaels tried and failed to hold some kind of a smile in place as he led Kelly from the restaurant floor and through the riotous smells and sounds of J35's kitchen.

Kelly watched the man ahead of him as they moved, preparing himself against the possibility that Michaels would grab something sharp or hot to fuck up Kelly's day. Kelly didn't know if the man he was following was dangerous, but the chef had come onto his radar when Danco had revealed that he'd seen him with Iris the night before she went missing. Michaels was a regular for the top-shelf coke and, as with all of his high-flying clients, Danco delivered in person – that night to the Englishman's penthouse. Danco had only seen Iris for a moment, but it was enough – he wasn't about to forget her beauty anytime soon, and so Kelly had been given a new lead.

A very irate, angry lead. Kelly found that out as soon as they stepped into the man's office, and the door was closed. 'You absolute piece of . . . of . . .' The man grimaced, seemingly on the edge of a stroke. 'How dare you come into my rest— my rest . . .'

Michael's words tailed away as his eyes seemed to boil in their own sockets. It was as if Kelly's impudence was on such a level that the chef couldn't even give voice to the crime, and instead the veins in his head and neck bulged like electrocuted worms.

'You utter cunt,' he finally breathed, almost collapsing with the effort. 'Are you police?' he demanded, not seeming to care that he might have insulted an officer. Kelly wasn't surprised at that – money didn't put people out of reach of the law, but it sure as shit gave them a head start.

'I'm not the police.' Kelly spoke evenly.

Michaels looked as though he was going to hit him then. Instead he punched a wall, recoiling in agony as the pain of the strike raced up his arm. Even Kelly winced.

'Then who the fuck are you, you twat?' Michaels steamed. 'Her pimp? Paparazzi?'

'Neither.'

'Bullshit! I've dealt with your kind before. Following other people around, just waiting for a slip. Just waiting for us to be fucking human! You're pathetic! A miserable fucking bottom-feeder, you twat! Now – how much do you want? Whatever your number is, fucking halve it.'

Kelly breathed out. He hoped that Michaels would pick up on his attempt at de-escalation.

He didn't.

'Well, fucking spit it out then!'

Instead Kelly put a hand on the man's shoulder and shoved him down into a chair as though he were nothing more than an unruly child. Then Kelly positioned himself so that his weight was looming over Michaels, pinning him in place with one hand. His second, prosthetic limb was poised to smash the man in his now terrified face.

'I'm sorry I shouted!' he apologized pathetically.

Kelly dismissed the words with a sneer. A girl was dead, and his reservoir of patience was dry. He would waste no more niceties on the prima donna of a chef and his fragile ego.

'I want to smash your face in,' Kelly told the man honestly. 'But I'll settle for answers.'

Michaels swallowed his pride. Fear was written into every line of his face. 'What do you need to know?'

'You were with Iris Manning on Thursday night.'

'I was,' Michaels confirmed nervously. 'When did she die?'

'Sometime Friday night,' Kelly revealed, knowing it would add the kind of pressure that his hands could not. 'So I'd say it's a safe bet your DNA's still on her, and maybe . . . maybe in the more intimate parts.'

'Shiiitttt,' the chef hissed, confirming Kelly's suspicions. 'Shiiiiittttttt.'

'So you did sleep with her?'

Suddenly, Michaels managed to look even more anxious. 'You're not wearing a wire, are you? How do I know you're not recording this?'

'You don't,' Kelly told him simply.

'Take off your shirt,' Michaels insisted.

'Fuck you,' Kelly snarled. 'Are you gonna keep talking or do I need to beat the answers out of you?'

'I'll talk, Jesus!' Michaels shuddered back. 'Yes, I slept with her! What else do you do with a fucking escort? Jesus-fucking-Christ.'

'Did you do drugs together?'

Michaels rolled his eyes. '*Yes, Mum*. Don't hit me!' he shouted quickly, seeing Kelly tense. 'Yes, we did drugs. Cocaine.'

'Did you see her again after that night?'

'No!'

'Do you know anyone who would do her harm?'

'No! I don't know. Shit. She was an escort! Who knows what shit she got into!'

'But do *you* know of anyone that she pissed off? That she crossed?'

'No! No, OK? She'd come to mine, we'd party, we'd have sex, she'd go. I don't live in a fucking Guy Ritchie movie. Christ!'

That last word was followed by the sound of a squeal. Even Josh Kelly had his limits, and the foul-mouthed degenerate had pushed him to it. Kelly twisted the man's ear as though they were on a school playground.

'Stop being a smart-ass and start thinking, *Chef*. When her autopsy gets done, I'll make sure the police know who she was with, and the police are going to want to know why your DNA's on a dead girl. Wouldn't you like to smooth things out before then?'

'How?' Michaels asked, his eyes closed against the pain of his twisted ear.

Kelly told him: answers to his questions.

How did Michaels meet Iris? How did he pay her? Was there anyone else involved?

At Rusa.

In gifts.

No.

'You're sure about that?' Another twist of the ear.

'Yes!'

'Did you ever get rough with Iris?'

'No!' Twist. 'A little! Shit, just a bit of choking! Who doesn't choke these days, fuck!'

Kelly considered closing the man's windpipe himself. The degradation of the case was wearing on him, and the compulsion for violence was a rising tide that he could not deny, no matter how slowly it had crept towards the barriers of his decency.

'I really don't like you,' Kelly told the man.

'I know.'

'I want to break every bone in your face.'

'I know.'

But wanting and doing were two different things. 'Maybe you got too rough with Iris,' Kelly thought out loud. 'A mistake. An honest mistake, and in your panic, you took her body out to the mountains. If that's what happened you should come clean to the police now. It's not too late.'

'Dumped her body in the mountains?' Michaels spat out. 'Are you fucking nuts? I might not want my private life splashed all over the tabloids, but there's a fucking limit, you dickhead. Don't hit me! Listen! I'm just saying that there's a limit to what someone will do for a reputation, and mine comes before dumping bodies in the fucking mountains!'

'And what about the reputation of Pandora festival?' Kelly asked. 'How far would you go to protect the reputation of that?'

He pulled his phone from his pocket, and opened the email that Sanders had sent him – William Michaels was listed below Sven Niklas as one of the stakeholders who had bought into the festival's parent company.

'Jesus.' The chef snorted. 'I've got less invested in them than half a dozen of my ventures! I want the festival to do well, of course I do, but to do what you're saying? You're mental, mate. Fucking mental.'

Kelly let go of the man's ear and stood back. Whatever he saw in the chef's eyes, it was not guilt or mischief. What he did see was a lot of anger.

'I'll fucking kill you for this,' Michaels promised as Kelly opened the office's door.

The big man turned, and smiled at the red-faced creature he was leaving in his wake. 'No you won't.'

But when he closed the door behind him, all confidence fled from Kelly's posture.

Iris Manning was dead, and he was no closer to knowing why.

81

Sanders's truck pulled to a stop in the wide parking lot. She turned off the engine and stepped down into the Nevada night, the heat wrapping around her in a warm, unwanted embrace. The neighborhood was quiet – no traffic, no dogs. Even though a couple of tired streetlights cast amber onto the cars around her, Sanders took a flashlight out of the back before pacing over to the reason that had brought her out here.

It was the Audi of recently deceased Blake Mathews. If the department were taking his claims of murdering Iris seriously, then the vehicle would have been taken in for evidence. The fact that it still stood on the warm tarmac told Sanders a lot – the LVPD weren't just dragging their feet on these cases, they were wading through tar.

On the day that Iris's body had been found, Kelly had pointed out that the Audi had been recently cleaned to a sparkle. That was at odds with Mathews's apartment, which still looked like a battleground weeks after he'd moved into the place. Something about that didn't feel right to Sanders, which was why she now moved about the vehicle with her flashlight beam carefully tracing over every inch. The Audi had been cleaned so thoroughly that it shone like a carriage of a royal wedding, and it was only when the detective shined her flashlight inside of the glass that she found the one blemish in the car's perfection – an open ten-pack of Marlboro Light cigarettes.

Sanders stood and looked up at the stars.

'Goddamn it.'

She took out her phone.

82

Josh Kelly walked from the casino that housed J35 and stepped onto the Strip. It was prime time for Las Vegas, and the sidewalks were packed with a colorful cast of tourists from all over the world. Bachelor and bachelorette parties looking for a blast of hedonism and infidelity before the 'I do's.' Patient grey-haired couples who had found 'the secret.' Waddling titans whose fanny packs disappeared beneath their guts. Photographing international visitors whose smiles were brighter than their camera flashes.

Kelly took it all in, and yet he saw nothing. He heard the cars' horns, the sounds of the slot machines, the dozens of languages, and the shouts of excitement. His senses were slapped, kicked, and punched, but he felt none of it.

Kelly was numb. And he didn't know why.

Despite the pain in his stump, he started walking. He looked back in his mind to the office of head chef William Michaels, and how Kelly had gripped his ear, and twisted it to get answers. It had felt good, Kelly acknowledged to himself. It had reminded him of the sense of power that he used to get from putting in a solid block on the football field, using his physical dominance to cow others. It *had* felt good, and Kelly knew that ramming his fist into the man's face would have felt even better.

Why?

Kelly had to walk a little longer before he had that answer.

Because Iris was dead, and Michaels had shown no remorse at that, only a hurried desperation to cover his own ass so that he wasn't implicated. Even under threat he had talked to Kelly as though he were above mere mortals, so why did Kelly expect that the man would show an ounce of decency and despondency for a girl he'd used as a plaything? Just another piece of entertainment, no more or less than tickets to Cirque, or a new TV? That was where girls like Iris fit in for men like William Michaels.

And you're surprised by this? Kelly chided himself. *You lived in Hollywood, for fuck's sake. You're not a child. Wake up, man. Unwrap your fucking brains.*

Kelly knew then why he had been so angry with Michaels. Over the past few years, Kelly had adopted a life philosophy where he tried to better himself daily. Where he tried to become a person without judgment, or hate. It was an impossible task, but one that Kelly strived for. Sometimes he forgot that the rest of the world wasn't on that journey with him, and when he was reminded of it, Kelly knew that – though he had come far – he was still as capable of immoral acts as the next person. He didn't like that fact. It made him angry, and feeling that anger made him more frustrated still.

It was a relief when he saw Tonya's name come up on his vibrating phone. 'Hey. What's up?'

Straight to business. 'Did you smell cigarettes in Blake Mathews's apartment?'

Kelly didn't have to think about it. 'No.'

'See anything like an ashtray?'

'No. Why?'

Sanders told him about the cigarettes in Mathews's car. 'I've seen mention of a ten-pack like that somewhere else today, Kelly.' The detective told him. Ever the teacher, she let him guess at the answer.

Kelly remembered it six seconds later.

'Iris's personal effects . . .'

83

'We have to consider the strong possibility that Blake Mathews did kill Iris,' Sanders told Kelly from the other end of a phone. 'His car was pristine, and if those were her cigarettes . . . I'm trying to find someone that's around and willing to help in the PD. We need those cigarettes in the car tested for Iris's prints.'

Kelly looked around him on the busy Strip for someplace more quiet. 'Hold up.' He slipped into a casino's gaping maw, spotting a quiet corner away from the coin-operated machines and tables. 'I thought you were off this case?' he asked his friend. 'Can you request things like that?'

'Not officially,' Sanders admitted. 'But I think Chaz Riggins has her head on tight. I think she'll listen.'

'Have you talked to her?'

'She's off shift. I don't think knocking her door down's the best way to get her onside.'

Kelly looked at his watch. It was getting a little late for personal calls, but . . . 'We need something, T.'

'Shit . . . OK. I'll try her when we get off. How did it go at the restaurant?'

Kelly told her, leaving out the details of how he'd gotten a little extra out of the head chef.

'Are you OK?' Sanders asked, hearing something unusual in his voice.

'Yeah.'

'Say if you're not.'

'I'm OK, Tonya, honestly.' But he wasn't, and they both knew it. 'I feel like I'm banging my head against a wall, and I can live with the bruises, but I just don't feel as if I've even made a dent.'

Sanders sighed. It didn't come from frustration, but because of concern for her friend. 'You really don't think Mathews killed her, do you?'

'I don't. I don't, Tonya. I think he was set up.'

'Your gut tell you that?'

'Yeah, my gut,' Kelly replied with a bit too much snap.

'Easy there, partner. I can trust a gut, but let's just take a step back, all right? Let's say that Blake Mathews was set up to take the fall for Iris. Well, we can't start letting the geeks loose on his Facebook until the department either charges him with the murder of Iris, or we get permission from his next of kin. Both of those things are out of our hands – quiet, Josh, they are out of our hands *at least at this moment* – and so all I can do is push Riggins, and we keep digging.'

Kelly ran his hand through his hair. 'I feel like we're digging in circles.'

'Well, maybe we are, but that doesn't mean that we won't get to the bottom of things. I know you've had tough times before, Josh. You got through those.'

Something in Sanders's words struck Kelly, and it wasn't that she had called him by his Christian name, a sure sign that she was beginning to worry about her friend. It was a flashback to dark days, and how Kelly had dealt with them. He'd done so in a woeful way that made him itch with self-reproach, but try as he might to dismiss the idea, the picture of Iris's torn body in the canyon screamed at him to consider it. The more that Kelly did, and the longer the image of death lingered in his mind, the more certain he became that he was willing to cross moral and legal boundaries to get to the truth of Iris's end.

'One moment,' he told Sanders, sending a message and breaking the law a few seconds later.

'Are you good?'

'I'm good.'

There was a pause as Sanders weighed her words. Eventually, she chose to bite back her concern – she wanted the mystery solved as much as Kelly did. 'I'm going to call Riggins,' she told him. 'See if we can get her on the program.'

'OK,' was all that Kelly said before the line went dead. Then he stood silently, picturing Iris in the canyon. A corpse beneath a brilliant blue sky.

Kelly was still lingering over the painful image when his phone began to vibrate. 'What did Riggins say?' he answered automatically.

But the caller was no officer of the law.

'My name's Ryan Fowler,' an irritated voice told Kelly. 'And I'm the owner of Pandora.'

Kelly opened his mouth to speak, but a strong Virginia accent beat him to it.

'I think we better have a little talk, don't you?'

84

'Get yourself to the Palms,' the festival owner instructed sharply, 'go to the VIP check-in, and tell them you're meeting Ryan Fowler at his suite.'

'Will they have my name?' Kelly asked.

He got a laugh. 'Half of Vegas has your name.'

Then the line went dead.

'Josh Kelly?' came a voice from behind him.

Kelly turned on his heel to find a young couple smiling awkwardly.

'We're big fans of your work,' the woman explained. 'Your documentary about sharks on the Barrier Reef was amazing. Do you mind if we get a photo?'

'Of course not,' Kelly replied automatically.

Selfies snapped. Kelly tried to smile.

'So how long are you in town?' they asked him.

'Just a couple of days.' He needed to get out of there. 'I hate to be rude, but I'm just on my way to a meeting . . .'

'Oh! Awesome. Well, it was a pleasure to meet you!'

Kelly shook hands with the pair and continued to the exit. He considered going back to get his car, but the traffic was thick, and nothing in Ryan Fowler's voice said that he was a patient man. Kelly decided that he'd make the twenty-minute walk despite the pain in his stump. He knew Vegas well enough that there was no need to turn to Maps to find his way to the Palms, and he waited at a crosswalk with two dozen others who were eager to cross the tide of traffic and get to the other side of the Strip. Unlike the revelers, however, Kelly put his head down and headed west. He could reach the Palms via the busy Flamingo Road, but instead Kelly opted for the quieter streets that ran away from the lights and between the tall buildings. It wasn't as if Kelly expected to be spotted by more fans – such a thing rarely happened twice in one day outside of Southern California – but he wanted space. He wanted to be alone. Kelly loved people, but he was what a friend had told him was an extroverted introvert – his social batteries could be drained very quickly, and when they were, he needed time alone to recharge them. Kelly hadn't ever realized how important surfing was to him until the shark attack confined him to a hospital bed. The day he'd gotten back into nature, it was as though he'd found the cable that plugged him into life's mains.

But hitting the waves or trails wasn't an option for him in the hot desert evening, and so Kelly took the side streets.

Ten years ago in the ocean, that inclination for solitude had almost cost Kelly his life.

This time, death came for him in a city's long shadows.

85

The first bullet missed Kelly's head and tore a chunk from the nearest wall before he even knew that he was in danger. By the time that the second shot sparked off the sidewalk next to Kelly's feet, the big man was running. He didn't know where, he didn't know why, but the animal instinct inside him had been triggered by danger. It was awake. Alive. And it told him: *Run before you fucking die.*

Two more rounds cracked through the air from behind. Then another two.

Kelly ran.

Ran for his life.

Active shooters were a cancer in America, but, just like the disease, they were a part of life that couldn't be ignored. Kelly's brother breathed war on all fronts, and once over the dinner table he had drilled the lesson into the more peaceful Kelly brother's head. *If someone's shooting, and you don't have something to shoot back with, you run. You run, and zig, and zag. Don't make yourself an easy target. First chance you get, you put hard cover between yourself and the shooter.*

Kelly saw the promise of that hard cover now. A five-foot-high wall behind a row of garbage cans. It was the kind of obstacle that Kelly would have cleared without even blinking ten years ago. Now . . .

Kelly leaped for the concrete wall, the flesh of his right arm grazing against its rough top. A split second later he was pushing himself upwards, the stump of his left arm grinding in the prosthetic's socket as two more bullets zipped through the darkness, the crack of the shots followed instantaneously by chips of wall sent scratching into Kelly's face.

They'd been close. So close.

The next would be fatal.

Over the sound of his shallow breaths Kelly heard footsteps running towards him, but there was no moment to turn and look, only one to push upwards and live. Kelly's body strained to lift him up and over the wall, and then he dropped heavily to the other side, his usual athletic grace lost in the chaos of a life-or-death pursuit.

He fell hard but there was no thought of pain in Kelly's mind, only escape. He saw passing traffic ahead of him, and pedestrians. Like a hero at the Games, Kelly sprinted hard and bust his lungs to reach the safety of numbers.

The strange sight drew stares from the tourists on Flamingo, but Kelly was only thinking about the relief that rushed into his shaking body. Adrenaline was pumping through his veins, and he breathed harder than he'd ever done on the football field. Kelly sucked in breaths of hot air, and thanked the universe and every God he could think of for his survival.

Someone just tried to kill me, Kelly thought to himself, almost as though he'd watched it on TV. *What the fuck?*

Then, with a revelation that was almost painful, Kelly realized that whoever'd tried was still at large, and their failure could be temporary. *Jesus fucking Christ.* There were sirens in the distance, but Kelly held little hope that whoever had fired the shots would be caught. He doubted most people would have even registered the shots. Tall buildings caught sounds, and fireworks were unleashed along the Strip with such regularity that gunshots were almost always discounted at first.

But Kelly was under no illusions – someone had tried to kill him.

And they were still out there.

86

Nineteen minutes after the shots were fired, Sanders joined Kelly in a quiet Irish bar on East Flamingo. She found him in the corner, his eyes on the door and a fire escape close at hand.

'What the *fuck*?' Sanders hugged him.

'I got shot at,' Kelly spoke evenly, repeating what he'd said on the phone.

'So you came for a *beer*?'

Kelly looked at the empty glass in front of him. 'It was a Diet Coke . . .' he said. '. . . with vodka.'

Sanders was about to tell Kelly that it wasn't the time for making jokes. Instead, she pulled her friend into another tight embrace. 'You dick,' she told him as she stood back. 'You're not the one that's supposed to get shot.'

'Well, I didn't.'

'You know what I mean. What the fuck happened, Kelly?'

He told her.

Sanders shook her head. 'And you're telling me this in a bar, and not to officers at the scene because . . .'

'The scene was a dark street with no one around. Once I made it to a busy area, I figured the shooter would have run too. Sticking around the scene just seemed dangerous.'

'You did the right thing getting someplace busy,' Sanders agreed. 'But it should have been nine one one before me, Kelly. They could have been with you in minutes. What's the situation with the police now?'

Kelly shrugged. 'I have no idea.'

'You . . . you have *no idea*?'

'What?' Kelly protested. 'I saw squad cars heading to the area, so I guess someone reported the shots.'

'But *you* haven't?' Sanders asked, and Kelly shook his head. 'Why?'

It took a long stern look from his friend before he confessed. 'Because I'm bait, T.'

'*Bait?*'

Kelly held up his hands. 'Whoever took a pop at me did it for a reason, T. No one's ever shot at me in my life. Isn't it a bit of a coincidence that it happened now that I'm asking questions about Iris?'

'No, it's not a coincidence! That's exactly why you should be reporting it, Kelly! It's why *I'm* going to!'

'Don't do that, Tonya,' Kelly said firmly.

'Why?'

'Because maybe they'll get scared. Maybe they'll run.'

'Good!'

'Not good. We want to find these people, T. Whoever took a shot at me, they weren't a pro. I think they fired like

311

six times. Maybe more. I don't know, it's hard to remember, but the point is they had me dead to rights and they missed. They weren't some kind of professional hitman like in the movies. I think it was someone amateur. They must have been following me, saw a chance, and tried to take it.'

'And what's worth killing you over, Josh?'

'The same thing that was worth killing Iris for,' Kelly said confidently. 'And the same reason for killing Blake Mathews, too.'

For a moment, Sanders simply bit her lip and chewed on a thought. 'Everything's getting out of control,' she finally said. 'I asked for your help because something was a little off at first, but now? You need to go back to California, Josh, and I'm going to go home. Tomorrow, I'll go see Captain Wolford, tell him everything, and Brovetski and Riggins and whoever else wants to fuck with this thing can have it. We're done.'

Kelly couldn't believe it. 'You're giving up?'

Sanders looked at him as though he were an idiot brother. 'No, I'm not giving up! I'm accepting that the game is over, Kelly. It's done, and we lost.'

'That's giving up. It's not over.'

'Fuck, yes, it's over. It was over the second someone pulled a trigger and tried to kill you. The truth of a dead girl is not worth your life. It's that simple.'

'I'm not going back,' Kelly said stubbornly. 'I'm seeing this through.'

Sanders tried hard not to choke her friend. 'Josh. Listen. You're being a jock right now. You're seeing a competition. You need to step back, and look at this like a

312

sane person. This is not game day at the Rose Bowl. This is Vegas, and someone tried to kill you. You want to know how many unsolved homicides we got from last year?'

Kelly didn't. Sanders told him anyway.

'Fifty. And the year before that? Forty-seven. And the year before that? Forty-eight. This isn't a game, Josh, and even if it was, it isn't one that we win much more than half the time, OK? So smarten up. We gave it a shot, but now . . . now this is done. For us, it's done.'

'Ryan Fowler called me,' Kelly said then, 'the majority owner of the festival. He wants to meet me at the Palms. I was on my way there to meet him when the attack happened.'

Sanders rubbed at her temples. Her scar seemed to twitch with irritation. 'Do you think that's maybe a coincidence, Kelly? That he invites you over, you get followed, and then someone tries to kill you?'

'Now who has the wild theories?' Kelly replied, delivering it with a smile.

'Fuck you, Kelly, you know what I mean.'

He did. 'I know you're just trying to look out for me.'

'Right,' Sanders said before she closed her eyes and exhaled. 'Look, I can see there's no way I'm gonna talk you off this path you're on, Kelly, and so the least I'm gonna do is walk it with you.'

Kelly smiled at that. 'And you'll bring guns, partner?' he asked her playfully.

Sanders rolled her eyes. She wanted to punch him, and hug him, but more than anything, she wanted to keep him alive. 'Yes, Joshua. I'll bring guns.'

87

The Sky Suites at the Palms Casino Resort & Hotel began at twenty thousand dollars a night, and when Kelly stepped out of the suite's personal glass elevator, he could see why – two pillars that looked as though they'd been taken from the Pantheon stood sentinel beside the glimmering waters of an infinity pool. The suite was enormous, tastefully decorated with modern furnishings. A wall of glass stretched two stories high, revealing the sparkling city that crouched below this dominion, a hideout for the rich and powerful, or a playroom for the rich and colorful – Kelly had heard stories about suites in the Palms Fantasy Tower that were home to DJ booths, saltwater fish tanks, and stripper poles in locker-room-sized showers.

Kelly heard the sound of glass on a hard countertop. He took it as a signal, and walked towards it.

'Take your shoes off,' Ryan Fowler told him.

Kelly obliged, slipping them off with his feet as he kept his eyes on the man who had 'invited' him here. Fowler was of average height, a slight paunch showing through his black T-shirt. He wore his hair tousled, with a dark beard trimmed tight and neat. He was only a few years older than Kelly, but Fowler hadn't seen as much of the sun, or the surf, and Kelly bet that the man had known some hard partying years. Now, though, it was Diet Cola that Fowler was pouring into a glass.

He didn't offer one to Kelly.

The dark liquid disappeared in four long swallows. During that time, Fowler's eyes never left Kelly's, and the taller man wondered what could have made Fowler leave his own festival. What could have rattled him so much that he would fly back to the city, and take time to talk to Kelly, instead of witnessing the grand orchestra that he had conducted?

The glass went back down onto the countertop.

Clack.

'I'm very loyal to my friends.' Fowler spoke up, surprising Kelly with his choice of words. 'I'm very loyal to my friends,' Fowler said again, professional hostility cutting through the air, 'and I love my friends, and I want to know why you've been upsetting them, Josh Kelly. I want to know who the fuck you are, who the fuck you think you are, and I want you to tell me why I shouldn't let the lawyers and police fall on you in a fucking avalanche that will suffocate the last living breath out of you.

'Tell me.

'Speak.'

Kelly said nothing.

He held his silence, and looked straight back into Fowler's eyes. Kelly saw the kind of paternal, familial rage that could only be unleashed when one's tribe is threatened.

'A girl is dead,' Kelly said simply. 'A boy too.'

Fowler folded his arms. No sigh, just determination. 'How much is it going to cost for you to go away, Josh Kelly?'

The words were delivered with near sadness. Kelly knocked them easily aside. 'I'm not for sale.'

'Then what do you want?'

'The truth.'

'Why?'

A heartbeat.

'Because they deserved it.'

Fowler took a deep breath, then. 'Are you sure about that?'

Kelly's look said that he was.

Fowler's said that his 'guest' was a fool.

'A girl who attended your festival was found dead in the mountains.' Kelly spoke up, leaving out that the bands which marked her attendance there had for some reason gone missing from evidence. 'There's no explanation for her death,' he said instead. 'Just suspicion.'

Fowler shook his head, and looked at his watch. 'Are you sure about that? You might want to check the news.'

Kelly stood still, but inside, his guts churned. *What fucking news?* he shouted at himself.

Fowler told him. 'Blake Mathews killed Iris Manning before killing himself,' he said confidently. 'I'm assuming they're the dead girl and dead boy that you're talking about?'

'How did you . . .'

'Suicide note went viral.'

The words hit Kelly like a cold slap in the face – how could he have been so stupid? How could he not have seen that coming?

'You look angry,' Fowler said.

And he was. So fucking angry.

With himself.

You're tired, Kelly's reconditioned soul tried to reason, *you're run down. Your stump is painful as hell and someone tried to kill you! Of course you're not thinking clearly! Give yourself a break! It probably* was *Mathews that did it! It's probably all like this guy's saying!*

But . . .

But Kelly couldn't buy it. He just couldn't. Who had tried to kill him? Blake Mathews's ghost from beyond the grave?

'Something's going on here,' he said with certainty. 'And I'm going to find out what, why, and who. Throw up all the smoke screens you want. I'm getting the truth.'

Fowler laughed then. It wasn't an angry laugh, or a scornful one. It was the kind of laugh you give when you're trying to convince a child that their scraped knee isn't that bad. That there will still be presents at Christmas, even though Santa isn't real.

'Just let it go,' he tried, but Kelly's expression told him that he wouldn't.

Fowler sighed. He worked his fingers against the air, and delivered his message with sadness. 'My people looked into you, Josh Kelly. They looked into the troublemaker, the nuisance, and they reported back to me about this guy who . . . who is, in all honesty, pretty fucking inspirational. The kind of person I *do* want to be in a room with. What you went through, what you overcame . . .'

He trailed off for a moment. 'And this cops-and-robbers shit you have yourself in now? I got it, at first, I really did. A great guy who wanted to be in the LAPD. You had that dream taken from you, right, Josh Kelly? The shark took that dream away, and so I could forgive you harassing my friends, and trying to throw shade on my festival. I could forgive that.'

Kelly's muscles stiffened. His throat went dry. With blinding certainty, he knew what was coming next.

'But that isn't the real story, is it?'

Kelly swallowed.

'So, Josh Kelly, why don't you and I talk about the real reason why you can never be a cop?'

88

Four years earlier

Kelly walked out into sunlight.

This was Hollywood, but he didn't see huge letters on a hillside. Or stars on the sidewalk. Behind him, Kelly heard the door of the house he'd just left lock shut, the message clear: party's over.

Kelly fumbled in his pockets for his sunglasses. His movements were slowed by drugs, but his cursing was sharp as he discovered the Ray-Bans missing, no escape from the California sun that beat the degenerate who had dared scar the most beautiful of days with his presence.

Kelly took out his phone, careful not to catch sight of himself in its reflection. He knew what he'd see there. Red eyes, red nose, chapped lips. Battle scars of three days without sleep. Three days of coke, Molly, K, and booze. Three days where Kelly had fought against going home, a final stand against the soul-crushing void that was the empty loneliness of his life.

He opened the Uber app in a shaking hand. He went to steady it with his other, but when he was fucked up he had about as much control over his prosthetic as he did the

319

direction of his life. Finally, Kelly entered his destination, and called the savior who would take him back to darkness. His apartment wouldn't have the company that provided legitimacy to his drug taking, but it had strong blinds, and Kelly had a pocket full of pills and powder. He had seen to that before he exited the house, buying whatever the crashing party-heads had left.

The Uber canceled.

Kelly frowned, and tried again.

Same result.

Payment declined.

Fuck.

Kelly pulled out his wallet. He had no idea where to find one, but maybe he could get a cab? A traditional one.

No. The wallet was empty, and Kelly knew that the credit cards in it were good for nothing except chopping powder.

And so he walked. He fucking walked. Josh Kelly put his head down into the sun, and he fucking walked.

How far could it be? Forty minutes? Forty minutes, maybe. What was the time? Nine. Shit. People will be up. They'll stare. Hopefully they'll be in work, though. In work or staying out of the sun. Maybe I could run? Run? Who the fuck are you kidding, bro? You've missed physio for four months. You probably don't even have one any more. Just put your head down. Walk.

Wait, over there. Some cover behind those trees. Go bump some coke off a key. That'll keep you going. It's only when you're coming down that you look shakey, dude. Keep doing little bumps and you'll be fine.

It was on the second bump that the cop found him. A squad car just rolling through the streets. At first the cop figured the tall guy was just taking a piss against a tree, and he was gonna chew him out before rolling on, but a hurriedly dropped baggy caught the sunlight, and twenty seconds later, Josh Kelly had his hands on the police car's hood.

His tears were on there too.

'Please, don't arrest me.' He pleaded to the officer as three days of drug taking, and six years of misery fell down onto his head. 'Please, it will ruin everything. I'm sorry. Please, don't arrest me.'

And the cop wished that he could let him go. Every ounce of his soul knew that the man he was arresting wasn't a bad one, but it was his job was to enforce the law, not interpret it, and so the cuffs went onto the wrists – one of them prosthetic, the other of flesh – and then the cop put the man into the back of his squad car.

When the officer shut the door and pulled away, Josh Kelly's dreams got left on the sidewalk.

89

Kelly knew that Ryan Fowler took no pleasure in speaking the truth about the demise of his dreams, but what did it matter? He felt as though a knife had cut his stomach wide open. He felt sick, raw, and wretched.

Kelly felt this way whenever he acknowledged that he was the architect of his own destruction. Not fate, not the universe, and not a shark. *He* was the one who'd blown it. Josh Kelly, party guy and drug addict. His dream had been out there, a possibility, a promise. Kelly could have crushed his physio, and shown that he was capable of carrying out the duties of an LAPD officer despite what he had suffered.

But instead, Kelly had chosen misery. Kelly had chosen drugs. With an arrest for possession on his record, his dream of becoming a cop had about as much chance of coming into existence as his missing arm and leg.

But then this. Iris Manning. A cause. A chance. A moment to be who he wanted to be.

Someone spoke. 'I'm sorry.'

It was Ryan Fowler. 'I really am sorry,' he told the tall man in front of him. 'I struggled with it myself. I went to rehab two times. I can't . . . I can't understand how painful it must be to lose your dream, but that doesn't mean I can let you try to fuck up mine.'

Fowler walked from the kitchen towards the balcony. 'This is your second chance to be a hero, right?' he asked over his shoulder. 'And to be a hero, you need to have a villain?'

Kelly said nothing, but something told him to follow Fowler to the balcony. Something told him that there would be answers there, and if not . . . at least there would be air. Kelly needed that, now. He needed it badly. The weight of his betrayal against himself drove daggers into his own heart.

He followed. The sky welcomed him. At this height, it had cooled to be a gentle embrace. A comfort.

Kelly was so wrapped up in it that he didn't see the two men who followed them out.

Not until it was too late.

90

There was nothing at Kelly's back but air and a four-hundred-foot drop. Between him and the suite's interior were two men who were his equal in height, but one look at their thick builds and dark eyes told him that they were his double in viciousness.

'What do you want?' Kelly asked, but *What are you going to do to me?* was the more honest question in his mind.

Kill me, was the craziest probability. *Try to scare me into silence,* was the most likely.

What Kelly didn't expect was for Ryan Fowler to start talking *football*.

'I went to college at USC,' the man said as he looked out over the city. 'My dad too, so I've watched the Trojans play since I was a kid.' He turned to face Kelly then. 'And I remember this *asshole* who caught a one-handed touchdown against us in the Coliseum. It was a hell of a play.'

A hell of a play. Kelly's play. A moment that had shut the mouths of eighty thousand Trojan fans, and brought the screams of the visiting supporters in blue. It was the pinnacle of Kelly's football career, a story he'd often be asked to tell in sports bars across LA. Usually, he'd make a joke that the shark which took his hand must have been a Trojan supporter, but Kelly wasn't feeling much in the mood for jokes right now.

'You know I've actually met a couple of your teammates from that year?' Fowler went on, as though there weren't two burly men stood just meters away, their eyes on Kelly. 'Maurice Jones-Drew and Marcedes Lewis? We have friends in common. Do you still keep in touch with them?'

Kelly didn't. Those guys had been the stars of the show, destined for a life in the pros. Kelly's interactions with both had always been positive, but he didn't feel as if he could call either a friend.

'If you're worried that killing me will upset them,' Kelly spoke up, 'then it won't.'

Fowler pulled a puzzled expression at the words. 'Kill you?' he asked quietly, before pointing into the distance. 'Look over there, Josh Kelly. You see those lights? They belong to *my* festival. When you made that one-handed catch? *You* were a hero that day, and what you're doing right now, this . . . detective stuff. I get it, OK. It's your chance to be a hero again.'

Fowler pointed back at the lights. 'And that is mine. *I* am the hero in this story, Josh Kelly. I have brought hundreds of thousands of people together for an experience they will never forget. They will make friends that will last a lifetime. This city? It will make over a billion dollars because of my festival. Money into pockets, people into jobs.'

Fowler enjoyed that thought for a moment. 'Did you know that I took a pay freeze as CEO years ago? That's right. Profits go up, but I don't take any more. I even sold forty-nine per cent of my creation so that I could spread the enjoyment with people I love. I could make more money, sure, but instead I put that money back into free water. More medics. In our European shows, we even provide access for people to test their drugs, so that they can avoid nasty shit. Do you know how much something like that costs? I pay for that, because I love this festival, and I love these *people*.'

Kelly remained silent. The man's words swirled around them; Fowler was a picture of colorful passion.

'Do I want the festival tarnished by the deaths of Iris Manning and Blake Mathews?' he asked. 'Of course not. And it *is* a tragedy, but tragedy is something that the festival can weather. We've lost people from ecstasy use – or heat-related deaths, to be more exact. We won't be badly hurt by deaths that didn't even take place on the festival's site.'

Kelly didn't respond to that. With Sven Niklas as a friend and co-owner of the festival, he expected that any words he had shared with Rusa's owner would have been passed on to Fowler.

Pandora's creator was quiet for a moment. He looked towards the lights of his festival, and then at Kelly. His words were measured. No threat in them, just a simple plea for calm. 'I've got a lot of friends in this town, Josh Kelly,' he said gently, 'but do you know what I don't have?

'*Skeletons.* Look into me. Look into my company. My festival is the hottest shit in Vegas. I admire that you're looking out for a girl you've never even met, but sometimes you have to call a spade a spade, and a whore a whore.'

Kelly bristled, but Fowler wasn't done, and he shook his head with sadness.

'Sooner or later, girls in that line get what's coming to them . . . and she got hers.'

91

Kelly met Sanders at the foot of the Palms' Fantasy Tower. Thanks to a concealed carry permit she had two guns on her person, but there was no hiding her worry.

'Shit, Kelly, are you OK?'

Kelly's lips didn't move.

We need to talk, his expression told his friend, and she followed in his troubled wake.

There was nothing glamorous about the place where Kelly chose to unburden his soul. It was a small food court within the casino. A half-dozen people stuffed their faces with fast food, oblivious to what the handsome man on the nearby table was telling his friend – that the reason he had never made the LAPD was down to a drug-possession charge.

'The shark attack took me out of the academy.' Kelly breathed heavily. 'But I was getting back on track. I was getting physio. I had the limbs. I was getting there, Tonya, I really was, and then . . . and then . . .'

And then something had put him on his back. A bite out of his life bigger than any animal could take.

'What was it?' Sanders asked him without judgment.

Kelly wasn't ready to say.

Instead, they sat for a few moments in violent silence, Kelly's hand gripping the edge of the table tight. Sanders was worried that at any moment he could flip it, and so she spoke.

She spoke quietly, evenly, and as a friend. A true friend. One who did not judge. One that only loved.

'You know, Josh, I've seen just about every talk you've ever given. You talk about the shark; you talk about the physio. You talk about what it meant – how it *hurt* – to get taken out of that academy by fate . . .

'But I knew there was something else. Something that you weren't ready to open up about yet. I'm glad that you can do it with me, now. I'm *honored* that you can.'

Kelly shook his head. 'Fate didn't take my dreams, Tonya, *I* did.'

'When was that charge?' she asked him evenly.

'Four years ago.'

'And do you use drugs now?'

He didn't.

'That experience,' Sanders said, 'I bet in some ways it was as hard on you as the shark attack?'

Kelly didn't answer right away. 'Worse,' he finally muttered. Surviving a shark attack, he'd been a hero. When Kelly was arrested, he was a pariah. There were friends – the old ones, who weren't living on a diet of coke and Molly – who stopped calling. Kelly's parents didn't turn their backs, but in their looks Kelly had seen fear. Not fear of what would become of him, but fear *of him*, as though he were a dangerous junkie on skid row. Kelly's grandfather, a veteran and a hero to his grandson, lost all interest in 'the family failure.'

'You had a lot going on,' Sanders assured him.

Maybe. But the result was the same: arrest; record.

So were the names: junkie; loser.

'I tried to kill myself,' Kelly confessed, the words as sudden as they were numb.

'I know,' Sanders said gently.

Kelly looked up at her. His eyes asked how.

Her answer came easily. 'You could never have talked me back if you hadn't been there yourself.'

Kelly's depression sat heavy and dark on his shoulders, but something in Sanders's words cut through his misery. It wasn't flattery, but a recognition of something. A recognition that good could come from even the greatest of failures.

It was a recognition of purpose.

Kelly's purpose.

'I thought I got over it,' he told his friend, something of the true Kelly she knew coming out in the words. 'I thought I got over it, Tonya, but I don't think I've ever really . . .'

'. . . accepted it?'

Kelly nodded. 'It eats at me. I know that what I do now helps people. I know that I'm not a piece of shit. But when I think back, when I remember that day, and those months, I just . . . I just don't feel like I deserve to be here.'

Sanders reached out and put her hand on Kelly's. He saw the love of a sister in her eyes. 'Josh, you've run yourself into the dirt for a girl – a dead girl – that you never met. Fuck those nasty voices in your head. You deserve to be here, and if they say any differently I will climb inside of your head and beat the shit out of them.'

Kelly laughed then. They both did. It wasn't loud, it wasn't easy, but it was something.

'Thank you, Tonya. I love you.'

'I love you too, dweeb.'

Kelly sat back in his chair. A ghost of a smile threatened to break free. 'Dweeb?'

'Dweeb. I'm sticking with it.'

'All right.' Kelly put up his hands. 'You've got the guns.'

If only they had somewhere to aim them.

'The festival owner was a dead end?' Sanders asked after a long moment. She tried not to sound despondent, but that was a tough ask.

'I thought his security guys were going to throw me off the balcony,' Kelly admitted.

'*What?* Why?'

'I've watched too many Bond movies, I guess.' Kelly shrugged. 'The guy's worth a lot of money. It shouldn't have surprised me that during the festival he'd have security.'

'Well, someone wanted to take away attention from his baby. The missing wristbands from evidence prove that, and maybe . . .'

Kelly sat straighter. 'What?'

Sanders thought on it a moment longer. 'Iris's body was found at the opposite end of the city from the event. That's never really sat right with me.'

Kelly nodded. 'Sure, but if that was a move to draw attention from the festival, wouldn't they have taken her bands, too?'

Sanders folded her arms. 'Shit . . .'

'Who could have taken them?' Kelly asked, trying to come at it from another angle.

Sanders thought on that. 'A uniform on the scene. The coroner. His assistants.'

'You,' Kelly joked.

But something in the lame jab caught Sanders. '*A detective,*' she corrected him, her eyes narrowing as she pushed back from the table.

'Shit, Kelly. I think I know who it is.'

92

The sports bar in Henderson was a far cry from the tourist traps of the Strip, with more TVs than customers. Late in the day, the dozen screens were showing highlights of the evening's baseball from across the country.

Kelly and Sanders drew stares as they entered.

'The Peg-leg and Scarface Show,' Sanders muttered under her breath.

Two people in the bar kept looking longer than most. One was the rundown server behind the bar, who looked at Kelly as though he was a piece of bacon. The second was a man in a booth. He had a friend sitting opposite, and a beer in his hand. He raised it in salute to Sanders.

'Hey, Bobby,' she greeted Detective Brovetski. 'You remember my friend?'

He did. Kelly was the bait that Sanders had dangled to get an off-the-books meeting with the younger cop. Not one for building social ties herself, it had been Brovetski's fascination with Kelly's injuries that had given them the opening. Brovetski had suggested that they grab a beer sometime to hear Kelly's story, and now here they were.

But a lot had happened since then.

'I hear you knocked a guy's teeth out?' the stocky cop asked Sanders. 'What the shit?'

She gave a smile that looked more like a grimace. Brovetski turned to his friend. 'Hey, Kevin, do you mind giving us a . . .'

'Sure.'

'Office stuff.' Brovetski smiled to his buddy as he cleared the scene, and the two newcomers took the open side of the booth. 'So you hit him?' The younger man's eyes were full of mischief.

'I did.'

'Why?'

'Because he lied to me,' Sanders lied herself. She'd hit real-estate developer Gavin Brown because he was a douchebag, but it wouldn't hurt to have Brovetski think otherwise.

'I don't know which of you has the crazier story.' Brovetski laughed, taking a pull from his beer. 'You hear about the mountain lion?'

'Yeah.' Kelly spoke evenly, picturing the dead animal. 'I heard about the mountain lion. So which was it?'

The younger man looked puzzled. 'Which was what?'

'The mountain lion, or the DJ with the suicide note,' Kelly explained, his mouth smiling but his eyes strangling. 'Which one killed Iris Manning? She was a popular girl, right? Alive or dead, everyone wants a piece of her.'

Brovetski's brow knotted. He placed his beer on the table, and looked at Sanders. 'You know I can't discuss a case with a civilian.'

'You told the press a mountain lion killed a girl,' Kelly said, regardless.

'That was different.'

'How?'

Nothing.

Sanders: 'Are you taking the suicide note seriously?'

'I have to.' Brovetski shook his head. 'Fucking thing went viral. I gotta tie in with Riggins in the morning.'

Kelly: 'That's gonna be difficult for you.'

Brovetski: 'Why?'

Sanders: 'Because she's gonna want to know why you tampered with evidence.'

There. Out on the table.

Brovetski: 'Fuck you.'

He got up to move from his corner. Kelly moved faster. Nothing to draw attention, just a slide and a friendly smile that said, *Stay in your fucking seat.*

Brovetski looked across to Sanders. 'What's the plan, Tonya? You gonna hit me too?'

Sanders shrugged. 'Fuck it. I'm already out of a job.'

Silence held for a few heartbeats. Kelly knew a trapped animal when he saw one, and Brovetski was a rat.

'I know why you did it,' Sanders told him. 'And I don't care. I'm not on any case, Bobby, I just want the truth.'

A snort. 'The truth, huh?'

'Why did you take the wristbands from Iris's arms?'

Kelly saw it then. *The truth.* It flashed across Brovetski's eyes and raced across his face.

'Wristbands?'

'I know why you did it.' Sanders shrugged. 'You did it to keep the captain happy, because the captain wants to keep the Mayor happy, and the Mayor wants to keep the city happy. Tampering with evidence is a serious offense, Bobby. Worse than punching a few teeth out of a slimy douchebag.'

Brovetski did his best to feign nonchalance, and took a pull from his beer. 'If you had anything more than conspiracy theories we wouldn't be here.'

Sanders smiled. 'How many cases you seen me drop, Bobby?' Kelly saw that one hit home – *not many.* 'And I'm about to have a lot of time on my hands.'

'Oh fuck you, Tonya.'

'Just tell me who told you to take it.'

'Eat a dick.'

'I'm already going down, Bobby, and misery loves company. Just tell me who told you to take the wristbands. That's all we're looking for. We want the people that killed her. We want the people that put her out there. That's it.'

Bobby Brovetski stopped fidgeting then. Kelly saw a surge of anger build up inside of the man, and prepared himself to fight, but the break of that swell caused no waves. Rather, it was an exhalation of regret.

Brovetski slowly reached for his pocket, and placed something on the table.

It was his police star.

'Take a look at that, Tonya,' he told the woman opposite him. 'You see Bobby Brovetski written anywhere on that star? I see "Las Vegas". *Everything* I do is for this city. *Anything* I do is for this city. I *serve* the city.'

Sanders stared into the man's eyes. She knew that it was as close to an admission as she was ever going to get.

She tried anyway. 'Just give me a name, Bobby. All I need is a name. Why did you take the bands from evidence? Just give us a name.'

The younger detective sat back in his seat. He looked at his empty beer, and then back to Sanders. 'Just a name?'

'Just a name.'

Brovetski smirked.

'*Las Vegas.*'

93

'I don't like your friend.' Kelly tried to joke as they walked out the sports bar.

It didn't land well.

'Oh, fuck off, Kelly,' Sanders spat, but she regretted the words as soon as they left her mouth. 'Shit. Shit, I'm sorry, Josh. Fuck this case. I'm really sorry.'

'Don't worry about it.' Kelly half smiled, feeling the same frustration that had caused his friend to lash out.

'Seriously . . .' Sanders sighed, leaning back against the thick bumper of her truck. Then she surprised Kelly by taking something from her pocket.

'Cigarettes?' He raised his eyebrows as Sanders unwrapped the cellophane from a packet of Newport's.

Sanders cursed, a smoke between her lips. 'Shit. Been so long I forgot to get a damn lighter.'

'Take it as a sign from the universe.'

Sanders looked in vain for someone else who was smoking outside of the bar, but the lot was empty. She threw the useless cigarette on the ground. Then she threw down the rest of the pack too.

Kelly could recognize a volcano on the edge of eruption. He held his tongue as Sanders stamped repeatedly on the pack as though it was a snake and banged her hand hard against the truck's hood.

'Blake Mathews killed Iris, Kelly!' she simmered. 'Fuck. He fucking fooled us when we talked to him, but he knew the game was up, so he killed himself. You think a guy like that could have handled prison? He knew it, so once we were gone, he made his plan, and took himself out. *He beat us.*'

'I don't think Blake killed her,' Kelly tried carefully.

'He left a note, Kelly! He was a lovesick idiot with an unsound mind from detoxing off of drugs and alcohol. He was capable of anything.'

'And – what? Me getting shot at was just a coincidence?'

Sanders ground her teeth. 'Maybe it was a mistaken identity.'

'Mistaken identity? I'm six foot three and I've got a plastic arm and leg!'

'You said it yourself. It was dark.'

'Come on, Tonya.'

'Crazy shit happens in Vegas, Kelly. A guy killed fifty-eight people, and for what? Why shoot up a music festival? For all we know, you were at the wrong end of a gang initiation.'

'I don't believe that,' Kelly said firmly. 'And I don't think that you do either.'

Sanders crossed her arms. She kept a lid on her frustration, but barely. It rattled as she steamed. 'Look, Kelly, this is exactly what it looks like. Boy meets girl. Boy gets his heart broken. Boy kills girl. Boy kills boy. It's Shakespeare one oh one.'

'I don't think that Blake had murder in him.'

Sanders couldn't hold her sarcasm. 'Based off of your experience? You haven't been a cop for fifteen years, Kelly. You haven't lived in Vegas for forty-five. Everyone – *everyone* – has a seed within them that can turn bad, and if they don't, then Vegas will plant one.'

The words hurt Kelly's ego. He took a few deep breaths to try and control the frustration. 'If that's true,' he said as calmly as he could, 'then why have you stayed?'

Sanders snorted. For the first time since knowing each other, Kelly saw ugliness on her face. 'You don't get to choose your family, Kelly, or your cases, but I'm done with this one. I'm gonna call it as I see it. Iris played with fire, and she got burned. R-I-fucking-P.'

Kelly said nothing. He didn't trust himself to speak.

'Get in,' Sanders told him, moving to the door of her truck. 'We need to get some sleep. Iris's parents will be here in the morning. I might be off the case, but I found her. I'm not gonna let that shit Brovetski be the one that talks to them, but they're not gonna want to speak to a zombie, either.'

It was too much for Kelly. Too much negativity. Too much anger. Too much judgment. Restless days and emotional waves caught up to him in one huge crash, dragging him under, pulling him into the riptide of rage.

'You're right,' he told the person he'd thought he knew so well. 'You're right, Sanders. Iris's parents won't want to talk to a zombie when they get here. They'll want to talk to a *fucking cop*.'

Kelly turned his back, and walked away.

94

Kelly heard a 'Fuck you' and a door slam as he walked away. Then he heard the big truck's engine fire up. As Sanders screeched out of the parking lot, he saw her hold her middle finger up in his direction, her eyes staring intently ahead.

'Shit,' Kelly snarled, but he was too angry to run after her, even if his leg weren't aching like a rotten tooth.

Kelly took out his phone and ordered an Uber. He needed to. . . he needed to . . .

Do what? What the fuck do you think you're going to do?

Kelly sat down on the sidewalk. The concrete was still hot, but the voice inside his head was hotter – he knew that he'd fucked up by snapping at Sanders, and if *she* wasn't a cop, then what was he? Did he seriously think he could just show up in town and fix the world's problems? He'd always been hard on himself for fucking up his shot at becoming a cop, but now, for the first time, Kelly wondered if maybe his criminal record was a blessing in disguise. Is this what he wanted? To bang his head against a wall? To make enemies? To lose friends?

You never had what it took anyway, Kelly told himself, his eyes on the ground and chin on his chest. *You never had what it took, so fuck it.*

FUCK IT.

There was only one thing left for him to do now.

It took Kelly less than five seconds to send the message that would change his life.

Are you awake?

Playing the hero hadn't saved him.

Maybe drugs would.

95

Aussie DJ Chris Herbert's suite was on the corner of the Cosmopolitan's tower; a dozen people lounged about on sofas or smoking on the wraparound balcony that peered down onto the center of the Strip. It was not the same kind of grandiose design that Kelly had seen in the Sky Suites at the Palms, but still . . .

'Not cheap,' Herbert told him after the red-eyed man had broken his embrace. The Aussie was wearing a Slayer T-shirt with cut sleeves, and swimming shorts that were still damp. 'Got a hot tub in the back,' he explained; then he winked and pointed towards a beautiful blonde girl on the balcony. 'What's up with you?' he asked Kelly when he realized that his friend's usual energy was absent. 'You look like your fucking dog died, mate.'

Not a dog, Kelly thought. *One of his closest friendships.*

'I fucked up,' he told the man simply.

Herbert shrugged at that. 'We all fuck up, mate, and the best way to get over it is to *get* fucked up. Want some coke?'

'Yeah.' The word was out of Kelly's mouth before he'd even thought about it. *You wanted this since the moment things got bad,* he snapped at himself. *Don't fucking kid yourself.*

342

'You really do look like you've been fucked with your own leg,' Herbert said, a statement of concern. 'You sure you want to party? We can go get a beer somewhere if you like? I don't even know who half this lot are.'

Kelly shook his head. 'I'm good.'

'Few lines, then?'

'Yeah.'

Herbert turned and faced the room. 'Oi, you cunts? Who's got my fucking coke?'

The DJ wandered off to find it, leaving Kelly by the door. He needed air. The suite's balcony was huge, and Kelly found a deserted spot. He leaned against the rails, and looked at the city below him, full of light and promise.

Kelly ran a hand through his hair. Like so many others, he hadn't beaten the odds.

'Where's my fucking coke?' Herbert shouted again in the room behind him, and Kelly knew that soon that powder would be going from a plate and up his nose. It wouldn't stop there. Kelly wasn't sure if it would stop at all. As he looked down to the ground below him, he didn't even know if he cared.

His phone vibrated. He ignored it at first. He didn't want to face Sanders, but . . .

But hope. A glimmer of it. A splinter. Enough to push its way into the darkness and to ask the question . . .

What if?

What if this is the call that builds a bridge? What if this is a call that breaks the case?

Kelly looked at the screen. It started with +702.

A Vegas number.

A splinter of hope.

'Hello?'

'Josh Kelly?'

A woman. A young one. A familiar voice that Kelly couldn't place.

'Yeah?'

A deep breath. A long exhalation. A moment of no turning back, for both of them.

'Josh . . . I know who killed Iris.'

96

Josh Kelly was on edge as he stood watching a steady stream of Ubers and taxis ferrying passengers in and out the Cosmopolitan. The evening was growing old, and giving way to true night. Legs were wobbly and laughs were raucous as Sin City's clientele looked to finish the weekend with a bang. Kelly watched every person come and go. Every peacocking young man, every hunched old lady. He watched them all.

He watched them all, because he was *scared*.

A few hours ago, someone had tried to take his life. He didn't believe those bullets had been fired because they were part of some gang initiation, or a case of mistaken identity. Someone had shot at him in that dark street because of the truth. A truth that he had given up trying to find until a phone call, and the promise of an identity. A promise of a killer. A promise of justice.

You really do want to be a hero, Kelly admitted to himself. *But this isn't about you. This is about Iris.*

But it *was* about him too, and he knew it. His shot at redemption. His chance to prove himself. A hope that bringing justice to one crime would wash away the stain of his own mistakes.

Concentrate, man. You're not safe.

He wasn't. Whoever had tried to kill him was still out there, but who was it? From the festival's owner to local detectives, Kelly's search for the truth had pulled feathers and bumped heads. Pride could be fatal regardless of circumstance, and Kelly had bruised enough egos in town that he was certain this weekend would haunt him, regardless of the outcome of Iris's mystery.

Josh Kelly was no spy or former Special Ops soldier, but he was doing his best to try and think that way. After taking the call on Herbert's balcony, Kelly'd asked his friend if he could use the concierge to bring him some new clothing. That kind of request was nothing out of the ordinary, and now Kelly had a 'Golden Knights' cap on his head, and a light hoodie over his tee. All were black, and Kelly hoped that any shots in the dark would be made a little harder because of his outfit.

You're actually considering the possibility that you will get shot at, a voice spoke up in Kelly's head. *Are you fucking crazy? You're not your brother! Go back to Orange County before you get yourself killed!*

But there was another voice in Kelly's head. One that was calm, measured, and intractable. It simply said . . .

No.

No. Kelly would not be leaving. He knew in his gut that this was the test that would prove his worth. If not? Well, there were drugs, and there was oblivion – and this go around, Josh Kelly had enough money in the bank that it could only lead to an early grave.

He saw her then, the driver's window down as she rolled the metallic-blue Mustang to a stop. Kelly moved to the passenger side so quickly that the driver jumped in her seat as he opened the door.

'Shit!' Stephanie Wilson breathed, Kelly seeing that the girl was flush with nervous excitement. 'You scared me.'

Kelly had no time to give his apologies to Rusa's bottle-service girl. Only questions.

One question.

'*Who killed Iris?*'

Fear tried to hold her lips together, but she bravely pushed it aside.

'Sam Chao,' Stephanie told him, her eyes burning into Kelly's.

'Sam Chao killed Iris.'

97

The Mustang came out the Cosmopolitan and took a right onto Las Vegas Boulevard, the Strip oblivious to the fact that two near strangers were talking murder.

'Why did you come to me?' Kelly asked as they settled into traffic. Jammed between other cars, beneath bright lights and in the open, Kelly'd figured that Las Vegas Boulevard was a good place for them to talk.

'I saw Blake's "suicide note,"' Stephanie replied. 'It's fucking bullshit. That's not him. He couldn't hurt a fly. He loved that stupid bitch.'

Kelly's gut was on the same page, but: 'Love makes people do crazy things,' he said all the same.

'Crazy like killing himself? Someone like Blake? I can . . . Look, I can see him doing some fucked-up Romeo and Juliet romantic bullshit like that, but killing *her*? No fucking way. It was Chao.' Once again she accused the high-rolling businessman.

'Why do you think that?'

'Because the guy's a fucking creep! And not like the losers that just want some attention. I mean he's the kind of creep on a power trip. The kind that thinks he can get whatever he wants.'

'Was he like that with you?'

'He's like that with *all* the girls! Guys like him, because they have money, they think they can have anything. They think because they're spending money at the club they own the girls, like we're fucking property. I swear the only reason he'd request Iris is because she put up with his shit. She probably encouraged it, too.'

'That's a long jump to murder,' Kelly tried to say as diplomatically as possible.

'Don't think I'm some ditzy bitch, Josh. Look, this one night at Rusa about a year and a half ago, Chao came in with a few buddies, and was doing his usual high-roller shit. I think Iris was his server, but whatever, that's not the point. The point is that he'd brought some girls with him, and one of these girls was blacked out at the table. I mean, I don't know if she'd had too much Molly, or G, or what, but she was gone, dude. She had no idea what was going on. So one of our staff sees this, and tells the bouncers. It's not a good look for the club, you know, but it's not good for the girl either! She needs taking care of.'

With sickening certainty, Kelly knew where the story was headed.

'So the bouncers report it up,' Stephanie went on, 'and everyone gets told not to interfere. The girl was at Chao's table, he was spending a lot of money, and he wasn't to be upset. Isn't that disgusting?'

It was. And it wasn't the first time that Kelly had seen or heard of it happening in the high-end clubs of Vegas and LA.

'What happened to her?' he asked, sensing that there was more.

'Chao left with her. The next day, she went to the police and reported that he'd raped her.'

Kelly let out a deep sigh at the sickness of the world. 'How do you know this?'

'Everyone at Rusa knew,' Stephanie explained. 'The police came to ask for statements. Can you guess how that went?'

Kelly could. 'No one had a bad word to say about Chao.'

Stephanie nodded angrily. 'And the girl was labeled a slut. A troublemaker. A gold digger.'

'Jesus.'

'Yeah. Chao's lawyers steamrolled her. I think they countersued for slander, or some shit like that.'

Kelly didn't know what to say, but the girl spoke for them both. 'That's just how it is here. Money talks. But this guy's a creep, I'm telling you, Josh. Blake didn't do it. Chao killed Iris, and framed him.'

Kelly thought that the story left no doubt that Chao was a dirtbag, but that didn't make him guilty of committing murder, or framing another for it.

'Why didn't you tell me this when we talked at the night swim?' Kelly asked, the memory nagging at him.

Stephanie turned to look at him, searching for judgment, and relaxing when she found none.

'Because I thought she'd died in some accident,' she said. 'But then I saw the note on Facebook. I told Rusa I

350

had an emergency with my kid so I could duck out and talk to you. I had to, once I heard the other girls talking.'

'Talking about what?'

'Blake, and Chao.'

'Why Chao?'

'He left the club the other night, and Iris scooted out thirty minutes after him without finishing her shift. She's done it before. You don't have to be a genius to figure out why.'

With a look, Kelly played ignorant.

'*Because she was fucking him,*' Stephanie spelt out.

It was a fact Chao had admitted to Kelly himself. 'That doesn't mean that he killed her . . .'

It did to Stephanie. 'He killed her. I know it.'

But she didn't. She *suspected* it. 'Do you know where Chao is now?' Kelly asked.

'The festival or his suite, I guess?'

Kelly looked ahead. The Grand Casino & Hotel loomed ahead of them, a glittering monolith of the Strip. Within it was Rusa, and the suite of Sam Chao. What Stephanie had told Kelly was a thin lead, but it was something, at least.

Kelly wasn't done with Vegas.

98

The Grand's front desk were helpful, but no help.

'I'm sorry, sir,' said the attendant with her phone to her ear. 'But I'm not getting any answer from Mr Chao's room. Is he expecting you?'

'No. Thank you,' Kelly added as he walked away, realizing that maybe the man's absence was a blessing – what exactly did he think was going to happen when he confronted him? That Chao would just blurt out a confession because Kelly would like one?

With a sickening lurch, Kelly grasped that he couldn't approach the accusations head on. He'd need to look for a point of weakness. A vulnerability. And to do that, he'd need to be on the inside.

He'd need to be Chao's friend.

Kelly took out his phone, and searched for a number. He hit call.

'Pandora VIP?' a young man answered, the background boom of bass coming down the line. 'How can I help you?'

'Hi. I'm a friend of Sam Chao's. He invited me to his VIP section, but I'm not really sure how to go about getting there?'

'Did you say Sam Chao?' the guy asked after a moment.

'Yeah.'

'Sam closed out already, I'm afraid,' the man explained, meaning that Chao had settled his bill and left the venue. 'I'd love to be able to let you in there anyway, but we already sold that section onto another client, I'm sorry.'

'No worries. Thanks for your help.

'*Shit,*' Kelly swore softly to himself once the line went dead.

Something about Chao leaving the festival bothered Kelly. The third and final night's closing ceremony was a firework display that cost half a million dollars to put together, and was not the kind of thing that people wanted to miss. Kelly doubted that Chao was keen to leave just to get a jump on traffic – if anyone was going to be flying in and out of a festival by helicopter, it was a baller like Chao.

Stephanie had promised to let Kelly know if Chao showed up at Rusa, but the night was young as far as clubs were concerned. No sign of Chao there, either.

So where is he? Kelly asked himself, refusing to believe that Chao would bail out of the festival's climax to go get a steak, or take in the Blue Man Group.

Running a hand through his hair, Kelly knew that he had a sniff of something rotten, but whatever caused the stink was hidden behind a brick wall. To break it down, Kelly would need a sledgehammer.

Swallowing his pride, he made the call for one.

99

Kelly leaned back against the wall and pretended to be interested in his phone as he watched the elevators that went up to the Grand's executive floors. Kelly'd already made one attempt at the sliding doors that could only be opened by key card, but the one gifted to him by Arabella Robins had expired, and Kelly didn't want to draw attention to himself by trying to get it renewed – an attempt that would no doubt require sanctioning from Rusa's management.

And so Kelly waited. He waited, he watched, and he thought about the woman that he had woken up beside that morning.

Those thoughts unsettled him.

They unsettled him because of what Stephanie had told him about the blacked-out girl at Chao's table. Vulnerable, the girl should have been escorted off the premises, either home, or into the care of law enforcement. She should not have been allowed to stay at the club. She should not have been allowed to be taken to the suite of a stranger.

And who had given those orders? Who'd told the bouncers and the bottle-service girls not to interfere, in case they upset the big spender? Stephanie had said that the incident had taken place eighteen months ago.

Arabella Robins was the club's manager at that time.

But Kelly shook his head. Everything that he had witnessed about the woman said that she was strong and passionate. He couldn't conceive that she was the person responsible for overlooking such behavior. That she could have been the one to back Chao, and to shut the door in the face of a girl who'd had the courage to speak out about what had happened to her.

Kelly had attended talks given by rape victims. Such awareness presentations had burned figures into his skull, and so he was aware that one in six women in the US would suffer either an attempted, or complete rape. He was aware that the chances of a rapist going to jail were pitifully low, and less than that of a robber. Kelly was aware of these things, but did he *understand* them? No.

But he understood courage, and for that girl to come forward had taken a lot of it. The courage to stand up, and demand to be heard. The courage to suffer the sickening slander of others. The whispers. The implied guilt. Was it little wonder that so few victims spoke out?

Kelly shook his head. If Arabella Robins had been a part of killing that courage for the benefit of a company . . .

If she had taken dollars over the truth . . .

Business over justice . . .

Kelly knew that he was going to have a hard time looking her in the eye. The truth was, he felt sick to his stomach from the whole thing, and – with a crushing admission of guilt – Kelly knew that he'd been a party to such things too. Football teams were not halls of saints. Neither were police locker rooms, even at the academy.

Kelly had heard stories that had offended his sensibilities, but had he spoken up? Maybe a handful of times, sure. The rest of the time? He'd forced a smile. *Boys will be boys.*

He ran the flesh of his right hand over his face, and hoped that it would wash his sense of shame away.

It didn't.

But Kelly forced himself to pause his self-recrimination as he saw a couple heading for the elevator. With his hoodie in his hand and his prosthetic arm displayed, Kelly began to follow them. Then it was a simple matter of fumbling with the hand into his pocket, as though searching for a key.

'We'll get that for you.' The man smiled. Like many, he mistook disfigurement for disability. It was a well-meaning trait that Kelly now took advantage of. 'What floor?'

Kelly gave them Chao's.

He took advantage of human nature again a moment later, once he was in the corridor, asking a housekeeper for fresh towels, and then dropping them clumsily with the prosthetic. The older woman looked sorry for the handsome young man so handicapped, and bent to pick them up for him. As she did so, Kelly nimbly took her key card from the cart. Preconceptions weren't all bad, especially when it came to breaking into someone's hotel suite.

A few moments later, Kelly was at the door that he had seen in the video shown to him by Rusa's owner. Kelly knocked, and prepared a smile should the door be opened by Chao. He had a story concocted about bros, and partying, but the fable wouldn't be needed. Kelly knocked again. Nothing.

Taking a deep breath, he ran the housekeeper's card through the strip.

The LED turned green.

Kelly pushed the door open, and broke into Chao's suite.

100

'Hello?'

There was no one home. No one that he could see, anyway.

Kelly stepped inside, putting his hands in his pockets so that he wouldn't be tempted to touch anything. He knew that he should wait, he knew that he should call a professional, but . . .

But housekeeping was working its way along the corridor, and Chao was a suspect to no one but Stephanie and Kelly. He had to act now.

Kelly decided that he should film it all. *Everything.* Document the room.

A well-stocked fridge. More drinks on the countertop, all unopened. The bed was made, but not to housekeeping's high standards. There were used condoms in the bathroom trash can. No blood. Nothing broken. The suite was tasteful and large, and from the preparation with the drinks, Kelly expected that it had been due to host a party that night. So why the change in plans? Where was Chao? Where were his clothes? His travel cases? Except for the used condoms, not a single personal item remained.

So where was he?

Kelly walked over to the window and peered out. He saw lights in the sky, descending towards McCarran International. At the back of the weekend, flights in were at their cheapest, while flights *out* of Sin City were at their premium. Sometimes, if your destination was in a nearby state, it could even work out cheaper to club together for a private jet.

The thought struck Kelly hard.

A private jet.

Kelly looked at the lights of the airport. Then he ran for the door.

He had to make it to the airport *now*, or Chao would be gone for good.

101

The stump of Kelly's leg burned hideously as he raced to the elevator, across the casino's floor, and out the Grand's main entrance. The hour was late enough that many were calling it a night after dinner, drinks, and shows, and the line for a taxi was long and winding.

'Sorry! My wife's in labor!' Kelly shouted as he cut to the head of the line.

'Congratulations!' someone shouted, and the entire booze-soaked line erupted into applause that followed Kelly into the back of the cab.

'Where to?' the cabbie asked him.

'McCarran private terminal.'

The cabbie was astonished. 'Your wife's having a baby *on a plane?*'

Kelly said nothing. Instead, he pulled the handful of twenties from his pocket and put them into the man's hand. 'Just go! Please! Fast!'

Kelly looked at his phone, and Maps. He was tracking someone's location. They were ahead of him, less than a mile from the private terminal.

Wait for me, he prayed silently.

A chain-link fence was Kelly's first indication that they were close to the airport. Then he saw the runway lights behind it. As the cabbie pulled to a stop in the isolated private terminal's parking lot, Kelly was already moving out of the door and shouting his thanks.

With relief, he saw that his prayers had been answered.

Sanders.

102

'Apologies later,' Sanders told Kelly. 'From both of us. I know what you're like,' she added with a short smile, 'and we'll be here talking about meditation retreats until sunrise.'

'Apologies later,' Kelly agreed, but there was still time for an embrace, which said everything that he could not. That Sanders was a true friend – family – and that Kelly hated himself for having lost his faith in her.

'Get in the truck,' she told him. 'I called ahead. Chao's jet was scheduled to fly out at five p.m. tomorrow.'

Her grimace told Kelly that had changed. 'How long do we have?'

'Twenty minutes. I've already talked to the security on the gate. We're good to go.'

The truck rolled to a stop alongside the security barrier to the airfield. People paying for private flights do it for expediency as much as anything else, and being driven to the door of your jet was part of the fun. A dozen planes sat on the tarmac now, and Kelly could see that two had their lights on, and were preparing for departure.

'Hand me your driver's license,' Sanders asked, showing that and her badge to the security guard. As she was on administrative leave, rather than suspension, the identification of her profession had not been taken from her.

After a cursory look into the truck's rear, the barrier was raised. Sanders was waved on, but her truck was not the only thing moving on the tarmac.

'Shit,' she growled.

A jet was beginning to taxi.

'It has to be Chao.' Kelly agreed. 'They're taking off from the far end of the runway. They'll have to taxi there.' He hit the dash then, the blow stinging through his hand. He could see that they were too late: 'Goddamn it! Goddamn it, Tonya, we were so fucking close!'

Sanders said nothing, but Kelly heard every word.

'No,' he said simply, seeing her eyes narrow, and her stare fix onto the taxiing jet. 'No, Tonya. No.'

Yes.

She floored the accelerator and the heavy truck pulled forwards like a charging bull. The private jet was still on the parking pan, short of the airport's taxiing lanes, but . . .

'Tonya, this will mean your career!'

Did she just smile?

'Fuck it. It's done anyway.'

'We don't even have facts! Just theories! What about evidence?'

'Fuck evidence.'

'You can't do this, Tonya! You're a cop!'

Sanders took her eyes from the plane, and fixed them on the man beside her. The man who had called her identity into question. Her *soul*. 'That's right, Kelly,' she said simply. 'I *am* a cop.'

The jet was close. Fifty meters. Thirty. Sanders passed it on the right, then hit a hard slew that brought her truck's back end around like a whip, leaving her side on to the aircraft's nose. A split second later, she was out of the cab with a badge in her hand and defiance on her face.

The aircraft stopped.

She was a cop.

103

The first thing Kelly noticed as he stepped out were flashing lights at the terminal, and the shape of a security car moving towards them. The second was the jet's opening door.

'Security's coming,' Kelly told her friend, as though she could have missed them. The car was rapid, and would reach them within twenty seconds.

'You go on.' Sanders spoke firmly. 'I'll deal with them.'

Kelly was already moving for the door, but he asked anyway: 'And what if Chao has a gun?'

Sanders shrugged. 'Then you'll get a cool scar.'

Kelly ran, and took the jet's steps in two, ducking his head as he boarded the aircraft.

No bullets came his way. Only a rapid fire of insults.

'Who the fuck do you think you are?' Chao seethed, standing in the aisle between the cabin's plush seats. He was alone, but he could swear for a dozen, and the words poured onto Kelly like acid rain.

Kelly waited until Chao paused for breath. 'I'm here for Iris,' he said. 'I think you probably want to talk to me about that.'

Chao looked as though he was about to turn purple. Then he violently shook one of the seats. Kelly didn't have time for the tantrum. 'Security are less than ten seconds away. Talk to me, or talk to them. I'll go down, Chao, but I'll take your miserable ass with me. Only way you leave Vegas right now is by talking.'

'Fuck you!' Chao shouted, but nonetheless he turned his attention to the pilot who stood open-mouthed at the cockpit door; the man had been in the private flight game long enough to know that you don't interfere with egotistical clients and their disputes.

'Get rid of them!' Chao ordered the pilot as the flashing lights of the security car began to wash through the jet's windows. 'Tell them that they brought me my fucking wallet or something! Go! Go!'

The pilot went for the steps. Kelly stared down Chao. After a moment of shaking, the shorter man slumped into a seat, kicking a glass of wine from a table as he did so.

'I thought we were going to be friends,' he said petulantly, the childish accusation striking Kelly with its absurdity – the big spender was more worried about his popularity than the sickening allegations that were about to be leveled against him.

Kelly shook his head. 'Did you kill Iris?'

Chao stuck up two fingers. 'I've never killed anyone, you piece of shit.'

'You're running from Vegas for a reason.'

Fiery eyes told Kelly whom he was running from. 'You didn't give me a choice!' The businessman folded his arms.

He really did look like a scolded child, Kelly thought. Either he didn't get enough attention as a kid, or maybe too much, and now life and the people in it were nothing but fuel for his ego. 'Talk, Chao.'

'I got accused . . .' Chao began, clearly sensing that it was a great injustice. 'Some bullshit accusation of rape eighteen months ago, from a girl I met in Rusa.'

'So?' Kelly didn't buy it. 'You were cleared,' he added, though he knew that cleared did not equal innocent.

'I was fucking Iris the night she died!' Chao said as if to an idiot. 'And I've been accused of rape in the same building. How does that look when it all comes out?'

Bad. That was why Kelly was here. 'Didn't you see his post on the news?' he asked. 'Blake Mathews killed Iris.'

Chao rolled his eyes at that. 'It's my DNA they're going to find on her, maybe inside her. I'm not waiting around for that. They can come to me, and come to my lawyers.'

'If you're innocent, stay and prove it.'

'And spend even one night locked up? Fuck you.' Chao shook his head in frustration. 'You heard about the girl. The one that accused me.'

Kelly gave a shallow nod.

'I paid for her flights here from Seattle. I paid for her hotel. I paid for the beach club. I paid for the nightclub. Did she think there wasn't a price? Can anyone be that stupid? No! She used me, and I used her. She let herself be bought like an object, so I treated her like one!'

Chao defied Kelly to say different; then he went on. 'Fucking idiots have made women think that they can behave like whores, then turn the tables once they have money and fame! Everything comes at a price! *Everything!*

Kelly's hands twitched with violence. There was almost nothing he wanted more than to put Chao's nose through the back of his head, but there was one thing, and that was the truth.

Chao had recognized that truth in his eyes, and played on it. 'You can try and stop me leaving,' the shorter man said, 'and I'll call my lawyers, you'll call the police, and we'll all suffer the shit storm. A shit storm that I, eventually, will walk out of.

'Or,' Chao offered, 'I can give you a name, a time, and a motive, and you can get out of my fucking way.'

Kelly's heart thumped. He wanted to see Chao humiliated, but he had come for the truth . . .

He unclenched his fists.

'Tell me who.'

104

'Sven Niklas.'

Kelly tried to hide his astonishment.

He failed.

'He was furious that Iris was fucking me,' Chao explained. 'And do you think I was the only one? She probably did it with most of the club's big spenders, and if people got wind that there was an "escort service" working out of that place? It could shut the whole thing down. Kill Sven's baby.'

Kelly could see that the man had more to tell. 'Spit it out, Chao. Neither of us has time.'

The businessman sneered. 'Sven had a thing for Iris,' he revealed. 'It was jealousy, too. Look what happened to Blake Mathews,' he went on as Kelly stayed silent. 'You see any other DJs getting fired for drink and drugs?'

Kelly hadn't.

'What more do you want?' Chao asked. 'I've told you everything. Probably make you a fucking hero.'

What more did he want? Kelly thought about everything that Chao had told him. It all made sense.

But there was something else in Kelly's mind. Something that he had been aching for since Stephanie had told him about the passed-out girl at Chao's table. How his lawyers had steamrolled her after she had had the courage to speak up.

'You wanted to know more about my arm?' Kelly asked Chao, who stared back in confusion. 'See what it could do?'

Too late, Chao realized the threat. In one swift movement Kelly reached out, grabbed the shitbag's head, and ploughed it into the nearest table. Chao bounced once, and then fell like a slinky onto the jet's carpeted floor.

Kelly used the foot of his prosthetic to turn the man's head up to face him. Chao looked up from his back, his nose smashed and his eyes fearful. Kelly hoped that he was still conscious. He wanted Chao to remember this lesson for a long time.

'Everything comes at a price, right?'

105

Kelly walked to the door of the private jet. The pilot looked from him to the slumped and groaning form of Chao on the floor, but one hard glance from Kelly told him that it would be a mistake to interfere.

Outside, Sanders waited behind the wheel of her truck, her cab bathed in the rotating orange light of the security vehicle that waited to escort them from the pan. There would be repercussions for their actions, Kelly knew, but sometimes it took sweat and tears to get results, and other times subpoenas and lawsuits. Nothing came easy, and as he took the steps down to the tarmac, Kelly could at least assure himself that it had been worth it. Even if all that he had gained was to put a shitbag's head into an expensive table, it had been worth it.

Kelly climbed up into the cab beside his friend. She looked at him for a long moment. At first there was relief, then: 'I've never seen you look like this.'

Concern.

Kelly didn't need to ask her what that look was. He could feel it in the darkest recesses of his soul. It was the law of the jungle. It was millions of years of survival and evolution untamed by suits and ties, houses and courtrooms. At best it was caged, but the bars of Kelly's mind were strong. There was a greater purpose to his actions than a moment of aggressive satisfaction. He would not give in to simple retribution.

He told Sanders what had happened. 'I shouldn't have done it,' he acknowledged. 'But I did.'

Sanders made no sign of judgment. She followed on behind the security car, the shape of Chao's jet becoming a nasty memory in the mirror. Having swung her fists herself in the cause of morality, she was in no place to judge, only to empathize. She sighed. 'Fuck him. But there's gonna be consequences, Josh.'

'I don't care.' They were maybe the most honest words he'd ever spoken. He looked at where they were. Thought of what they'd done. 'They're not gonna just let you skate on this either.'

'We're OK for now,' Sanders told him, meaning the security. 'They think we did it for a client, and that's all they care about.'

'For now.'

'For now.'

Kelly almost smiled then. He saw the look on her face. The set to her shoulders. She was a hunting dog with a scent in her nostrils, and nothing would distract Sanders from her prey. Kelly told her all that Chao had said. They were out of the airfield's gates by the time Kelly had finished. At best, they were on borrowed time.

'Do you think Niklas could have killed Iris?' Sanders asked. She was driving them towards the Strip. Like so many others, they felt an irresistible pull towards the bright lights.

'I don't know,' Kelly said honestly. 'What Chao said made sense, but . . . I just didn't see it in him.'

'Sometimes you don't.' the experienced cop shared gently. 'Sometimes the killer is some skin-headed prick that just oozes violence. Sometimes he looks like your favorite uncle.'

'Do we have enough to take it to your captain?' Kelly asked in hope, but Sanders shook her head.

'Everything we have is circumstantial. And the next time he sees me he's as likely to throw my ass in a cell as listen to me. We need something, Kelly.'

They sat in silence as they turned over every moment, every conversation, every action. In the end, it was one of Kelly's questionable ones that produced the lifeline they needed.

'What's going on?' Sanders asked as his phone began to vibrate urgently, a series of messages streaming through.

Kelly paused a moment before he told her. 'I may have broken the law.'

The detective took in the measure of her friend. 'How badly?'

He looked out the window. 'Badly enough.'

Sanders breathed out . . . 'Was it worth it?'

It was.

'I know how to get Niklas to talk.' Kelly held up his phone, scrolling through a dozen messages. 'I just need to show him these.'

Sanders tried, and failed, to be positive. 'Just like that, huh, Josh? You'll show him some messages, he'll confess, and he gets arrested. Sure.'

'No, T.' Kelly shook his head. She'd completely misunderstood him. 'You'll arrest him when he tries to kill me.'

106

Kelly walked alone into the Grand Casino. He was a worm on a hook, but he wasn't wriggling just yet. With dozens of cameras in the ceiling, and witnesses on the carpet, Kelly was calm enough to know that what he was about to do was dangerous not just in a physical sense, but in the legal too. Kelly's journey to find Iris's killer had started with a need to uphold law and order, but in the past twenty-four hours he had himself become guilty of trespassing, assault, and more. Kelly'd always known that the lines blurred in 'police work,' but his own picture of right and wrong was beginning to resemble a Jackson Pollock. If it wasn't for the image of Iris lying dead and abandoned in a dusty canyon, maybe Kelly would have questioned such actions, but remembering her dead eyes, he knew that there were a lot of laws that he'd break to bring her justice.

And there was more.

It made him uncomfortable to even acknowledge the thought, but Kelly could not deny that he had always wanted to be the hero. The knight in shining armor. The cowboy in the showdown. Here, the beauty on the train tracks had already met her maker, but Kelly believed in the soul, and if he could not save the girl's life, then maybe he could save her spirit. Maybe bringing justice to Iris's killers would see her at peace in the next life, in whatever form that took.

'Are you OK?'

The question came from a woman's voice. One that he knew.

Kelly turned. As he took in her olive skin and feline eyes, he felt a reassurance from her presence.

'Arabella.' He smiled. It wasn't a strong one. It was a show of trust. A signal of his vulnerability.

Robins took in the sight of him. 'You look . . .'

'Yeah.'

'What happened?'

Kelly left out the details. He left out the shooting, and the threats, and the fights. He needed this woman. He needed her to think that he was in need of assistance, but still at the controls. That was important. She didn't need to know that the plane was going down in flames. 'Can we talk inside?'

By inside he meant Rusa. The line for the nightclub was shorter than it had been the night before.

'We expect to get busy from about two till five,' Robins explained, mistaking his look – Kelly wasn't looking for customers. He was looking for witnesses.

'The festival has its finale at midnight,' she went on. 'Nobody wants to miss the fireworks.'

Nobody except Chao, Kelly thought to himself.

'I really need to speak to Sven,' he said as Robins led them into her office.

Instead of acknowledging that, Robins leaned back against her desk. Just enough so that her chest was pushing forwards, and an elegant arch appeared in the line of her neck. There was no mistaking what she wanted.

She said it anyway. 'Sven can wait.'

A million other times, yes. But—

'Not now.'

Robins's eyes narrowed.

'I really want to get together after all this is done,' Kelly said, not knowing if he meant it. Robins softened . . . a little.

'Why do you want Sven,' Robins teased, 'and not me?' She gave him a look that promised so much.

It almost worked.

Kelly took a half-step back. 'I think I've found something that confirms Blake's guilt,' he lied. 'I need Sven's opinion before I take it to the police.'

Her feline eyes met his and flashed wildly. 'You did?' She shook her head. 'That piece of shit. I used to think he was such a great kid. Troubled, but . . . yeah. Jesus. I'll . . . I'll go find Sven.'

Kelly was expecting a goodbye kiss. Some stamp of Robins's to remind him that he was hers for later.

None came. She closed the door, and left Kelly alone in her office.

He looked at his phone and checked the service: good signal. That was important because Sanders was tracking his location, waiting armed and ready inside of the casino.

If he called, she'd come. If he didn't call by thirty minutes past midnight, she was coming in anyway.

'He won't pull a gun in the casino,' Sanders had promised her friend, trying to reassure him. 'If you're right, Sven will either run, or bribe you, but you'll be safe so long as you stay on the casino's property. Stay in sight of the cameras. Stay where there are witnesses.'

Kelly grimaced as he thought back on that advice, and looked at his surroundings. Robins had been willing to fuck him on her desk – there were no cameras here. There were certainly no witnesses, either.

'Shit.' He'd made a mistake. Kelly thought for a moment about leaving, but to where? The guts of Rusa would be 'off the grid,' and Kelly needed Sven to feel comfortable enough to come to him. That wasn't going to be at the center of the dance floor. No. Kelly was sure that Robins's office would work to lull Sven. At the very least, Robins could be Kelly's witness . . .

But where was she? Five minutes had gone. Eight. Ten.

Kelly knew that it was a big club, but it was a quiet time, and what was more important to the owner than pinning blame on the supposed killer of Iris?

Fuck.

Escaping – Kelly realized – *if you were the real killer.*

'Jesus,' he breathed. Not for one moment had he considered that Sven might smell the trap, and Robins was the person who – unwittingly – was trying to lure him into it. What might he do to her?

'*Shit.*' Kelly knew that the time for waiting was over. He'd wanted to end this with subtlety. With decency. Like the cops he'd watched on TV as a kid, Kelly had thought that if he could just get the man in a room, and lay out his crime, then he would see him confess.

But life wasn't like that. He'd fucked up, and now a man he thought a murderer was about to smell a rat. An unwitting rat who'd delivered Kelly's bait.

Robins.

Kelly flung open the door and ran.

107

Rusa was far more than a dance floor. It was a labyrinth of offices, storerooms, kitchens, and locker rooms, and through these rooms and corridors Kelly ran in desperate search of Robins. The building was quiet, but still he drew stares from janitors and bottle-service girls who were arriving for work, and Kelly knew that it wouldn't be long until security were hunting him down.

He had to find Arabella before then. He had to find Sven Niklas.

Breathless, the stump of his leg burning like fire, Kelly pulled up short in another of the long corridors that wrapped their way around the club's heart. He could hear bass, but see little. The lights were dimmed to protect employees' eyesight as they went in and out to the dance floor and tables. A soft, purple light washed over everything. It could almost have been soothing, if Kelly weren't worried sick for the life of Arabella Robins.

Could Sven really hurt her?

Yes. Kelly had no doubt. If Niklas were guilty, and if Robins stood in the way of his escape, then Niklas *would* hurt her.

Kelly tried her cell again. Nothing. Again. Nothing.

'Fuck!'

He should call Sanders. They should show their hand now. Drop the net. If Sven wasn't already spooked then he would be after that. They'd probably lose him, but at least it would happen before he could harm anyone else.

But . . .

But Kelly needed to see justice.

More than that, he needed to deliver it himself. He knew it was pride that was making him think that way. He knew it was ego, and that it wasn't the way that he should be thinking.

But Iris's body . . . torn at by animals . . . ants on her eyes . . .

Kelly wanted this. If there was going to be an endgame, he'd be the one to play it. No more dancing around.

Kelly dialed a number. It didn't belong to Arabella Robins. It didn't belong to Tonya Sanders.

It was the number of Sven Niklas, and calling it bought Kelly two seconds of life.

108

Kelly heard a phone vibrate. His instinct screamed that he was about to be attacked, and so he spun on his heel and gave a half-formed prayer that he was not—

Too late.

There was a gun in Sven's hand.

A gun in his hand, tears on his face, and savage instinct in his eyes.

For the second time in his life. Kelly stared death in the face. He hadn't gone without a fight the first time.

He didn't now.

Kelly swiped with his left hand. The prosthetic limb hit metal. That gun spat flame, and pain. Kelly knew that he was hit.

He roared something that had no meaning but defiance. Instinct was all he had now. It told him to grab the gun. It told him to smash his attacker's face apart. He wasn't a surfer or a motivational speaker in these moments. He was more of an animal than the creature that had once tried to eat him. He was fighting for survival, and no beast is more deadly than the one that feels its life bleeding away.

Kelly took Niklas down to the floor in a savage pile of flailing limbs and gnashing teeth. Both men were six three, but only one had been a football player and Kelly landed on top, his right elbow crunching into Sven's face. He felt the Swede's nose burst immediately, the club owner howling in pain as he tried to bring the gun to bear – anywhere! – on Kelly. He fired again. This time he missed. Kelly had his left hand on the firearm, and his grip was steel. Niklas couldn't pull it clear, or turn it against the American on top of him.

And he didn't need to.

Instead Niklas shoved the thumb of his left hand into the wound on Kelly's shoulder. He pressed it, pushed it, and Kelly felt the long digit touch bone.

It felt as though there were a million razors cutting through Kelly's body. He shook. He screamed. He wanted to curl up. To cry. Maybe even to die. Only two parts of his body escaped the torture. Parts manufactured in a workshop, not formed in the womb. It was this that kept Kelly alive. No matter the agony as the Sven dug his thumb deeper, Kelly's hand would not give up on the pistol.

But he did give up his position, and, like a snake, Niklas worked his way out from under him. Kelly clung to the pistol as if it were his child, and Niklas tried to fire, but the trigger clicked harmlessly – Kelly's grip had stopped the top slide from moving forwards and feeding in another round. There was none in the chamber, and until there was, the gun was useless.

'Let go!' Sven shouted through a mouthful of blood. 'Let go!'

Kelly would not. And there were voices now. Cries of alarm. Niklas knew that his time to kill Kelly was short. His time to escape the casino shorter still. He looked at the gun. It was useless so long as Kelly held it, and Niklas knew with certainty that there was no way he could pull the weapon free.

He had one choice. Take the magazine out of the gun, and run.

He did.

With the pistol in his hand, Kelly bled into the carpet.

109

Kelly didn't want to move. He didn't want to *think*. He just wanted to close his eyes, and pant, and swear, and wish that the racing pain in his body would go away.

And so that's what he did.

He closed his eyes . . . but he found no peace there.

He found *her*.

Iris. Dead. Abandoned.

And Kelly knew that she'd always be there until someone answered for what had happened to her. Until someone was made to say *why*, and pay for that crime.

And that man was getting away.

Kelly pushed himself onto his knees. He saw his blood on the floor. There was a lot of it. In the center of the crimson lake, something caught Kelly's eye. He reached for it. At first he thought it was the empty casing of the bullet that shot him.

It wasn't.

It was a 9-mm round. It was the one that should have been fed into the chamber when Kelly had blocked the top slide. It had come loose and fallen when Niklas ejected the magazine.

And now it was Kelly's. He cocked back the blood-slicked top slide, and fed the bullet into the chamber with shaking hands. He depressed the release catch, and the slide thumped forwards. There was an authority in that tone. A message.

Kelly had one shot.

One shot to bring down a killer.

110

Kelly might have only had one shot, but he had a decade of points to prove, and a body full of adrenaline, and this carried him through the club's corridors like an Olympian. Niklas wasn't a hard man to track, blood and an open doorway leading Kelly quickly into the hot night air.

Kelly knew where he was. It was the location of the night swim, where he had first met the club's owner. Tonight, the dance floor was empty, the water in the pools serene.

Kelly saw blood on the floor. His own, picked up by Sven's shoes.

Kelly saw where they led: the VIP bungalows.

He knew that it was time to call for backup. He pulled out his phone, but one look told him it was out of action, bent out of shape in the fray. The antenna within was snapped. No service. No Sanders.

'Shit.'

Two options ran through Kelly's head. Wait it out, and hope that there wasn't some back door out of the bungalows that he couldn't see, or push on, and keep pushing until Niklas was cornered, or cuffed.

Two options, but only one real choice.

Kelly pushed on.

He tried to hold the pistol up and in a steady aim, but his hands were shaking from blood loss and fear. Instead Kelly held the weapon tight to himself. His brother had taught him to 'punch out' into the aim, and that's what Kelly would do when Niklas was in his sights, but it had been a long time since the ranges . . .

'Sven! Come out! Give it up!' he tried, hearing the futility in the words even as he said them. 'I know about Blake! The police know about Blake!'

Tired words, but what else could he say? At that same moment, on some hard street corner or in some suburban neighborhood, a cop would be saying the same thing. They'd be saying it tomorrow. They'd be saying it in a decade. In a century. A last cry for decency. A bet against all odds.

'Sven! Just come out, man!' Kelly's voice began to break. 'Do you want to die?'

Real question: *Did Kelly want to kill him?*

He wanted justice. He wanted the truth.

But did he want to kill another human being? The answer hurt Kelly, because he knew that he might have to.

He reached the bungalows. Kelly couldn't see a pretty way of doing things. On the football field, he'd learned that you could run as many patterns and routes to outsmart a defense as you wanted, but sooner or later, you had to put your head down, and get hit.

Fuck it.

He pulled back the first curtain.

Nothing. Kelly's stomach felt sour. He forgot all about the pain in his shoulder, and tried not to puke.

He was terrified.

Second curtain. Nothing. Just a rising tide of nauseous nerves.

Third curtain. Nothing.

Fourth—

Niklas hit him with a bull rush before the curtain had moved back an inch. He was lighter than Kelly, but the Swede had the power of a man with death in his eyes, and he carried the two of them over the railing at Kelly's back. The smash of the metal into his muscles was a split second of agony before they were both falling the ten feet to the ground below, the deep cushioned sofas breaking their fall before bouncing them onto the hard tile.

Niklas was the first to his feet but, seeing the gun still in Kelly's hand, he made no move to fight. Instead, fueled by fear, he ran.

Kelly followed.

'Sven!'

In his panic, Niklas ran to the right of the waters, but it was a mistake – the exit was on the left.

Kelly could beat him to it.

And then Niklas slipped.

111

Niklas went down as though he'd been hit by a sniper, but it was a wet patch on the poolside that dropped him. The Swede's head bounced off the floor, and now, with the water between himself and his prey, Kelly dropped to one knee and took aim.

'Don't try and run!' he warned breathlessly. 'I will fucking shoot you, Sven!'

But even Kelly heard the lie in those words.

He couldn't shoot an unarmed man. Not even one who was dripping with guilt.

'Fuck you,' Niklas groaned. 'Fuck you.'

He was crying.

Kelly looked at his surroundings. It was ten meters across the pool. With a pistol, that was no easy shot even for someone who was well trained and uninjured. Kelly was neither of those things. It had been over a year since he last went to a range. His left shoulder continued to leak blood. His head and limbs ached. He just wanted to lie down. He just wanted to close his eyes and sleep.

He thought about moving, but that would simply flush Niklas in the opposite direction.

They were at an impasse.

'Don't move,' Kelly growled. He would wait for security, he decided. Wait for the police.

Niklas sniffled. 'Fine by me.' As he wiped at his face, a whisper of confidence came into his voice. 'You know, maybe it's best that *you* move, Kelly. What are they going to see when they get here?' Niklas asked him. '*You* pointing a gun at *me* in *my* club.'

Kelly scoffed. 'And I suppose they'll think I shot myself.'

'I had that gun for self-defense. After what happened to Chao . . .'

So Niklas had heard about Kelly's visit to the airport. *Shit.* Kelly knew that didn't look good for him. Assaulting one person linked to Iris, and now having a gun aimed at another . . .

'Where's Arabella?' he asked. He could worry about himself later. Niklas pushed himself to his knees. He was unsteady. The fall had rocked him. '*Where's Arabella?*'

Sven tried to laugh, but failed. Instead he looked into Kelly's face. Even across the width of the pool, the Swede's tortured soul shone through.

'Just let me go, Kelly,' he pleaded.

No.

'*Please, man.*'

No.

A moment. A near-sob.

Then hope. 'I don't think you can kill a defenseless man.'

Kelly wasn't sure he could kill *any* man.

'You tried to kill me,' he said in an attempt to steel his heart. 'Twice, you motherfucker.'

'I tried to *scare* you,' Niklas sobbed. He was openly crying now. Pathetic. Broken. If this was a killer, it wasn't how Kelly had pictured one to look.

'I know you killed them,' Kelly declared.

But he hadn't known. He really hadn't.

Not until he saw those tears. That look. Kelly believed in soul and spirit, and he was seeing this man's laid bare. It was all the proof that *Kelly* needed, but the law would need more. A lot more.

They would need a confession.

'You know it's all over, don't you?' he told Rusa's shaking owner. 'You might skate some of the charges, but what you've built, you've lost. It's done.'

Niklas shook his head. He couldn't accept that it was gone, and so it was time for Kelly to beat him down.

'I had someone hack Blake's Instagram,' Kelly revealed. A crime that would likely see him punished by the law, even if it did bring a killer into its grip. 'The police have a transcript.'

At least, Sanders did.

'I know what happened that night,' Kelly told him.

But he didn't. Not all of it. He needed Niklas to fill in the final pieces, and he could only think of one way to do that.

'Give it up on tape,' Kelly offered. 'I'll record your confession on my phone. All of it.'

A sneer worked its way onto the Swede's red face. Calculating. Dangerous. 'Why the fuck would I do that?'

Kelly was ready with his answer. So ready it scared him. 'Because once you're done . . . I'll throw this pistol into the pool.'

Niklas swallowed as he grasped the implications.

'You're finished in Vegas, Niklas,' Kelly delivered the verdict. 'But beat me to this gun, and you've got a shot at a life someplace else.'

A heartbeat.

Five of them. Fast, and fearful.

Niklas spat. 'You're a righteous cunt.'

But that was why he trusted Kelly to honor the deal.

That was why he spoke, and spilled his guts about a death in Vegas.

112

Two days earlier

Iris Manning did not enjoy being told what to do.

She was sitting on the edge of the unmade bed, and looked at the man who was pulling on a black T-shirt. 'This is fucking bullshit.'

'It's business,' Sam Chao reminded her.

Iris didn't think so. 'It's no business of his who I sleep with.'

Lies, and they both knew it. Who Iris slept with was every bit of *his* business when it jeopardized a multi-million-dollar company.

'You know what the rules are about sleeping with clients,' Chao said patiently, wondering how much it would cost him to smooth things out.

'I know what the rules about sleeping with employees are too,' she shot back, 'but that doesn't stop *him*.'

Chao said nothing as he poured himself a Jack and Coke. He offered one to the beautiful girl on his bed, but she shook her head. Ten minutes ago they'd been in the thralls of ecstasy – at least Chao had; he couldn't give a shit if Iris was faking or not – but then the suite's phone had rang off the hook. It had been for Iris, and the message had been clear: *Get your ass out of that fucking room.*

She cussed. 'I hate him.'

Chao knew that wasn't true. He'd made his money by reading people, and when he saw her look at *him*, he saw the lust there. The desire to attach to a winner.

'What do you want for tonight?' Chao asked. 'Jewelry?'

Iris blew him a kiss. 'Surprise me.'

Chao took in the girl's beauty and lines. Even her tattoos seemed to hold her body tight, afraid of losing her. It was a shame Chao would never fuck her again. It had been fun, but . . .

'I'll surprise you,' he promised. She was worth that. She'd been worth risking his relationship with Rusa, after all. Chao knew that such girls were poison, but they were also the antidote to life's banality. Flame and fury trapped within skin. Beautiful creatures that devoured partners too slow to escape.

Chao would not be consumed. But yes, he would miss her.

One final smile, for old times' sake. 'Shall I order you a car?'

'I'm good,' she tells him. She believes it, too.

'OK. Goodbye, then.'

He opens the door. Iris walks out of his suite.

The time is 03:08 a.m.

113

Iris walks through the Grand Casino. The pissed-off mood that she'd had since the phone call persisted, but she knew that she'd be OK. She was always OK. She was just fed up of massaging men's fucking egos. Why did they have to be such *pussies*?

She left the Grand and pulled a face as the heat of the night embraced her. Living in the desert was something that she tolerated because of what Las Vegas could give her. She missed California. She wanted to move back there, but . . . she was making *so much money*. And the gifts? The gifts alone could buy a house when she moved back. Not along the coast, but inland. Corona, maybe. Someplace her parents could retire. They'd never owned a place, and though they'd never complained – not once – she knew how hard they'd worked to keep a roof over the family's head. Soon it would be Iris's chance to turn the tide. They wouldn't agree with how she'd done it, but had their own parents approved when they got married at sixteen and hit the road? At some point, every child would make a decision that they thought was in the best interests of the family, but would upset the older generation. Iris knew that was just how things were. She was OK with who she was. Comfortable in her own skin. If guys wanted to throw gifts and attention at her, then why should she turn it away? It had been that way since junior high. Fuck 'em.

She crossed the street and passed through the next casino. He was waiting on the other side, just as she knew he would be. Just like a little bitch. She called, he answered, but she didn't want anyone to see them together close to Rusa. It wasn't good for her look, and she knew he'd get jealous if he saw her get attention from another guy. Shit, she knew he was jealous, regardless.

And yet here he was.

She climbed into the car. As always, it was immaculate. Iris laughed inside at the effort. He was a bird trying to fluff its nest, but how could a clean Audi compare with the private jets that the other little birdies were offering? The yachts? The villas?

First thing she says to him. 'You get my cigarettes?'

He has. A ten-pack, Marlboro Lights. First thing he says to her, 'You look beautiful.'

She snorts. She hates him really. Hates him for his lack of spine. He can probably smell the sex, and yet he compliments her. What he should do is grab her throat. Push her out of his car. Fuck every other girl at Rusa until she's red in the face with anger and jealousy.

But he won't. And so she tells him where to take her. She sees a little of him die inside. That little piece of hope that it would be *his* place. The rekindling of a dying flame.

'Don't fuck around, OK? Get me there fast.'

He does as she tells him. He always does. She can feel his hate. She can see how tight his hands are on the wheel. He hates her more than almost anything in the world.

But he loves her that little bit more. Soon, he thinks. Soon she'll realize that she was wrong.

But she won't.

They pull up at a mansion outside of town. Not a gated community – this place has its own walls. They didn't talk during the drive. He tried. She smoked, and played with her phone. He's just a taxi to her. A plaything. Hers and no one else's.

'You don't have to go in there.' One last attempt. He's looking at the steering wheel as he says it. 'I can take care of you.'

She laughs and gets out. Forgets her cigarettes.

'I'll wait here for you.'

'Don't.'

He does anyway. His guts turn to acid as he sees the man in the door.

His name is Sven Niklas.

The time is 03:40 a.m.

114

Sven Niklas closes the door. He is furious. He turns to unleash hell.

Iris is on her tiptoes. She grabs his collar. Pulls him down. Kisses him. She knows how to disarm a bomb. When they're finished, panting on a sofa, he tries to regain the upper hand. It's gone. Iris has won. He knows it, but he tries anyway.

'You shouldn't jeopardize my business like that. Do what you want in your own time, but when you bring it into work, it puts Rusa at risk.'

Do what you want? She knows he doesn't mean that. He's told her after too many vodkas. Begged her to stop. Begged her to just be his. But she knows how to treat a man who tries to control her. She turns to her phone.

'Hey. Who are you texting? I'm trying to have a conversation here.'

'Just a friend.' A shot across the bow. A painful one.

'Who is your friend? Iris. Hey. Who are you texting?'

The friend is Blake Mathews. He's sitting in the car outside, begging her to come out. Begging her to leave. In two days' time, a stranger will see these Instagram messages.

He'll see them, and know that Niklas lied about where Iris was that night. When he had last seen her. When he had last seen Mathews.

Iris please, you don't have to do this!

Please just come out and talk!

OK. I'm sorry if I'm upsetting you. I just want you to be happy.

I'll go if you come out and I know you're OK. I promise.

She plays them both. Niklas thinks she has a lover. Mathews thinks she's at the whim of a tyrant. Desperate, the kid outside leans on his horn.

'Who the fuck is that?'

Niklas storms out. Iris follows. They're half-naked. Mathews's heart has already been shattered. Now he just feels sick. What makes it worse is that Niklas is the only one of the pair to show emotion. Iris pouts like it's all a game.

'Get the fuck out of here!' Niklas roars.

Iris says nothing. Angry and tearful, Mathews drives away.

Iris leads the club owner back into the house. She doesn't expect what is coming next.

'You are a piece of shit,' the tall man curses, looking at her as though he means every word. 'You are a fucking piece of shit!'

Something she doesn't hear from guys. Something she never expected.

'How dare you treat that guy like that? Are you fucking sick? Bringing him out here? Making him sit there as . . . He loves you, you fucking cunt!'

His words sting more than her slap. '*You* fired him! You fired him, Sven!'

'For Rusa!' he yells in her face. 'For Rusa, not for you! Did you know that I offered to pay for his rehab, huh? Did you know that? Of course you didn't, you selfish bitch! You're too caught up in Iris's world!'

Not a slap, then. A punch. A flurry of them. The tall man takes them. Soaks them up. He would have taken them all, but he couldn't take her venom.

'You're no better than he is, Sven! You're a fucking loser! You've always been a loser! The only reason anyone would ever think about fucking you is for your club. You're a joke. It's pity sex. I pity you. I could have whoever I want! Why would I ever want you?'

It was just one push. Just one push to get her out of his face, and give himself a clear path upstairs. One push, but he is six foot three, and she is drunk, and angry, and violent. The sound of her leg hitting the table is sickening and sobering.

'Jesus, Iris!' He's aggrieved. He's . . . 'Jesus!' He doesn't even mind the punches. He doesn't mind the taunts. Seeing her lying there, he just wants to help her. To comfort her. 'I'm so sorry.'

She has him again. She knows it. Every time they dance this dance. He can't escape her. He's done enough now that his heart will be in her pocket for months.

'I want you to run me a bath,' she tells him.

Niklas nods. 'I need some coke.' She wants some too.

A mile down the road a car pulls over. Behind the wheel is a sobbing man. Through the tears he sends one more message. The last that Iris will ever receive from him.

This is all my fault. I'm sorry. Call me if you need me.

The time is 04:14 a.m.

115

Josh Kelly stares at Niklas across the pool. The Swede is crying. Shaking. The story has fallen from his lips quickly, Niklas desperate to afford himself the chance of gaining Kelly's pistol, and potential freedom, before security comes onto the scene.

Kelly thought about that. How long did he have? He could only hope that, in the event of gunshots, the club's policy would be to evacuate into the casino, and that the night swim area would be one of the final zones to be cleared.

So far, the club's owner had not told Kelly anything he didn't know either from intuition, or from Blake's Instagram messages. He needed more, and so he would goad.

'So you killed Iris because she pointed out who you really are behind the suits and the mansions? A nerd from Sweden that no one has ever given a shit about? Just a stack of cash for people to use and abuse? You killed her because you were her fucking bitch, weren't you, Sven? Why don't you do the first man-like thing you've ever done in your life, and just admit it!'

'It wasn't like that!' Tears. Grief. 'It wasn't!'

Kelly thought he heard shouting – he was running out of time. 'Thirty seconds, Sven. Either I get an answer and the gun goes in the pool, or we wait it out here.'

Animal desperation. Fleeting eyes. Panted breath.

Sven Niklas rubbed his bloodied hands over his shaved scalp . . .

And then he talked.

116

She was in the bathtub when he found her. He'd just snorted a line, and even though she'd asked him for some privacy, the coke in his veins compelled him to talk.

And so he'd knocked. 'Iris?'

He'd waited. 'Iris?'

He'd entered.

No words, that time. Just that horrifying realization that a person gets the first time they see a body. The moment when they learn that they have the ability to tell life from death with just a look. Niklas didn't need to check her pulse. He didn't need to shake her, or shout at her. He just knew. It wasn't possible for a person to be that still and live, the air around her a vacuum.

She was fucking dead.

He cried a lot then. He floundered with her in the bath. He made plans. Changed plans. He thought about her. He thought about an ambulance. He thought about coke. He thought about consequences. In the end, through tears and fumbling fingers, he called the one person who could make it all OK. The one person who had been his rock. His anchor. His right hand.

She didn't slap him around the face when she arrived. She didn't hold his head under the bathwater. Not physically, at least. She sobered him with words. Brought him to earth with truth: 'Iris is dead. Do you want Rusa to die with her?'

All the blood, all the sweat, all the tears. Would it be for nothing? Torn down in the scandal of the club owner who had an overdosed bottle-service girl in his bathtub? Rusa would never survive, and Sven Niklas would never survive without Rusa.

'What do we do about Iris?'

A drive into the desert. A grave amongst the rocks. The woman wished it could be different, but the dead were the dead, and the living were the living, and she could live with herself. That was all that mattered. She hadn't killed the girl. Most likely Iris had OD'd. Why should she suffer for that? Why should Sven? Why should the dozens of Rusa employees?

Fuck that. Iris could go out into the desert, and rest there. It wasn't like it was some monstrous act. They did it in other countries, for fuck's sake. Sky burials, or some shit.

So the woman pulled her car close to the house. Sven helped lift Iris in. She didn't weigh much. That was the last memory that he had of her.

Arabella Robins put the car into drive.

It was 04:50 a.m.

117

Stumbling in the dark was a blur. A nightmare. But Robins was strong, in body and mind. Sven would have broken without her. As the sun threatened to bleed onto the horizon, they dumped Iris's body. Sven wanted to say some words. Robins said them instead.

'We need to get the fuck away from here.'

Sven followed, numb. She tried to give him Valium. Instead he blew coke. He did a lot of it on the drive back to his place.

'You're gonna need to sleep,' his right hand told him.

How the fuck would he ever sleep again?

But he did. He gave in. Took the Valium. Drank some vodka. Robins stayed in the guest room. She checked on him. He was her boss and baby brother. As the warm blanket of the sedatives wrapped around him, he knew that things would be OK. Iris was dead, but Rusa would live on. He could make things right. Support her parents, maybe? It wasn't like Sven had killed her. He wasn't a murderer.

The next day was a nightmare. No way to avoid it, though. The festival comes first. Rusa comes first. Business comes first. Smiles and handshakes. How relieved he was when Josh Kelly came to the club to 'break the news.' Finally, Sven had an excuse to cry.

But later . . . later he knew that things were not OK. The visitor to Las Vegas was hungry. He was relentless. Robins promised they could throw him off the track. He wasn't even a cop. They could show him just enough. It would all be fine. They didn't need to prove their innocence, just not get caught in their guilt.

But someone *was* guilty. Iris was dead, and something – someone – was at fault. Sven was a gram of coke and ten shots of vodka deep when he realized who.

Blake Mathews.

That cunt. *He* killed Iris! When Mathews met Iris, she was pure. A diamond. Mathews took that precious stone, and made her ugly. How?

How? By not being the man she needed him to be! By letting her run wild! If Mathews had been a real man, Iris would never have turned into the . . . slut that she became. The gold digger that she became. The drug addict that she became. It was all on Mathews.

And he had to know it.

Sven took his gun. It wasn't even loaded. He just wanted to scare the guy. To make him realize that he had cost the world one of its greatest children.

But Mathews must have realized it first.

The note that he had left behind an unlocked door said as much. Page after page of it. Apology after apology. Sven screwed it up and put it in his pocket. Then he used Mathews's thumb to unlock the dead kid's phone. Niklas was numb from coke and grief, and he hadn't come to be a wealthy club owner by missing opportunities. He saw one here. Poetic justice. Cosmic karma. The man truly responsible for Iris's death could take the blame. Because he was a decent man, Sven set the publication time to be early that morning. Not even Blake Mathews deserved to rot and swell in the heat.

Sven closed the door without a backwards look. And breathed out in relief. Rusa would live.

It was 04:24 a.m., a little over a day since Iris's death.

Across the city, Josh Kelly was in bed with the woman who had disposed of her body.

118

The man who had begun the confession was not the one who stood across from Josh Kelly now. Sven Niklas had aged a decade as his grief and guilt shook him like jilted lovers.

It was all for business, Kelly realized with a lump in his stomach. Love of flesh and blood had been trumped by a deeper desire for dollars.

'I didn't kill anyone,' Niklas begged, his words more to the heavens than to Kelly.

'But you didn't try to save them, either,' Kelly passed judgment. 'And you'll get whatever you deserve.'

Niklas looked at the gun in Kelly's hand. He'd been promised a chance. He'd delivered on his end.

It only took a look to get Kelly to deliver on his.

You want this, Kelly told himself, recognizing the tide of anger that was rushing through him like California wildfire. *You can't shoot a man in cold blood, and so you want this.*

He tried to deny it. He tried to pretend that what he wanted was just the truth.

It was a lie.

Kelly lowered the pistol.

He wanted *justice*.

'Here's your chance, Sven.' He held up the pistol. 'There's one bullet in there.' And a whole magazine full in Niklas's hand.

Then, with the image of Iris's body filling his vision, Kelly tossed the pistol into the water.

One man's life had run its course.

119

Neither man moved as the pistol hit the water. Sven's eyes were red welts in his face, cried out and beaten. His limbs shook like a cornered coyote's. Kelly didn't expect that he looked any better. His tongue felt huge, dry, and stuck against the roof of his mouth. The acid in his stomach felt as though it was burning a hole through his body. He didn't want to die.

But he didn't want to kill, either.

'We don't have to do this,' he tried.

Sven opened his own mouth to speak. The words never made it out. Terror had sewn his lips shut.

And so they stood. As the pistol sank to the bottom of the pool, they faced off across its waters, two wounded, terrified animals that did not know whether to fight or flee.

It was a production engineer ten miles away that changed that. In his observation tower at Pandora festival, and with a bank of controls in front of him, the engineer turned the master key that would begin one of the most expensive firework displays on the planet. A crashing crescendo of color. A riot in the sky.

Kelly was the first to turn his head at that distant sound. Instinct made him do it, and Sven saw his chance.

He could see the shape of the pistol in the water. His salvation.

He leaped.

Kelly had no time to curse. No time to think. He just dived. Beaten and bloodied, it wasn't his best, but even a dull blade cuts into water.

They met over the pistol.

Sven knew that the gun was his only chance, and reached for it with his right hand. His left wasn't strong enough to stop both of Kelly's hands from gripping his face, and pushing his head backwards. Bubbles streamed to the surface as Niklas gave an agonized wail, his fingers brushing atop the gun's barrel, but gaining no purchase to hold it.

His best chance was gone.

The pistol lay dormant as the men broke the surface, gasping for air. Kelly was the first to land a punch. Then he felt Sven's hands grasping for his bullet wound. If he could get a finger in there, then Kelly would be pinned down by pain, his own nervous system condemning him to water-filled lungs.

And so Kelly wrapped his arms around the man in front of him, and took him under.

Face to face, no hiding from the terror in Sven's eyes. The Swede knew what this meant. His arms were pinned beneath Kelly's, and so he tried to throw his head, gnash his teeth, but Kelly had been caught up in riptides and dumped in hundreds of tons of white water. Nothing that Niklas could do to him beneath the surface could compare to the power of nature, and they both knew it.

Those moments were the longest in Josh Kelly's life. Underwater, he heard the garbled pleas as a man begged. He felt the air bubbles against his cheek as Sven screamed. He felt him thrash, shudder, and give in.

He held him down until he was sure. Then the body rose up to the surface as the last of Pandora's fireworks arced into the sky. The festival was over.

So was a man's life.

Kelly rose through the water and gasped for air. He didn't have time to take in the canvas of colors painted in the sky. Just the six police officers, and the weapons that they held pointing towards him.

When Kelly saw the open, accusing eyes of Sven's floating body, he prayed that they would shoot.

120

The heat. The heat was all-encompassing. It was the master of this domain, and the man on the hot rocks was a guest. Nothing more. The heat could crush him. The desert could crush him. For a while, he had hoped that it would, but now, as the man opened his eyes and emerged from his meditation, he knew a kind of peace that had been denied to him in the days that had followed the drowning of a club owner in his own pool.

Kelly got to his feet. He tried not to wince at the pain in his shoulder, his dressed wound dry from so many hours in the scorching sun. He tried not to wince at the memory of Sven Niklas's body floating alongside him like a listless ship.

The memories of what happened next were a lot easier to bear. Kelly knew that he shouldn't be proud, but . . . fuck it. He was. It hadn't been an easy thing to ignore the shouts of the police officers and their pointed weapons, but that's what Kelly had done, dragging Sven's body to the side of the pool, where he had begun CPR. There was a lot more screaming. Confusion. The officers didn't seem sure what to do. In the end they stood back as Kelly pumped the water from Sven Niklas's lungs, the Swede spluttering back to life, if it could be called that – he was in a cell now. Attempted murder, among other things. The life as he knew it, over.

But not by Kelly's hand.

As Sven regained consciousness, Kelly himself had been treated like a criminal, and with good reason. He was bloodied. There was a gun in the pool. Even Sanders's arrival on the scene had done little to calm things, and Kelly had been cuffed to the bed as they stitched up his wound.

But there was one wound that they couldn't stitch, and that was deep inside of Kelly's chest.

He felt like a fool. An absolute fool. Arabella Robins had played him from the beginning. She'd read him, and she'd shaped him. That final night, Kelly had let something slip. Maybe a word, maybe an emotion that played across his face, but Robins had read it. Seeing the endgame, she had set Niklas onto Kelly, and fled. A search of her house had found an empty wardrobe and desk. She was gone, and on the run. At least Kelly could take comfort from the fact that the woman's high-flying life was over. He wasn't proud to feel that way, but Robins had put business before decency. She had been willing to dump a girl in a canyon – this canyon – to protect the reputation of the man that cut her checks. Kelly had no doubt that justice would follow her, be it the legal kind of the United States, or the karmic kind of the universe. One way or another, Robins would reap what she had sown.

'Feeling better?'

Tonya Sanders. She'd been watching and waiting. Kelly smiled. She'd been doing that since she arrived poolside. His big sister.

'I am.'

Sanders walked over and stood by his side. No hugs. Not her style. An unbridled smile, though. A rare thing, and beautiful. She joined Kelly in looking out across the desert. To the metropolis in the sand.

'I spoke to the DA while you were speaking to . . .'

Kelly shrugged. 'I don't know who.' That was the truth. Maybe just to himself. But the meditation had worked. He was unburdened. At least, unburdened enough to smile.

'Well, the DA is all about making this public. Now that a big fish is on the line, they want to fillet him so that everyone can see that Vegas doesn't stand for that kind of shit.' It was bull and they knew it, but what did it matter? Kelly had gotten into this for Iris Manning, and later, Blake Mathews. They were all that mattered.

He told her as much.

Sanders nodded. 'DA says that you'll be fine for the Instagram hacking. I didn't know you could do that stuff?'

'I can't, but he had contact details on his DJ page. I sent the details to a guy in LA, and paid him to hack the app. I had a feeling we'd get something out of it. He didn't seem the type to stay quiet.'

Sanders stopped smiling. She turned her back on the city. She sensed something . . .

'Why do you know this hacker?'

Kelly fought against the drop in his shoulders.

'I lost more than being a cop when I got busted with the drugs,' he admitted, the words coming out like razors.

'I . . . I did some things that I wasn't proud of. That's how I know the hacker.'

'Like what?'

Enough razors. Kelly's mouth stayed shut. His eyes told Sanders all she needed to know: pain. And lots of it.

'OK,' she said. 'You know, in a way, Blake helped solve what happened to Iris. Those messages were the breadcrumb trail that tied Niklas to her with time and place. I hope he can know that, and find peace.'

Kelly nodded at the sentiment. 'They both died before their time.'

They had. But not how Kelly had suspected. Iris's autopsy had revealed a blood clot in her brain. From the large bruise on her leg, the pathologist concluded that the clot had formed there. The cocaine in her system had likely contributed to forming the clot, as it had the effect of thickening the blood. It would be down to the lawyers to decide whether it was an accidental death, or manslaughter caused by Niklas pushing Iris into the table of his home.

'Either way, we never would have known it without you, Josh,' Sanders told him. 'You would have made a great cop, and . . . you make an even better friend.'

There was barely a moment of silence before Kelly ripped out a burst of laughter so harsh that it hurt his shoulder. He didn't care. 'How hard was that for you to say?' he beamed.

Sanders grimaced. 'I feel like throwing up.'

'Ha! If they do end up firing you, maybe you could become a counselor?'

'You're a dick.' Sanders wasn't out of the woods for her assault and airport stunt. Time would tell on that.

'At least you're not behind bars.' They knew that they were both lucky to be that way, but success has a way of shaping attitudes and opening doors. Especially the ones on cells.

Kelly took a deep breath. They'd come to the canyon for more than meditation and clearing the air. 'Shall we do this?' he asked his friend.

Sanders nodded. 'They're waiting up the trail.'

121

Two dozen people waited at the spot where Iris had been found, that space between the rocks now a cascade of flowers and tributes. Kelly looked over the faces, and recognized many. Adam and Amy, the two friends in the photo that had given him their first lead. Zakhir Khan, the 'drug dealer' who had pointed a gun at Kelly in the after party. Even Stephanie Wilson, the bottle-service girl who had traded punches with Iris over her treatment of Blake Mathews.

She caught Kelly's look, and moved to join him. 'Vegas does funny things to people,' she said to explain her presence. 'I didn't agree with a lot of what Iris did, but she didn't deserve what happened. She just got caught up in the money and the lights. Nobody deserves to die for that. She was still a person.'

There was little Kelly could say to that. In trying to solve her death, he had come to see the slide of Iris's morality, but Stephanie was right – nobody deserved to die for making those choices. They didn't deserve to be chewed up and spat out. Kelly had made bad decisions of his own. It was good fortune and friends that had brought him through it. Iris had been tainted by the corruption of a city, and she had died as a result, but it was no more deserved than any other death in the world. Like all others, it was a tragedy that left a void in humanity. Looking around at the assembled faces – many of them people who had been wronged by Iris – Kelly could see that there were some who understood that. No matter what Iris had done, they still *loved* her, and they would miss her.

Amy stepped forwards. She was an old friend of Iris's, and her cheeks were cut through with tears. She had a phone and a cordless speaker in her hands. She placed them by the flowers. On her third attempt, the words came out. 'This was her favorite song. I'll miss her so much.'

She pressed play, and in the melancholy lyrics Kelly heard the story of the girl he had come to know through chasing ghosts.

It was too much for Amy, but Adam came forward and held her. So did Zhakir. So did a dozen other people who didn't even know Amy, but who recognized the love and suffering in her heart, and who wanted to protect her.

When Kelly saw that Sanders was among them, he lost his own battle with emotion. As the tear trickled over his cheek, he thought back over the two days where he had grasped for truth. He thought about how he had searched for the sin of others, and instead had been confronted by his own. He thought about the pain and misery, but looking before him now he saw love and purpose, and he knew that the world was a beautiful place. A place of second chances. Life and Las Vegas had consumed Iris Manning, but her death was a sacrifice for others who would now right their own ships. Make the hard decisions. Face the demons. Kelly was among those people, and as he walked away from the gathering, Sanders followed.

'You're leaving?'

He was. Leaving with gratitude flooding through his body, because Kelly realized that a death in Vegas had given him his own life. His *real* life.

'Back to California?'

Kelly smiled as the sun began to set, and the stone of the mountains turned bloody red. His reply was the most honest thing he'd ever told her.

'I don't know.'

But he did know one thing. The truth that, more so than any shark attack or drug bust, the events of the past weekend would shape his life forever.

Because, badge or no badge, Josh Kelly was a detective.